Boston Burning

Eric D. Salin

DISCLAIMER AND COPYRIGHT

ACKNOWLEDGEMENTS

First, I need to thank my primary editor Dr. Laura Cameron. She has both a global overview and an incredible eye for detail. Laura not only knows the finer points of English and writing but seriously "gets" the elements of a good novel. If this is not a great novel, it isn't Laura's fault. Awesome! Other serious help has come from Charla Arabie, who has been both a friend, an initial editor and wonderful with her feedback. My beta readers, particularly Dr. Erin Tempelton, Dr. Angelica Gopal and the many family friends who helped. My graphics were done by my old friend, David Boomer, who has done much more for me than graphics. Final editing was done by Chris Cameron, a great editor and a craftsman in his own right.

READERS TAKE NOTE

There is a list of characters and technical terms at the end of the book. If you have an eBook, you can reach this easily by clicking on the link in the table of contents.

CONTENTS

PROLOGUE

"English, speak English," Major Yitzak Markus said to himself as he dropped his heavily laden F15I Ra'am in towards the water. Closer, then closer. Fifteen meters. Dangerous in the predawn haze. A glitch in the altimeter, a wiggle of the control stick, and they would both be nothing more than an oil slick. "English, speak English," he told himself one last time. He could barely see his wingman, Captain "Fast Freddie" Friedman, against the star-filled sky. He watched the countdown timer, almost mesmerized, for another minute before blinking his red-filtered flashlight briefly at Freddie. Almost instantly, a dim red light blinked back. Markus smiled in satisfaction as his friend dropped from his wingman position, off his right side, to the slot position almost directly behind, but safely up and back. "I'll kick his ass into his brains if he doesn't speak English," Markus muttered as he began a gentle turn towards the coastline.

All electronic systems were passive, sensing only, no transmission, so no stray electronic signals leaked to the enemy. He checked his infrared camera. This would show anything hotter than the surroundings. "Freddie, if your infrared breaks down, you and I are going to be closer than two queers on Saturday night," Markus thought with a grim smile as he imagined Freddie ramming his F15's nose up his own F15's engine. It was unlikely, though—the rehearsals had all gone extremely well.

One hundred and twenty miles off the coast in a U.S. Navy E2 electronic surveillance plane, Petty Officer Second Class Douglas called over Lieutenant Junior Grade Brian Crosby. "Sir, those two Israeli F15s just dropped into the clutter. Should we report it?"

Crosby thought for a moment. "The clutter" consisted of false radar signals reflected off the waves. The Israelis had done the equivalent of dropping down into the high grass. Still, Crosby, who had recently been reprimanded for lack of judgment, did not hesitate for long. "No, I'm not getting my ass burned again for crying wolf, but keep a damn close eye on things. We were warned that the Israelis are on a training exercise. They might just try sneaking up on us for fun." For insurance, Crosby told the rest of the watch to stay sharp, though this was probably a waste of time. When the fleet was this close to the coast, everyone stayed sharp.

5:13 A.M.

The coast was coming up now. Soon they would have to switch to active sensing to get through the rugged terrain. Their powerful radars would splash the high mountains with radio signals and echoes would paint the picture they needed for navigation. It shouldn't matter, Markus thought, with the short energy echoing pulses that we're using. The enemy shouldn't be able to pick us up on any of their middle-aged Soviet equipment. Anyhow, there really wasn't any choice. If they flew over the low coastal range, they would be picked up by coastal radar, and that would be deadly. The terrain map flicked by perfectly as the autopilot jerked them through the first low range. It was time.

"Bat Two, stand by," Markus spoke into his microphone. He smiled. Their transmissions were unscrambled. Later, and not much later at that, someone would hear them speaking American English.

"Affirmative," acknowledged Fast Freddie. Good, Markus thought: he had remembered to work in English. It was easy for Markus—he'd been brought up in New York—but Freddie was a *kibbutznik*.

This would be a single-pass mission. Freddie had Rockeye bomb clusters for the softer storage-tank farms. The Rockeyes would spread hundreds of individual bomblets over the terrain. Markus had four 500-pound conventional bombs on his hard points. The rest of his weapons points were occupied with defensive air-to-air missiles. Being the senior pilot, he got the tougher target: the chemical plant. That suited him fine. He hated chemical weapons. He had once been maced by a New York cop, and somehow, this was his revenge on all chemical weapons. He had almost flunked out of college because of his hostility towards his chemistry class. Only his decision to switch to engineering had saved him. The expression *Payback is a Mutha* came to him, and he smiled.

Markus angled along the wispy river, which showed up well in the infrared as it was warmer now than the cold mountainous desert. He blinked his running lights, waited five seconds, then banked sharply to the left, flying over the river fork—Initialization Point. This was the beginning point for a bomb run.

He knew that behind him, Fast Freddie was banking sharply to the right. Watching his timer carefully, Markus counted ten seconds then slammed the throttles forward and banked so sharply to the right that he would soon be flying inverted and have to look up to see the target. There it was, vivid in the infrared camera display, tall hot chimneys, exactly where they should be. He looked through his canopy and saw the chimneys clearly, the rising sun at his back. A dawn raid. Perfect! Freddie would come five seconds after him from a different direction to confuse the anti-aircraft batteries.

Markus straightened the aircraft and locked in the bomb sight system for automatic release. "Piece of cake," he mumbled. Still no anti-aircraft radar on them. This was unbelievable, he thought, just as he heard the low boom in his earphones that meant his electronic countermeasures system had detected sweep radar. "Too late, assholes," he said to himself, as the plane surged up, two thousand pounds lighter. Markus slammed in the afterburners, banked left, and then dropped the aircraft down to within meters of the ground. From the corner of his eye, he saw the speck that would be Fast Freddie dropping down for his attack run. He banked sharply to the right to orient his F15 back towards the coast. Cameras would record it all, but he had to be able to see. Against the five gravities of the "mild" turn that were smashing him down in the seat, he twisted his head just enough to see the chaos of the chemical plant. A mushroom-shaped cloud was moving towards the sky as flames licked at the base of the wrecked building. Farther away, the tank farm was nothing more than a dense brownish-yellow cloud moving downwind. No flames? Maybe nerve gases didn't burn.

His earphones were alive with the sound of search radars. The warble of a missile radar lock galvanized him. Markus punched the chaff button twice and flicked the lighter and more nimble F15 down behind some low hills. He retarded his throttles to 30 percent power and slowed to wait for his wingman as the warble fell away. Scanning while contour flying was damn near impossible. He flicked on the autopilot and let it find its own way using his aircraft's ground search radar. Despite the violent jerking, he searched for Freddie. He was just about to try the radio when the crackle of speaker in his helmet interrupted him. "Bat One, Bat Two on your tail, let's boogie."

Markus, delighted that Freddie was back, waggled his wings and pushed the throttles forward. No more afterburner for now, fuel was going to be tight. A quick bank and they were safe, for the moment, in the mountains.

* * *

Ensign O'Toole, on the FM tactical scan system of the E-2 aircraft, jolted in his seat and grabbed his earphones. "Crosby! Crosby! Holy Shit! Something's coming down!" Crosby put his hand on O'Toole's shoulder.

"Correct reporting procedures, Ensign."

"Jesus, Lieutenant. There are two people, sounds like Americans, talking unscrambled and lots of Arabic. The rag heads, excuse me, Arabs, are excited as hell. They're all over the air defense bands." Crosby tensed. This coast was usually dead quiet.

At the next console, Petty Officer Third Class Campbell grabbed Lieutenant Crosby's sleeve. "Sir! Look at the display." She gestured towards her console. "A lot of search radars in the Al Bahah valley just lit up, and they're staying on. They'd never give away their positions like that unless they were under attack."

Crosby had just straightened up when Petty Officer Jones on the main radar called him over. "Sir, those Israelis are back, and they're just under Mach 1, going directly for the fleet."

"Oh shit," muttered Crosby as he flicked to the command link channel. "Something's gonna hit the fan." Mach 1, he thought, the speed of sound. These guys were seriously moving.

5:27 A.M. Combat Information Center
USS Carl Vinson, Carrier Strike Group Three

The Fleet Watch Officer, Commander Franks, responded immediately as the information came into the CIC. "Wake the Admiral, I'll be up to brief him immediately," he said into the microphone. He shuddered slightly. Admiral "Cool" Cole was not called "cool" because of his pleasant disposition. Most of the sailors thought the nickname came from his icy demeanor. But older hands, like Commander Franks, knew that it was a hangover from the Admiral's days as a naval aviator. Many times he had demonstrated his ability to respond coolly in tense situations. His gift for finding superb solutions to nasty problems with only wisps of information at hand was one of the reasons he had been assigned command of the "oil slick" fleet. Many believed that Admiral Cole would be the next Chief of Naval Operations, but Commander Franks had his doubts. The Admiral might make all the right decisions, but he had an intolerance for incompetence, a bad temper, and a razor-sharp tongue. He would never make it in the Puzzle Palace. Commander Franks was dreading his meeting with the Admiral. It wasn't that he woke up nasty; it was simply that there was bound to be something that Franks had missed, something that the Admiral felt was important.

He knocked on the hatchway. "Franks, sir."

"Enter!"

Franks wondered how the Admiral could look fresh whenever he was hauled out at a moment's notice. "Yes?" with raised eyebrows.

Franks didn't waste any time. Stalling wasn't the way to survive exposure to the Admiral.

"We have two Israeli F15s heading towards us. They claim they need to overfly us to reach their tanker. I checked. It's on the other side of us."

"So?" snapped the Admiral.

"They just came off the coast near Al Bahah. From the radio and radar intercepts, it looks like they hit the chemical weapons facility there."

The Admiral bolted up and grabbed the telephone from the bulkhead. "Watch Officer." Franks listened carefully to the Admiral's clipped commands. "Launch the alert 5 aircraft immediately. Get the CAP out to those incoming F15s and force them away. Get everything that's configured for air-to-air combat up in the air now. Sound General Quarters. I'll be up in five. Do you understand?" The Admiral nodded as the watch officer, at the other end of the line, repeated his orders.

"Okay, Franks," the Admiral said as the General Quarters klaxon began to hoot through the ship. "I want the Fleet on Full Alert immediately. Pull the CIC together and prepare for air combat."

"Is it an assault on the fleet, sir?"

"No, idiot! In about five minutes every MiG on standby is going to be chasing those Israelis our way. If we can't get rid of those F15s, we're going to get tangled, bad. Got it?"

Franks thought he had grasped the implications. "Yes, sir."

"I'll meet you in CIC. Dismissed."

* * *

Moments later, things were just settling as Franks stepped into the CIC. Helmets and life preservers were being tied down as the men settled back to their stations. "Any new information?" he asked loudly.

Lieutenant Chan handed him a yellow message sheet. "Just came in before the message from the E-2"

Commander Franks read the message and grimaced. "The Admiral's going to love this."

"What am I going to love?" Franks spun around at the sound of the Admiral's voice and handed over the message, wondering how he had gotten to CIC so quickly. "They just sent this? Full cooperation for this training mission? Shit!" The Admiral clenched his fists, visibly struggling to control himself. But within a moment, he appeared calm.

Son of a bitch, thought Franks, He really is cool.

"Chan," called the Admiral, "can you reach those Israelis?"

"Yes, sir, we have them talking to the CAP boys now."

"Get me on," growled the Admiral.

Chan handed the Admiral a microphone then looked at the operator of the tactical band radio. The operator nodded back. "You're on, sir. They're using the call sign 'Bat Flight.'"

"Bat Flight, Bat Flight, this is Admiral Cole, commander of the United States Navy Carrier Strike Group. Get away from my fleet. Do you copy?"

From the air, Major Markus nodded at the sound of the nasal voice. He had been briefed on Cole, a real hard case. "Admiral, this is Bat Flight leader. I read you Lima Charles, loud and clear. Sorry we cannot comply. We are almost out of fuel. Repeat, we are almost zero on fuel. I believe our government received assurance that you would allow an overflight."

"That was for a training mission," snapped Cole.

"This is a training mission," countered Markus.

"Don't shoot me that crap, Bat One. You just shot up Al Bahah."

"Sorry, sir. This is a training mission, and we have permission for an overflight."

Commander Franks was impressed, yet again, as the Admiral retained his composure at the blatant lie. Instead of anger, his face took on a calculating expression as he handed the microphone back to Lieutenant Chan. He stepped over to the long range plot. "Look, there they are, the hounds of hell."

Franks could see the MiGs coming onto the screen as the E2 downlinked the information to the CIC computer. The Admiral turned to him. "We've been suckered, well and truly fucked." Franks was shocked. In eighteen months together, this was the first time that he had ever heard the Admiral swear.

* * *

Running on full afterburners, the MiGs were within air-to-surface missile range in less than ten minutes. As required of fleet policy, they were warned off. The results were almost inevitable given the technological differences. Fifteen minutes later, eight MiGs had been destroyed at a cost of two Navy F15s. The Admiral watched the entire battle in grim silence. It was all out of his hands. Even the news that one of the downed Navy air crews had survived failed to cause any visible reaction.

Finally the Admiral turned to Franks. "Get me a scrambled link directly to Admiral Pauling, not one of his flunkies." Commander Franks watched the Admiral's back as he walked to his cabin—the loneliest man in the fleet.

CHAPTER 1: BEGINNINGS

December 3
The Meeting

Hassan Bucheri prided himself on his ability to disguise himself to play any part. Today, he looked like a midlevel Arab civil servant. He admired his reflection briefly in the glass door. Simultaneously, as a matter of habit, he used the reflection to check for watchers. Satisfied, he entered the main office building of the Ministry of Agriculture.

The guard at the reception booth checked his identification and then the authorization list. When he saw who the appointment was with, he straightened slightly and nodded politely. Hassan had excellent hearing and could discern the muted buzzer that allowed him access past the second, hidden guard. He was pleased that he hadn't been recognized. He was, in fact, known to all the major intelligence services. The Russian FIS, Foreign Intelligence Service, which had formerly been the KGB, considered him a star pupil gone astray. The Mossad classified him as a prime target. The CIA and FBI thought that he might be responsible for the bombing of the Marine barracks in Lebanon. He went way back. Now they were sensing his hand in the Nairobi Embassy. After two facial reconstructions, one in Moscow and one in Miami, not even Hassan's family recognized him—not that it mattered now. His older brother had died fighting with the Syrians against the Israelis on the Golan Heights. Hassan should have taken better care of him. There had been golden times, playing as children in the streets. His older brother had always taken care of him, protected him. Now it was too late, lifetimes to late, to repay the favor. There were greater enemies to fight than the Israelis.

Bucheri's memories weren't all old: some still carried their raw, jagged edges. Only nine years ago, the Israelis had flown an airstrike against his family's settlement in Lebanon, perhaps even in retaliation for something that he himself had done. His sister had been killed in that raid. His younger brother, the warm scholar who admonished Hassan about his violent ways, had been blinded by the Rockeye cluster bombs. His father was now little more than a vegetable. And then there was the worst, his recurring nightmare: his mother, a screaming tortured end. Oh, yes, Hassan thought as he considered his many debts to be paid, so very many.

His father had been a village headman when he was very young. The Israelis forced them out of their village to make a new settlement. His father had always been wise and just. Hassan remembered his father's beard, how it moved when he smiled. Even then, when times were hard, he smiled while discussing the world with Hassan, his favorite son. In the beginning, when the family still had some money, Hassan's father financed his studies at Harvard. The turbulent sixties were a time of revolution and hope for the oppressed peoples of the world, and Hassan's father committed the last of his family's wealth to his son's education.

But Hassan's superb intellect and background in English private schools had not prepared him for the abuse from the Harvard Jewish community. At every opportunity they had taken steps to discredit his achievements. Despite the proclaimed liberality of the times, few would listen to stories of his homeland. The politically aware focused on the war in Vietnam, while the rest focused on adventures with drugs and sex.

His only real friend and companion during this period had been Martha Lowell, a vibrant, petite, blond woman from the "old money Lowells." They had met in Harvard Square while looking at posters in a small store off campus. The latest craze at the time was posters with fluorescent colors, illuminated by black light. In the eerie glow of the back room, Bucheri had been distracted first by her vividly fluorescing white shirt then by her rich laughter as she viewed a poster picturing a solider under fire, sprinting across a field. The title said, "Fly South East Airlines and Vacation in Sunny Vietnam." Her response to the poster piqued his interest. She seemed equally intrigued with his intensity and European charm. Their relationship lasted about a year and a half, the last six months of which they lived together. Sometimes, Hassan felt that she stayed with him for his novelty. At other times, they seemed spiritually close. Overall, he thought, Americans are rich, spoiled people. They had never really fought a foreign aggressor on their own soil, nor had they suffered the dramatic losses in war that other countries had. Eventually Martha left him. They had fought over the Vietnam War. Martha was against the war and believed in the power of protest. Hassan argued that American leaders were weak to bend to the chants of a few students, to insignificant losses in war. "Truly," he told her one day, "you are the weak led by the weak."

He studied the remains of his cigarette as he waited now in the Director's outer office. The Director had invited him with the suggestion that he had a very large project to be undertaken, and that Hassan was the perfect man for it. He called himself Professor Montasser, the Assistant Director of Agriculture, but he was, in reality, the Director of Intelligence. A silly disguise, Hassan said to himself, adjusting his brown striped tie, but the Director was not a silly man. The lack of a receptionist or, indeed, anyone else in the waiting area was particularly interesting. Perhaps they are learning about security, he thought, as the electromagnetic lock clicked on the Director's door: his signal to enter.

The Director, a small balding man, greeted him energetically. As they moved through the coffee-pouring ritual, Hassan realized that the Director was waiting for someone—moving slowly so as to buy time. This was odd considering that there weren't many people higher in rank than Montasser.

As Hassan lifted his cup to take a first sip of coffee, a buzzer sounded. The Professor jumped up and hurried to his desk. Again, the massive electromagnetic lock clicked smoothly in the door. Out of instinct, Hassan put his cup down and stood.

As the visitor entered, Hassan was jolted. Allah save us, it's the Leader, he thought. Hassan considered himself a well-educated man—an intellectual of sorts, certainly a thinker. There were few people that he truly feared. This was one of them. A man of enormous ambition, the Leader had personally killed his own family members for resisting him. Hassan found himself torn between admiration, apprehension, and disdain. He found the naked ambition, deceit, and treachery of this man as disturbing as his repression of any group that suggested the slightest opposition. On the other hand, as an Arab, in a world where life was harsh and the weak were crushed, Hassan admired the strength and stature of the Leader, his willingness to fight against incredible odds, opposing all challengers. Most important, the Leader had succeeded in the scorpion's nest of Arab politics and was offering a vision of Pan-Arab unity. He was truly formidable.

"Please," the Leader said, gesturing to the circle of low couches by the coffee table.

Hassan walked ahead, feeling the chill from those cold eyes. As he sat, he noticed that the Leader had no intention of sitting; instead, he began to pace.

"You have heard, by now, of the Israeli and American raid on my chemical plant?"

"Yes," Hassan replied, wondering what that could have to do with him.

The cold eyes watched him. "Do you think the Americans were dupes of the Israelis as they claim?"

Uncomfortable, Hassan decided on the truth. "Probably. They haven't the strength of will to take a step like that. They need endless discussions and allies to hold their hands."

"Perhaps you are right, my friend, perhaps you are right." The eyes gave away nothing.

Hassan kept his face expressionless. Perhaps he had not appreciated the intelligence of this man. The Leader pivoted and pointed at Hassan. "But they are the source of all our troubles, do you not agree? They shield the Israelis, manipulate oil prices, inundate the world with their pornographic filth, and exploit the masses."

Hassan nodded. While this sounded like the propaganda of the Revolutionary Council, it was also close to the truth.

The Leader began pacing again. "The Americans must be made to realize that they are part of the world community; they are not the world themselves. They must see suffering. They must suffer as they have never imagined they could. They must live with the fear of the unknown, as we do. They must be humbled. Do you agree?"

This time Hassan had no trouble nodding. Americans were the weak riding on others' misfortunes. He smiled in anticipation. In a moment of gestalt, all of his years of experience told him that something momentous was about to happen. His dream was within reach.

Again the Leader pointed at him. "You, Hassan Bucheri, are to be my sword! The Sword of the Oppressed." He paused and put his hands on his hips. "You are a man of genius. Bring me my revenge. Do not fail me, do you understand?"

Hassan met his eyes and stood slowly. It was time to take control or his dream would never materialize. "I understand, but the plan will be mine alone. You may approve, or disapprove, but the plan is mine. Do you agree?"

The wait was short, but vibrant with tension. "I agree," the Leader answered with a shadow of a smile.

"There is more. The method of execution is mine, to be done my way, with the people I select." The Leader paused for a moment, and then nodded his agreement.

"We will meet again to discuss your plan," smiled the Leader, ever the skillful politician.

"No! You are too well-watched. I will meet with the Director."

"You are wise. There must not be a whisper. This is too important. Allah is with us. They will dance in hell."

Bucheri watched the Leader's eyes and saw the truth. The rhetoric was cheap, but the way was clear. A lifetime's ambition was within his grasp. "Dance in hell," Hassan repeated, nodding. Indeed they would, and Hassan Bucheri would play the tune.

CHAPTER 2: WARNINGS

10:30 A.M.
January 3

The President clearly enjoyed his private security briefings with the CIA and FBI directors. The intelligence was stimulating beyond anything he had experienced before. Sometimes the news was deeply troubling, but at least these small meetings got to the point quickly without the fuss and egos of the larger National Security Council meetings. The last item on the agenda was New Business.

The President leaned back now that the meeting was almost over. "Well, gentlemen, anything else to report?"

David Lam, the new Director of the CIA, shifted slightly, betraying his extreme discomfort. "Mr. President, we may have some fallout from that Israeli air strike last month."

The President clenched his jaws. That affair had been a cheap, dangerous shot from the Israelis in response to his policy on the Palestinians. Anything that affected the Arab world could cascade into another war. Damn, he hated both the Arabs and the Israelis. "Please elaborate."

The Director of the CIA cleared his throat, another sign of discomfort. "Rumors are rapidly building in the Middle East of a massive terrorist strike against the United States. We've deduced this mostly from phone intercepts and a few hints from lightweight sources. Also, globally, a lot of potential troublemakers are disappearing."

"That's it?" asked the President. Before the CIA director could reply, the President exploded. "You people haven't been able to penetrate that area for twenty years. One of your mandates was to get a network there. You've got to stop counting on satellites and NSA electronic eavesdropping. Those people aren't going to do something that shows up from orbit, for Christ's sake. I should remind you, I gave that same mandate to your predecessor, and you know what happened to him."

The CIA director shifted again. Since the Twin Tower bombings, all agencies were under fire concerning their anti-terrorist intelligence capabilities.

The President watched him for a moment, then continued. "Do you think that you could set your rivalries aside for a little while to accomplish this small mission?"

The CIA and FBI directors nodded.

"You know, I've always wondered whether we should combine the CIA and the FBI for a nice seamless intelligence effort. Save some money too. Hopefully work out a lot better than the Homeland merger."

Charles Wesson, a veteran of many bureaucratic battles and director of the FBI, kept his face expressionless. "Perhaps it would be best if we got on this immediately. A mission-specific joint task force might be appropriate."

The President, now in a pit-bull mood, rose to signal the end of the meeting. The directors waited for any last words.

"Try and keep this out of the press. That's really half the battle, isn't it? That's what these people really want, and we won't give it to them, will we?"

"No sir," they replied.

Wesson paused at the door and turned. "Shouldn't we be bringing in Homeland on this?"

The President flushed red. "Are you serious?" he hissed furiously.

Wesson thought to answer. He opened his mouth and then closed it. "No sir."

The President glared for a moment then said, "You'd better get someone really good for this—really good. Someone who can handle all aspects, if you catch my drift."

Wesson paused for a moment before he realized, or thought he did, what the President was saying.

* * *

"Don't call her 'Loony Tunes,'" the President snapped at Harvey Betworth, his best friend and Chief of Staff.

Harvey smiled. "You're right, maybe 'Calamity Jane' is a better term."

"Damn it Harvey, you know what would happen if it got out that either you or I had called her that? Especially with her psychological problems."

Harvey Betworth stopped smiling. "Melody Jane is a problem, boss."

The President sat down. "Well, no shit. How did we ever get into this situation?"

Harvey Betworth sighed. "Well, she's conservative. The Teapots loved her. Hell, most of the Republicans did. She was a trade for the Consumer appointment, and they hated that."

"Christ, Harvey, it was a rhetorical question. I guess it was. What I mean is, why did we not know that she had problems?"

Harvey shook his head. "As the Assistant Attorney General I guess they kept her in the closet. She had a good record but that could be her staff. She is just so fixed-minded and scary. Have you ever had her stare at you? She could freeze a martini. I think the previous administration left her for us—a ticking bomb."

The President started to pace. "The Republicans pushed the vote over the edge. Could they really have wanted a nutcase as head of Homeland Security? Did they set us up to fail on something as important as that?"

Harry shrugged. "Maybe they didn't know. We won't find out soon. Why worry? We just need to contain her. She's a disaster. She keeps holding doom and gloom press conferences and people are leaving Homeland in droves. She works them like dogs on nonsense assignments and shrieks at them when they fail. Three top team leaders quit this week alone. How do we remove one of our own nominees after only a month?"

"I think she's clinically paranoid," said the President. "I'm not surprised the name Melody Jane Harmony got turned into Loony Tunes."

Harvey watched the President pace a few more steps. "Do you have a plan?"

The President stopped in his tracks. He turned slowly to face his Chief of Staff and gave a wolfish grin. "Don't I always?"

12:15 P.M.

The Director of the CIA and the Director of the FBI were observed by a Washington Post reporter meeting at the Army-Navy club for a hastily arranged lunch. This was very unusual, given their competitive situation, but with no additional information the reporter shrugged his shoulders. Mini news was no news.

Inside the private dining room, both men were concerned.

Dave Lam sipped his Perrier and wiped his brow. "Charley, he was serious about combining us. I don't want you to take this lightly."

"Dave, the Bureau wouldn't function right if we lost the intelligence capability. I'm surprised he didn't threaten to combine you with the NSA. Hell, they could swallow us both with their budget." Charley Wesson was upset too, because he knew that the "police" function of the FBI could easily be pared off, leaving it a weak shadow of its present self.

Charley leaned forward. "What did he mean about 'finding someone special'?"

Dave reflected for a moment. "I think it was triggered by my mention of Homeland. I think he flipped out thinking about Loony Tunes."

Charley tapped his chin for a moment. "I think I have the man."

"He'd better be quick on the uptake," Dave said. "I think there's going to be a lot going on. Our intel suggests that this is going happen very quickly and be seriously big. Bigger than 9/11. Whoever is orchestrating it is really good, based on his ability to hide something this big for so long."

Charley nodded. "My guy has been on the shelf for a while, but we've kept him around because he's brilliant and ferocious. He's just not your standard Special Agent type climber."

Dave squinted, "What if it gets really ugly? Just to start with, Homeland is going to shit a brick, and I would not want to mess with that wacko."

Charley laughed. "Well, he's past our normal retirement age," he said, and shrugged. Dave took that as an admission that this agent, whoever he was, could be sacrificed. "But if you mean can he handle himself in a shit storm?" Charley added, "I'd have to say that he's more likely to make one. He's un-PC, which is one reason he hasn't gone up very high. He's mission-oriented and just blows past the politics. Not a good way to rise in the system."

Dave leaned back. "He sounds ... interesting. Well, I guess your agency will have the lead, if there is such a thing on a mess like this."

Charley leaned back too and looked at Dave for a moment. "OK. We'll use my guy. But realize that he can be unorthodox—in your face one moment while plotting like Machiavelli the next. The outcome you might be able to guess, but the path you can't. He really should have been with you guys. We're both going to have to back him up."

There was a moment of silence. Then they both stood up and nodded, each deep into his own understanding of the situation.

2:30 P.M.

Harley Jones was uncomfortable sitting in one of the leather chairs around the coffee table in the Director's office. It wasn't that he had done anything wrong—at least as far as he knew. It was that old hangover from the Hoover days. It just wasn't good to be summoned to the Director's office, even for the head of the Special Research Unit. He rose as Charley Wesson came out of his private bathroom, drying his hands on a towel. The Director stopped for a moment, then absently flicked the towel back into the bathroom.

The Director gestured to Jones to sit back down as he flopped into a chair himself "Pour us some coffee please, Harley, and tell me how the SRU is doing now."

Jones frowned slightly at the strange request. He had just turned in his semi-annual report on the new team. "Well, sir, as I reported…"

The Director's head swiveled rapidly towards him, like the turret on those Phalanx anti-missile guns Jones had seen in a news video. "I read the report, damn it! I want to know how things really are."

Oh shit. "We're doing as well as can be expected. We've downsized by 40 percent under the new budget and, quite frankly, we've lost some good people, especially young blood. We've got most of our old expertise and that helps with the liaison linkages…"

The Director raised his hand. "I'll cut to the chase, Harley. I know that you've done well. You built the SRU from nothing. It's tough to be downsized and maintain a capability. Now that you know I'm not after your hide, let me light up your life. There are going to be some big changes. The Bureau and the Agency have decided to form a joint task force to handle intelligence and action on terrorist groups and individuals when they present a perceived immediate danger. We will share a common database. Active measures inside the U.S. continue to be our responsibility while the CIA continues to hold the power for outside the country. Understood?"

"Yes sir, that's astounding. How did they ever agree to that? In fact, why did we? And, what about Homeland?"

The Director paused a moment with his pale blue eyes on Jones. "You are to form a group which would control all of the police and intelligence assets in a specific area, like a city or even a state. Similar in some senses to the Homeland Fusion Centers, but leaner and mobile. You've studied the problem theoretically; now it's time to pull together a team that could actually do the job, instantly. No call up, build up … none of that. The next point is this, and I want you to take me seriously: I want you to prepare to meet a larger-scale threat than those you've gamed before. Think big, really big."

"Is there something you're not telling me?"

"Lots, but nothing that you need to know yet."

"It's going to be tough with our present staffing level."

The Director rose and extended his hand to Jones. "Congratulations on your appointment as the task force commander and as an Assistant Director of the FBI. Remember, think big."

Jones was stunned. An Assistant Director, with a force of less than one hundred agents. It was the strangest thing that he had ever heard of in all his years in the FBI. While his mind raced over the possibilities, he stood up and took the hand of the Director quickly, as he had been taught to do by his father, an old-time FBI agent. He looked into the Director's eyes for a clue, a hint of deceit, a flash of bravado, but there was nothing.

Homeland Security Headquarters
Nebraska Avenue Complex, Washington D.C.

Susan Page, Deputy Secretary of Homeland Security, looked across the large clean expanse of Melody Jane Harmony's desk. Melody Jane Harmony was the Secretary of Homeland Security and knew how to keep people in their place. Susan Page had come with Melody Jane from the Department of Justice. It wasn't that she was a friend of Melody Jane, because Melody Jane had no friends. Susan had seen a chance to ride the rocket of her boss's unexpected windfall. Susan's mission was to keep the missile on course. Melody Jane thought that this was her responsibility, but Susan knew better.

Susan put an organizational chart on the desk. "There it is, the mess that you inherited. KPMG's audits still aren't signed off, and we have more than 30 organizations, some not linked, all fighting for a chunk of our budget. You have almost a quarter of a million people working directly for you and almost two million first responders under our umbrella." She sighed. "I know we've talked about this before but you've been busy visiting the organizations, and I wanted to make a point now that you're back. In short, you have everything from the Border Patrol to FEMA. If anything goes wrong, anywhere, it will come back to you."

Melody Jane shook her stringy dishwater blond hair out of her face as she sat back. "I should have the FBI too. I'd be willing to give the CIA to the Pentagon for that." The Defense Department was one of only two departments with a bigger budget than hers.

Susan wondered whether Melody Jane had lost focus or, perhaps, had a plan. "How would that make things any better?"

Melody Jane nodded. "Then we would split into two sub sections, making things easier to control." She liked control.

"There would be law enforcement, everything from Border Patrol to the Coast Guard and Secret Service, even the TSA." She paused. "We've got to get the TSA guns," she added as an afterthought, which Susan dutifully wrote down.

"Then there is just FEMA and Immigration," Melody Jane continued. "The FEMA could certainly be dumped. All the cyber warfare stuff really is law enforcement." She paused again for a moment. "We've got to get more control over the networks. We should have central nodes that can lock down the net. We can peel a billion off the budget for that. That's only one percent."

Susan sighed again. It was going to be a long day. She would have to explain congressional oversight and executive approval again. It wasn't that Melody Jane Harmony was stupid, but she sometimes focused on one thing to the exclusion of all else.

January 7
Recruiting

"Of course you want the best people," snapped Professor Montasser, the Director of Intelligence. "Everyone wants the best assets. But these requests will devastate our—"

Hassan Bucheri cut off the Professor with a wave of his hand. "Director," he said, "must I go to the Leader? You are aware of the importance that he places on this project aren't you?" Bucheri stared hard at the Director. He was tough, yes. No one rose to be director of the intelligence service by being weak, stupid, or squeamish, but a confrontation with the Leader would be unthinkable, if not terminal.

The Director made a pushing gesture with both hands as though trying to force Bucheri back into the armchair in which he was already comfortably seated. "Perhaps if you could explain why you want some of these ... things." Again he held up his hands, this time as though to ward off a reply. "Not enough to compromise security, just so that I can satisfy myself and the Leader that these ... things are ... worthwhile."

Bucheri sighed. God but he hated nosy bureaucrats, but sometimes they must be accommodated. "What specifically were you curious about?"

"Well, for example, I understand why you don't want to use more of our people, but why so many Europeans and Asians?"

"First, this must appear to be an international effort. Second, if there is no obvious ethnic group, it becomes much more difficult for the police to put out a general description."

"I see." The Director nodded. "And why soldiers as well as freedom fighters?"

"There are two phases of this operation. The first is best done by terrorists—what you call 'freedom fighters.' These people are quite happy killing civilians, men or even women and children. They are not happy working against armed men. Soldiers, on the other hand, will not willingly kill civilians but are well suited to fight armed men. Is that satisfactory?" Bucheri raised an eyebrow.

"Well, it certainly is a different approach from what I have come to expect of these affairs. I must tell you quite frankly that I was not initially pleased with the Leader's desire for revenge. I'm feeling much better now that it is in professional hands."

Bucheri watched carefully, but there was no sign of patronization.

The Director continued, "I'm still concerned about these foreigners. Why Koreans, Vietnamese, and worst, the Japanese?"

"The North Koreans are from their Special Forces. They are skilled with explosives and other useful tools but, even better, they are absolutely superb at hand-to-hand combat. Their lifetime training of Tang So Do karate makes them deadly. As for the Vietnamese, after fifty years of war, they are the best killers of all. The Japanese are included because they are a classic terrorist group. To the Americans, all Orientals look the same, so the Japanese are convenient. If necessary, they can be sacrificed."

"I see." The Director nodded again. "Do you think that will be necessary?"

Bucheri hesitated a moment. "I have made a number of contingency plans. With the proper financing there is no question of failure. It is only a question of how successful it will be. There won't be any problem with the financing?" Once again, Bucheri fixed the Director with his stare.

The Director hesitated, but the Leader had been quite specific. "There will be no problem. It is just unusual to pay the whole amount before the operation is completed."

Bucheri nodded. "Nonetheless, that is the way it must be. This will be my last battle. There must be no question of a lack of commitment from any party."

The Director nodded, wondering whether Bucheri believed that this was a battle against the infidel or simply another mission. In any case, it didn't matter. If this worked, it would be worth every penny. But with everyone able to speak English, it would cost a fortune. Then again, the blood would flow like oil. The Director smiled at the analogy. Bucheri took the gesture as a sign that the interview was over and rose to his feet.

Startled, the Director rose quickly too. "There is one more thing. There is a volunteer for your mission. I want to introduce him to you now."

A spy, thought Bucheri. God damn these transparent amateurs.

"You don't have to take him, but I think you'll find him passionately motivated, highly intelligent and, as a bonus, there is no possibility that he has a record."

"Who is this treasure?"

The Director ignored the remark as he pressed the button and ushered in a man with thick glasses and a middle-size frame, about the same as Bucheri's but with the soft look of the unexercised.

25

"Let me introduce you to Dr. Kamal, the former manager of our chemical facility at Al Bahah. He speaks faultless English, knows a great deal about chemistry, and his wife and two children died in the tragic chemical release. He could be very useful."

"Please, I will do anything you say to strike back in some way." The man's eyes begged. "Revenge is all I have to live for."

Bucheri hesitated a moment as he examined the soft man. "Lose twenty pounds in the next three weeks and I'll take you," he answered with a smile.

CHAPTER 3: TRAINING

January 28
Somewhere in the Somalian Desert

"My apologies, Mr. Buch— excuse me, Hassan, but it all seems so backwards from what I had expected."

"Ali, I will not call you Dr. Kamal and you must not call me Mr. Bucheri. You simply must grasp the concept of security. Now, Ali, what exactly bothers you? I will explain everything I can to you since it is important that you be able to act in my stead. Deceit is everything. Deceit and knowledge. How convenient it is that you, too, were educated in the United States. That is one of the reasons that I decided to allow you to join me in this mission. It will give you a broader frame of reference." Bucheri nodded approvingly at Dr. Kamal. "This may work out very well indeed. Now, what is wrong?"

"Well, to start, why are we spread out in tiny groups all over this cursed desert? Shouldn't we be together to build a team spirit and better coordination?"

"Ali, if this was a football game, or even, perhaps, a conventional military raid, you would be correct. We have isolated the groups so that none of them can compromise us if they are captured. They all know that this is a large operation. That's enough. We have far too many secrets that they could deduce just from seeing each other."

"Of course. Just the knowledge that we are using Asians could give something to the enemy."

"And our Europeans are treasures not to be given away lightly. So we isolate them in cells. They will become very cohesive and self-sufficient within these cells. That is as it must be."

"If I am to act for you at times, perhaps you could tell me more about the groups and what they will do. That sort of knowledge would seem appropriate, wouldn't it? I don't know quite what you expect of me."

"It's simple. I want you to pose as the leader of the operation."

"But why? Surely your name has drawn them to the banner of the oppressed?"

Bucheri smiled indulgently at Dr. Kamal's jargon. "It's simpler than that. Terrorism of the type that we have known is fading. The intelligence organizations of the world powers, particularly the Mossad, have infiltrated almost every potent organization. Every group that has committed forces to this operation has done so for money or to satisfy a

27

debt to the Leader. Every individual in these groups will be paid a large sum of money. For many, this will be their last operation. Time has run out for our kind. This will be the last bright flash of the freedom fighter. With luck, it will be a blinding flash."

Dr. Kamal blinked in surprise. Bucheri, as was his habit, watched his subordinate's response closely. Finally Bucheri said, "You think me cynical?"

Dr. Kamal swallowed but said nothing. Bucheri sighed and gestured with his hand for Dr. Kamal to sit down. Dr. Kamal would have sighed too, for this usually meant a lecture, but he was intensely curious and slightly apprehensive.

Bucheri started to pace, his eyes on the ground. He spoke slowly, searching carefully for his words. "Terrorism is simply the application of military force by those who have no formally recognized national status." He stopped to make certain that Dr. Kamal was listening, and then continued, "If France bombs a German railroad station, it becomes an act of war, and warfare is just one of the methods of extending national policy. If one is not a nation, and one performs the same act, then it must be banditry, no matter the motive. Do you understand the rationale?"

Dr. Kamal hesitated, then shook his head. "Of course not," said Bucheri. "It's not a logical argument, it's simply self-serving. If you have a patch of land that I can bomb and a flag of your own, then you can be a nation. If I wish, we can fight by whatever rules we agree, and if I take your land then you cease to be a nation and are no longer a player in the game of nations."

Bucheri paused for a breath and squinted. "If you are a group without land, not a nation, then you have no legitimacy. There can be no prisoners of war, no treaties, and no negotiations. None of the amenities of nationhood. The Palestinians are only one example of such a group. These groups are not allowed to arm, and all their acts become criminal rather than political. All nations publicly condemn the actions of these groups, although they may approve of their motives. Do you see why this is, Ali?" Bucheri was clearly getting to the point now; Dr. Kamal could feel the tension from the man, as he shook his head.

Raising his hands in the air, Bucheri said, "It's obvious. If nations recognized these groups in other countries, and their right to arm themselves, they would have to recognize the same type of groups in their own countries. Every religious, economic, and political group would arm and fight for its cause. So the lesson is simple—" Bucheri paused for effect— "You cannot be recognized as a nation unless you are a big terrorist. The Israelis are the prime example. You must be more than a terrorist, you must be lots of terrorists. Then you become a revolutionary power, which the Americans have made acceptable, and then you have semi- legitimacy. If you seize power, then you may finally have succeeded. The important point is, radical political movements starts with terrorists, then grow to revolutionaries and finally they can form governments."

Bucheri exhaled loudly. "As for us, we are the last of the professional terrorists. Many of us were trained in state schools to be the nuclei of revolutionary change. We are modern in the sense that we do not attack military targets but, instead, attack civilian targets. This is simply a reflection of modern methods of warfare. We are no more evil than Winston Churchill, Roosevelt, Truman, or any other wartime leaders. Those last three, idolized by the west, killed hundreds of thousands civilians with fire bomb raids on Tokyo, Dresden, and..." Bucheri threw his hands up again. "The mind boggles. It didn't end in Japan with Hiroshima and Nagasaki, completely civilian targets. Look at the complete destruction of North Vietnamese and Iraqi society."

Turning to Dr. Kamal, Bucheri shrugged. "So you see, civilians have been legitimatized as targets by the west. As modern soldiers, we go for the nerve center, the maximum effect with public opinion: we go for what the financiers call 'leverage' by attacking appropriate civilian targets. Maximum effect calls for maximum media impact, as you will see."

Dr. Kamal's expression shifted. Bucheri nodded encouragingly. "Ask!"

"But all of these different groups, they do not seem ideologically sound together. It is just so ... odd."

Bucheri leaned down to put his face close to Dr. Kamal's. "You're not putting this together, Ali. We're professionals. I've told you. This is what we do. We don't bake cakes, and we don't drive trucks. Some of us have personal reasons for this job—certainly you and I do—but for most of us, it is the last job, a way out. State-sponsored terrorism is dying with the last of the ideologically based states. Only Iran plays this game. We have entered the era of the amateur terrorist, the eco bomber, the ignorant religious zealot, the Tylenol crazies. For us, the professionals, this will be the last statement."

Bucheri was looking into the distance as Dr. Kamal finally worked up the courage to ask another question.

"But, still, why am I pretending to be the leader?"

"So that I can be in two places at once. If I must leave this desert, you will carry on, and the Sword of The Oppressed will continue to be honed. When we are at the target, we will have the same advantage. The

Americans do not like things that they cannot explain, and a terrorist in two places at once will make them uncomfortable. During training, there are other advantages. I will pose as your driver. While you talk to the leaders, I will talk with the troops. Leaders lie, but troops do not. Soon I will know the truth."

"It is no wonder that they call you 'The Fox.'"

Bucheri paused. "Actually, they call me 'The Butcher.'" He smiled gently. "But I like the name. You may use it. You had more questions."

"The Europeans, what should I know about them?"

"The Germans are versatile. They are former East German Secret Police, *Stasi*. They speak English well, will take orders like robots, and are capable as both terrorists and soldiers. They are also extremely mercenary, so their motives are clear. The Germans will pose as businessmen that have come to buy computers in order to run a factory in Germany. They are mature, older, as are many of our people. That too is outside of the profile that the police agencies use. They were once important and well paid, but after the fall of the Berlin Wall they were lucky to get jobs as janitors. They were humiliated and impoverished. They need this job for many reasons.

"The Romanians were secret police also, but their English is weak. They will serve well as soldiers, as they have demonstrated in their own defense. These men are survivors. The Italians are a different story. They are emotional. They must be pumped up with rhetoric. They will probably be good for only one set of killings. They may hold together or they may collapse. They are still communists, so treat them that way. Use terms such as 'world solidarity of freedom fighters' and 'strike against the ultimate imperialist.' We will use them as terrorists; they do not have the training to be soldiers. They will pose as businessmen that have come to open up an Italian food store chain. They will move into an Italian neighborhood and rent space."

Dr. Kamal nodded, trying to capture the essence. "And the Asians?"

"The Japanese are very well-disciplined terrorists. They will be the point of our dagger. Good fanatics, they will not allow themselves to be captured."

"That seems rather old-fashioned."

"That is exactly what these Japanese think they are—reincarnated samurai. They seek honor above all, and that is what you must sell them … the honor of it all. Be very forceful with them. They will want to think of you as their new liege lord."

"And the Vietnamese?"

"Yes, the Vietnamese." Bucheri contemplated the shimmering desert for a moment. "These are mostly intelligence officers caught allowing too many boat people to get away. They took too many bribes and didn't pass enough on. Greedy. After their experience with their own prison camps and those of Cambodia, they will kill anyone without a second thought. They will not be willing to be shot at, so they must be used as terrorists, and…"

"Yes?"

"Never touch them, especially on the head. That is a terrible insult. Just give them their orders. They are in this for the money."

"And the Koreans. The North Korean Special Forces. They are soldiers. Yes?"

"I will handle the Koreans. They have a special task."

"Our own people will be much easier."

"I hope so. The former Republican Guard troops are all well-educated, many of them in America. We should have no trouble with them. Naturally they must be kept away from the Iranian Army groups. The Iranians are professional soldiers, not Revolutionary Guard cannon fodder. You can see the problems that could arise if those two should meet on a training exercise. The Syrians are former secret police. They may still be secret police for the new regime. Probably they are spies. They are certainly not trustworthy, but they will make good sacrificial lambs. Understood?"

Dr. Kamal was smiling. Bucheri lifted his eyebrows. "I believe that you are beginning to enjoy this."

"All my life I have worked with chemicals," Kamal said. "Now I am seeing more of the real world, people, politics… I am fascinated, yes, and excited. I am only saddened with the cost, my family. It adds a bitter taste which will make victory all the sweeter." Kamal pulled out a notebook. "And the training?" he asked.

"The training will be similar for both the soldiers and the terrorists. Firearms work with semi-automatic rifles and pistols. Hand-to-hand combat with emphasis on knife work. You will bear the primary responsibility for teaching them about your specialty: chemical improvised weapons. I will have others instruct them on military and civilian explosives. They will be critical to our work and everyone must be skilled with military, civilian and expedient types. They must also become thoroughly familiar with our communication methods. The theory can be learned here, and we will practice on site. Transportation is another problem. I have acquired one motorcycle and one automobile for each group. I expect everyone to learn to drive and ride a motorcycle. Several groups will have to provide a truck driver. We have one large truck here, the supply truck, which they can practice with."

Bucheri glanced at Kamal's notebook. "You are taking notes, good. But this must be memorized before you meet the teams. Also, those notes will be destroyed before you leave here. I will search you myself."

Dr. Kamal looked up from his notes, blinked, and nodded. After a moment he asked, "The question of equipment might arise. What should I say?"

"Tell them that the Americans will provide most of what we need. We will swim in their wealth. Chairman Mao would have liked that expression."

Dr. Kamal looked up quizzically. Bucheri shrugged his shoulders at Kamal's ignorance.

"And if that doesn't satisfy them?" Dr. Kamal asked.

"Smile enigmatically. It is something that leaders do." Bucheri smiled. "And there is one sacrifice that you alone will have to make."

"In addition to my weight loss? That was very difficult. I am a shadow of my former self."

"Yes. You must finish your portion of the training early. You will leave in ten days for Mexico. There you will get plastic surgery. You can be recognized now, and that would lead the Americans straight to the Leader. You can understand that?"

"For my wife and children I will do this. Who will I look like?"

Bucheri put his arm around Dr. Kamal's shoulders and smiled slightly as they gazed out across the desert. "With luck, Ali, you'll look like me."

CHAPTER 4: COUNTDOWN: SUNDAY

13 April
Stirrings

The SRU had morphed into the new CIA/FBI Counter-Terrorist Unit—CTU to the insiders—and was now housed in the old FBI building in downtown Washington, D.C. The meeting room was in the middle of the building protected from laser bugging devices which could pick up vibrations from windows. Long, narrow, and dirty light beige, it was standard issue government in every way. Some members of the team considered the building and room a bad political omen, but Harley Jones only shrugged. He had other things to think about.

Theodore Browner was second in command of the CTU. People in the CTU tended to call him Ted or Teddy. Ted didn't know whether the heavies in the CIA took the CTU gig seriously, but he certainly did. Browner was a Company Man to the core and proud of it. He tugged gently at the vest of his Armani navy blue suit. His hair had been razor cut the day before. He believed that a manager should always look and act the part. His experience at Yale, Princeton law school, and fifteen years in the Central Intelligence Agency had given him confidence in his leadership style.

Browner watched the section heads as they filed into the dingy meeting room. Jessica Williams laughed warmly and playfully elbowed George Alvarez. The informality of the CTU grated on him like fingernails raking across a chalk board. As he watched, he analyzed. Browner wore two hats in the new CTU, second in command and head of operations. Both were positions of considerable strength. Charley Montresor, head of intelligence, was also a CIA man, giving the CIA a strong share of the power. Montresor, a small, slim man with wire rim glasses and a quick smile, was joking with George Alvarez. Alvarez had a warm Latin charm which was complemented by an encyclopedic knowledge of electronic surveillance techniques. Alvarez was short, like Jones, but his stockiness had given way to softness and he had faint acne scarring on his face. Rumor had it that the ladies loved him. He vibrated with life as he settled back in his chair and flashed a brief smile at Harley Jones. Montresor and Alvarez: two more pawns on the board.

Tall and lean, Jessica Williams moved with an attractive economy of motion, her long brown hair pulled back in a casual tie. Her eyes swept the room and locked momentarily with Browner's. Browner's memory shifted back to the briefing file the Agency had collected on the FBI SRU personnel. There were hints that Williams and Jones had been involved in the past, before the SRU was formed. Strangely, the relationship seemed to have broken off soon after she came to the SRU. Browner closed his eyes and shook his head almost imperceptibly. As an analyst, he knew that the data was so skimpy that it shouldn't be taken too seriously.

The last person, John Woods of the FBI, was more to Browner's taste. His blue suit was nicely complemented by a maroon tie. Woods sat down primly and placed a clean yellow pad on the desk before pulling out a gold fountain pen. He arranged the two items carefully on the table top as the room settled down. Woods headed Support Section, an organization which would provide everything from equipment to transportation. Browner nodded: Woods was perfect.

As an officer of the intelligence community, Browner's job was to evaluate data and look for patterns and anomalies. Harley Jones was just such an anomaly. In his baggy gray trousers, wilted white shirt, and leather flying jacket, he couldn't be meeting the FBI dress code, Browner thought. His shaved head and glasses made him look like a professor. The biggest anomaly was that Jones was an Assistant Director of the FBI. There was only one rank higher, Director. Jones outranked Browner considerably, and it just didn't fit with all the other data in his history. Jones hadn't followed any conventional path to promotion. In fact, he appeared to be a bit of a maverick, based on the slim file the CIA had compiled on him.

Browner's reverie was as interrupted as Harley Jones shifted up from his deep slouch, leather jacket creaking. Suddenly Browner realized that Jones had been watching him the whole time. Without a word being spoken, all eyes shifted to Jones. Browner couldn't help but be irked. At six foot three inches and two hundred and some pounds, he should have dominated the room. He didn't. One-hundred-and-sixty-pound, five-foot-eight-inch Harley Jones did. Nonetheless, Browner listened very closely. Harley Jones's mind clicked like a super computer, and he had all the interpersonal skills of a barracuda. Despite the friendly way his subordinates treated him, the rumor mill said that he was a dangerous man to cross.

His black eyes centered on Browner. "Ted, please summarize the overseas data."

Just as Browner was about to start there was a brief knock and the door opened. A small Asian woman slipped in with an embarrassed grin and a nod to Jones. She was quite pretty, Browner thought, and about his age. He glanced across the table and saw a look of puzzlement in Jones's eyes. Jones gestured around the group.

"Ladies, gentlemen, Jeannie Kawai, our liaison with the forensics labs." Jones paused for just a moment. "Just back from a tour with Scotland Yard?"

Jeannie nodded and answered as if in apology as she slipped quietly into the nearest chair, "Just off the plane. Sorry."

Jones nodded and turned back to Browner. "Please continue Ted."

As the highest ranking CIA representative and second in command, Browner was responsible for overseas data. "There are two sets of interesting but uncorrelated data. First, a suspected training camp has been spotted very deep in the Somalian desert. It's so deep in the desert that the Somalians may not have authorized it. They may not even know about it. The reason it took so long to spot is that there are a number of sites. Each site is tiny, one or two tents, one vehicle and the infrared signature of a generator or small motor. We didn't do a high resolution scan until yesterday, and most of the sites are empty now. All of the personnel we photographed at low resolution were wearing wide-brimmed hats, so we can't tell much, but by their shadows we estimate that at least twelve of them are shorter than five foot six inches. Ten of the shorties were in two groups of five. We estimate that these are Asians of some kind. Too small for Chinese.

"There are several firing ranges for various distances, but that's standard stuff. There are a number of holes blasted in the ground, suggesting demolition work. That's not common. The dispersion of the sites is unusual. And I guess that's it. Questions?"

Jones held up his hand. "We'll hold with the general questions. Can we get somebody in to check out the site and perhaps snatch someone?"

Browner felt his triceps flex involuntarily. Controlling was where the promotions were, but he had loved his days of field work. "I've asked the Navy to put a Marine Force Recon team in the vicinity as soon as possible." Browner looked at his watch for a moment. "They might even be there now."

Browner had taken a risk in authorizing the Recon insertion on his own. This would serve as a test of Jones's leadership style and the CIA's commitment to the joint CTU project. He had forwarded his request through the CIA, directly to the Director. He was pleased with this double-edged sword. If either party came at him, he could always claim it was a test for the other. He watched Jones carefully.

Jones nodded slightly, apparently in approval. "Give us the rest."

"Well, obviously we don't know what every individual in the terrorist community is doing, but we do have ways of watching the overall flow as well as some individuals. At the 95 percent confidence level, there is a disappearance of over forty known or potential terrorists." Chairs squeaked as the team tensed. "Our estimates are bound to be low, so something big is going on. In some cases, like in Italy, entire cells have disappeared. There has never been anything quite like it on the international scene, although we've certainly seen this happen in a given country. Something big is happening. There is one solid indication that this might be coming our way."

Browner paused and Jones nodded. "They all speak English."

Groans filled the room. Jones waited, but Browner shook his head slightly. Jones nodded an acknowledgment and began, "Good, we need to know more about these people, both as individuals and then any common threads, like the English. All of you are on the network, so start familiarizing yourselves with these files. Next time we meet we'll want some answers, either based on hard facts or first class extrapolation. Who, What, and Why? Most important is What: the target. Next item."

Jones paused for a moment as the team members digested what he had said. "I'll summarize some of the local and almost local news. Under normal circumstances, these items would pass unnoticed. First, today at the Toronto airport, a man of Asian extraction killed two RCMP officers in hand-to-hand combat. He was unarmed. Unfortunately, he was killed when he tried to escape with one of the officers' pistols. Public speculation is that he was a hijacker, but he had just come in from Seoul, so that theory doesn't float because he was going through Immigration on his way out of the airport, not in."

John Woods chipped in, "Sounds like he thought he was Bruce Lee."

George Alvarez leaned over, "This guy *was* Bruce Lee. Strictly baaaad."

Jones raised his hand for silence.

"His passport is Chinese, but his features are not. Second, as Mr. Alvarez points out, this person did not learn his skills watching movies. Next, a truckload of bulk explosives is missing. It was sent in from ICI in McMasterville, Quebec and should have arrived at the Burlington Marble Quarries in Vermont yesterday."

Browner looked quizzically at Jones. "What are 'bulk explosives'?"

Jones paused. "They are used in mining. They are delivered in a truck that works somewhat like a cement truck. It mixes the explosive to about the consistency of oatmeal and then pumps it down into holes in the ground. It won't explode by itself. It needs an 'initiator' like TNT."

Browner nodded. "Doesn't sound too handy for terrorists."

"Yes, it would be unprecedented for them to use something like this. But then again, a truckload of this material has never disappeared before. Granted, it's only been missing for twenty-four hours, but a truckload is a big bang."

Jones took a sip of water, then started again. "Next item. In the vicinity of the missing explosives truck, a gun shop was cleaned out. The Green Lantern Gun Shop just north of Plattsburg in northern New York State. The shop didn't carry any paramilitary weapons, but everything high powered including at least ten large-caliber pistols is gone. The operation had a very professional look to it. A dog was killed silently and a security system bypassed. The only unusual thing reported in the vicinity was a group of diners at a restaurant down the road, the Royal Savage Inn. The waitress remembered a group of four men, because they had German accents and none of them drank anything. That area is close to Quebec. Lots of Quebecers come down across the border to shop and beat their taxes, but they have French accents and drink like fish."

John Woods rolled his slim body forward. "Doesn't all this hint at New York again? Either the U.N. or Wall Street. Those big glass buildings are deadly when a bomb goes off out front. The Bogotá police were decimated when the druggies blew up only two hundred pounds of explosive in front of their headquarters. It hailed glass slivers inside, just hamburger left."

Jones nodded. "Thanks. That's the kind of extrapolating we can use. Unfortunately, this last bit of news doesn't confirm your hypothesis, although it doesn't deny it either. The Border Patrol has informed us that a well-known smuggler was killed in San Diego last night. He had been tied up and executed with a single stab up into the brain. This sort of dispassionate killing is uncommon in that area—not a classical Mexican knife fight.

"I'm going up to New York to see what can be done on the Green Lantern weapons case. See Browner with any problems. Questions?"

There were no questions. Harley Jones stayed in his chair as the team filed out. They were a good team, he thought as he watched them talking among themselves. The new CIA personnel were integrating nicely with his Bureau agents. Each of these staffers had four or five people working for them as well as access to other Bureau or Agency services. It should be enough.

CHAPTER 5: PLAYERS

Jeannie Kawai

Monday morning, FBI Special Agent Jeannie Kawai woke to the click of her music system starting up. She stretched luxuriously as the theme from Flash Dance reverberated through the apartment. This was the way she started every day. She loved mornings, and she loved her work. "Life is good," she told herself, as she did every morning.

Perhaps it wasn't always so, but one must struggle to make it so. Her family wasn't happy with her career. Mostly, though, it was her father, the master of the house and of the family. It wouldn't be so bad if he was a jerk, but he was a great man. She remembered his warmth and strength, the blanket that had covered her for so many years. He was disappointed that she had refused to join in the family business, karate. He said she could have been great, the best woman in the islands, his masterpiece. In that way, he was very un-Japanese. He believed that women could do anything. So, with a sigh of resignation, he had allowed her to go on in school. Even her decision to go on for a PhD degree in chemistry hadn't been enough to cause a rift. She was the tolerated, even indulged, little black sheep.

When she had announced at dinner one night that she had applied for a position in the FBI, her father had simply left the table. She had followed him out immediately He was about to learn that while her brothers were great fighters, she was the child with steel in her soul.

"What's wrong, Papa?" she had asked.

He was standing braced against the rail of the balcony. "The FBI? The creatures that rounded us up for the camps, America's Gestapo." He turned to face her, his eyes narrowed in anger. "How could you?"

She hadn't flinched. "Times have changed in the FBI, Papa, in the whole country. With enough minority agents it won't be possible for them to discriminate like that."

He turned away again, looking out across the valley towards the ocean. "The whole country discriminated. You know what they did, how we paid."

To a stranger listening, it would have seemed that he was talking about Manzanar and the other camps in which American citizens of Japanese ancestry had been held while their former communities robbed them of their possessions. Perhaps the stranger might also think that Jeannie's father was referring to those same Japanese-American men who had formed the 442nd Army Regiment and fought in Europe to become the most decorated unit of World War II. But Jeannie knew better; it was much more personal. Her father's mother, her grandmother, had died of pneumonia in the camps, unable to get medical assistance. Her grandfather had been with the troops in Europe, so her father had failed, he felt, as the man of the family, at the age of thirteen. It was a terrible shame that even her grandfather had not been able to remove when he came home to raise his son.

Jeannie slipped out of bed now, and pulled her nightgown off over her head, symbolically shedding her father's disappointment. She had own sense of *giri,*duty. Hers was to her country and to herself, to being the best she could in her life. Sometimes she wondered if she was really so different from her father after all.

For a moment, she checked her body in the mirror. She tensed her leg and watched the muscular definition as she rotated. Then she winked to herself in the mirror. A lifetime of working out was showing. She was aging gracefully—all anyone could ask.

She pulled on her body suit and went out to the living room. The music reverberated along the wooden oak floors: one of the reasons she had chosen this apartment. As always, she moved up within a few feet of her picture window and started her stretching as the rising sun cast long shadows across the city. Now she was swaying to the music, stretching her lats before getting down to the serious leg work. Briefly she glanced at her watch: 6:15. Right on time. Fifteen minutes more stretching, then an hour of dancing. A quick shower, then off to the Bureau. It was good to be back where she belonged.

Harley Jones

The corridors were endless, branching left and right, going on to infinity. He was running. Someone was after him and getting closer. He branched to the left and kept running. Bells were ringing everywhere and the someone was getting even closer.

Harley Jones woke groggily and slammed the alarm clock into silence. Only the ringing of his backup alarm clock in the kitchen kept him from fading back into sleep. It had been a terrible night again. He was slipping back into a clinical depression. The drop had been dramatic, almost instantaneous. His heart had sped up and his right hand had tensed almost to the point of clenching. His whole body chemistry had shifted. Now he had a metallic taste in his mouth and sleep was a disaster. He could get to sleep, but a few hours later he would wake up. Then he would skim the surface of sleep until dawn, his mind racing. At the moment it was racing over his baby, the Counter-Terrorist Unit. He had spent seven years building the SRU, the FBI part, and then watched it slashed in Bureau budget cuts. Now a major problem was coming down the pike and no one would, or could, tell him anything.

Jones groaned as he got out of bed stiffly. As always, only a long hot shower could make him feel human. Naked, he padded over the cold floors and started the shower, stepping back carefully to avoid the initial cold rush. Then he stepped numbly into the stinging spray, waiting for life to enter his body.

As his mind started to work, Jones thought about the recurrence of his depression. It was no comfort at all to know that five percent of the population was in a major depression at any given time. There was only one word for his relapse: depressing. He shook his head. Now he was getting depressed about being depressed. That was the way it went when you were depressed: every thought turned to shit. Maybe he should go back to Dr. Mayer, his psychiatrist. It had taken over a year to find him, a stress specialist who could really cut right to the problem, no mumbo-jumbo hypnosis or detailed histories. Jones shook his head, thinking about his first experience with a stress specialist, Dr. Christine Trudeau, the blond bomb. Jesus! Four weeks just getting a history, then "How do you feel now?" "How did that make you feel?" Feel, feel, feel, what a pain in the ass. He didn't know how he felt about things. He just felt like shit, that's all. He had known what the problem was then—the death of his best friend, Tom Coyle. How did he feel? What a stupid question. How would anyone feel when they let their negotiator get blown away? What a miserable morning.

Jones stepped out of the shower and toweled himself in front of the foggy mirror. Zoloft. He'd have to go back on Zoloft, the antidepressant. He'd call Dr. Mayer for the prescription right away. The cost of care from Dr. Mayer came right out of his pocket, not the Bureau health plan. It had to be kept out of his records. There was no way that the Bureau's psychology department was going to get hold of him. Dr. Mayer understood that. It wasn't paranoia. It was fact. Nobody with any psychological problem on record, even depression, ever made it far in the Bureau, despite the propaganda of the psychology department. The agents had an expression for it, "shrunk for life." It wasn't even supposed to show up in your file, but somehow, the word was out. Burnout, alcoholism, divorce, death of a partner, drug addiction, all cop problems, to FBI agents as much as to anywhere else. Just don't let anyone know that you were seeing a shrink, and especially, don't ever see the Bureau's shrinks. It was just one more bit of carefully concealed bullshit that the Bureau could never quite break past.

As he laced his shoes, Jones sighed. Thank God for work. When he was depressed, it was the only place where he felt decent. Work kept him too busy to be depressed. It was the end of the work day that he dreaded. Nights were the worst.

Sharif Al-Hawari

Sharif Al-Hawari lay in the rumpled bed, stroking the inside of Karlene Davidson's thigh as she lay half asleep. Karlene was his American treasure. A graduate student in geology at M.I.T., she had decided to take him on as a project; the sexual education of an underprivileged Palestinian, she had called it. Surprisingly, they had gotten along well outside of bed too. As his ignorance turned to expertise, Karlene was pleased with the imagination and skill of her protégé. "Fucking good," she had called it until he had finally convinced her that her rough language was unfeminine to him. To their surprise, their sexual relationship had turned into a love affair. Karlene enjoyed a kindness and sensitivity difficult to find in the company of the egotistical, driven graduate students at M.I.T. Sharif bathed in her depth, fascinated and pleased that a woman could be his equal. Perhaps that was the real source of his discomfort as he remembered his call from "Uncle Paul" this morning.

"Sharif Al-Hawari?"

"Yes," answered Sharif sleepily.

"It's Uncle Paul."

Sharif jolted upright in bed, eliciting a groan from Karlene. "Yes. Thank you for the fruit." This was the response meaning that he had not been captured.

"You've gotten all of them?" He must be referring to the apartments that he was supposed to have rented. The cars had been purchased months ago.

"You sent four types didn't you?" Sharif asked, checking the number.

"Yes. Were they good?"

"Yes. Everything is, ah, was, perfect." All four apartments were furnished and the rent was paid for four months.

"Excellent. I'm in the country now. Things will be happening soon, so I expect we will be together again. Your mother sends her regards."

His mother probably did send her regards from Beirut, where Sharif had learned his fighting skills from the old men of the last war, as they prepared him for the next.

"Goodbye."

"Goodbye."

Sharif cradled the phone carefully, and then settled down quietly next to Karlene. He snuggled into her, spoon fashion, and put his arms around her. He couldn't, however, sleep at all.

Private John Miller

Private John Miller, of the Massachusetts National Guard, Company C, 182nd Infantry Battalion (Mechanized), was eating his Raisin Bran as his mother fried two eggs over-easy for his father.

"George, these eggs will kill you with that cholesterol and God knows what they feed chickens these days. Half of the ones I buy have broken legs or something."

"They're mutants, Mom. They're growing on Mars now because the gravity is lower so they grow bigger." John and his father exchanged smiles.

"Don't give me that moon stuff, John. They're pumping them full of drugs like … those Russian Olympic winners that lost their medals..."

"Mom. If the chickens were full of that stuff, they could run away and we wouldn't be eating them. They'd be eating us."

"Don't be making fun of me. You know what I mean. I can read. I know what's going on."

"Right, that's why you think I'm going to be sent to Russia with the National Guard. We're going to keep the peace in Red Square."

"Don't laugh. The National Guard got sent to Iraq, didn't it? I read in Newsweek that they were also the first sent to Korea during that war. The extra dollars you get for playing soldier could get mighty expensive."

"Mom. The last time my unit was even put on alert was when we were almost flooded with Hurricane Irene. Now, will you have my uniforms ready?"

"Don't I always?"

"You always come through, but we're going to have to restrict your reading." John gave his mother a kiss as he picked up his lunch box. "Dad, try Wheaties, the Breakfast of Champions."

Patrick Henry Johnston

Pat was on the couch again. His Kodiak bear, all eight feet of him, looked down at him. Damn, he thought, I should have brought Margie along for that hunt. I could have shot her, stuffed her and mounted her. Oops! Accident.

Sleepily he rolled over and saw some of his other trophies. A head from the alligator he had shot with a .357 pistol. That thing had been fast. What a rush. There was the white mountain goat head, a 400-yard cross wind shot after a four-day hunt. He had been so cold he could barely work the action. And finally, his only trophy from Africa, a Cape Buffalo head. Stopped at five meters after that idiot Slowinski had wounded him. That time, he remembered, he had been truly frightened as the buffalo moved around them through the tall brush. The Cape Buffalo was supposed to be one of the most dangerous animals to hunt, and it sure as hell was smarter than Slowinski. Slowinski was lucky to be alive and he still walked with a limp. No more hunting for him.

Pat swiveled his head a little farther around. The famous thirteen gun rack. He used to bring girls back to the apartment, and they'd see the rack of guns. Whether they liked hunting or not, it seemed to turn a lot of them on hotter than a Saturday night special. Once, two at the same time. True, they were teeny boppers, but it was one more trophy.

His life was in the rack—from the .375 Holland and Holland to the .222 varmint gun, they were beauties. Husqvarna, Remington, Mauser, and Beretta: he had some of the greats. He swung his legs off the couch and padded over to the window, touching his 870 Remington briefly as he went by. He always put the short slug barrel on it and loaded it up with double OO when he was at home. It was his house gun, his friend in need. The only one he kept loaded. For close encounters it was all he would need.

Downtown Boston was already stirring. He watched his neighbor, Joyce LeBeau, climb into her BMW. She had been lucky to get a parking place right in front. Pat counted the parked cars to the end of the street and then multiplied by three. One hundred and twenty yards. At that range he could shoot a two-inch group with his 6mm varmint gun.

Hassan Bucheri

Hassan Bucheri put down the dossier and moved to the hotel window. Below people streamed through the streets, the ants of Boston. Soon it would be time to kick this ant hill over. His mind ran back to the camp in

Gaza, the smell of his mother's cooking on the kerosene stove while he played outside with the ants. His mother had been strong and kind, never harsh despite the coarseness around her. She didn't mind him playing with the ants, and he told her what he had learned. A few ants were special. Disturbing them affected the whole nest.

The cell phone beeped, disturbing his reverie.

"Yes?" he answered. "Oh! Excellent. Thank you very much. You are so kind. Would you like to have lunch when I'm in town again?" He paused again. "Yes, I'm sure he'll be surprised. Bye now."

Bucheri smiled faintly. It was time to perturb an ant, a very special ant.

Nadia Nikolsky

The steady pace of her run was soothing. Among other things, Nadia Nikolsky was a professional athlete and she enjoyed demanding workouts. Her hair was loose now, flowing behind her like a horse's mane in the breeze. Men stopped and stared as she ran past. Below her dark red team shorts, her leg muscles slid easily under her smooth skin. Her breasts were clearly outlined through her tight top with the old Soviet CCCP letters still on it. Nadia ignored the men, as she always did. Beauty was a tool and she wanted nothing from them. She had an assignment and would excel, as she always did, but this time would be different.

Twenty kilometers, a good light run. She stepped up the pace as she passed the high school where she taught part-time. For the first time during her run, Nadia smiled. As the grimy walls slid past, so would the rest of her grimy life. Again she picked up the pace.

Pamela Clark

As always, the radio-alarm startled her when it started with the seven o'clock news. Eddie Herman's voice was terrible and she knew she could do it better. The man just had no style. She grunted and gently lifted her sleeping mask off. The room was completely dark, but Pamela Clark had seen Greta Garbo wear a sleeping mask and been caught up in the extravagance of it. She stretched against the silk sheets, luxuriating. Languidly she got out of bed for her shower. In the bathroom she had a series of yellow Post-Its stuck to the mirror. They fell like yellow snow as she showered. She reviewed them as she brushed her teeth and then rinsed with whitener. The last note galvanized her: an appointment with

Geri this morning. A girl in her business had to look good, and Geri would do it for her. She'd been waiting months to become one of his clients, and she certainly wasn't going to miss her first appointment. She straightened up for a moment and caught herself frowning in the mirror. "Stop that" she told her face and the wrinkles disappeared. Was it fashionable to be late for an appointment with someone like Geri? She shook her head. She just couldn't take the chance.

As she walked out of the bathroom, she patted a varnished carved wooden sign which read, "Today is the first day of the rest of your life."

Melody Jane Harmony

The alarm woke the Secretary of Homeland Security, Melody Jane Harmony, at 5:30 exactly. A quick shampoo and blow dry, and she would be ready to dress. Dressing was easy—she had only three suits. One was beige, one was gray, and the other was navy blue. All of the colors had been selected after reading *Dress for Success*. They were all power colors, and the suits were cut for a stern no-nonsense look. Frivolity was not in her nature. Her driver, a Secret Service agent, would pick her up at 6:30. She would be at her desk by 7:00, setting an example. Her driver would bring her breakfast, yogurt, cereal, and black coffee at 7:30. Using a Secret Service agent as a waiter was a slight indulgence, she felt, but they were hers to use.

As she dried her hair, she wondered if the drying couldn't be done in the car, saving fifteen minutes. That would get her to work before 7:00. Now that would really be setting an example. She also decided that she could get an additional edge by using another agent to read the news to her as she dried her hair in the car. With almost a quarter of a million people working for her, she had to optimize. She would need two secretaries, she decided, both men. Men were less moody and catty.

Jik Kang

Captain Jik Kang examined himself in the mirror. Briefly, he allowed himself a moment of satisfaction. At thirty-nine, he was as strong and fast as he had ever been. His lean body rippled as he moved, muscles sliding effortlessly as he shifted from one form to the next. His thighs were pillars of strength, yet he was as flexible as a ballet dancer. Finally, he finished his forms and dropped to the floor to stretch again. He was mildly dissatisfied with the exercise, as he hadn't been able to jump or do anything that might cause a thump on the floor. It was essential that he not attract any attention.

As he stretched, Kang let his mind drift. The floor was a cheap linoleum. It gleamed now, with the multiple scrubbings and waxings that Kang had put into it during the last three days. Americans were filthy. It was inconceivable to him that anyone could have lived in the room as it had been before. The landlord should have been ashamed. He shook his head faintly. He had scrubbed the walls and washed the windows, all for just a week's total occupancy. It was worth it. He had his pride. In North Korea, the lowliest peasant would be embarrassed to live in a room so filthy. A Korean private would be beaten senseless for not cleaning up his section of the barracks.

Kang shifted to a sitting position on the floor to begin his mediation. His breathing slowed and shallowed. He didn't notice the sweat cooling on his body as he steadied his mind with the image of clear calm waters. With his eyes closed, he sensed the room. All of the room was in his mind: his cheap suitcase, the shotgun under the blanket, the knife under the pillow. He felt the vibrations of someone walking down the hallway before he heard the soft thump on the cheap carpet. He could smell the insect killing spray that he had applied around the baseboards. Behind it all, he could hear, smell, feel Boston. The cars, the people, the parks, the buildings, all a giant hunting ground for Captain Kang. When this was done, he would be a rich man, and life would no longer be hard. Perhaps he would use his false Canadian passport and immigrate to South Korea. Wouldn't that be a joke? Kang smiled for the first time that day.

CHAPTER 6: COUNTDOWN: MONDAY

9:10 A.M.

Harley Jones stepped out of the elevator and walked across to his office. He checked his watch and grimaced slightly. The Bureau liked people on time, especially supervisors. Still, he ran the CTU differently. People could work from their computers at home as far as he was concerned, as long as they got the work done. Work, especially smart work, was what Harley Jones wanted. Clock punching was for drones, he thought as he opened the door.

Nancy Coyle looked up and greeted him cheerfully. "Morning Harley, you look like hell. Why don't you sack out on your couch? I'll hold your calls."

Nancy Coyle was a great secretary—administrative assistant really. Once they had almost made love on that couch, but Jones had stopped it in time. Nancy was special. Because she was Tom Coyle's widow, he had found a job for her. She had turned out to be a treasure with a keen mind, but more than anything else, she was a reminder. Every day that Jones came into the office and saw her, he would flash back to Tom Coyle's death. For just a moment, he would see Tom Coyle buckling forward as the rifle round passed through his stomach. That was enough. Jones didn't need to remember watching him bleed to death as they tried to retrieve him while a firefight raged. He didn't need to remember all his other mistakes from that day. He never should have allowed Tom to go out at all, let alone without a bulletproof vest. The situation had felt wrong. Over the phone, the kids had sounded hyped up, but Tom, ever compassionate, was convinced that he could talk them in. Jones had allowed the whole thing to unravel against his better judgment. Seeing Nancy was his reminder: never again would he allow someone to challenge his judgment. Jones knew he wasn't God, but he wasn't going to let anyone slack off around him. Not once. New people either shaped up quickly or disappeared. He wouldn't take second best from anyone. He knew that he had a reputation for a vicious temper, but it wasn't true. He would far sooner thrash someone verbally than watch them die later. If they couldn't handle the heat, they could move to someone else's unit. Nancy understood his "temper" without ever having been told. She just didn't realize that she was his daily reminder of the kind of mistakes that made her a widow.

"Nancy, get somebody from Operations to find out who dedicated a song to me this morning on 99.0 FM. They played it about fifteen minutes ago."

Nancy arched her eyebrows. "A song?"

Jones nodded. "*White Rabbit* by the Jefferson Airplane."

Jones went in to his office and slammed the door. Son of a bitch, *White Rabbit*. Gracie Slick echoed through his mind as he flopped into his chair. Fucking pills making me larger and smaller...

Somebody was watching him, onto him like a glove. His hands shook. As long as the Bureau didn't find out about the depression—or worse, the Zoloft.

Jones sat slowly back in his chair and closed his eyes, breathing deeply as he struggled for control. Slowly he pulled himself together. They must be following him. Who? Why? Chasing rabbits, falling in holes ... the song was haunting him.

It was a puzzle, perhaps a clue. He could handle it. Who was he chasing? Was he going to take a fall? "Men on a chess board telling him where to go"—who was the chess piece, who were the players?

Maybe it wasn't about the Zoloft at all. Maybe it was about perception, versions of reality. Did he care what the dormouse said?

Jones bolted upright with understanding. It didn't really matter who or what. What really mattered was that he was personally targeted, and that could only mean that the CTU was going to get into something heavy, deep, and very bad. Jones experienced a thrill of fear.

The phone rang, jarring Jones from his thoughts. Relieved at the interruption, he picked up the receiver.

"Jones," he said.

The phone was silent for a moment, then a smooth voice with the polish of an educated man said, "Did you like the song?"

Jones felt as though a bolt of electricity had hit him. "*White Rabbit?*"

"Of course," the voice replied with a silky smoothness. "I know all about you, Harley Jones. I know more than anybody, even your friend Dr. Mayer."

Jones had thought after the last shock, that there could be nothing worse. Hearing Mayer's name was worse. No one knew about his visits to the psychiatrist.

"Oh yes, Harley Jones," the voice continued, "I'm going to play you like a chess piece. You're going to dance to my tune, as you will soon see." There was a moment's pause and then a click.

Jones remembered the one time when he had known absolutely that he was going to die. The Huey had lost power at a thousand feet and fallen like a stone after the 12.7mm caliber bullets had shredded the fuel lines. The pilot had laughed later and explained that helicopters could autorotate by getting their blades spinning as they fell, then use the spinning blade to land. The stark terror of freefall gripped him again.

10:45 P.M.

Dr. Kamal now called himself Ali in all his dealings. He was pleased at the way everything was working. Now he understood what Bucheri had meant when he said, "The Americans will provide the tools for their own destruction." He was enjoying his role as a terrorist. At his fourth warehouse, this one on Cottage Street near Central Square in Cambridge, he received another shipment. This time it was chlorine gas cylinders from Lynde Chemicals. Beautiful yellow cylinders, all lined up against the wall. Twenty Soldiers of the Oppressed, waiting to serve. When he had gone to George Washington University in Washington, they had had a saying: "Better living through chemistry." Now he had coined another: "Better killing through chemistry." The environmentalists would probably tie up the legal system for years instituting checks, and the chemical industry would stagger after the attacks. Meanwhile, his credit card was his weapon. The Americans would sell anything.

He glanced at the barrels of ammonium nitrate against the other wall. He was curious about the boxes from Radio Shack and Mass Army-Navy store, but the nervous Korean was always around. He wanted to look, but it wouldn't be wise to disobey Bucheri on this, or any matter, with the Korean around. The infidel was useful, though. Some of the filthy young neighborhood blacks had been curious. The Korean had caught two of them as they tried to look in the windows last night. Ali had giggled as the Korean beat them just badly enough that they wouldn't have to go to the hospital. It was the methodical nature of it that had terrorized the blacks. After a disabling kick, each was dragged into the warehouse, tied by the hands and feet and then hung from the center beam by their arms, racked meat. The Korean then taped their eyes and mouths and circled them, pinching, punching, and twisting as his victims tried to scream through the tape. That Korean had an extraordinary knowledge of human anatomy. Dr. Ali Kamal shivered. What the Korean could do with just a finger!

49

CHAPTER 7: COUNTDOWN: TUESDAY

5:30 P.M.
Massachusetts Avenue, Cambridge

Sharif was weaving his bicycle through traffic as he moved towards the Harvard Bridge. Two minutes on the bridge, three through the streets and he would be back with Karlene. Maybe there would be time for a quickie in the shower before dinner.

He had shown every site that he had rented to the man who introduced himself as Uncle Paul, although he knew it wasn't the same Uncle Paul that he'd encountered before. Similar, but not the same. The voice was different and the manner was different. The original Uncle Paul had met with Sharif only once, in a dark basement in Beirut. He had power, a presence that was tangible even in the dark. When the original Uncle Paul had given Sharif the chance to study in the United States, he had taken the offer immediately. Beirut taught you to make decisions quickly. His records would be faked, but he would try his best. Sharif knew that he was good—he had always been the best in his class—but Harvard? Indeed, Harvard had been too difficult. But failing at Harvard had a certain prestige to it, and he had eventually been admitted to Boston University in downtown Boston. Surprisingly, Uncle Paul had not been upset about the change. He just urged Sharif to do well in his studies.

And now everything he had worked for was in jeopardy. The cause of his people, the oppressed of Palestine, might be highlighted, but his own life, for which he had worked so hard in Boston, might be in danger too. He had friends and, in another year, a degree in Business Administration, and most important, he had Karlene. How long could this last? Would the secret police, the FBI, come for him? Would he go to prison, be deported, or simply be shot in a dark basement? Would Uncle Paul continue to fund him? How could he live without the money? He gripped the handle bars rigidly in panic.

Sharif was wondering whether he should discuss this with Karlene when he swerved in front of a Ford delivery van. The driver braked, and Sharif came alert to the howl of burning rubber, but it was already too late.

Spiders Sporting Goods
11:23 P.M.
Massachusetts Avenue Near Porter Square, Cambridge

Detective Paul Andrews of the Boston Police Department elbowed his partner, Detective David J. Maloney. "What are the Feds doing here?"

"Fucked if I know. Why don't you ask them? Then ask why we're here. This is Cambridge."

Detective Andrews shrugged. Who gave a shit about the snotty Feds? What was the big deal, anyhow? Organized crime didn't need to knock over a sporting goods store. Still, it had a certain touch of class. Strangely, though, they hadn't taken any of the cash, just the guns and ammunition. Down in the little basement shooting range, all five of the staff were lying side by side, legs and arms tied with wire, and their elbows pulled back tight with wire too. Andrews tried to remember where he had seen someone tied like that. Even tidier, they had their eyes taped and their mouths stuffed with bandannas. They'd each been shot twice in the head with a .22. No noise from the sound-proofed range. The only sign of a struggle was one clothes rack which had been knocked over. It had all been done right at closing time. Neat.

But there was no reason for the FBI to be here. The Suits had barely glanced at the bodies; they were having a party with the store records. Andrews snorted in disgust. That was no way to solve a crime. Ledgers, invoices, receipts. They didn't tell you diddly.

CHAPTER 8: COUNTDOWN: WEDNESDAY

2:43 A.M.
The Conversation

Hassan Bucheri used the encrypted cell telephone, just like a dope dealer. It was almost impossible to tap as long as he kept moving from one transmission cell to another. The occasional glitches in the conversation as he drove by buildings and trucks were an annoyance, but only that. He carefully punched out the number as he drove down Interstate 93. With no one in sight, this was as safe as it could be.

There were several clicks, and then the voice known to millions of Muslims answered calmly. "Yes?"

"Brown Fox here," Bucheri replied.

"An appropriate code name, Brown Fox. Mine will be Black Knight," the Leader said.

"The unpredictable piece."

"Let us hope so, for all our sakes. Perhaps you can answer a question for me? Can I name the cities? Would that be a breach of security?"

Bucheri answered without hesitation. "Yes. It would. But at this point it does not matter. Please ask your question?"

"Why have you selected Boston? Why not New York?"

"The answer is simple. New York has been done. Anyhow, they have a very effective police system now. They could be a problem. And only New Yorkers care about New York."

There was a short pause, then a burst of laughter from the other end. "Tell me, does all the rest go as we planned?"

"Yes. As well as can be expected with an operation of this size. I lost one piece, but it was not critical."

"I hope to hear your stories later."

"If it is possible, that would be entertaining. As for now, we are ready to begin. It is daylight where you are. You must make the final deposit."

"It is an extraordinarily large payment, Brown Fox. I would prefer to pay after the mission."

Bucheri had expected this, but he was nonetheless disappointed at the cheap gamesmanship. Still, considering who he was dealing with, it was no surprise. "As I explained before, this is my last mission. It may also be the last for many of my associates. If it seems like a great deal of money, then consider how much money you lost in the ten minutes of the dog fight over the American fleet. Every MiG 29 cost at least ten million dollars. You lost, what, eight?" Bucheri paused for this to sink in. "If the money is not deposited within twelve hours the operation will be canceled. We are running on a critical schedule; there can be no failures on anyone's part, including yours."

Talking like this to a man with the Leader's ego was risky, but it had to be done.

After a pause, the Leader replied, "You are a mercenary, Brown Fox."

"I am a realist, Black Knight. That is why you hired me. Ours is a marriage made in heaven. You just paid the dowry. Now I will do the honors."

There was a pause, then the Leader spoke with a more commanding tone. "Well put, Brown Fox, wave the bloody sheets. She will be a virgin no more."

Bucheri nodded as he hung up, surprised at the Leader's command of English. Perhaps he wasn't as crude as some claimed him to be. He smiled as he thought of the Leader's terminology, "virgin." That was precious. But America was not about to lose her virginity, she was about to become a rape victim.

What did they say on that television show? He wondered. Ah yes, the proverb, "Revenge is a dish best served cold." Bucheri selected Janis Joplin on his phone music player's list of favorites.

Baby bye bye

Bucheri hummed along then sang with her on the last stanza.

Just like her, he'd have to "face it alone."

CHAPTER 9: COUNTDOWN: THURSDAY

9:35 A.M.
His Master's Voice

Pamela Clark leaned back in her swivel chair, pushing off the lower desk drawer which she had pulled out to use as a foot stool. She leaned back carefully to avoid touching her hair to the wall. Geri had given her just the right look for a hot TV reporter, and she didn't want anything to mess it up. A small smile curled the corners of her carefully painted lips. She didn't need to look in a mirror. She had watched her face a thousand times on video. It was great—not perfect, a bit thin, but great. Her body was a little lean too; maybe a boob job would help, she mused, as she changed the image in her mind from almost flat to model size.

Her smile grew when she remembered the time that she had shown genius and worn her white dress to the anti-abortion riot. One of the rioters had splattered her with chicken blood, but no one in the audience had known that when she taped in front of the ambulance while wounded riot police and rioters alike were being carted away. It was really just a question of insight. It was going to carry her to the top.

Sighing, she gave up the moment of self-indulgence and settled in to study the potential stories for today, looking for a winner. By the end of the list she was disgusted. Another day of mugging victims, building openings, and state financial disasters. Her telephone rang.

"Hi, Ms. Clark. This is Louise at reception. There's a man that wants to talk to you but he won't say what it's about and won't give a name. He sounds foreign. Shall I put him on?"

Pamela didn't hesitate. She was safe at work and her home phone was unlisted.

"Sure, put him on." She fumbled only briefly as she put the suction cup microphone onto the telephone earpiece and pressed the record button on her tape recorder. It was illegal as hell, but who cared. It saved taking notes. "Yes? Pamela Clark here."

"Hello Ms. Clark, are you listening very carefully?" The tone was crystal clear with a slight foreign accent that she couldn't quite place. It felt like the man was in the room with her. Eerie, somewhere in the background she could hear the Doors song,

Hello I love you.

And then something about "tell me your name…"

Something warned her and she grew more alert.

"Yes. Who am I talking to please?"

"I am the hand that wields the sword." Pamela groaned silently. Another nut case. Might as well jerk him around for a few laughs.

"Which sword is that?"

"The Sword of the Oppressed."

Pamela perked up a bit. This was getting more flavor.

"What can I do for you Mr. Hand?" said Pamela, barely able to keep the laughter from her voice.

"That is very good, Ms. Clark. You may call me The Hand. That will be the code name that we will use to authenticate our communications." Pamela chilled slightly. Something in the tone caused her to look around to see if anyone was watching her. "You have been selected because you are ambitious. I am going to lead you to a series of stories which can propel you onto the nation's television screens, but you must work hard. I am giving the same opportunity to several of your competitors. That is the American way isn't it—competition with only the best surviving?"

The tone was entirely rational and deadly serious. Pamela sat up. "What do you have to say Mr. Hand?"

"It is very simple. The official message that we wish made public is the following: *America must pay for its sins. Boston, the birthplace of America, will burn for America's aggression. Everyone must leave Boston or be burned with it.* Did you get that?"

"Yes. I got it. But it doesn't carry much weight."

"I understand. Be at the east end of the Harvard Bridge at exactly five o'clock today with a camera crew. If the police are there, you will have lost your chance. Is that all quite clear?"

"Yes, but I need to know what will happen."

"Anticipation is an excruciating pleasure, Ms. Clark. Your footage will get you on national, perhaps international, television. That's what will happen."

"Who are you? Really?"

"We are the Sword of the Oppressed, Ms. Clark. And you will see the first slash. For us, the joy of enlightenment. For you, fame or obscurity."

The click of the receiver echoed in her ears like the clash of cymbals.

She knew that he had cut off the last of the Doors' lyrics, something about jumping into the game. It was just plain creepy the way that had been timed.

Gently she placed the receiver down. She placed the suction cup microphone in the drawer and turned off the tape recorder. Slowly she moved her chair back into her thinking position. The news director would never go for it, she decided.

She rocked forward again and resumed her perusal of the list of possible assignments.

9:45 A.M.

Dieter Schmidt was relaxing in front of the television admiring the legs of Maria Shriver, the smart, rich Kennedy, Arnold Schwarzenegger's former wife. There was one man who had made it into the big time. Soon, Dieter nodded, soon. He wouldn't marry a Kennedy, but he would have a comfortable life, perhaps in Cuba, where dollars went a long way. Gerta wouldn't mind moving, although the boys might. Reunification had been a disaster. At least before, they had been their own masters, despite the Soviet influence. The carpetbaggers from the West had taken over the East—incompetent leaches. Any former communist was excluded from any decent position: they were the new Jews. As for Dieter and his kind, vanishing seemed the best idea.

The phone on the coffee table rang. Dieter slid his feet off the table and leaned forward to pick up the phone. His movements were calm and deliberate—those of a professional.

"Yes?" His accent was heavy.

"George?"

"Yes. I am speaking."

"Fox here. I have a game for the Golf team."

Dieter knew that this wasn't the man that he had originally been introduced to, Bucheri. Bucheri was supposed to use the code name Brown Fox, but this man's voice was different, even though the accent was similar. It didn't matter though. Things like this were done in the business, as long as the verification procedure was followed. If someone had gotten into that … well, like the Americans said, "Shit happens."

"How will the weather be?"

"Overcast but warm, I'm told."

Dieter exhaled a sigh; the code was correct.

"Where will the game be?"

"It will be with Harvard at a place of their choosing." So it was to be the east side of the Harvard Bridge. An excellent choice.

"When will it be?"

"That's not exactly settled. But I'll come pick you up at sixteen-thirty." Sixteen-thirty plus half an hour. Seventeen hundred. This Fox fellow was careful, using European time to make absolutely certain that he wouldn't be confused by the American a.m and p.m.

"Anything else?"

"As we planned, there should be some news people there. I think you should get there early, as we discussed, to make certain that everything suits you." There wasn't anything new in this message. Perhaps The Fox was an old woman worrier, but at least he was thorough. That was important to Dieter. A good planner was worth ten hard men.

"I understand."

"Good luck."

The phone went dead. Dieter walked into the kitchen where his three colleagues were checking their equipment. The table was neatly covered with newspaper while Hans cleaned the pistols, American revolvers with enormous impact and penetration called .357s. He and Hans carried their 9mm Mausers as backups. He felt more comfortable with the automatic, but orders must be followed. The kitchen cabinet was slightly open, and he could see the plastic explosive neatly stacked on the shelves.

Dieter followed the procedure The Fox had insisted on, always speaking English. "We will make the attack at seventeen hundred as planned."

They all nodded quietly. Hans asked, "Where?"

"The Harvard Bridge. There is supposed to be news coverage. We will go in any case. Chris, you have our video camera don't you?"

Chris nodded. He was uncomfortable speaking English but understood it well enough.

"Well then. How about a game of cards?"

4:37 P.M.
M.I.T., Cambridge

"Jeremy, come on."

"Jesus, Pam. What's the rush? No one is going to give a damn about a new library at M.I.T. There isn't a chance in hell that the boss is going to air this. You would have had a chance at that rape victims' convention. You must have bent your antenna getting up this morning." Jeremy had been Pamela Clark's cameraman for seven months and he had never seen her behaving so energetically *after* a taping.

As they started for the van Pamela said, "I'll drive."

Now Jeremy was truly confused. He hadn't even known that she could drive. Then he relaxed. She must have a hot date.

"Got a hot rod all lined up?"

Pamela looked at him blankly, then realized what he had said. Her voice tight, she answered, "Just keep your camera in your lap." Now

Jeremy knew that something was up. The bitch wasn't going to tell him, so he wasn't going to ask.

As they pulled onto the Harvard Bridge, Pamela slowed to a crawl and scanned carefully from side to side between anxious glances at her watch. Jeremy watched her briefly, then decided to join her in watching the traffic. He was the first to notice the smoke from the far end of the bridge. Already traffic was jamming in their lane while the opposite side was deserted.

Pamela hissed, "Damn! Get out. We're going to check this out." She pulled over to the right of the lane, and then bolted out of the van and started running up the bridge sidewalk. Jeremy jumped out to follow, but even despite her high heel handicap he could barely keep up.

As they got closer Pamela could see the source of the smoke: a white Cadillac with open windows. Flames were coming out of the driver side door. As she got closer, she saw two men beaten back by the heat as they tried to open the passenger side door. Finally, opposite the Cadillac, Pamela could see what they had been trying to get out: a burning corpse. She could see the glasses still resting on the nose of the victim as she moved closer, glancing back briefly to be certain that Jeremy was taping. Even more clearly, she could see the shape of a scimitar spray-painted in vivid red on the door of the Cadillac. Just then, the gas tanks exploded, knocking her down and singeing her eyebrows. As she fainted, she hoped that her underwear wasn't showing.

6:02 P.M.
Harvard Bridge

Pamela took her cue from Jeremy. She was excited, but it wouldn't show. She would be the headline story on the Six O'Clock News on her station and probably all the Boston stations. With a little luck, the nationals would pick it up.

Short and powerful, that was the key. Let the anchor ask the questions.

"This is Pamela Clark reporting from the Harvard Bridge in Boston. At five o'clock a man was tragically burned in his car, apparently the result of a Molotov Cocktail fire bomb attack. A scimitar outline was painted on the side of the car. Based on a communiqué received by this reporter earlier today, we believe that this attack was perpetrated by an organization called 'The Sword of the Oppressed.' We have no further information at this time, but we believe that this is a foreign-based organization. Back to you Sam."

Sam, the anchorman, was primed. "Why do you believe that this organization is foreign based Pamela?"

"I talked to their representative for several minutes this morning, He called himself 'The Hand'—that is, 'The Hand that Wields the Sword.' He seemed to be well educated and he had excellent English vocabulary, but he spoke with a slight accent. Definitely foreign."

"What did he say to you?"

"My notes state that he was calling to warn us that 'America must pay for its sins.' He went further to say, 'Everyone must leave Boston or be burned with it.'"

"Pamela, we have just learned that there was another burning on the Expressway. The car had similar markings but we have no tape. Do you believe that this is from the same organization?"

"Sam, given the timing and the painted symbol reported on that car it would seem very likely. The caller indicated that there might be multiple acts of terror."

"Now we'll go to some scenes taken by your crew during the incident. Pamela, will you please narrate."

She checked the position of the small lapel microphone as she watched the playback monitor.

"We had finished a taping at M.I.T. and had just turned onto the Harvard Bridge. Traffic was jammed so we left our van and went forward to check it out. It was obvious that this wasn't an ordinary jam, because we could see smoke rising in the oncoming lane. Here we've just reached the vehicle. There's the victim inside and you can clearly see the sword, the scimitar, painted on the side. I tried to get the victim out, but there was an explosion … yes, there. That's all I remember of the incident."

She was relieved to see that she only showed a good stretch of thigh when she passed out.

"Pamela, thanks very much for that on-the-spot reporting. We're glad you survived."

"You're welcome Sam."

The red transmit light was barely off as Jeremy pulled her around.

"You bitch. You knew something was going to happen, and you sure as hell didn't try and save that guy's life. He was already crispy."

Pamela fixed him with her most direct stare. "Jeremy, do you like your job?"

Harley Jones snapped off the television and turned to the CTU team gathered in the grubby conference room of the Annex. The silence was broken only by the sound of the disk being ejected from the player.

He raised his head and spoke softly but very distinctly. "That's it. Boston. That's where it's happening."

Ted Browner grimaced. "Happening? Happened! Hell, it's over. Three road kills and now they're gone. Too bad we missed 'em."

Jones had a contemplative, almost serene expression on his face. "They haven't gone. This is just the beginning. It's going to get worse."

"How do you figure that? Terrorists always cut and run. Basic guerrilla warfare tactics."

Jones didn't change his expression.

"Let's look at the evidence. First, we get multiple reports of a massive terrorist assault. The last one was a big multi-part effort, quite complex. Second, we've gotten a terrorist demand, but only after an initial act. That act was to get our attention. Clearly they want something, and they've established their credibility. Third, multiple attacks were made simultaneously. That indicates a very high level of organization. Not the sort of thing that's thrown away without getting something in return. But they haven't even asked for anything yet. 'Everyone must leave Boston or be burned with it'—that's just rhetoric. Fourth, and very important, that news woman didn't just happen to come across the killing on the bridge. She was set up. That implies a long-term plan. The questions are: Why? Why Boston? Why television coverage? Why car killings?"

The other section heads nodded thoughtfully, but Browner seemed skeptical. Jones looked over the group. "Pack your bags and plan on being at work in Boston tomorrow morning at 7:00 a.m. Any questions?"

Browner looked Jones in the eye, "Isn't it a bit risky to move us all to Boston? What if this is a diversion? We've got all our equipment and space and, well, everything all set up here. Shouldn't we just have an operational unit on site?" Browner was safe quoting protocol. He'd written it himself.

Jones smiled benignly. "Would you like to stay, Ted?"

Browner straightened up abruptly. He certainly didn't want to miss any action. "SOP is for the commander to stay at the Command Post. I was thinking that I should go to Boston."

Jones continued to smile. "Actually, Ted, a leader should be at the front. An executive officer should stay behind and shuffle papers. Use your best judgment. I'll be having lunch tomorrow at Legal Seafood on State Street." Jones looked up at the section heads, who had been following the discussion with some interest. "Saddle up folks. We're going for a ride."

The rest of the CTU filed out as Ted Browner sat back in his chair, looking at the blank screen, flexing his powerful hands.

8:30 P.M.
Arlington, Virginia

Melody Jane Harmony pushed her Shih Tzu off her lap as she reached for the telephone. "Yes?"

Her phone display told her that it was Jerry Price but she couldn't remember who that was. "This is Jerry Price," said the voice on the other end. "We've had an incident of interest."

Damn the man. How was she supposed to know who he was with thirty-three different organizations? "Yes Mr. Price. Go ahead."

"Well, I have a report from the Boston Fusion Center." She knew that the fusion centers were supposed to collect intelligence from the various agencies and provide a single coherent advisory capability. The fusion centers only collected intelligence; they didn't coordinate or act. If action was needed, a state Emergency Operation Center, EOC, would be activated. They had received considerable criticism for the idiotic warnings some fusion centers had transmitted; since there had not yet been any *real* major events, the EOCs had not really been tested yet

Jerry Price continued, "They picked up something on the television that the Boston Police Department is handling."

"Television?" Melody Jane asked.

"Well, yes. It probably wouldn't have popped up on our radar at all. The Boston P.D. thinks it's just a wacko. Someone burned a person in his car and painted a scimitar shape on the side. Then they called into a radio station and identified themselves as 'The Sword of the Oppressed.'"

She sighed. "That could be anyone."

"I agree. The FBI is looking into it apparently," he noted.

"Well, they should belong to me, but this is silly. Let them waste their time on it. They're trying to make themselves relevant."

Jerry Price waited a moment. "Should we activate the EOC in Framingham?"

Melody Jane was pleased that she remembered something about this EOC. "That's a newer opening isn't it? An old bunker from the sixties?"

"Yes."

"I don't think that's really appropriate at this time, do you? This seems to be the FBI just puffing itself up."

Jerry Price paused, "Yes, Madam Secretary. I think I understand completely."

"Jerry, next time, go through my deputy, Susan Price. Good night," she added as she hung up.

Who was Jerry Price? Why did he call her directly? The department needed more structure. She'd work on that in the morning.

10:07 P.M.
Massachusetts General Hospital, Boston

Sharif Al-Hawari stared at the television, transfixed. Karlene Davidson was holding his left hand; his right arm was broken. "Honey, what is it?" she asked.

He started to turn towards her, but stopped abruptly with a groan from the pain of his concussion. She leaned over and kissed him gently on the left cheek, the one not covered by a bandage. "My poor baby, you've had a rough day."

Sharif moved his head carefully back to watch the last of the show. Pamela Clark had just fainted and he could see the sword painted crudely on the side of the car. He would have been sick at the burning figure inside the car, but he'd seen such things before in Beirut. Still, his stomach churned. He closed his eyes and leaned back. Karlene sensed that he was tired and tried to let go of his hand, but he tightened his grip. Was this the end? Thinking of the stockpiles he had seen, he knew it wasn't.

CHAPTER 10: ENGAGING THE ENEMY

Friday: 10:15 A.M.
The Office of the Mayor of Boston

The mayor's assistant, a slim black woman with an air of competence, introduced herself as Marci Clayborne. Tim Blackwell, the Boston Special Agent in Charge for the FBI, whispered into Jones's ear, "That's *Ms.* Clayborne to us." Blackwell had briefed him on the characters they were likely to encounter. Marci Clayborne was an up-and-comer in Democratic state politics and would likely be run as a congresswoman. She was politically astute and paranoid. The mayor used her as a hatchet man and watchdog. The mayor was old upper-class Bostonian with linkages all the way back to the Boston Tea Party. A patrician, he despised disorder.

As Ms. Clayborne ushered them into the room, Jones noted the elegant woodwork. People said the mayor had paid for the woodwork from his own pocket. He was tall and slim with carefully cut silver gray hair to complement his elegant navy blue pinstripe suit. He extended his hand. "Hello. I'm Charles Stone." The mayor motioned them towards plush leather chairs arranged around a large low table. A conversation table, not a working table, Jones noted.

The mayor wasted no time. "I understand that you believe there is an emergency."

Jones was about to respond when a large florid man in a rumpled brown suit hurried in. "Sorry Mr. Mayor. I was delayed."

Jones remarked a brief expression of displeasure passing over the mayor's lips as he stood up. "Gentlemen. Brian Delaney, Police Commissioner." He gestured for them to sit then looked at the FBI group expectantly, clearly not sure who was in charge. Ms. Clayborne nodded towards Jones. "Mr. Jones is head of the new FBI-CIA Counter-Terrorist Unit in Washington."

Jones nodded his thanks. "Mr. Mayor. We have very strong evidence that a large-scale terrorist attack is beginning in your city. We would like to centralize the command of police and military agencies so that—"

The mayor held up his hand. "Military? There are no military units active in Boston, and there will be none." He looked at Commissioner Delaney expectantly. Abruptly, Delaney caught his cue.

"We've got SWAT teams as well as an intelligence unit. The attacks that took place yesterday, hell, that was peanuts. It looks to me like you're closing the barn door a little late." He smiled.

Jones turned back to the mayor. "Mr. Mayor, if my intuition is correct, Boston is going to suffer from an attack which is far in excess of anything an American city has seen since 9/11. Possibly beyond anything that we've seen anywhere."

Ms. Clayborne broke in, "I think that 'intuition' is insufficient to warrant a change in our policing policy at this time. Perhaps you should return when you've done some police work."

Jones turned to face her, uncomfortable in the low leather chair which out-gassed every time he moved. "This isn't just intuition, we have—"

The mayor raised his hand. "Gentlemen. Thank you for your warning. We have excellent procedures in place now. We don't want to disturb our city with unnecessary speculations in the press. I would be pleased if you turned over any information you have to Commissioner Delaney for use by his intelligence unit." The mayor rose, signaling the end of the meeting.

Jones had to try one more time. As he was shaking hands with the mayor he said, "Mr. Mayor, this could be a bad one. Please call us immediately if things start to happen." The mayor nodded towards Commissioner Delaney, who in turn nodded towards Jones.

As they left the mayor's office, Jones leaned over to Blackwell and said quietly, "We're in serious trouble."

10:30 A.M.

Deputy Superintendent Eddy Yeager sat in his bathrobe at the kitchen table, sipping his first morning coffee while carefully reading the paper. His wife, a lieutenant in the narcotics unit, was working the day shift in Roxbury, and the house was quiet. There was one thing different this morning: Eddy Yeager was worried.

He was the commander of the "ash and trash" detail, as his buddies called it. This included the mounted detail, the motorcycle patrol, the boat unit and, uppermost in his mind, the Arrest and Apprehension Team, Boston's SWAT unit. He was especially proud of them. Most were motorcycle officers who would be pulled from their traffic assignments if the Arrest and Apprehension Team was activated. Boston was cheap, as most cities were now, and they couldn't keep a standing SWAT unit. Although they had been trained by the best, including the FBI Hostage Rescue Team and the Army Delta Force, there were problems. It wasn't the men. They were keen and smart, even better than the Marines he had led in Iraq. It was everything else. They were consistently getting nickel-and-dimed to death. They had finally managed to get Glock 9mm pistols, but they were still using ancient 9mm Uzi submachine guns. It was pathetic. Instead of having a clip-on arrangement for a laser spotter light, they had to tape mini mag flashlights to their Uzis. As long as the light was on, they made themselves targets. With the laser arrangement on the Heckler and Koch, his weapon of choice, the laser only came on when the stock mounted switch was pressed. They hadn't even had helmets until one of his enterprising lieutenants had "acquired" some from the local National Guard unit. The sniper situation was the worst. They had to use the lightweight 5.56mm round that was used in M-4 rifles. It was a nice flat shooter, but a high wind or a blade of grass could send a round halfway to New York. Previously they had used M-14s. They were much better, but the civilians had complained that the heavy 7.62mm .30 caliber round went through walls and just plain traveled too far. Well, maybe it did, but when you targeted a man through a window, you hit him, not the wall, which is what happened with the featherweight 5.56mms. "Gone with the wind" was the expression his snipers used.

The training was good, but there wasn't enough. Even their training with gas had been reduced after some had drifted across the harbor into the University of Massachusetts Boston Campus air conditioning system. What was the matter with these people? Couldn't they take a little joke?

Eddy put down his cup and stared at the headlines again. Car fires. Sword of the Oppressed. Something was going on. He stared blankly at the page now, his mind cranking up. He worked the night shift as the area commander for half of Boston, like all the other three-star Deputy Superintendents. It didn't leave much time with Barbara, his wife. There was one advantage though: it left time to plan some training today. He had the queasy feeling that he used to have when going into a hot landing zone. Definitely, training tomorrow.

10:45 A.M.
Pamela Clark

Pamela snatched the phone before it finished its first ring.

"Hello."

"Ms. Clark. You did quite well yesterday." This time the voice was less clear, but the same aura of power and confidence came over the line.

"You killed those people."

65

"Yes and you used the opportunity quite well. I noticed that you managed to get on CBS. I presume you would like another opportunity."

There was a pause. Pamela didn't want to become an active part of terrorism, but she desperately wanted the exposure. Would she be making news rather than reporting it if she participated?

"There are others if you are not interested." The voice came through coolly.

"No. I mean yes. I want to know."

"Good. You read the written message that I sent you this morning."

Pamela looked at the plain white paper with the typed message that a bicycle courier had delivered moments before:

Citizens of Boston: Today will be your second warning. You may call it strike two. Leave Boston or burn with it.

The message was signed as before, "Sword of the Oppressed," but this time, a scimitar symbol underlined the typed signature.

"Yes," she answered, "I've read it. It's quite clear."

"At 11:30 your station must put out that message. At 11:50 you should have a crew at Charles Station."

The line went dead. Pamela looked at the receiver, slammed it down and moved into action.

11:45 A.M.
Charles Subway Station, MBTA

Jeremy stumbled as he tried to keep up with Pamela on the stairs. The lighting man was dragging behind.

Pamela reached for a cigarette. The platform was empty. Damn. Was it going to be something to do with the station or on one of the trains? Inbound or Outbound? Damn that man.

"Jesus, Pamela, what's happening this time?" Jeremy was worried that it might be something serious, but he wasn't going to look weak in front of Pamela. The man frying in his car last night had been horrifying. But if she could take it, so could he.

She could see the inbound train coming in and glanced down at her watch. 11:47. Everything looked normal. The train stopped and the doors opened. People got off. "Damn that man," she thought again when she noticed one of the passengers stop to stare at one of the cars. He said something which she couldn't hear. Then she noticed that no one was getting out of that car. The middle driver of the train, a sharp-eyed black woman, had been watching her curiously. Now she leaned out looking first towards the front then towards the rear. She had her hand on the door control when Pamela yelled, "Stop!"

Three people were now staring into the silent car. Pamela ran down until she could see through the open doors. She staggered to a stop. There were bodies everywhere. She could see two children on the floor as she walked farther forward. Jeremy jerked her back, waking her from her trance of horror.

"Look," he pointed.

She could see a small cylinder just in front of the door. It was green with black lettering. "What is it?" Jeremy had excellent eyes.

"Phosgene. It's a deadly nerve gas," he answered quietly, staring into the car. "Oh shit, back up," he added, pulling her back.

She could smell it now, the smell of grass or maybe freshly mown hay. She moved back until she couldn't smell anything. For a moment, Pamela sagged back against the station wall, then noticed a crowd gathering. She straightened herself, adjusted her dress and turned to Jeremy. "We're going live. Get the station ready." She turned to the lighting man, "Set up. I want a good clear shot of this."

12:00 P.M.
Pirate Radio 960, 14 Miles East of Boston

"Whoa, yes indeed folks it's high noon and this is Big Al on Pirate 960 on your dial. Yes indeed, fifty thousand watts of Pirate Power broadcasting to you from somewhere out in the Atlantic in a yellow submarine, just off your shore, invading with tunes from the past. We have a new sponsor today, maximally cool. He says tunes are his message. All right! My kind of sponsor, cool name, 'The Hand.' Here's his first advert, hope he's not a pervert or I'm a convert. Whoa! Big Al kicking into gear with a message from the Hand to the CTU, whatever that is. Maybe it's an IUD in sideways."

There was a slapping sound and a squeaky voice said, "Bad Al. Bad Al. Go home now."

Al's voice started again, "No way! Pirate radio. Ninety-six is just sixty-nine backwards, and you all know what that is! Now the Beach Boys and *Shut Down* from 1963. No, boys, that's not about some thighs squeezed tight."

The music faded in with the Beach Boys and their epic drag race song about a Corvette and a 413 Hemi.

A massive engine howl dominated the music soundtrack and then,

"...buddy gonna shut you down..."

12:22 P.M.
FBI Field Headquarters, Boston

Harley Jones slammed the digital recorder on its side, sending it sliding down the polished table and crashing to the floor. The picture, a frozen image of the gas cylinder, remained on the screen. The CTU section team heads and Ted Browner stared at Jones, startled by the uncharacteristic display of violence.

"Damn that bitch. That's the second time. She's in touch with whoever is running this thing, and she hasn't given us any warning."

"She doesn't have to. The First Amendment protects her. She doesn't have to reveal her sources," replied Jessica Williams. Jones gave her an intense but not unfriendly look for a moment before turning to George Alvarez.

"Follow her and bug her. I want bugs everywhere. If she farts it had better be on disk, in stereo."

George nodded and wrote in his pad. "I'll get a court order. Who is our judge here?"

"Judge? George what's the matter with you? Get her bugged now. I don't give a damn about her rights. This doesn't require a judge's order. This is a question of national security. The CIA doesn't get court orders, right?" he turned to Ted Browner.

"Right," Browner answered, "but the CIA doesn't operate much in the continental U.S.A., so that's an interesting point."

"Harley, it's the 'tainted fruit' principle," Jessica Williams said. "You know that. We might use the evidence to capture them, but it will destroy the whole chain of evidence. We can't use it in court." She leaned back and adjusted her skirt over her knees.

There was a moment's silence, then Ted Browner spoke up. "It's time for prophylactic action. We can try for the court order, but who cares." His glance shifted back to the frozen video picture, a small hand evident next to the gas cylinder. "They'll never be captured alive."

Jones's complexion had almost returned to its normal unhealthy white from the beet red shade it had been a minute earlier. "All right folks. It's time to get real smart. First, pass the word to the Boston Police Department that any suspected terrorist must be captured, not shot. We must interrogate. I presume you have some specialists for this sort of thing Ted?"

Browner paused. "Well, since we had all of these Guantanamo problems, rendition would probably be better. But," he paused, "we could probably find some of the old timers."

Jones nodded. "Get them and whatever equipment they need for rapid extraction of information."

Browner looked up from his notepad. "Wouldn't it be better to fly them to Langley? All the equipment is set up there. For testing only, of course," he added.

Jones looked disgusted. "Ted, you still don't get it, do you? We're on a roller coaster here, and someone else is at the throttle. We don't have time. They'll move as fast as they can to obtain their objective. We can't afford to lose two hours in transporting a prisoner to interrogation."

Jessica sighed. "Harley! Two things. One, torture doesn't work and, two, we'd get fried if we attempted it."

Jones stared at her for a moment. "Jessica! Two things. One, it sometimes works and, two, we may get fried later anyway. The 'we' will be 'me,' so—" and he turned to look at everyone in the room— "if you can't handle it, pack your bags." He faced Jessica again. "Enhanced Interrogation works. Ask Ted."

She turned to Browner. He paused for a moment then said, "A politically unpopular truth."

Jones broke the somber mood and turned his attention to the whole team. "Now, listen up people. We need ideas and we need some action. Here are my thoughts. First, I believe that the leader of this operation, possibly this whole operation, is from an Arab country, probably Islamic. I have two reasons for saying this. The first is the name of the organization, or his name, whatever—Sword of the Oppressed. The second is the symbol, a scimitar. My second conclusion is a long shot, but the use of phosgene spells chemist. They could just have easily thrown a couple of Molotov Cocktails in there and toasted the bunch. The phosgene allowed them to get away quietly. Finally, the leader has got to be a professional, either military or from an intelligence service. Things are too big and going too well for this to be run by any half-baked terrorist. Anyone want to comment?"

Ted Browner stared up at Jones. As a professional in the intelligence business, he felt he shouldn't be surprised, but the extrapolations from the limited data were brilliant. They might be wrong, but they were a great shot in the dark. Anyhow, no one ever really knew what was going on until it was all over. He definitely agreed on one thing: they'd only seen the tip of the iceberg.

The FBI people were familiar with Jones's leaps of deduction, but they had never faced a case as dramatic as this. Still, none of them had any better ideas. Jones was met with silence and shrugs or nods.

Jones turned to Jessica, "OK. Get into your database with that speculation and see if you can find out who might be running their show.

Match that against..." Jessica waved her hand in a gesture familiar to Jones. It meant, "don't tell me the obvious."

Jones turned to Browner. "Get me—" he began, when the phone rang. Since it was impossible to dial that phone directly, someone had transferred it despite the importance of the meeting. Jones picked it up. "Jones here."

There was a brief pause. "Well, yes Mr. Mayor. I do seem to remember warning you about the possibility..." The expression on Jones's face changed to one of impatience. "Mr. Mayor, we have turned over all solid information to Commissioner Delaney. We expect much worse to come."

Jones held the receiver slightly away from his ear. "Yes sir, my intuition, which has served the Bureau well for—" He looked at the receiver in disgust and placed it down gently in the cradle. He seemed to contemplate the phone for a moment, then turned back to Ted Browner.

"Ted, I want you to have your people synchronize directly with Jessica. I don't want any bureaucratic data filtering going on. They've got to give us the latest on who is where and anything that the recon team gets from the site in Somalia."

Jones turned to the Alvarez. "George, plan on setting up a unified command structure. Don't worry about the mayor. Make the plans and find out what assets are available locally and what high class talent is available internationally." He continued through each of the section leaders, briefing each in general, and expecting them to carry forward with their own initiative.

12:37 P.M.

From his hospital bed, Sharif Al-Hawari watched the news broadcast quietly. The tears ran down his cheeks when he saw the child's small hand by the gas cylinder. He remembered a hand like that—his brother's hand, as he had been found after the Israelis shelled the south end of Beirut. The picture of the hand was still vivid in his mind. How could he have forgotten? It was his last remaining nightmare, come back to haunt him.

* * *

Patrick Henry Johnston was in his car on Highway 93 headed south to visit a client interested in whole life insurance. He snorted in disgust. "Leave Boston or be burned with it." What a crock. No one was forcing him out of anywhere. He reached across and flipped open the glove compartment of his Nissan Pathfinder. Without taking his eyes from the road, he pulled out the four-inch barreled Colt Python .357. It was still in its clip-on Bianchi holster. With his thumb he pushed off the holster and then pulled the cylinder catch back. With a flip of the wrist, the cylinder swung out. Only then did he look down. All six .357 rounds were there, primers undented, ready to go. His Python wasn't a hunter's pistol, it was a self-defense gun. Patrick Henry Johnston believed in the right gun for the job. If you were going to have to shoot it out with someone, you were going to be scared, so you needed a gun without any fancy switches or gizmos. That made it a revolver. Very few pistol encounters were at a range greater than ten feet, so you didn't need a long barrel, and, most important, you wanted the animal down, permanently. The Python was the right gun for the job. The recent police and military love affairs with 9mm pistols didn't impress him. Unlike the 9mm bullets, it didn't take a double tap, two hits, with the Python. One hit anywhere at all and the target was no longer a problem. The only thing better was a Dirty Harry .44 magnum, but there were limits, after all. Carrying a .44 was like having one of those small cars in your pocket, just too damn big.

With his eyes back on the road, Patrick Henry Johnston closed the cylinder with his thumb and gently pushed the revolver into its holster. Again without looking, he slid the gun and holster into his coat pocket.

* * *

Private John Miller of the National Guard didn't hear the news until 1:45 when his cement truck pulled into the construction site on Concord Avenue in Somerville, in the Greater Boston Area. Since his father drove to work and his mother only took buses, the train gassing didn't worry him at all.

1:45 P.M.

Liz Martin tapped on Harley Jones's door frame.

Jones looked up from his computer screen and waved Liz to a chair. "What's up?"

Liz remained standing in front of his desk, her hands behind her back.

"Probably nothing Harley, but one of the secretaries records one of the local radio stations for her boyfriend. It's one of these offshore high power pirate stations. Anyhow, it's probably nothing, but here." She brought a small recorder from behind her back, put it on his table and pressed the play key.

71

Jones looked at it for a moment as it hissed, and raised his eyebrows. After the complete Beach Boys song had played, Jones leaned back and stared at Liz. "Get the full scoop from that station."

Liz shuffled her feet and then sighed. "We can't. They're offshore. Jurisdiction is completely muddled. The FCC can't touch them, that's why they can run high power. They're anchored way out so the Coast Guard can't go after them. I called their office in town, but it was just a message service. Probably they'll call back." She didn't sound very hopeful.

Jones rubbed his forehead, then leaned back. "Have someone record everything that comes out of that station."

Liz shrugged. "What good's that going to do? We don't have enough manpower to listen to it constantly. They could say anything and we wouldn't know."

Jones looked exasperated and then calmed himself. "Split the listening into shifts, get the secretaries into it. They don't have to listen— you know what I mean, *really* listen. They just have to listen. Got it?" he snapped.

Liz shrugged and left. "His will be done," she thought.

2:45 P.M.

Jik Kang, former Captain in the North Korean Special Forces, still thought of himself as a soldier. Now he was a soldier with a mission, and he was enjoying himself enormously. His pleasure in no way reduced his efficiency. He felt somewhat foolish in his workman's overalls and would have preferred to do this job at night, but his leader's timetable was tight. It had been explained sufficiently to him. He did not want to know it all. He believed in compartmentalization, but having some idea of the mission concept was helpful. The one known as "The Fox" had earned his code name in Captain Kang's book, and Kang was excited. If the concept was valid, it would open up a world of opportunity for people like him, not that he would need money after this mission. He could disappear in Thailand. Nonetheless, it was stimulating. He breathed deeply, bringing the sea air down into his lungs.

As he approached the gate he slowed, checking his rearview mirror. He pulled the van up within four feet of the entrance, effectively blocking it from view. He reached between the van seats and pulled out the long bolt cutters, still with their Ace Hardware price tag gleaming a brilliant yellow against the shiny red finish. It was amazing, he thought. In North Korea, the distribution of such a tool would have been carefully controlled; here, any thief could buy one at a hardware store. He stepped from the van with the bolt cutters; then, remembering, he reached across the seat for his other important accessory, the yellow construction hat. American workers always wore these, so he must as well.

Kang walked quickly around the front of the van to the gate. A smile crept over his normally passive face when he saw the chain and lock. The lock was strong, but the chain wasn't hardened. What fools these people were. Strong locks and weak chains. He held the bolt cutters out with both hands and tried to cut the chain as though the bolt cutter was a giant fingernail cutter. He grunted with effort, but could barely dent the chain. This chain, while unhardened, was bigger than the one on which he had practiced. Even more important, this chain was not on the ground, but hanging and hard to stabilize.

After several more muscle straining attempts, he dropped to his knees and put the blade over one-half of a link. Then he carefully placed one handle of the bolt cutters against his chest, stabilizing it with the side of his face. He placed both of his hands on the other handle and pulled carefully but strongly towards him. It took only a few seconds before the 120 pound Korean heard and felt the satisfying snap while the bolt cutter arms closed. In less than a minute, the chain was cut and the gate opened. In another minute the gate was closed. The chain had been carefully placed to look intact. In fact, the gate was held together by an almost invisible piece of fishing line which would offer no resistance if Kang had to drive through the gate later.

Kang drove to within 200 yards of the BosGas natural gas storage tank where he turned the van around so that the rear faced the red and white 150-foot tower. He then got out still wearing his construction hat, and opened the back. His excitement was so great that he literally bounded in. He was instantly gratified that he had worn the construction hat as his head hit the van roof. Still, he was chagrined that his excitement had caused an error. He was a fourth degree black belt in Tang So Do style karate and didn't like to lose control of his body. To gain self-control, he dropped into a cross legged position, closed his eyes and breathed deeply. Within a minute his pulse had dropped thirty beats per minute. After a glance at the tower behind him, he partially closed the van doors, leaving an opening of only twelve inches.

Satisfied, he moved towards the front of the van and reached for the rifle under the blanket, an old U.S. Army Springfield in .30 caliber, what the Americans called thirty-aught-six. They sold many bigger guns, but this was the biggest that you could conveniently get armor piercing ammunition for. Once again, Kang was amazed by the stupidity of the Americans. Guns, ammunition, even gas masks were available to the public. He had bought the ammunition in Vermont at a store which specialized in surplus weapons. The ammunition had been stored in a large wooden crate. The black tips had marked them as armor piercing. They were old and some might be duds, but they wouldn't jam in the rifle. It was a reliable bolt action weapon with enormous strength in the breech. If one round failed to fire, he would just eject it and load another. Of course, he could have reloaded these, but it just wasn't worth the effort. He had a whole box of ammunition if he needed it.

Since there wasn't room to stand, and there was no need for great accuracy, Captain Kang took a kneeling position with the Springfield in his hands. Then he remembered his practiced procedure and pulled the hearing protector down from the construction hat and placed it over his ears. The rifle was incredibly noisy inside the van with the doors almost closed. The advantage was that the rifle shot could hardly be heard outside the van. At worst, it would sound as though a large tool had been dropped. The insulated van interior acted as a very effective silencer. He could have built a silencer, but, again, it wasn't necessary. The Fox was a master of the field expedient. Kang smiled in appreciation of another professional's expertise.

Without waiting, Captain Kang raised the rifle to his shoulder and worked the first round into the chamber. Slowly he brought the battle sights to dead center of the tower and about three-quarters of the way down. The recoil rocked the slight Korean back; he was more used to the lighter recoil of an AK-74. He looked carefully at the region where he had fired, but saw nothing. It was a double-walled tank, but the armor-piercing ammunition should still penetrate. He worked another round into the chamber and shifted slightly to the right. He sighted carefully through the gap between the doors and pulled the trigger. Once again, there was no sign of damage. This was expected, but still disappointing. Next, he shifted to the other side and fired another round. Again, no visible effect. Now there were three holes in the tower, and they should be squirting out liquefied natural gas. Shortly after reaching atmospheric pressure, the pressurized fuel should go from liquid to gas and be very flammable, if not explosive. Kang waited for a moment and eyed the cross bow with its "flaming arrow" arrowhead made of tightly wound cloth which he would dip into gasoline. He had not tested this, and he was not sure that it would work. For his last two shots, Kang would fire between the three holes that he had already made, or that he assumed he had made. He sighted carefully again just to the right of his center hole.

This time, he was lucky. The armor piercing steel head struck a small spark as it penetrated the thin steel of the tank. A small amount of vapor from the center hole ignited.

He would never forget what he saw next. The stream from the center hole ignited in a finger reaching thirty feet towards him. In less than two seconds, the second hole had contributed its fuel and a giant fan of flame spurted from the side of the tower while the liquid fuel running downwards became a flaming skirt. The wind flicked the flame up, and then to the right. The fire didn't reach the hole on the right side, but it did ignite the jet of liquid from the hole.

Kang leapt out of the back of the van and ignored his construction helmet as it fell to the ground. Even at this distance, he could feel the intense heat. "Too close, too close." He hastily slammed the rear doors before running to the front of the van. Briefly, he paused to etch the beauty of the scene into his mind. Then he jumped in and drove away. In his rearview mirror, the entire tower was sheathed in flame.

Captain Kang slowed down, but didn't stop, as he drove through the gate. He allowed himself a moment of glee before reporting on the cellular phone. This was more fun than the time that he had killed a student in hand-to-hand combat training. The student was the son of a Party apparatchik. That self-indulgence had cost him his career in the North Korean Army, but he sure as hell wasn't out of business. Boston was now burning.

3:00 P.M.

Harley Jones had turned to Pirate 960 out of curiosity. Despite the inanities of the disc jockey, the music was to his taste. Old rock and roll. He sat back for a moment and turned his eyes away from the image of yet another terrorist on his computer screen.

"Whoa, Big Al is slowing down." Loud sniffing sounds came through the twin speakers on Jones's small but high quality Sony radio. Jones smiled at the imitation of cocaine snorting. "Whoa, Big Al is slow no mo. Now, another tune from the Hand. This one for all of Boston. Now ya'll listen real closely 'cause this Hand has got taste. Ahhhh, terrible. Wonder where the Hand was? Agh! What if the toilet paper broke? Agghhh!" — and the music faded mercifully in to cover Big Al's wails.

The sweet sound of *Light My Fire* came through the speakers. Jim Morrison's voice rang out. Harley Jones smiled until he heard the words, "light my fire." He mused for a moment over the line about setting the night on fire. Jones smiled at his memories of the Doors. The messages that Jim Morrison had tried to pass onto an unsuspecting world.

"Oh, how right he was, a gifted artist…"

Jones ran back through his mind for some of the other greats of the Doors, wondering why the "Hand" had chosen this particular song.

All about love becoming a funeral pyre. Setting the night on fire.

The musical bridge drew Jones back to his first college love, Lynda Sue Dunham, a psychology student who experimented with his ego as well as his body. After it was over, she had said to him, "Harley, you know I never loved you." Jones shook his head. To this day, he could not understand why she would say something so cruel. He shook his head and turned the radio down a notch.

3:15 P.M.

Pamela Clark was getting the most excruciating roasting of her life, but she wasn't sure she cared. She had tuned out a few moments ago, but pulled herself back.

"...and furthermore, I don't believe that you were trying to save anybody at yesterday's incident, and I sure as hell don't believe that you 'just happened to be there.' Do you think that I was born yesterday? You are one glory-sucking, unscrupulous..."

The phone rang. The boss picked it up. He listened, and then stared at Pamela. "This had better be a goddamned emergency." He handed her the receiver.

Pam listened for a moment and paled. She dropped the phone and ran to the windows of the boss's corner office. Even before reaching the windows, she could see it. "Look," she said, pointing to a faint black smudge on the horizon.

The boss put on his glasses and stood frozen for a moment, then dropped back into his chair. He stared at Pamela, then at the smudge. Slowly he waved towards the phone. Pamela picked it up, listened for a sound, then put it back in its cradle.

The Director of News, a veteran of twenty-seven years of reporting, was pale.

"Was it him?"

Pamela nodded.

He swallowed and then waved his arm. "Get out there."

As Pamela raced through the doorway, he yelled after her, "Report it, don't make it," but she didn't hear him.

CHAPTER 11: FIRST EVIDENCE

Special Agent George Alvarez threw open the door of the small conference room that Jones had taken over as an office. Alvarez ignored the cot in the corner and stepped over the piles of printouts as he worked his way towards the conference table that Jones used as a desk. They had worked together for three years, but this was the first time that Jones had seen Alvarez so agitated.

"What?"

"He called—The Hand. He's lit a big damn fire over by Highway 93."

"The trace?"

"Liz is cranking it. She'll come in when she gets it. The call is only," he glanced at his watch, "four minutes old."

"OK. The fire?"

"Some sort of natural gas storage facility." Alvarez slid sideways to look out Jones's minuscule window and then moved back shaking his head. "That Hand dude told them to look out their office window. I mean, the call was transferred, get me, it wasn't Clark's phone but her boss's. Anyhow, the Hand tells them to look out *that* window. How did he know? He must have the floor plan or have visited their office. See what I mean?" Further comments were cut off by Liz Martin who knocked twice and walked in.

She grimaced slightly. "Burner phone."

"Damn!" Jones slammed the palm of his hand down on the table. A cheap prepaid cell phone would be untraceable.

"Smart fuck. I told you." Alvarez turned to Liz. "See what you can find out."

Jones was up and reaching for his jacket. It clunked against the chair as he banged his new 10mm automatic. "Get the chopper cranked."

"Already running, boss. I warned them before I came in."

Jones nodded. "Get Browner up to the chopper and Kawai with the forensics kit. If you three aren't there in five minutes, you miss the ride." Jones halted in mid-stride.

"What?" asked Alvarez.

"'Light my Fire'—that son of a bitch is jerking me around."

Alvarez shook his head as Jones brushed past him.

Pamela Clark winced as the helicopter flew overhead, hoping that it wasn't another newsie. They were almost there, but they had been forced to drive on the shoulder of Highway 93. Traffic was jammed on both sides of the expressway as drivers pulled off to see the spectacular sight. The flames were heating the sides of the tank, forcing the gas out even faster. A huge black pillar of smoke trailed up into the sky. Dripping liquid was converted to sheets of flame on the side of the tank, while the jets continued to point angry fingers of flame. None of the spectators were tempted to move closer than the highway, half a mile away.

Exasperated by the full stop in the traffic, Pamela jerked open the door and yelled to Jeremy, "Bring the stuff." She started walking towards the inferno. Jeremy, panting, caught up just as she was about to climb the fence. He had finally had enough.

"You're going to look mighty small."

Despite her fascination with the inferno, something in his tone caused her to turn towards him. "What?"

"I'm not going over that fence, so you're going to look awfully small." Pamela needed this scene, and she needed it now before the other newsies got hold of it. There would be another time to tame Jeremy. Maybe she would fire his ass.

"OK," she said. "Let's get on that mound so we don't have the fence in the background."

Jeremy nodded, relieved. Just as they reached the mound, the helicopter settled in near the gate. Three men and one woman emerged. "Jeremy, zoom in on that. Get those faces." Jeremy complied, surprised that Clark wanted anything other than her own face on the air. He watched through the zoom lens as one man stationed himself by the gate to keep people away. The other two men followed the woman. She carried a large briefcase, like a pilot's map case, and walked slowly, watching the ground as she went.

Pamela said, "Cops. They're trying not to screw things up. I wonder if they know what this is all about. They sure got here quickly."

Jeremy took a moment to scan back to the helicopter. On maximum zoom he could barely make out the seal on the side of the helicopter. "Feds I think."

"Neat," was Clark's reply. "FBI."

"I guess. Can't read the print." Jeremy scanned back to the party. "They've stopped by something yellow, a hard hat. Only the woman is out there now, she's taking pictures of the ground. OK. Looks like they're leaving."

"No shit, Sherlock," said Clark before she could stop herself. She didn't need a zoom to see that. Jeremy twitched one side of his mouth but said nothing. Clark straightened her blouse. "OK. Let's do this while it's hot. How does my hair look?"

4:00 P.M.

"Hey folks, Here's Big Al with another tune from our friend Cool Hand Duke. Oh, man, did that puke. That Hand really grabs me. *One in Five* from the Doors, 1968. Can he pick 'em?"

The cymbals crashed and a heavy bass beat synchronized with the cymbals and the air rang with the notice that no one here gets out alive. The cymbals crashed again. The tune thumped a savage message ending with a warning that "their ball room days were over and night was drawing near, yeah … and no one is getting out alive…"

All across Boston listeners looked at each other. Was this the same Hand?

4:15 P.M.

Jeannie Kawai was uncomfortable. She shifted slightly after knocking twice on Jones's door. She had gone out with Jones twice a year ago before her "Golden Opportunity," as she called the tour at Scotland Yard. She had enjoyed their dates. There was something special about him, but the relationship hadn't had a chance to flower. Now she was back and immediately reassigned to the CTU. Was this the hand of Jones, or just luck—perhaps bad luck? Before, she hadn't been working for Jones. Now, one of the local agents, Jake Black, was describing Jones as a man with the interpersonal skills of a chainsaw. Then again, Jake Black was an asshole, making comments about how nice her waist-length hair would look on his pillow. During the helicopter ride and visit to the crime scene, anyway, Jeannie hadn't been able to read Jones at all. He had been quiet; the CIA man, Browner, on the other hand, had been a real Chatty Cathy. Based on Browner's eyeballing, Jeannie was certain he was going to hit on her. He didn't realize that she never mixed business and pleasure. Still, she thought, there was something about Jones.

The door swung open, startling her. Jones smiled instantly and waved her to a seat as he moved behind the table that he used as a desk.

Jeannie decided to stand; it would signify that she didn't have much to say and make for an easier getaway.

Jones flopped into his chair but didn't look surprised that she was still standing. "OK."

"From a hair fragment in the helmet I can conclude that it was an Asian. From the size and depth of the footprint I estimate between 110 and 125 pounds. The gate was cut with conventional bolt cutters. Based on the chain size, I would estimate that this is an unusually strong male for his weight. Based on that, and I'm reaching here, I guess around five foot two with good shoulders."

Jones nodded slowly, digesting, and his eyes came into focus. "Anything else, even a guess?"

Jeannie hesitated for a moment. "I really think that this guy was unusually strong—someone who works out a lot, probably most of his life."

"Why?"

"Well, partly it's a question of strength. I had several of the guys try to break the chain with our cutter. It was tough even for the biggest of them. Second, our guys cut it on the ground. This man had to do it at waist level; it wasn't pinned down. It would have been tough, real tough. The guy must be an athlete. An estimate, of course," she added.

Jones nodded, his eyes focused on some distant place. After a moment, he looked directly at Jeannie. Eyes like an eagle, she thought. Jones continued to watch her. To her surprise, Jeannie wasn't disturbed. Jones was somewhere between vision and thought. It brought back a memory of something her father had once told her about karate. "The mind must be as calm as the morning waters, controlling the rising storm."

His eyes cleared as he returned from his distant place. He gestured, "Please sit."

Jones watched her sit before starting, "You've been with the Bureau fifteen years now?"

"Just about. It's time for me to get back to the lab, I guess, though I've enjoyed being a field liaison and Scotland Yard was really interesting."

Jones leaned back and looked into the distance for a moment before returning his gaze to her. "Look Jeannie. That was an excellent report. Just the right amount of fact and extrapolation. You've got an excellent record. Your supervisors say that you're very candid. We're going to need a lot of that here for a while."

Jeannie nodded, surprised that he had read her file. Then again, perhaps he had checked her out first before he requested her.

Jones smiled briefly. "Don't be surprised. I liked the way you handled yourself on the crime scene, so I took a look at your record."

The smile disappeared as he leaned forward. "I want you to sit in on all our meetings. Your science background will be valuable, but what I really want is a fresh viewpoint, an analyst's mind. Is that OK with you?"

Jeannie nodded, her heart pounding. Finally, some excitement was coming into her life.

"It won't be easy," Jones warned. "There will be a lot going on."

Jeannie nodded, not really understanding, but alert. Jones smiled and stood up, extending his hand. Jeannie took it, surprised by the electricity in the touch, the eyes.

"Welcome to the CTU. Stand up! Hook on!" Jones said like a paratroop jump master.

"Airborne!" she returned the right reply. Jones's smile grew into a wide grin that lit his whole face. He nodded as she turned to go.

As Jeannie was leaving, Jessica Williams of the CTU team came in. Jeannie couldn't keep herself from checking the other woman out, then shook her head as she realized what she was doing.

Jessica caught the look as she went by. Closing the door, she turned to Jones and said, "I just finished talking to Liz Martin. The linguistics people say Middle Eastern native Arabic speaker. Probably learned his English in a British private school, traces of a New England accent." Jones bolted upright at that. Jessica held her hand up using Jones's characteristic "wait" expression. "The acoustic signature of the background is that of a car, probably a medium size General Motors with a six-cylinder engine."

"We can use that, excellent, but the Middle Eastern is a problem. We just got some forensics on a possible perpetrator, Asian."

Jessica looked thoughtful. "Doesn't mix with the eye witness reports, Caucasian on the Harvard Bridge. All these different ethnicities, it just doesn't make sense if this is some type of home grown group from ... well, anywhere."

Jones slumped into his chair, shaking his head. "Damn. What a can of worms."

Jessica pulled up a chair and sat down, watching him carefully. "Harley, forget business for a second. You don't look so good. Are you getting depressed again?"

Jones started to snap, but restrained himself. There was silence for a moment as they watched each other. "Yes. I'm getting memory dreams too. It started last week. It'll pass when this thing is over."

Jessica leaned forward, putting her hand on his. "It's hard, Harley, I know, but you've got to let him go. No one is perfect. We need you here one hundred percent. Tom is dead and gone. You've paid for him. We've paid for him."

Jones nodded, knowing that she was referring to their relationship, which had just been budding when Tom Coyle had been killed.

"Harley, you were the Agent in Charge—the man—of the HRT. You just..." she paused, looking for words, "disintegrated."

Jones nodded, uncomfortable with the history.

"And then they gave you the SRU. It was nothing, Harley, a joke, an office and a secretary. *You* made it, Harley." She squeezed his hand hard. "We died, but the SRU and now the CTU were born—your idea, your baby." She slid close to the table pulling his hand up to her cheek, kissing it once.

"Harley, I've moved on. No guilt. No recriminations. We had our good times, and that's all I choose to remember."

"I know Jess, and I miss you," Jones answered.

"I miss you too, Jonesy, but we both moved on. Now you've got to take the big leap, the one that matters. You've got to give up Tom."

"You didn't let him go in after those kids."

Exasperated, Jessica stood up and started pacing.

"Jones, that's crap and you know it. We all know that we can get hurt. It's just like the goddamn Army." She turned fiercely towards him, pushing her face next to his. "You remember the Army don't you?"

Jones nodded. He remembered all too well.

"Well pull it together Jones. People died in the Army, didn't they? Special Forces, Recon, all that crap you told me about. They died, didn't they?"

"By the score."

Jessica grabbed Jones gently by the ears, pulling him up, a gesture he remembered from their days together. "And the beat goes on, Jones, the Army lives, you live, life goes on. Get off your self-indulgent, pitiful ass and join us here in Boston. We need you." She released him and walked out of the room without a backward glance.

* * *

Jones was quiet minutes later when Alvarez came in and pointed to the television. Somehow Jones knew that it had to be Pamela Clark. He flipped on the television as some of the section leaders drifted in. Footage of their helicopter landing was followed by an upper body shot of Pamela Clark with the burning tower in the background.

"The terrorist group, Sword of the Oppressed, has struck again. The leader of the group, known as 'The Hand,' or 'The Hand that Wields the

Sword,' told this reporter that 'Boston is now burning, and all those remaining shall burn with it. You have failed to heed our warning, walk the fires of Hell.' Police do not yet know the exact cause of the fire but FBI investigators —" Now the screen switched to footage of Harley Jones, Ted Browner, and Jeannie Kawai walking out to the site. Jones heard gasps. " — were on the scene. They left before local police arrived."

"Damn!" Jones slammed his palm down on the table again. "The mayor is going to be steaming. He's going to think that we know something that we don't, and the wiretap is questionable. Damn." He turned to Liz. "Get the team in here."

Minutes later, everyone assembled around his table, Jones hit the mute button on the television. The room was silent. "Any ideas?"

The section heads settled back for a rough session. Jones wasn't fond of section heads with nothing to say. The only thing worse than nothing was bullshit. That got you fired, silence only got you scorched. Jones started, "So far we have The Hand as being Middle Eastern, one oriental male probable perpetrator and several Caucasian males at the Harvard…"

"Hey—" Alvarez was pointing at the screen. Jones hit the Pause. There was a freeze frame blow up of Harley Jones. Jones hit the Play button.

Pamela Clark's voice came purring over the speaker, " …as Harley Jones, Assistant Director of the FBI, head of the new CIA-FBI Counter-Terrorist Unit with" —the picture changed to a shot of Ted Browner— "Theodore Browner, his assistant in this revolutionary new unit…" The screen went silent again as Jones hit the mute button.

"Perfect. Counter-terrorists with their faces on television. Where did she get that information from? There's only one place…" Jones' voice had the ultra calm that his team had come to recognize as extreme anger.

The phone rang. Jones stared at it, knowing it must be urgent.

"Jones here." If anything, his voice was even more silky.

"Yes, Mr. Mayor. In fact, since it was a terrorist act, we *should* have been the first on the scene. As I remember, you decided against a unified command, so it's natural that your police department should be delayed in getting the news." He held the receiver slightly away from his ear, then started again. "Mr. Mayor, you must realize that it is not your jurisdiction. Failing to cooperate may be hazardous to your re-election. I also suggest that you restrain yourself in the information that you pass to the press."

There was a moment of silence. "Yes sir, what I mean is that both myself and Ted Browner were identified on television. The news person

83

certainly did not get that information from this office. I suggest that you check your office for leaks, or I'll have to plug them for you."

Several section heads winced, but Jones's face changed only slightly for a moment. "All right, sir. I'll look into it."

Jones put the phone down thoughtfully. "Clayborne, Delaney and the mayor were together all day. He says none of them leaked our identities. Now we've got a real problem. How did she get our names?"

A knock on the door interrupted the meeting as Liz Martin put her head in and pointed at George Alvarez. Jones waited for a moment while they whispered. The door closed and Alvarez said, "The Hand called just after they aired the first footage. He's the one that identified you to them. He said something else that they didn't put on the air."

Ted Browner broke the silence. "What?"

"He said he's going to kill you both."

Ted Browner's throat constricted, but he felt comforted by the bulk of his .45 Colt Commander pressing into the small of his back. Jones's reaction was quite different.

"That's it. This man is an intelligence professional. He is either with or has recently been with some intelligence service. The CTU is new. He has to be in the business to get that kind of a briefing. And what's more, he knows our faces. He's made his first mistake by giving out that information. This guy's got a blimp-size ego."

Ted Browner, graduate of Yale Law School and first in his CIA Clandestine Services class felt alive as he hadn't since his last work as a field operative. He looked up at Jones and shook his head. Jones nodded for him to speak.

"What if this guy is playing us all the way?"

Jones nodded again for him to continue.

"Maybe he knows that we'll tap Clark's line. He's doing a psych job on us. Jerking us around."

Alvarez broke in. "Jesus! That's spook double-think. Criminals don't work like that—even the mobsters don't play games like that."

Jessica Williams smoothed her skirt over her long legs. "Maybe Ted's on to something. If Harley's right and this guy's a soldier or a spook, then he could be playing mind games with us. These songs on the radio certainly suggest something. Anyhow, if he is a professional, it certainly makes my job easier. If we've got the information somewhere in the database, I'll figure out who he is."

Jones nodded his agreement. "With respect to these tunes he's putting out, if any of you get ideas, come see me. The only thing I've come up with so far is that I own a Corvette Stingray. If he knows about that, and he does know my name, then maybe he's challenging us to a race." Jones paused for a moment and decided not to mention the playing of the Jefferson Airplane's *White Rabbit* back in Washington. The interpretations from that would hit too close to home. No one needed to know about his use of antidepressants.

Jones looked around the assembled team. "I don't expect a lot of respect from this guy. The Bureau has never had to deal with a serious foreign threat quite like this and the Agency's tactical operations have often been done through third parties like the Mossad or the French. I expect this will change things, but that's for later. For now, we'll just keep it in mind and try to be as efficient as we can. The mayor is sending over a liaison officer, spelled s-p-y, and as far as I'm concerned, he or she can see anything they want. A chief with Delaney's reputation probably won't do anything no matter what information he gets. Now, start grinding."

The CTU section heads filed out of Jones's office. Jones signaled Browner to stay behind.

"What do you think, Ted?"

"Well. I wasn't an analyst for long, but I think I can give you my projection in two words."

Jones nodded wearily, knowing that those words would express his own fears.

"Shit sandwich," finished Browner.

5:15 P.M.

There was a solid knock on Jones's door.

"Come in," he responded, looking up from his littered table top.

Ted Browner slipped in and closed the door behind him.

"You ain't going to believe this," Browner said in an exaggerated Texas drawl.

Jones raised his eyebrows.

"A Russki come to help." Clearly Browner was very suspicious, but that is exactly what Jones would have expected from a CIA man. Jones was intrigued.

"Show him in."

Browner's smile broadened farther than Jones had ever seen it go as he opened the door wide.

Centered in the doorway, clearly waiting, was a striking middle-aged blond woman in a navy blue business suit. Browner stepped aside and she stepped confidently into the room, her movement a poem of downplayed sensuality. Jones stood up and she held out her hand as she stepped forward.

"Nadia Nikolsky, FIS," she said in a husky voice with just a tinge of accent.

Jones shook her hand, appreciating her very strong grip. Her eyes, he noticed, were a startling deep blue, almost a match with her navy suit, and her cheekbones were high, Slavic.

"Harley Jones," he said. And gesturing towards Browner, "My associate, Ted Browner."

"Yes," she replied. "I recognize you both."

Jones's eyebrows shot up.

"On television," she answered with a hint of a smile.

Jones sighed. "The joys of a free press."

Nikolsky nodded. "We are learning also of the pleasures of a free press. It can be an embellishment at times."

Jones stared at her blankly. "Embellishment?"

She looked puzzled for a moment, then laughed at herself. "So sorry, *impediment.*"

Jones smiled slightly "What can I do for you?"

She leaned forward slightly. "I hope it is I who can do something for you."

She paused for effect then continued.

"My situation is somewhat difficult. I am with the Foreign Intelligence Service, what you used to call the KGB. There have been rumors throughout the terrorist network—"

"Which you helped set up years ago," interjected Ted Browner.

She hardly paused: "—about a large-scale attack to be made in the United States. As you know, the Russian Republic was a power in the former Soviet Union."

Ted Browner snorted at the understatement.

She continued with barely a glance in his direction. "The Russian Republic is not involved in any of the training missions that were formerly run in the Soviet Union."

Browner raised his eyes to the ceiling, but Nikolsky missed the gesture as she continued on.

"In a gesture of goodwill, we would like to help you in your situation; however, you must understand our position."

"Your position?" Jones echoed.

"Yes," she replied earnestly. "Many of our training clients were from Muslim countries. Our southern neighbors are also Muslim Republics. We cannot afford any unrest or misunderstandings with any of these countries. We still conduct a great deal of trade with them and, even though we produce oil, we also buy large quantities. I think the linkage is obvious. All information that I can give you must remain secret. I myself am secret."

Browner leaned towards her, "You are secret?"

She nodded, "I have come straight from Saint Petersburg, my home, at the request of my supervisor. I am not from the embassy and will have no linkages there. I have extensive experience with our clients from the Middle East, and I also speak Arabic. My only communication with home will be to my supervisor through the telephone, if it is necessary. You can understand the limitations, but I have excellent memory and may be quite useful."

Jones cocked his head slightly. "Why do you think that these terrorists come from the Middle East?"

She hesitated for only a moment. Jones suspected that this was a ploy to get his full attention.

"We know many of the terrorists are from Iran and Iraq. We believe that their leader is Hassan Bucheri."

Ted Browner laughed outright. "Lady, Bucheri's been dead for three years."

Jones nodded. Bucheri's death had been a great relief to all of those in the counter-terrorist business.

Nikolsky stood up, "Well, perhaps I am out of date; however, as I said, I do have experience in the area if you would like some assistance. Perhaps when you get some more information? I have been an analyst for many years."

Jones stood up and shook her hand. "Thank you very much. Where will you be staying?"

She smiled, now obviously tired. "I don't know yet. I just came in and haven't found a place to stay. I'll call back later and leave my number."

As the door closed behind her Browner turned to Jones. "Analyst my ass. That's a field agent, and I should know."

Jones was looking down at his hand. "She's sure got a grip."

He looked up at Browner. "So what's going on?"

Browner shrugged. "Well, FIS doesn't exactly carry credentials so we'll just have to take each piece of information as it comes. Putin and the gang aren't happy with us so we can't really call FIS for confirmation on her. Let's just see what she gives us." He paused. "That Bucheri thing was a blast from the past. I wonder if the Russians are in this themselves, and this is some sort of disinformation game."

Jones shook his head. "Politically it would be nuts for the Russians to jerk us around. I can't see what they would have to gain."

Browner nodded. "I agree. It doesn't make sense." He turned back towards the door. "Did you see that movement?"

Jones smiled, enjoying the chance to rib Browner. "Remember the poison needle that the Soviets used in umbrella tips?"

Browner looked up, ready for the punch line.

"That was one deceptive umbrella," said Jones

Browner smiled back and returned in a Texas drawl, "Boss, that weren't no umbrella."

5:45 P.M.
Homeland Security Headquarters,
Nebraska Avenue Complex, Washington, D.C.

Susan Page walked into Melody Jane Harmony's office without being announced. Melody looked up sharply at both Susan Page and the short, squat man who followed her. "Sorry, your secretary is gone," she started and took a breath, "This is Jerry Price."

Melody Jane nodded. "Of course, I know Mr. Price, we talked last night." A faint reproof seemed to come from those words, but Susan Page couldn't be certain.

Susan continued, "We have some concerns about Boston. I'll let Mr. Price brief you."

Melody Jane put down her pen and leaned forward expectantly.

"Well," he began, hesitating, "You'll remember I mentioned the car burning yesterday in Boston. Today things have gone crazy. There was a gassing in the subway and—"

"What?" Melody Jane exclaimed. "When?"

"Just before noon," Jerry Price replied, surprised.

"Why didn't you tell me? That was six hours ago."

Still surprised, Jerry Price replied, "You told me to go through your deputy, Ms. Page."

It was Susan Page's turn to look puzzled. She looked at her cell phone. "Oh goddamn it. I was flying back from New York, my phone is turned off."

Melody Jane's face became brilliantly red as Susan's turned white.

Jerry Price noticed the exchange and continued, "Ahem. The gassing killed a fair number of people—the reports are still confused, but over ten. It was a subway car. Done with a gas cylinder. But there's more," he paused to catch his breath. "A huge natural gas tower outside of Boston has been set on fire. We got the report just now."

Melody Jane inhaled deeply and exhaled slowly, "What's the cause? Is anyone injured?"

"Not at the tower. Cause unknown, but apparently it's spectacular. We're getting some news clips off CNN as we speak. They also stated that the FBI was investigating. They even named the man in charge, Harley Jones."

"Harley Jones?" Melody Jane said. "Sounds like a drink, or maybe a motorcycle."

Jerry Price smiled. It seemed to be called for. "So far the FBI hasn't told us anything, and the Boston P.D. isn't telling us much either. Their Mayor and Police Commissioner have been unresponsive. The Boston police liaison in the Boston Fusion Center is mystified. After all, the fusion center is in police headquarters."

Melody Jane Harmony, the Secretary of Homeland Security, stood up and walked over to Jerry Price. She tapped her finger into his chest. "You'd better get down there and kick those people into gear. We've got a lot riding on the fusion concept, and it doesn't appear to be working. I'm counting on you, Mr. Price."

She watched as he left the room and then turned to Susan Page. "Remind me, who is he?"

Chapter 12: "Night time is the right time"

6:00 P.M.
Pirate Radio 960

"Hey folks, this is Terry the Pirate picking up for Big Al. Would you believe it? Yes indeed, another tune from the Hand. If you haven't had your nose plastered to the tube, the Hand is a maximal bad guy that says he's been doing all the evil in Boston these last few days. Me, I don't know, but I'm gonna listen real close and pick my spots. Yes indeeeed…"

The lyrics of Dire Straits, *Ride Across the River,* flowed like a poison over the airways. Ready to pay with their lives if they must…

Deputy Superintendent Eddy Yeager shuddered as he pulled his specially equipped unmarked Ford sedan over to the side so he could listen for a clue, any clue. Just what we need, a religious nut, he thought.

The song rolled on: …they were the dogs of war, and didn't give a damn who the killing was for… Oh yes, thought Yeager. This could be really bad.

* * *

Private John Miller of the National Guard raised his eyebrows as he looked across the dinner table to his father, a veteran of Vietnam.

"What do you think, Dad?"

His father looked up from his meat loaf and shrugged. A sad expression drifted over his face for just a moment as he remembered Jim Martin, his assistant gunner, on his last day of life, over forty years ago. Jim had liked music too.

* * *

"Fucking communists," cursed Patrick Henry Johnston as he slammed his fist down on his steering wheel.

* * *

All across Boston listeners drew their own conclusions and called their friends.

6:04 P.M.
The Six O'Clock News

The CTU team gathered to watch the news program that had become known as the Six O'Clock Horror Show. The Boston police had not allowed them onto the crime scenes, although they were required by federal law to do so. They were not treating the crimes as terrorism. The news, then, was to be the CTU's chance for a preliminary look at the latest subway attack.

The anchorman immediately turned the show over to Pamela Clark at Park Street Station of the MBTA subway. The scene behind her looked like a backdrop from a disaster movie: bodies were lying on the platform or being carried away by stretcher bearers wearing gas masks. Pamela Clark, however, was not masked. She looked ill and subdued.

"Without any prior warning, the Sword of the Oppressed has struck again. About twenty minutes ago, this reporter monitored intense police activity on the radio. From this, we learned that something had just happened at this subway station, only five minutes from our downtown office. When we arrived the scene was chaos. Police still do not have any count of the dead in what appears to have been another gas attack. Seven plastic buckets containing some kind of liquid were placed at various exits. Some glass jars are lying by the buckets, but police have not yet allowed us to move close enough to read the labels. This reporter has seen at least sixty bodies. The scene can only be described as gruesome."

Pamela Clark made a throat cutting gesture and the television switched back to the anchorman, who was caught unprepared. "Some on-the-spot reporting from Pamela…"

Jones hit the mute button. "Comments?"

Jeannie Kawai, the forensic expert, spoke first. "Probably cyanide gas," she said. "The bucket is filled with an acid-like hydrochloric. It's plastic so the acid won't eat it up. They probably threw in potassium or sodium cyanide. You get hydrogen cyanide gas out, that's the real killer."

"I've heard of that before," commented Browner.

"It was used in the California state gas chambers when they did executions. The Nazis used it under the name of Zyclon B in their death camps. They used to—" Jones interrupted her by turning up the television.

The screen was showing an aerial view of the downtown area. Jones recognized the view from the maps he had studied. The anchorman spoke excitedly. "We've just had an unconfirmed report that police on several of the bridges into the downtown area have been attacked. The report, and I repeat that this is —" the reporter stopped momentarily to listen to his earphone— "Yes, it is confirmed by another call and our traffic monitor is sending you the picture. It appears to be total gridlock. Police have not yet issued a statement" —the picture switched back to the anchorman— "but we'll give you a news highlight as soon as—" He touched his hand to his earphone: "Some more late breaking news from Pamela Clark at Park Street Station."

The picture showed Pamela Clark up at street level, holding a microphone out to an elderly black woman. "...so I turned around," the woman was saying, "they was all being so noisy behind me and all. I looked down the stairs and three men came up them stairs real quick like. One had a gun in his hand so I sure enough stepped aside, you know." The woman looked at Pamela, who nodded, "Well, these boys—well men really, they weren't so young—they were taking off gas masks and putting them in briefcases." The woman looked helplessly at Pamela.

Pamela asked, "What were they wearing?"

"They had on suits, just like everybody else at this time-a-day but me."

Pamela leaned forward. "Did they look foreign at all?"

The woman looked at Pamela. "You mean, like black? Lady, this here is Boston, we got everything. But I know what you mean, were they white? No, they had dark hair but kinda light skin. Maybe they was Jews or A-rabs."

Pamela Clark turned to face the camera. "That's the latest from Park Street Station, Jim—back to you."

Jones hit the mute as the news changed to weather. He looked at the team and said quietly, "That's it folks. This guy won't leave until he's forced out. We've got to—"

The phone rang. Jones flinched. Every call was a disaster. After three rings, he picked it up.

"Assistant Director Jones? This is Ruth at the front desk. I have a call from a woman who says she'll only talk to you. Will you take it?" Jones thought for a moment, wondering who knew that he was here, then he remembered the news broadcast. Everyone knew he was here.

"Yes. I'll take it. Try and get Liz Martin to trace it please." All calls were recorded.

There was a momentary click. "Assistant Director Harley Jones here."

"Hello. I have a friend that knows something about this Sword business, but he can't be prosecuted, I mean I want to make a deal. In fact, I want him allowed into the country—you know, a green card."

Jones thought for only a moment. "OK. I guarantee not to prosecute for anything having to do with the present situation. As for the green card, if he helps us substantially, I can guarantee it. How's that?"

There was a pause before the woman spoke again, "OK. Only you. Come to the Mass General Hospital. The waiting room on the fourth floor, East Wing."

Jones started talking quickly, not wanting her to hang up, "How will I know you?"

The reply was rapid and concise: "I'll know you," followed by a click. A moment later the receptionist came on the line. "Mass General Hospital sir, one of the pay phones, that's all we know."

Damn, Jones thought. Everyone knew him now. He would always be in danger as long as he was with the CTU.

Browner stood up. He had followed enough of the conversation. "I'll go. It could be a set-up."

Jones thought briefly. Browner was right, it could be a set-up. What a coup that would be for the terrorists. But it was too good an opportunity to miss, and he simply couldn't take a chance that the person might know the difference between him and Browner. Finally, Browner wasn't an investigator. Jones looked up.

"Get me a wire and assemble some bodies with radios. You stay here and run our show. Tim Blackwell can run the team on me. It's his turf. He has the clout and the bodies. We'll just have to wing it. We need information now more than we need security. Have them ready in ten minutes." Jones reached for his jacket and was reassured by the weight of the Glock 10mm pistol. After a moment's thought, he pulled the Glock and its holster out of the jacket pocket and clipped it onto his belt in the small of his back. The weight was heartening. He glanced at the team as they watched him. "Into the valley of the shadow of death..."

Jeannie Kawai felt a warm tension as she watched the man. Maybe this one was different.

6:20 P.M.

Jeannie Kawai brushed her hair distractedly in front of the mirror in the small women's restroom down the hall from Harley Jones's office. Jessica Williams pushed open the door and moved up to the mirror. Behind her, the door hissed closed.

Jessica squinted at herself as she reached into the purse. "Some meeting, eh?"

Jeannie nodded to Jessica in the mirror as she put away her brush. "I've never been so excited in my life, or so scared."

Jessica nodded as she leaned forward to freshen up her lipstick. "Life with Jones. It's a rocket. That's for sure. Did Harley ask you to sit in on the meetings?"

Jeannie looked sharply at Jessica. "Yes, why?"

Jessica smiled faintly. "Just curious. Harley's a very smart man. Let me guess." She was silent for a moment as she rubbed her lips together. "You're a scientist aren't you?"

Jeannie nodded.

"Well then," Jessica continued, "I'd guess that he wanted you for a different perspective. Am I right?"

"That's what he told me."

Jessica snapped her lipstick shut and turned to face Jeannie, "Harley's a good man. If that's what he told you, then that's the way it is, but you have to realize that he's very complex."

Jeannie cocked her head slightly. "Complex?"

Jessica dropped her lipstick into her purse and snapped it shut. Then she looked down at Jeannie, who was a full six inches shorter. "Harley could do you a lot of good."

Jeannie flushed. "I don't work that way."

Jessica's expression didn't change. "You're not reading me right. You could do him a lot of good too. His world is very dark right now. He could use a friend." Jessica turned and left.

Jeannie stared after her as the door shut.

6:45 P.M.
Massachusetts General Hospital

Jones stood uneasily in the center of the waiting room. Everyone seemed to be ignoring him. Team members were stationed at the far ends of the long corridors, out of sight. A nurse rolled a cart by, ignoring his existence. "My, I really love street work," he thought as a wave of fear rolled over him. From the corner of his eye, he saw a door open a crack. He swiveled to face the threat and dropped into a Weaver stance. Unfortunately, of the rear sight of his pistol got caught in the lining of his coat with a sharp ripping sound. A young woman in jeans with long brown hair stepped through. Her hands were held in the air.

"Is it supposed to make that sound?" she asked.

"Nope. I'm just out of practice. Normally my pants fall down," He straightened up and fumbled the pistol back into place. She said nothing but waited for him to get the pistol in the holster and then tuck the holster onto his belt in the small of his back. The desk nurse, who had witnessed the incident, shrugged and turned back to her work. Nothing really odd for Mass General.

"You're really an FBI man?" the young woman asked, apparently unconvinced after his clumsy quick draw effort.

Jones nodded and showed his identification. That seemed to satisfy her. She inclined her head down one of the corridors and Jones followed her, still nervous, despite the delicious fit of her jeans— absolutely no room for a weapon there. She led him into a four-person ward room with only one bed occupied. The occupant was a young man in an extended "airplane" cast, which indicated collarbone as well as arm damage. Jones thought he looked like any other college kid who had crashed his motorcycle.

The woman, still not identifying herself, said to the young man, "It's him."

Jones paused for a moment before deciding to take a low-key approach. He flopped down tiredly next to the patient. "How did you pick up the bruises? You must have really pissed her off." He nodded towards the woman, who smiled slightly.

This brought a weak smile from the young man too. "I fell in front of a truck. I was riding a bicycle."

Jones smiled and nodded, encouraging the patient to continue. "My name is Sharif. I am a student at B.U. I think I know something about the stuff that's been coming down these last two days. Do we have a deal, like Karlene said?"

Jones took no notes; this was all going into the wire which would transmit it to a van in the hospital parking lot. It would all be recorded there on duplicate recorders. "Yes. Green card and no prosecution for anything having to do with this incident. Fair?"

"Yes, thanks. Actually, I probably haven't done anything illegal, but, well, you know?"

Jones smiled slightly, "Sure. Do you mind if I have a couple of my people in to help, so that we won't miss anything? Also, do you need protection?"

Sharif swallowed. He hadn't thought of that. "Yes. These people are very dangerous." Sharif jumped slightly despite his casts as a man stepped into the room with a short deadly looking Heckler and Koch MP5 submachine gun in his hands. Immediately behind him, walking almost backwards, was a stocky woman wearing a smart blue business suit that seemed incongruous with her own H&K. They nodded to Jones and then moved quietly to opposite corners of the room after wedging the door shut.

After everyone settled in, Jones turned again to Sharif. "OK. The cavalry has arrived. Go on."

Sharif looked to Karlene then back to Jones. "Well, it started two years ago in Beirut. I was..." Jones settled back to listen after placing his own small recorder on Sharif's bed. Harley Jones was a careful man.

8:30 P.M.
FBI Field Headquarters, Boston

"So, that's what we know so far. He has stashes all over the Boston area, as you can see..." he gestured towards a map in which red pins marked the locations reported by Sharif and blue pins marked attack sites. "The local police have been alerted and will go in and clean them out. We have asked them not to muddle the scenes. As soon as we have gotten a feel for what's in them, we'll decide what level of forensic assets we wish to commit." Jones winked at Jeannie Kawai. She cursed silently for flushing at a gesture which probably meant nothing. Uncomfortable, she crossed her legs. She noticed Jones glancing at her as she adjusted her short skirt; well, maybe it did mean something.

Jones continued. "As I said before, it's war. Ted has requested that everyone available from the HRT be moved to a staging area just outside Boston." Jeannie's eyes widened slightly. The FBI Hostage Rescue Team, which could be up to eighty people, was far more adaptable than its name implied. "Both the Bureau and the Agency are contributing helicopters. We now have a direct satellite link to Langley and Washington, so database work should go rapidly. Our agents will be taking some faces over to our witness to see if he can identify this 'Uncle' who might be 'The Hand.' We will also have him listen to the recordings we've made and see if he can ID him on voice. Then we'll work from any *modus operandi* that we have on him. That's the good news. The bad news is that I'm sure it's going to get worse. I've talked again to the mayor. Unfortunately, he doesn't agree. Now, any ideas?"

Browner, who had been watching the map intently while Jones was speaking, started immediately. "There's something funny here. All the blue pins, the attacks, are centered in the downtown area, while the reds, the equipment caches, are scattered around."

Jones turned to follow his glance. "Yesss... But what does it mean?" He looked around the team for suggestions. There were none. He turned and stared at the map while slowly rubbing his index finger along his nose. He closed his eyes and leaned his head back, then swiveled and pointed at Browner. "Get hold of Commissioner Delaney. Tell him that

96

we want our liaison officer right now, minimum rank of captain. I don't want any lightweights. Then tell him that we think that the attacks will continue in the downtown area. He should concentrate his forces there. Finally, tell him that ... no, hint." He paused for a moment, "No, don't hint. He's too stupid. Tell him that we're going to spill that he isn't cooperating to Pamela Clark. That should get him warmed up."

Browner nodded, taking notes. "All right, how do I justify this if he asks why we we're making this force positioning recommendation? This guy doesn't sound either trusting or bright."

Jones smiled and settled into a chair. "Tell him it's a computer extrapolation."

Despite the tense atmosphere, Browner broke into laughter. Within seconds, the walls echoed. Finally, Browner continued, "So why, really?"

"Harley's intuition, Teddy Bear," Jones said "It tells him that The Hand is going for the big show. I think that we are in a giant media event being orchestrated by someone who takes us for fools." Several of the FBI members of the CTU nodded. They had seen Jones's long shots pay off before. The CIA members looked less convinced.

"Jesus," Browner said. "That's two big jumps—first, that it's going to escalate, and second, that it's going to stay downtown. What else does the crystal ball tell you?"

Jones turned sober. "That we won't get much sleep for a while. So, I'm going to crash down the hall. Blackwell's people are setting up cots and bringing in food supplies. We're also going to mount some security downstairs." Jones, with his customary grace, turned and left the room without a backwards glance.

Browner listened to the door whisper shut on its hydraulic dampener.

9:50 P.M.

Ted Browner moved quietly into Jones's office. The lights were off and Jones sat in a chair, eyes closed, his feet propped up on the conference table. Browner touched Jones gently on the shoulder, and Jones sat up, apparently awake. "I heard you come in. What's up?"

"Do you want the good news or the bad?"

"The bad."

"The Boston and Cambridge Police have refused to go into any more of the stashes, but they will stake them out. The second one was booby-trapped and they lost a man. This is going to take forever."

"What was in the first stash?"

"Civilian weapons mostly—hand tools, some chemicals, and some surplus clothing."

Jones squinted at Browner. "Surplus?"

"Yeah, Army surplus. Boots, pants, that sort of thing."

Jones nodded, storing it away. "OK. How about some good news."

"We've identified The Hand. Jessica sent photos of her best computer matches over to the kid in the hospital. No ambiguity. It's Bucheri."

Jones groaned and put his head in his hands. "God in Heaven. You call that good news? Bucheri was supposed to have died three years ago."

Browner nodded sympathetically and turned on the lights. "You know the funny part?" Jones shook his head. "We're the ones who tried to terminate him. He's one tricky operator."

Jones sighed, stood up and walked over to the cot in the corner. He flopped down on his back, and shielded his eyes from the bright overhead lights with his arm. "Get that Nikolsky woman in. Maybe the Russians do know something."

Brown scribbled on his pad. "She hasn't called in yet. We'll get her as soon as she does."

Jones sighed. "OK. Run down what we know about him."

Browner hesitated. "Shouldn't I brief the whole team?"

Jones nodded slightly from the crook of his arm. "Yeah, just give me the highlights, especially your impressions."

"Well, the first thing we know about him is that he's damn smart. He got into Harvard on a scholarship in 1965. Some of his professors describe him as 'brilliant' or 'genius,' and that doesn't come cheap at Harvard. The best part is, many of the profs thought he was a Jew. The next really important thing that comes up, and this is real touchy because the Mossad didn't give it to us ... he was in the Israeli Army during the 1972 war."

Jones sat up and swung his legs off the cot, rubbing his eyes. "Let me guess, he was a paratroop officer." The Israeli paratroops were the elite light infantry troops that staffed most of the commando units. They were considered among the best in the world.

Browner smiled, "Nope, worse, he trained with the paratroops and then transferred to military intelligence. He stayed with the Israelis through the war and then disappeared. They say that he was the one who provided all the intelligence to the Egyptians on the Suez positions."

"Worse and worse," groaned Jones. "A trained spook and soldier."

Browner waited for Jones to look up. "So, the rest you probably know. The bombing of the Beirut Marine barracks was the big one, but there are many more. The interesting thing is that he seems to operate as an independent. He wasn't with Islamic Jihad, but he did the reconnaissance for them disguised as a Marine and then designed the detonator system. Probably the idea was his, but no one is admitting that."

Jones took on a faraway look that meant he was thinking very hard. "We've got to find out who he's working for. When we know that, we'll know what the target is." He sat up and slapped his thighs. "Call the team together. We have some more puzzle pieces. Send the photo of Bucheri to the Boston P.D. Let's get moving."

10:00 P.M.

"Well folks, it's Big Al, back again to make your day. Yes indeed, it looks like the Hand is doing the Dirty Harry on us. Now it's time for the latest word from the man. He dedicates this to Boston's finest. *Bad Moon Rising*, from Credence. Maybe so, maybe so."

Across Boston, Credence Clearwater brought the bad moon rising, with troubles on the way, earthquakes and lightning, pounding with the beat.

Deputy Superintendent Edward Yeager pulled his unmarked car over to the side of the road to listen. He agreed with the song: bad times today. He was even surer that it was bound to take life. He flexed his hands on the steering wheel in time to the heavy drum beat. In his mind, each powerful flex was another punch into the miserable creep.

Yeager got control of his breathing and forced himself to calm down. A dangerous creep, he acknowledged. Still, the guy hadn't met the first string yet. Yeager thought of his Arrest and Apprehension Team. They were good guys, the best. With a little more time and money, he could — He cut that line of thought. It didn't pay to worry about what might be. After a year as a Marine Corps platoon commander in Iraq, including scenic Fallujah, Yeager didn't believe in dreaming about what might be. He listened some more. He could feel the bad moon on the rise. Yes indeed, he could hear the voice of rage and ruin.

Could this guy actually be trying to say something? Yeager closed his eyes to the flow of traffic past him, the red lights leaving a dim bloody streak on his retina.

He shrugged and pulled out into traffic. Time would tell.

At the corner Yeager recognized Motorcycle Officer Gates, the Arrest and Apprehension Team clown, in full uniform including helmet, dancing on the sidewalk with a small black woman, her hair done up in a wild afro, while two friends kept time, clapping and laughing as their radio blared.

Yeager turned on his siren briefly. Gates turned and waved, then spun back to his dancing. Yeager shook his head. Gates would never make sergeant, but he was a hell of a sniper.

10:10 P.M.
FBI Field Headquarters, Boston

Jones and the CTU team were washing down stale Dunkin' Donuts with tepid coffee and cold Diet Cokes. The initial excitement over the identification of Bucheri had died down as the team tried to analyze the data.

"OK, OK," Jones raised his hands in his own defense, "I admit that it's reaching, but the discovery of gas storage cylinders and chemicals in the first stash has me thinking that something smells very funny here. Look, we haven't seen a single use of explosives, the traditional terrorist weapon; and second, or maybe first, we haven't seen any use of advanced weaponry. No rocket launchers, machine guns, not even an Uzi, yet this has been the most destructive terrorist strike since 9/11. Everything is home grown. Those chemicals were from a local supplier, the weapons we found were stolen in Vermont from the gun shop, and all were legal. It's like they're strangling us with our own pantyhose." Jeannie Kawai snorted but the rest had gotten used to Jones's special expressions.

Browner started slowly, "It's like they've given us a puzzle."

Jones jolted upright. "No!" he exclaimed. "The message isn't for us. It's for the public. That's why he's been so careful to make certain that there is media coverage."

Alvarez held up his hands. "Whoa, boss, so what's the message?"

Jones pointed his finger, quivering with excitement. "It can happen to you. That's the message. It can happen to you. Everything they've used is commonly—"

The door burst open and an agent leaned in. "The Boston P.D. have got a sniper trapped in a maintenance building at Boston University. I thought you'd want to know, especially since they were warned by a phone call before the shooting started."

Jones looked at Timothy Blackwell, Special Agent in Charge of the Boston Field Office, who replied, "Let's roll."

10:15 P.M.
Maintenance Building 7, Boston University

Captain Kang stood up with a grunt, satisfied with the wedges that he had pounded into the last door. He adjusted the 9mm Smith and Wesson automatic pistol in its shoulder holster and picked up his rifle, an AR-15, the civilian version of the military M-16. The only difference was the selector, which didn't have a position for full automatic fire. The AR-15 fired the military 5.56mm NATO round which gave it very light recoil. This would allow him to switch rapidly between targets. The 5.56 round had an extremely flat trajectory out to 400 meters due to the high velocity of its light bullets. In Vermont, he had tested the weapon on a groundhog. He had been impressed by the cloud of blood. He was certain the police would be impressed too. The "cherry on top," as the Americans said, was the Starlight telescopic scope. It was surplus, a relic of the Vietnam era, but the faint lights of downtown Boston and the light amplifiers inside would make it as bright as day. Kang was pleased. This was much better than igniting targets. Now he would be killing them.

Flasher lights reflected through the windows from the police cars that had already arrived. It was time for action. He looked around once more to make absolutely certain that there were no lights turned on anywhere on the floor. All around him, the dark shapes of boxes and occasional pieces of machinery loomed indistinctly. The entire wall was windowed with standard industrial windows, one foot square panels. Kang moved behind a crate near the windows and switched on the Starlight Scope. The faint whine whispered in his ear as he moved the plastic stock up to his cheek and began a scan of the nearby rooftops.

There, immediately across from him, he could see two men walking, crouched over, both with weapons. One had the characteristic shape of a submachine gun while the second had a longer rifle with the distinctive shape of a hunting scope. Amazing, Kang thought; they didn't even have intensified scopes. He smiled as he worked the action on the AR-15. He now had one enormous advantage. He was inside a completely dark building, while they were illuminated by city lights, stars and the moon. The reflections off the windows would shield him. He was safe because of their limited technology. "The aggressor chooses the place of battle," his instructors had said again and again. They would be proud of him now.

He sighted in on the sniper first. They had just dropped to a kneeling position when he fired the first round. The target was only seventy meters away, filling his scope. Despite the close range, Kang missed. He

101

had been aiming exactly at the center of mass, the solar plexus. The window pane had deflected the bullet slightly down into the sniper's groin. From the way he fell, Kang guessed that he didn't have armor over his groin. Within two seconds Kang was back on the spotter. The spotter's face was greenish white in his scope as he looked back towards the flash from Kang's rifle. A second later, firing through the broken panel, there was no error at all. The soft nose 5.56mm round traveling at 3200 feet per second hit the second man in the forehead. Within milliseconds he was dead. Later, seasoned policemen would look at the body of Officer Gates and vomit.

Kang dropped down behind the crate, wondering now what was inside it. He should have checked. He only chided himself mildly; in fact he was enormously pleased. These American police were amateurs compared to the American and Korean forces that he had played tag with along the DMZ in Korea. This was hardly any challenge at all. The end would be the best part.

10:20 P.M.

Hassan Bucheri and Dr. Kamal sat with their feet up on a coffee table, enjoying the view of the Charles River from their rented apartment. There were two police wavelength scanners, both purchased at Radio Shack, sitting on the coffee table. One scanned the entire police spectrum, its red eye hopping from channel to channel. The other, an identical model, was locked onto the tactical frequency of the Arrest and Apprehension Team. Kamal eased down comfortably with his coffee while Bucheri scanned the television channels, muted now, looking for a news broadcast. Finally, he couldn't help himself.

"The news is important?"

Bucheri nodded and smiled politely before reaching into the bag of Smart Food, a disgusting mutant popcorn in Kamal's opinion. "It's everything. What good does it do if people die and no one knows?" He looked squarely at Kamal, expecting an answer.

"Why, none I suppose."

"Good. Now the next question, my friend. What good does it do if none die but the news announces that many die?"

Kamal pondered a moment. "None, I suppose, in the long run. The truth would be put out and—"

Bucheri silenced him with an angry wave of his hand. "The news media never recant what they report. Even if they did, the truth doesn't matter. It is only the impression that matters. America is not a land of substance, but a land of impression. Americans are weak and have the memory spans of children."

"I don't think that Saddam Hussein would have agreed with you, and neither would the people of Baghdad."

Again, Bucheri made an impatient gesture. "You're missing the point. You can't fight American technology. That is superb. It is their moral fiber. Their country has never been invaded. They have never had to struggle, because they were protected by their oceans and their technology. They have no religion or fundamental beliefs on which to fall back when the world becomes ugly. Their heroes are celluloid images on a giant screen, John Wayne and Arnold Schwarzenegger. Their religion is comfort, money, and automobiles. They are a people of no substance."

"You seem quite certain of this."

"Mark my words, the mayor and governor are typical American politicians. They will react like a knee to a rubber hammer."

"What about Harley Jones?"

Bucheri shrugged. "He is a fly among elephants. He will not be a problem."

Kamal nodded politely, as he knew he should.

10:35 P.M.
Boston University

Harley Jones and Tim Blackwell screeched to a halt behind the Arrest and Apprehension Team van. Motorcycles and patrol cars with their flashers running were parked around the van as police officers pulled on black jumpers and extracted weapons from the van while two sergeants supervised. Within minutes they finished and moved into a defensive perimeter. The officer in charge of the assault unit, a captain, decided that the area was clear and signaled to his men on their earphone radios. Quietly they slipped into a loose column, each man alternately facing to the left or right as a guide came up. Jones watched, fascinated. In less than a minute, the second Arrest and Apprehension Team was jogging off towards the maintenance building. Jones and Blackwell followed them, looking for the officer in command of the operation.

Up ahead, crouched behind a police car, they found the command group. A uniformed officer with a three-star insignia was in charge. Jones and Blackwell ran up and crouched next to him. He nodded at Blackwell. Blackwell gestured quickly, "My boss, Assistant Director Harley Jones of the Counter-Terrorist Unit." Then, remembering, he gestured towards the officer, "Deputy Superintendent Yeager." Jones nodded and held his hand out for a brief shake.

"Anything out of the ordinary about this sniper, Superintendent?" Jones asked. Yeager raised his eyebrows. "No shit, Jones. He's killed seven of my men so far. He's one bad motherfucker. As far as I know, we're out of his line of sight, but I'm still hiding behind this goddamn car."

"Look, Superintendent," Jones said, "this guy may be a professional. I urge extreme caution. I've got a very bad feeling about this. I think it's linked up with some of the other killings in the last twenty-four hours. We'd be miles ahead if this guy could be captured."

The Superintendent stared hard at Jones then turned away and said bitterly, "Right." Jones knew then that there would be no suspect to interrogate. The Superintendent turned back to Jones and pointed to the second Arrest and Apprehension Team, which was crouched against the wall, deep in the shadows. The Superintendent continued, "No one pulls this kind of shit in Boston. You watch."

Jones started to speak, but Blackwell squeezed his arm and shook his head.

Yeager waved to the captain of the second team. Within seconds, two men carrying grenade launchers ran to the corner of the nearby building and peeked around briefly to the right. Quickly they set the range on their weapons' sights. It was obvious that they were right handed shooters as they put their weapons awkwardly onto their left shoulders. One squatted low while the other moved back, staying out of sight of the maintenance building. Simultaneously, they both moved out, one high and one low. They exposed only half of their bodies for the brief two seconds it took them to aim and fire. Coincident with the thunk from the grenade launchers, Jones heard the crack of a high powered rifle. He recognized the sound from his Vietnam days—an M-16. The standing officer spun around, hit in the arm, but crawled quickly into the shelter of the building. Two regular uniformed officers carried him back to the waiting ambulances as the rest of the team rushed up to the protected corner.

Yeager was listening intently in his earphone. "They're giving the gas thirty more seconds. Then they're going in."

* * *

Captain Kang put on his gas mask, just as he had done a thousand times in drills with the North Korean Army. The mask was odd, the old American style, but he had tested it with ammonia fumes and knew that he could get a seal on his face, even though it was much smaller than the average American's. They would be laying down a base of fire in a moment so he put on his surplus helmet too. The eyepiece of the gas mask would protect his eyes from flying glass. He checked his gloves and then put the AR-15 down gently. He allowed himself a growing sense of excitement as he picked up the second weapon, a Remington 12 gauge auto loader with an eight round extended magazine. Loaded with double-aught shot, he could put out seventy-two .30 caliber balls in less than five seconds. Not that he would do that, of course; he would aim. It might take as long as ten seconds if he got enough targets.

Ready again, he moved to one of the broken panels and watched the corner. He shouldered the shotgun and waited. A hundred meters was far too long a range for the shotgun to guarantee a kill, but those lead balls would still cause damage at that range.

There was a shadow of movement in the corner of his eye. Kang dropped behind the wall, just as a burst of submachine gun fire splattered the glass all around him. Damn, he should have thought that they would send up someone else to the roof of the adjacent building. Still, someone with a submachine gun was a surprise. Kang huddled against the brick wall as the volume of fire picked up. Glass splinters flew as every window shattered under the hail of lead. Kang crouched lower as a ricochet hit his leg, not penetrating the skin, but hurting like a bee sting.

The hail of fire had dropped to a drizzle when Kang heard the thump of explosives.

* * *

Jones watched from a basement stairwell as the entrance team breached the steel double doors with a flash of explosives. The volume of fire picked up again as the supporting fire team switched from semi-automatic to burst firing. While half the Arrest and Apprehension Team, eight men, provided the base of fire, the rest dashed for the now open door. From behind the cover of the adjacent building, the original Arrest and Apprehension Team, which had been decimated, stepped out to provide fire support as the last of the squad moved up in a patter of boots which could be heard over the gunfire. Surprisingly, there was no return fire. Maybe, Jones thought, they'd been lucky and gotten the sniper. This was just too easy now. It didn't feel right. He ran back to join Yeager behind the police car. The car radio had been reset to the Arrest and Apprehension Team frequency, and he could hear the harsh breathing of the men as they ran up the stairs.

* * *

Kang debated killing some of the police team as they broke through the door into his immediate area. It would be fun to play hide and seek with them in the jumble of crates and machinery. Then again, this group was being much more professional than the last. They might get lucky. He decided that he might jeopardize his mission if he indulged in combat now. It was too bad, he thought, he'd always wanted to see just how good he was in a close-quarters gun fight. He shrugged his shoulders and ran for the supervisor's office next to the door. Even over the gunfire, he could hear the men setting small charges on the door as he moved over to the small hole that he had cut through the concrete floor. His tools were still there, the pick, the acid he had used to soften the cement, and the hacksaw that he had used when he hit the reinforcing bar. He wriggled through the small hole feet first, leaving the shotgun behind and pulling a small rug over the opening. Below him, as he hung from the ceiling, he could just barely feel the crate that he had placed there earlier. Silently he dropped to a crouch, not expecting to find anyone in the dark machine spaces of the heating room, but not taking a chance. All his senses alert in the pitch black, he listened.

* * *

"Ready," came over the speaker from the assault leader. There was a clatter of boots as the demolition team thundered down the stairs, then a sharp crack. Then more boots moving more slowly, up the stairs. Immediately the flash of stun grenades reflected off the ceiling as the team spread out to sweep the top floor. "Stand by for lights," said the speaker, and the top floor lights came on. Jones could imagine the team spreading out in a skirmish line, the tension high, hands shaking.

After several "clear" calls the team leader ordered the sweep team to silence in order to minimize the distraction.

"Team Two," the assault leader addressed the downstairs team. "There are some wires running along the walls. Otherwise it looks normal."

Yeager nodded in acknowledgment. Jones wondered about the wires, something stirring in the back of his mind.

"Leader, Kowalski here—there's a hole in the office floor."

* * *

Kang crawled rapidly through the steam tunnel, his flashlight beam waving against the walls. He cursed himself for not having worn elbow and knee pads, but the end of his journey was in sight. He sighed and stood up as the steam tunnels met to form a larger single tunnel. Within thirty steps he was at the ladder, rungs imbedded in the cement. He put the flashlight, pointing up, down the front of his trousers, and pulled a pry bar from his tool belt. Carefully he climbed the ladder. Holding on precariously with one hand, he forced the pry bar into position. Then he turned off the light and settled down to wait. Realizing what he had forgotten, he held on with one hand while putting his ear plugs in with the other.

* * *

Suddenly, it clicked in Jones's mind. He yelled to Yeager, who was still behind the car. "Get them out."

Yeager looked over, startled. Jones yelled again, "It's a trap. There's a bomb, get—" but it was too late. With only a slight rumble, the corners of the building crumbled. Within seconds, the rest of the building had collapsed.

Ted Blackwell was crossing himself as he stood up, saying, "Oh my God! What have we gotten ourselves into?" Jones was staring, his jaw clenched, as a brick dust cloud moved over the roadway between the buildings. He tried to fight back tears. Yeager was less successful. A scant minute later, one of his captains was walking him back to his car, comforting him as he stumbled and wept. The medical teams and scores of police officers were sorting through the wreckage as they backed out through the pandemonium.

* * *

Kang decided not to kill the couple that had been fondling each other on the bank of the Charles River. It would have been fun, but a breach of discipline. His sergeant was waiting with a stolen motor boat just off the bank, only slightly downstream from the optimal position. He had navigated well in the strange area. With his hand cupped over the lens so that it gave off only a dim red light, Kang gave the recognition signal. The reply was immediate. He set the flashlight down on the bank, a reference point in case he should become disoriented, and then slipped into the dark waters, invisible in the night.

CHAPTER 13: THE ENDLESS NIGHT

11:00 P.M.
CNN News Special

Ralph Holcombe:
Tonight we have a news special from Boston. CBS affiliate WXTV reporter Pamela Clark has become deeply involved in the story that is unfolding there. Pamela will be speaking to us from their studios.

Good evening, Pamela Clark.

Pamela Clark:
Good evening, Ralph.

Ralph Holcombe:
Pamela, perhaps you could tell us how you became involved in this event.

Pamela Clark:
It started, Ralph, when I was coming back from a reporting assignment at M.I.T. We were crossing the Harvard Bridge, and I saw something going on at the other end. I told my camera man to follow me.

Ralph Holcombe:
That was the Scimitar Incident in which you tried to save a burning man.

Pamela Clark:
That's correct Ralph.

Ralph Holcombe:
You've been in contact with the spokesperson for the group that committed that act. Do we know what is behind these actions?

Pamela Clark:
Well, Ralph, as you know, the spokesperson, who seems to be the leader, calls himself "The Hand" or "The Hand that Wields the Sword"—the sword being "The Sword of the Oppressed." He has a slight accent but is extremely articulate. His statements are terse and very dramatic. I get the feeling that he is playing to a climax of some sort, but that is just an impression. As you know, he has claimed responsibility for a number of other acts in Boston including two subway gassings.

Ralph Holcombe:
Pamela Clark, have you ever met this person face to face?

Pamela Clark:
No Ralph, I haven't.

Ralph Holcombe:
He seems to be speaking just to you. Is that correct?

Pamela Clark:
Yes, Ralph, so far that is correct.

Ralph Holcombe:
Do you have any idea why this might be?

Pamela Clark:
(*Pause*) I can only speculate on his true motivations, Ralph. He did say that he wanted a reporter who would, and I quote, "tell it like it is," and it may simply be because I have a large following in Boston.

Ralph Holcombe:
It seems that you've been selected to be his intermediary to the world. How does this feel?

Pamela Clark:
It's a terrifying responsibility. I hope that I can come through for my audience.

Ralph Holcombe:
We'll look forward to your reports, Pamela Clark. Good luck.

Pamela Clark:
Thanks Ralph.

11:05 P.M.
FBI Field Headquarters, Boston

Harley Jones and Tim Blackwell walked quietly into the reception area.

"Jesus!" murmured Blackwell to Jones. "I just can't get over it. Just 'Boom!' and they're gone. I mean, Jesus! I've got to wash my hands."

It was Blackwell's third hand wash since the explosion. Jones nodded patiently. "It's OK Tim. It will pass. You'll be all right." He put his hand on Blackwell's arm. Blackwell shook his head violently. "Jesus. Just gone." He moved off to the bathroom.

As Jones moved past the central lounge, a disturbance caught his attention. George Alvarez came up to him, almost running. "There you are. Have you heard?"

Jones frowned. "Heard what? Calm down. You're being unprofessional."

Alvarez looked chagrined. "Unprofessional" was a very strong word with Assistant Director Jones. "The National Guard has been called in. The first units will be here before dawn."

Jones paled. "God help us. It's going to be Kent State all over again. Those people aren't equipped for this. Damn!"

When he walked into their meeting room, he wasn't surprised to find Browner behind a desk, talking on the phone. Immediately Browner waved an acknowledgment and finished the conversation. He turned to Jones. "That was my Director. You can have anything you want. If we haven't got it, we'll steal it. I've never seen him make such a strong statement. Someone must have...."

The phone rang. Again, they looked at each other, wondering what this was going to be. Jones picked it up. "Jones here."

Browner and Alvarez watched Jones tense. The voice on the other end of the line was distinctive.

"You are the Jones that's running the Counter-Terrorist Unit of the FBI and CIA?" the President asked.

Despite himself, Jones came to a position of attention. "Yes sir. I am in charge of that unit. What can I do for you, sir?"

"At Mayor Stone's request, the governor of Massachusetts has called out the National Guard. Brief me quickly Mr. Jones. Where do you think this is going?"

Jones paused only a moment. "Sir, I believe that the governor has played right into this group's hands."

"Tell me about their leader. What do you think he's up to?"

Jones didn't like giving speculative reports, and this was one of his thinnest. "Sir, the Hand is playing a very sophisticated game. I don't know his goal yet, but every time we respond in a traditional manner, we get burned. We've got to separate him from his targets."

There was a pause at the other end. "You mean evacuate Boston?"

Jones smiled faintly. "It's too late. In fact, I suspect that an evacuation is one of his goals. Were you briefed on who the Hand is?"

"Yes. I can't believe that our first efforts failed to eliminate him. I'll have to look into that."

Jones smiled grimly. When this President looked into things, they generally got unpleasant for someone.

110

"Mr. Jones, do you have some recommendations? I want this situation clarified." Jones knew what "clarified" meant: finished. He also knew that it was unusual for the President to jump the chain of command, and there were several very heavy links, including Homeland Security, the Attorney General, and the Director of the FBI, that had been bypassed. "I've talked to the Director. You have my full support. The CIA will, of course, also give you full support. Do you need anything else?"

A wish list. Jones hesitated only a moment. "Yes, sir. I need control of the situation here, and I will also need military support."

"Mr. Jones, I can't give you control of the city until the governor and the mayor authorize it. As for the military, what's wrong with the National Guard if you need guns?"

Jones was ready for that. "Sir, I understand about the control. With your permission, I'll simply put the machinery in place. As for the military, I want much more sophistication than we can get from National Guard units pulled out of bed. I'm going for quality and sophistication. I don't want to say more over an unsecured line."

Jones could hear the President breathing at the other end as he read between the lines. It was just like those telephone advertisements, Jones thought, you could hear a pin drop.

Finally the President spoke, "Mr. Jones, I've got good news and bad. The bad involves a … domestic issue." There was a long pause. "Like you I can't say much, but you remember your oath when you entered military service? About '…enemies foreign and domestic'?"

"Yes sir."

"I recognize your need for control, but you may have competition. That 'competition' poses a threat as great as the terrorist himself. In this situation it would be like a match in gasoline—very bad. Do you follow me?"

Jones wasn't sure, but he had an idea. Did he mean Homeland Security? "How should I deal with this problem? Isn't that more your domain?"

There was a momentary silence. "If this pans out as quickly as you suggest, there won't be any time for me to act. You'll have to handle it too. I'm sorry about this added complexity, but you may have to be imaginative."

Jones paused this time before replying. "Imaginative, yes sir."

"Now for the good news," the President said more confidently. "I'll send you General Bradley, the Deputy to General Power of the Joint Chiefs of Staff. He will provide all the military assets you need. Do you remember him?"

Jones was pleased that he did. "He commanded the Marine assault units that went into Afghanistan."

"You'll like him, I think. He's got a reputation very similar to yours. Good luck." And the line went silent. Jones put the phone down thoughtfully. A reputation similar to his? Just as the receiver settled in the cradle, it rang again.

"Assistant Director Jones speaking."

"Well, Jones, you know who this is." He certainly recognized his director's voice. They were not friends, but they enjoyed a mutual respect.

"Yes sir."

"I'll keep it short and to the point. The President was just on my case. You have *carte blanche* for anything that we can provide. Browner will soon be getting notice of the same from the CIA. The President has lit a fire under our proverbials. Your main problem is going to be getting cooperation from the locals. There isn't much that I can do. Perhaps the President can help, but it's a jurisdictional problem. I don't need to tell you how important your performance on this will be."

No, he didn't. Jones knew that his proverbials were on the line as well as the whole combined operations concept. The CTU was his baby and the end result of seven years of sweat. He would far sooner have his own career terminated than see the CTU die.

"So, Jones," the Director continued, "start sweet-talking those locals. They're a serious problem."

The phone went dead before he could reply. Even the Director seemed to have missed the point. The locals weren't the problem, it was Hassan Bucheri.

11:35 P.M.
CTU Meeting Room

"OK Ted, here it is. You guys have a computer system which does real-time voice transcription, right?"

"Yep! It's classified Top Secret though."

Jones smiled indulgently. "I believe the Director talked to you."

Browner blinked and then rubbed his chin, contemplating. "I see what you mean. That changes the way we look at this."

"What I want is this: get ready to tap into every phone conversation possible with your system. I presume that it can multitask. If you can't handle them all, then jump around. All of the attacks have been in the downtown. As a first approximation, listen to only downtown calls."

"Wait! Wait!" Alvarez was shaking his head. "You can't get that many warrants. No way in hell."

Jones looked from Alvarez to Browner. "Do you see a problem?"

"Nope. I'm sure they're in the mail," Browner showed only a whisper of a smile to Alvarez. He was going to get his hands dirty with a little field work. He liked that.

Jones started soberly, "It gets worse."

Browner raised his eyebrows. "I thought it might."

"I want you to be prepared to cut all ground phone communication. You'll have to get someone at the phone company to do that for you."

Liz was clearly getting agitated. "Wait. Legalities aside, what about all the emergency calls? Fire, ambulance—everything will turn to mush."

Browner answered her. "It's omelet time Liz. We probably won't be able to monitor them all, but if only mobile phones are working, we might be able to monitor those at least. Too bad we can't track them."

Jones surprised everyone with a quiet "Maybe we can." He continued, turning to Ted Browner, "You will identify the bad guys by filtering the calls in the computer. Use appropriate key words like 'operation, hit, kill, assault, police' —you know. Anything that gets caught in that filter gets taped. If it sounds important, then we have a voiceprint and maybe some intelligence. We'll also monitor the CB and commercial radio bands if we get the manpower."

There was a lull as everyone tried to grasp the magnitude of the task. Jeannie Kawai broke the silence. "What about these acid attacks on the police? Acid in the face, then the assailants disappear. What's the point? The Sword clearly has more potent weapons. What are they trying to do?"

Jones turned slowly towards her. "Jeannie, you've got something there. Bucheri doesn't do anything without a reason. Have you got any psychologist friends? Maybe he's trying to invoke some primal fear that we don't know about."

Jeannie nodded, although she had some doubts about Jones's armchair psychology. She had studied some psychology at university and his suggestion just didn't have the ring of truth. "I'll look into it," she said. Suddenly she looked up at Jones. Why didn't he call on the FBI psychologists? The FBI had an entire section of them in Behavioral Science out at Quantico. She started to speak but he had already turned to another problem.

12:00 A.M.

Dr. Ali Kamal woke up suddenly and reached for the pistol under his pillow as he had been trained to do. He slipped the safety off the .45 automatic and padded quietly over the carpets into the living room. Music was coming from the living room. The music was alien to Ali Kamal but he listened carefully; it was often an indicator of Bucheri's moods. Bucheri seemed to like old American rock and roll music—no doubt the songs brought back memories from his earlier time in America. It was dreadful the way he would set his tablet computer to play the same song over and over. Now he was listening to the radio station that played songs for him. Kamal didn't understand the reason for playing the music over the air. Somehow, it was blasphemous. He shuddered as the music swept through the room. Now there was something about seasons and purposes under heaven.

Hassan Bucheri was framed by the large window overlooking the Charles River. He stood with a glass in his hand, silhouetted against the city lights in the dark room. Ali Kamal hated it when Bucheri drank. He could be so odd then, profound but convoluted. Dr. Kamal did not consider himself stupid. He had a PhD, but he felt like a moron next to Bucheri. The man was brilliant, and when he drank he said the most difficult things. Dr. Kamal could feel another one of these sessions coming on.

"Ali," Bucheri said over the music, "You have the stealth of a garbage collector."

Dr. Kamal heard the music talking about reaping, killing, and healing.

Dr. Kamal nodded. There was really no reply in these sessions.

In Bucheri's reflection from the window, Dr Kamal could see a smile pass across Bucheri's face as the music went on to laughing and weeping.

Ali didn't understand the reference at first, then decided to ignore the jibe. He swallowed because he had something difficult to say. "Hassan, should you be drinking? It is forbidden."

Bucheri laughed. "Ali, there is a time for everything." He paused, in sync with the music.

"And now it's my time."

He smiled sadly.

"A time for me to mourn, and dance, and gather my stones together, like you Ali."

114

Bucheri spun to face Dr. Kamal. "And my stones are gathered, my friend. So many stones, so little time."

Bucheri turned back to the window. "Anyway, Ali, what makes you think I'm a Muslim?" Bucheri asked.

Ali stammered at the bizarre question, confused by the disordered cadence of the conversation. "Well, I assumed…"

"Ali. Too many assumptions. As a scientist, you should know better than that. There are many Christian Palestinians. Then again, how do you know that I am Palestinian?"

Again, Ali stood puzzled and uncomfortable. Where was this going? The next twist was even more amazing.

"Ali, I'll wager that you think that the Americans are evil."

Ali was more comfortable with this. "Of course. They are the Greater Satan."

Bucheri cut him off. "No, Ali. The United States is the Greater Satan."

Ali shrugged. What was the difference? As though reading his mind, Bucheri continued. "The Americans are a fine people. They try not to be racists. They work hard and take pride in their skills. They worship their God and allow others to worship theirs. They have a sense of humor and are kind to their neighbors. They protect their families and appreciate education. So what is wrong, Ali?"

Ali was dumbfounded. This was absurd. Before he could reply, Bucheri cut him off again.

"It isn't the American people, Ali." He gestured towards the flashing lights across the river. "Those people could have been our friends. They were fathers and warriors, perhaps church-goers. So what's wrong?"

Ali just shook his head.

"It's the government, Ali. The Americans are so naïve. While they allow immigrants to become true Americans, despite their race or religion, they ignore the rest of the world. They allow their government to treat us as subservient races, slaves to the dollar. Imagine, whole governments in South America controlled by fruit companies. And to think that now they complain that the Chinese are doing the same thing to them. What a joke. No, Ali, the Palestinians were sold into purgatory so that Israel could exist. Israel exists now to provide a power base in the Middle East, but remember, it wasn't always so. When Israel came to be, the Middle East was well under the control of the oil companies. They saw no danger, no need for a base like Israel. No, Israel was a sop to the conscience of the West, especially America, for the destruction of the Jews by the Nazis. Unfortunately, Americans have no endurance. If they can't have something quickly, they lose interest. Israel became a monster and they chose to ignore it. The Israelis became the Nazis of the Middle East, the master racists, all because Americans chose not to be bothered by details. All of the human rights which they are so quick to bestow on their own—they have no interest in seeing these spread throughout the world. Certainly not, it might be an inconvenience if Arab peoples decided to sell oil for what it was worth. Oh no! Not that!"

Ali shook his head tiredly. The constant background of the music was bothering him. "Hassan, I'm confused, what is the point of this if the Americans are good people?"

Hassan Bucheri was in full vigor now, despite the hour. "Because they are naïve, my friend, dangerously naïve. They have never lived in the shadow of fear. They cannot for a moment understand life as a Palestinian, a Serb, or a Kurd, or any of the other peoples that live in terror. With all their power and influence and statements about equality and justice, their government watches only the almighty dollar and the next election. They are children led by the worst of politicians. They consume more, pollute more, and manipulate more than any other country on earth. In their name, they do in other countries what would not be tolerated within their own borders, hypocrisy of the worst sort. They claim to allow others the freedom of choice, yet you and I both know what happens if a communist government emerges. The Americans think that they are safe in their sandbox. It's time that they came out to play, to find out what has been done in their name."

Ali thought he understood. "So you love them and you hate them."

Bucheri turned back to the view of Boston and sipped his drink. "I loved one American, but in the end, she was a child too."

"So you hate her now?" asked Dr. Kamal. Hassan Bucheri remembered Martha Lowell of the beautiful blond hair. Vibrant and warm, unconcerned that he was poor and she was rich. Cape Cod and the family yacht, *Extravaganza*. Wonderful memories from a turbulent time, a time of self-discovery. Bucheri had often wondered whether he should call on her in her Beacon Hill home, meet her children and her rich husband. Ideology had eventually driven them apart. She had none, just the vapor of the times. He had ambitions and desires for a whole people.

Bucheri paused before replying, "No. I don't hate her, and I don't hate Americans. The Americans, though—they are the most dangerous people on the planet. With their power they can build or destroy. Now, they are building on the bodies of others. The people of Boston will tell the rest of the country what it is like to feel fear, to know that one has lost control of one's destiny. Then they will understand our desperation, our pain."

Bucheri spun to face Ali. "And Ali, there is always revenge, sweet revenge. That makes it personal." Bucheri leaned forward and pointed his finger at Ali. "Revenge alone would be enough for what they did to my mother."

Inwardly, Ali rocked back at this insight into Bucheri's motives, but he kept his face expressionless.

Bucheri straightened up and seemed to calm himself. He breathed deeply several times. "I want to punish them as I would a naughty child, without emotion, but the pain of my people gives me a savage pleasure in destruction. Every brick that falls here, every person that dies, will be a stone cast at Israel." Bucheri leaned forward again towards Ali as a wicked smile appeared on his face. "And Ali, it's going to rain stones—a flood."

12:05 A.M.
FBI Field Headquarters, Boston

Harley Jones snapped off the radio. "Son of a bitch."

Jeannie knocked gently on the partially open door. Jones looked up. "Yes?"

"I brought you some fruit juice," she said, holding out the Styrofoam cup.

"Come on in." Jones leaned back and rubbed his eyes. "That sounds good. Why juice?"

"All of this caffeine is bad for you. You'll get the jitters," she smiled.

Jones closed his eyes as he rolled his head around. "Wouldn't want the jitters." He opened his eyes and smiled tiredly.

"Does your neck hurt?" she asked.

Jones nodded. "Shoulders, everything."

Jeannie walked behind him and started rubbing his shoulders. "Don't tell anybody about this. I don't want anyone to think I'm your Japanese house girl. You know, walking on your back, that kind of thing."

Jones groaned with relief. "God, that's great. I won't tell anyone. I promise." He sighed. "Oh Lord. Promotion, your choice of assignment, anything, just don't stop for another minute."

"My God, your muscles are rigid."

They were silent for a moment as Jones relaxed, trying to control the tension in his shoulders.

Finally Jeannie spoke. "You know, you can control the tension. Exercise, compartmentalizing your problems, learning to flow."

Jones didn't answer, so she went on. "Csikszentmihalyi wrote about it, flow I mean."

Jones opened his eyes, "Wow. That's a mouthful, and what did he say?"

Jeannie laughed, a low chuckle, "I can't express it in ten words or less. Basically, you have to find things that you like to do and do them."

Jones straightened up and Jeannie moved around to the front of his desk. "Jeannie, I love my work."

She watched him for a moment, "You are your job, that's different."

He closed his eyes and shook his head before gesturing with his hand. "Please take a seat."

She sat carefully, arranging her skirt. Jones waited, his eyes locked with hers.

"Jeannie, you're new to the team." He waited for a reply, an acknowledgment, but she waited silently, her gaze unwavering.

Finally, he gave in to her composure. "What do you think of the team? How are they forming up? I wouldn't ask, but we've been thrown into a sink-or-swim situation and, well, I'm worried."

Jeannie smiled faintly. "You want me to spy?"

Jones looked startled. "Spy? No, I just want an objective perspective on the team. I'm closely tuned to the old members and that makes it hard to get a feeling for the team as a whole."

Jeannie raised her eyebrows. "So you want a psychological evaluation?"

Jones shrugged. "Sure."

Jeannie stood up. "They're professionals and behaving like it. They'll do fine." She paused a moment. "Do you want some more psychology?"

Jones nodded.

"That suggestion that you gave me about deep psychological fears and the acid attacks on the police, it's bull." She smiled widely as she rose to leave.

Jones called after her. "Jeannie? Wait a moment please." He gestured for her to sit.

"First, thanks for your, ah, candid reply."

Jeannie gave a slight nod.

He continued, "Look, this is hard for me to say, but before you went to England we went out a few times and..." He paused and closed his eyes, searching for words. "I thought things were going well. I had ... well, you know, I thought things were going well." He looked directly in her eyes. "I'm your supervisor now and that makes things difficult. You know that, don't you?"

118

Jeannie was very familiar with the sexual harassment regulations of the FBI. There were regular briefings on them. It was difficult for someone to ask someone else out who worked in the same group. It was almost impossible for a supervisor to ask a subordinate out. Jeannie felt a pang of disappointment, then decided to take control of the situation.

"Perhaps it would be best if we considered that we had already started a relationship before I transferred. Would that be acceptable to you?"

Jones smiled in relief and winked at her. Jeannie felt a thrill of warmth go through her. Harley Jones was a real gentleman. They didn't make them like that anymore. She nodded to Jones and turned to leave, but the doorway was blocked by Ted Browner and a woman.

Jones signaled for them to come in. "Stay please Jeannie," he added.

Jones rose and extended his hand. "Ms. Nikolsky, thanks for coming." He remained standing as the rest took chairs, then he took his seat again.

"You know my associate Mr. Browner." Nikolsky nodded pleasantly. Jones gestured towards Jeannie Kawai, "This is Ms. Kawai, our forensics expert." The women nodded to each other, although Jones sensed an antagonism which baffled him.

Nikolsky smoothed the skirt of her blue business suit as Jones started, "Much to our surprise, it has been confirmed that Hassan Bucheri is involved in these terrorist acts."

Nikolsky nodded, expressionless. "She knew," thought Jones. "Absolutely, positively, for sure, she knew."

After a moment's pause, Nikolsky said, "He is the leader."

Browner leaned forward. "How do you know?"

Nikolsky answered, completely unfazed by Browner, "He is always the leader. Men and women follow him willingly because he has developed a reputation as an outstanding leader and planner."

"Planner?" queried Jones.

"Beirut for example," she answered. "Everything from the dead man's switch on the detonator, the route through the guards, the time of day. It was meticulous. All his planning and training. A mock-up compound had been set up in the Bekka Valley. The candidates were trained there for a week."

"Candidates? For a suicide mission?" asked Browner, disbelieving.

"There were many volunteers," she replied coolly. "You simply do not appreciate the Muslim religion or the glory of martyrdom." She shuddered slightly. "You have no idea."

Jones wondered at her emotional response, but decided to move on. "What can you tell us about Bucheri?"

She hesitated. "The military training, as you probably know, came primarily from the Israelis." She smiled faintly. "He was doing quite well and would probably be a general if he had stayed. His intelligence training came through the Egyptians and, at their request, through us. He was an excellent student although it was obvious at the time that he was not truly a Marxist-Leninist. Because of his excellence, he was allowed to continue to advanced schools, primarily those having to do with espionage." She pursed her lips slightly. "You have to appreciate that even at that time many of the people we trained were not Marxist-Leninists, simply nationalists, people who wanted to free their homelands."

Jones waved his hand, indicating that he was unconcerned with their initial motivations, despite Ted Browner's clear desire to pursue the topic.

"What can we expect from Bucheri?" Jones asked.

"Deception and game playing," Nikolsky answered. "Most of his efforts have been single strikes, like Beirut, but he always likes to give a clue. Did you know that he had a local fruit peddler deliver a section of the Koran to the Marine guards the day of the bombing?"

Jones and Browner both shook their heads.

Nikolsky shrugged. "I don't know what it said exactly—it was in Arabic—but apparently it was a section which tells a story similar to that of the Trojan Horse. The Marines never bothered to have it translated."

She sighed. "I'm sorry I can't tell you much more. I've read reports on many of his operations, so perhaps I will see a pattern for you as things go along."

Jones didn't move for a moment and then stood up, extending his hand. "We would really appreciate the help. Would you please wait outside for a moment with Ms. Kawai?"

After both women had stepped outside and the door was closed, Jones turned to Browner "Well?"

Browner shrugged. "I don't see what we have to lose, but we can't let her know what we're doing."

"Agreed." Jones paused for a moment and pursed his lips. "I think Ms. Kawai would be perfect for this job, don't you agree?"

Browner looked blank. "Sure, why not?"

Jones nodded, and Browner opened the door to let the two women back in. "Ms. Kawai will brief you on what is going on and find a desk for you here," Jones told Nikolsky. "I'm sorry but we won't be able to include you in our planning sessions."

Nikolsky bowed slightly and gave a brilliant smile. "I had not expected to be part of your private sessions. I am pleased to be of service. I will inform my superiors."

Nikolsky turned and left with Browner on her heels. Jeannie Kawai paused at the door and turned back, her eyebrows asking the question, Why me?

Jones gave a smile and a small goodbye wave as he sat down again behind his table. He settled back and watched the door with narrowed eyes for a moment before returning to his work.

12:05 A.M.
Conference Call

Jerry Price:
Madam Secretary I'm really sorry to wake you. I'm at the Boston Fusion Center and—

Melody Jane:
Wait! Susan, are you connected?

Susan Page:
Yes ma'am.

Melody Jane:
OK, Mr. Price. Go ahead.

Jerry Price:
Things have gotten ugly here. I—

Melody Jane:
I've watched the news.

Jerry Price:
I doubt that it's on the news. The Boston P.D. SWAT team got ambushed. They have many casualties. The governor has called out the National Guard.

Melody Jane:
Shouldn't I be doing that?

Susan Page:
No. They belong to the states unless they're federalized.

Melody Jane:
Well, two things seem to be in order. We should activate the Framingham Emergency Operations Center, and we should have the National Terrorism Advisory System send out an Imminent Alert. We have to be in the game here. This is our show now.

Jerry Price:
I can get the EOC warmed up. We can have the Boston Fusion Center feed them. I don't know about the NTAS alert. That's way out of my league.

Susan Page:
Ah, Ms. Harmony, I'm not so sure that you want to ring the NTAS bell. The old alert system brought us so much static. People claimed there was political use … it was a nightmare. Maybe we should talk with the people on the ground and see what they want? Also, do we want a local or a national warning to go out? They're supposed to be focused.

Melody Jane:
Susan, we are the people on the ground, and the American people need to know. We'll make this a national level alert. We can always back off, but it's really not good to raise it later. It makes you look unresponsive. Remember that famous saying, "It's easier to get forgiveness than permission." Use everything. Facebook, LinkedIn, all the news networks. We'll get some profile with this.

Susan Page:
Madam Secretary, there are consequences—

Melody Jane:
Susan, do it now. I'll see you at the office at seven.

There was a sharp click.

Susan Page:
Jerry, what do you think? I mean … Imminent Threat nationwide?

Jerry Price:
Excessive.

12:15 A.M.
Chinatown

Lee Zhang burst out of the tiny family apartment and ran down the stairs into the street. Upstairs his parents were shrieking in both Vietnamese and Cantonese. They had been boat people who were fortunate enough to get to the Promised Land. Unfortunately, the Promised Land offered little opportunity for those who didn't speak English. There was even less opportunity for ethnic Chinese-Vietnamese refugees with no family to help them. Life had been difficult and Lee Zhang's mother and father had been fighting for months. This time his mother had slashed his father across the ribs with a kitchen knife. Lee Zhang had run then, knowing that his father was a violent man and that things could only get worse. Down at the corner, he could see two dark figures, police by their hats. He sprinted as fast as he could, the blood pounding in his ears as he ran.

Patrolman Craft heard the patter of racing feet behind him. He and his partner, Patrolman Charley Green, had just been discussing the acid attacks. Between them, they had decided that no one was getting closer than ten feet. Patrolman Craft had seen the face of one of the patrolmen in the emergency ward. He was certain that he was going to have nightmares for the rest of his life. The jaw bone and teeth had shown through. Flesh just shouldn't look like that.

Patrolmen Craft and Green spun simultaneously. Craft reached for his pistol while Green reached for his club. Craft dropped into the approved two-hand combat stance and both patrolmen yelled "Halt!" The running figure didn't slow in the slightest. Craft dropped slightly lower and tried to lock his trembling arms and hands. Green yelled "halt" again, and then stepped behind Craft, dropped his club and reached for his service pistol. The figure ran through a pool of darkness then finally into the light, no more than a second away. Patrolman Craft had one last impression of an upraised hand with a bottle before he began firing as rapidly as he could pull the trigger. Once, twice, three times he pulled the trigger before the body slowed and fell.

Patrolman Green almost had his service pistol out, but now he forced it back. He stepped out from behind Patrolman Craft and moved to check out their possible assailant. He moved carefully around to stay out of Craft's line of fire. He kicked at the outstretched hand, which flopped open to reveal a handkerchief. Still careful, he straddled the body and reached down to check the pulse. In a moment he looked up: "Dead."

Patrolman Craft stood up slowly and tried to reholster his weapon, but succeeded only in dropping it. Patrolman Green was calling in on his radio as his best friend, George Craft, clutched a light pole and leaned into the gutter to vomit.

The sirens started up in the distance almost immediately. Green put his arm around his friend. "George, be cool. It's just one of those things."

Within four minutes the first police car arrived. Within ten minutes Pamela Clark and a camera crew were on the scene.

CHAPTER 14: RIGHTEOUS SATURDAY

6:30 A.M.
Manchester, New Hampshire
Sixty Miles North of Boston

Shapour was proud to have this assignment, the most important of all. Even though he appeared only to be a truck driver, he was, he told himself, a revolutionary of the first order. The cell phone, a miracle of Western decadence, chirped softly on the seat. He picked it up. "Yes?"

"Hormuz, Hormuz. Do you understand?" Shapour recognized the authorization to go and replied.

"Dakar, Dakar. Yes I understand." Now they knew that the message had gone to the right man. One couldn't be too careful, he had been told.

He and his friend, Ashraf, had stolen the truck for this most important of missions. They had repainted the necessary portions with spray cans and installed the additional features needed. It had not been too taxing. Ashraf was a mechanic and he had also been a Revolutionary Guard. No one would ever say that he lacked either courage or luck, having survived the Iraqi guns three times in that long-ago war. He was awake now. He gave Shapour a fierce warrior's smile. They would drive a dagger into the heart of Satan.

Shapour started the engine and moved the truck out smoothly.

7:43 A.M.
The White House
Washington D.C.

"Mr. President. I think you should put down your coffee."

The President sighed, "Harvey Betworth, you'd better not be pulling my chain."

"Sorry, but I don't want you spraying coffee all over the place."

The President finished a sip and put the cup down, signaling for Harvey to go ahead.

"Loony Tunes put out an Imminent Threat alert last night."

The President reflected for a moment. "Well, that isn't so radical."

Harvey smiled. "Over the whole nation."

The President flushed and jumped up. "Jesus H. Christ. That threat is localized in Boston. An Imminent Threat over the whole country will freeze us harder than a new groom's..." He paused. "She's just crazy. This will cost us millions, maybe billions, every day. Airlines won't fly. Trains will stop. People won't go to work. What was she thinking?"

Harvey pursed his lips. "She says the public has the need to know. She's new in the job, probably doesn't get the implications."

The President shook his head as he paced back and forth. "She's a fucking idiot. She's doing what every terrorist wants, giving them attention. Damn her to hell. The ramifications are impossible to predict." He paused, clenching his fists for a moment. "She's got to go. She's going to do more damage than the Sword of the Oppressed."

"Well, you said you had a plan for her."

The President shook his head slightly. "I don't know Harvey. Things are way out of control."

8:00 A.M.
JFK Federal Building
Boston

Harley Jones woke with a groan and looked around. Slowly, as his eyes focused, he realized where he was. Somehow, two hours ago, he had moved from his desk to his cot. "Levitation," he thought to himself, but was unable to raise a smile. He swung his feet off the cot and sat with his face in his hands. He should know better. Sometimes it was better to stay awake. Last night he had dreamed about Tom Coyle again, had seen him double over again, heard that single rifle shot echoing across the meadow. A sorrow of infinite depth had overwhelmed him. Twice he had woken up, his throat choked with the pain of loss. Once he had cried himself back to sleep. Poor Tom, he had trusted Harley Jones. He had trusted in Jones like some people trusted in the Lord, and Jones had loved him like a brother.

Harley Jones and Tom Coyle had been roommates at the academy. Jones had just come out of the Army and Tom was a freshly minted PhD in psychology from Tulane. The FBI academy was physically very difficult on Tom but, to Jones's surprise and pleasure, it was a breeze compared to what he had undergone in Ranger training. At first, Tom was a project—someone to help, but no one special. In fact, for Jones, there was no one special. The war had turned him into a loner.

One night, Tom woke Jones up from one of his ugly recurring dreams. "Son," the younger man said, "Y'all need a drink and a talk."

126

With that, he pulled a bottle of Southern Comfort from underneath his mattress and said, "This here is therapy. I'm the doctor, you take your medicine."

Any alcoholic beverage in the dormitories was grounds for expulsion, so Tom was taking quite a chance, but that was Tom. He had a way with trust. By six o'clock in the morning they were both drunk, Tom knew about Jones's Vietnam fears, and Jones had a friend for life.

Soon it became clear that Tom would not be able to pass the physical fitness test. He was both overweight and in poor condition. Jones kicked in by sitting next to Tom at every meal, removing all the "excess" foods from his tray. Before dinner, Jones took Tom on ever lengthening runs through the Virginia woods. Exercise was new to Tom, but Harley knew from his own experience that anyone could pass the FBI physical fitness test if he worked hard enough. Soon they were running beyond the small area occupied by the FBI academy and into the much larger area occupied by the Marines at Quantico. They ran together until the day of the physical fitness test. Jones put it bluntly: "Tom, if you don't past the test I'll kick your ass over every mile that we ever covered." Tom just smiled and hugged Jones. Jones had been deeply embarrassed but shouted with delight when Tom crossed the finish line with fifteen seconds to spare.

They had both gone on to pass high in their class at graduation. Tom had shown an enormous physical improvement and Jones had come to grips with some of his demons. After graduation Tom had gone to the Hoover Building in Washington, and Jones had been assigned to the west coast where his Vietnamese language capabilities might be useful. They had kept in close contact over the years. Eventually Jones had been assigned to the Hostage Rescue Team back in Washington. It was an incredible stroke of luck for Jones. Many good men waited years for a choice assignment like that, but Jones had done outstanding work and the higher-ups were grooming him for advancement. A year later Jones had been the best man at Tom's wedding. It was the happiest single day that Harley Jones could remember. He loved Nancy and Tom as the closest of friends. They were as good as a family and the marriage didn't change anything.

Finally, after years of maneuvering, Jones had gotten Tom onto the HRT. Tom had a gift with frightened people, as Jones well knew, and he displayed it time after time with the team. Jones became the man, the Agent in Charge, of the HRT, and Nancy and Tom introduced him to Jessica Williams. That initiated the golden era, when nothing could go wrong. Tom Coyle and Harley Jones became known as the Carrot and the Stick: their combined abilities allowed them to handle almost any situation. Tom was the smooth talker, the warm human, while Harley played the hard boss who had to be convinced. Their record was unblemished for almost three years.

Jones shook his head now. One giant fuck-up.

His trusty clock radio kicked in with a snap and Pirate 960 came on. "Yes, folks, it's Big Al, hairy Al, back on with Pirate 960 to carry you through this beautiful Saturday. We'll start running with another tune from our sponsor, the Hand that Wields the Sword. Yes, folks, you heard it first here. Weirder things have happened, I just don't know when. Our sponsor dedicates this to 'You know who'. Now, you and I know who that is don't we? Shit, I might. Well, it ain't me, so it must be you."

Jones opened his eyes as Jackson Browne sang especially for him about the road rushing by. He covered his ears and shook his head, but the refrain came through. It didn't matter, he knew it all anyhow. The rest of the world might not know, but Jones did. Bucheri was playing it for him.

Jones dropped his hands and snorted. "Running on empty"—wasn't that the truth.

"Believe" —Tom had believed in him. Jones paused; what did he believe in? This was important, he realized. Something was missing. Jackson Browne sang about looking for the friends that he counted on.

Jones blinked back a tear and stood up. He took a deep breath. It was too early for this bullshit. Today would be better. He grabbed his towel and went looking for a shower, firmly closing the door on the last refrain, knowing that it was true: just like the song said, he was *running behind*.

Cambridge

After five hours of sleep, Jeannie Kawai woke to her alarm. She lay in bed for a minute, trying to recall the previous day, the best parts, as she always did. There was so much. Excitement, danger, new people, decisions, responsibilities. It was exhilarating. She slipped out of bed and padded to the shower. There would be no dancing this morning. Her life had moved to a new plane. She could feel it in her *hara*.

As she showered she couldn't help thinking about Nadia Nikolsky. Why had Jones assigned her to be Nikosky's liaison, and why did that woman give her chills? She shook her face in the warm spray. Maybe it was the way she looked at men, as though she was leaning over a pastry tray, wondering which one to eat. Jeannie shivered despite the warm water.

Harvard Bridge

Shapour slowed the truck as they came across the Harvard Bridge. Police cars were moving rapidly along one of the cross streets. Shapour had a map, but he didn't read very well, so he counted streets very carefully. His English was weak, so he would use his portable telephone to call The Fox, if it became too difficult.

Shapour had been a low-level Iranian government operative for years. As a young man, he had worked for SAVAK, the intelligence arm of the Shah. The new religious government, like all governments, needed a secret police to root out dissidents, so there was a job for him after the revolution. Unfortunately, his original service in SAVAK had kept him from rising in the new agency. Others, seemingly more devout and more cunning, had climbed the religious ladder to control, leaving him out in the streets at night, watching the homes of the possibly unfaithful.

In the beginning, the service under the Ayatollah had been good. Shapour had removed several potential threats to himself, a business challenger to his father and, the ultimate test, his brother-in-law. A filthy cheating scum who beat his sister publicly and played with whores. Shapour remembered the smell of urine in the back of the car when that wretch had finally realized that he wouldn't make it to the police station. A bullet in the head and a bed in a trash heap, exactly what he deserved. His sister inherited the property and her freedom, at least temporarily. Women really shouldn't be too stressed, so Shapour managed the business end of things. With the money he made from this operation, he would become one of the more powerful men in Tehran.

It was satisfying, he thought as he downshifted for the corner.

The traffic was heavy, even though it was Saturday. Shapour reached under the dashboard and flipped the switch that would inject the initiator into the bulk explosive. The whine of the two large pumps vibrated the steering wheel in his hands. It was the feeling of power.

The bulk explosives were liquids, about the consistency of porridge, that were pumped into deep holes. The main component wasn't explosive until it was mixed with the initiator. The two reacted together to form a compound that was an explosive, but still very stable. It would take a fast blasting explosive, something like TNT, to start the explosion.

Shapour was especially pleased with the arrangement that they had made to mix the chemicals. The truck had two tanks, a small tank for the initiator and a large tank for the bulk explosive. They had pumped out the large tank leaving just enough room for the additional volume of the liquid from the initiator tank. Then they had taken the hose and placed it back into the loading port. It would keep pumping the initiator into the top of the tank until the initiator was consumed. Then they could mix it more by just running the bulk explosive pump and cycling the material through the hose and back into the loading port. It was beautiful, thought Shapour. It reminded him of a print that he had once seen in the home of an intellectual they had eventually shot. It had been a scene of a peculiar dragon which was eating its own tail. Now their truck was eating its own tail. He laughed out loud.

8:20 A.M.
Boston Police Headquarters
Tremont Street

Patrolman Arthur Church, at the entrance desk to the Tremont Street headquarters, wasn't a guard. His job was simply to monitor all the video cameras on the building security system. As the white tank truck with Boston City markings pulled up front, he wasn't worried about anything other than where it could park without disturbing the normal flow of traffic. He checked his other monitors and then looked back at the screen, wondering why the building would need a tank truck. Shouldn't it be out back? Maybe the sewers were backed up. The urinals certainly stank. He could see the driver standing to the side of the truck, while his assistant did something out of sight on the other side of the truck. Then Church saw that they were walking to the entrance, perhaps to get some guidance. There was something about this that he didn't like, but he couldn't leave his desk. He picked up the phone by his side, "Dispatch? Hi Eddy, I've got somebody funny out front. A white truck. Roll a unit to check it out will you? Thanks." It wasn't his assignment to check these things out. He'd gotten his ass chewed out once for leaving his desk and investigating someone snooping around the cars parked out back. Procedure required that he call a patrol car, and Sergeant Clayborne lived for procedure.

As Patrolman Church watched, the driver and his assistant walked right through the building and out of the camera viewing zone towards Albert Street. "I'll be damned," he said to himself.

Shapour held the radio detonator, a model airplane controller, in his hand as they started to walk across the grass towards Albert Street. He was excited and relieved now, his mission almost accomplished, his responsibilities handled. He was acutely conscious of the details around him, more alive than he had been in years. They would walk several blocks to the subway station, where they would get on a train and ride to the airport. Ashraf was excited too, Shapour could tell, as he gripped Shapour's arm. Just as Ashraf began to smile, Shapour heard a roar that filled his world with a shock wave and threw him spinning through the air. In those last moments he knew that his neck was broken, but he didn't worry. The mission was successful; he would ride with the triumphant in heaven.

Patrolman Church didn't have time to be surprised between the time of the flash from the video camera and the shock wave which crushed him to the wall. Farther down Tremont Street, Hassan Bucheri watched in awe the damage that he had triggered with his own radio detonator. Even a block away, the shock wave rocked the rented Cadillac Escalade. It would have been ideal to have placed the explosive inside the building, perhaps in a garage, but there wasn't one. The headquarters building was a rectangle with a walk-through archway in the center. The truck had been parked exactly in the middle of the arch. In the first instants of the explosion, the shock wave blasted through the windows facing Tremont, then ripped down the hallways, knocked down interior walls, and expelled itself through the windows on the Albert Street side. Those who were not killed directly by the shock wave were mutilated by thousands of flying fragments of glass, steel, and masonry. Only the documents clerk in the vault would survive. The slow blast velocity explosive sheared the face off the center of the building, causing it to collapse. The communications center on the fifth floor crumbled into a pile of stones and cables, exposed to the sky.

"Astounding," thought Bucheri as the dust cloud rose above the rain of heavier fragments pelting his Cadillac. "This is even better than the Marine barracks." He shook his head, trying to clear away the exultation, to be rational again. Of course, he realized, this was more explosive than Beirut. Still, he thought, this was a gift from Allah. He turned off the video camera, picked up the cell phone and punched the preset memory button.

"Miss Pamela Clark please. This is an emergency."

CHAPTER 15: MID-MORNING

9:00 A.M.
Private John Miller

Private Miller and his squad were standing by in the loose formation that Sergeant Gomez called a "clusterfuck"—that is, no formation at all. After all, this was the National Guard, not the Marine Corps Drill Team.

Alan Coster, the driver, pulled out the earphones from his radio and turned up the volume on the speaker. He yelled over the din, "Hey, guys! It's for us! Pirate Radio."

"...didn't even know that the National Guard was in town. Wouldn't that be cute, all the boys and girls in their high topped leather running shoes, a vision in green, running through the streets of Boston. For you people, our 'Home Guard' our '*Force de Frappe*' our 'last line of defense'—this one's for you. Me, I prefer Bud Lite."

The characteristic back beat of Credence Clearwater playing *Run Through the Jungle* came through with crystalline clarity, thumping about a nightmare and the devil on the loose.

Alan Coster started dancing with Ferdinand Genaro, his gunner on the M113 armored personnel carrier.

"Shut that shit down," bellowed the First Sergeant over the beat. "Mount up!" Credence filled the land with smoke.

Sergeant Gomez yelled, "Get inside, you weenies." He paused for effect, then shouted, "Move! Move! Move!" as sergeants have for thousands of years.

Captain Thorn, the company commander, turned to the First Sergeant.

"I don't like this radio business. It's likely to spook the troops."

The First Sergeant nodded. It was just like PsyOps Iraq, but now that it was someone else operating on *his* psyche, he didn't like it one bit.

Credence warned them to not look back.

9:20 A.M.
A Call from On High

Teddy Browner knocked and walked into Harley Jones's office with an encrypted military model cell phone that Jones only recognized vaguely.

He raised his eyebrows to Browner. Browner replied, "I ain't Martha Stewart and this ain't a good thing."

He put the phone down on the desk and plugged into the audio jack of Jones's portable radio. When he was done he said loudly, "I'm connected to a small speaker. Assistant Director Jones is in the room with me. No one else is in the room and it is unlikely that anyone can hear us."

There was a hiss as the two encrypted instruments synchronized, then Harley Jones heard the President's voice. "Mr. Jones. I don't like having flunkies give bad news and, also, I need to take your pulse. First, I heard about the bombing. I'm sorry. Things are in a terrible state, but I fear they're going to get worse."

Jones was tired, very tired, but this statement jacked up his pulse rate. "I'm listening," he said.

Jones thought he actually heard a sigh, but maybe it was static, before the President said, "You know that the Secretary of Homeland Security has issued an Imminent Threat warning."

Jones nodded, "Yes sir. We wondered about that."

"Well," the President said, "A national alert is, to put it bluntly, insane. That, however, may be an indicator of what is to come. I'm afraid that the Secretary may try to take over the operation. She has no personal experience with this kind of thing." He paused. "Well, hell, none of us does, but she is ill-equipped to direct anything that is as fast-moving as this appears to be. To once again be blunt, I think that she poses a danger to your efforts. I can't tell you what she will do because..." he paused for a long-time, "she's nuts."

Harley Jones waited and then said, "What do you want us to do?"

There was another silence before the President replied, "Jones, you're sitting on a powder keg, and I'm afraid that she's going to start running around with a match."

Teddy Browner leaned towards the phone. "Browner here, sir. Since neither the CIA or the FBI is under her control, do you think that she can interfere?"

The President replied immediately, "Yes. If she stays in Washington and talks on the phone, I think we can handle it. But, if she flies up there with some of her people it's going to be very bad for your mission."

There was a long silence. Finally Harley Jones said, "It would seem that our options are limited."

"Jones, I've been told that you are a man with both brass balls and a vivid imagination. You'd better come up with something ... and that 'something' had better be non-lethal but deadly effective. It isn't just careers on the line. There are tens of thousands of people who will be put at considerable risk if this plays out as I see it."

There was a pause. Thinking back to the Tom Clancy book, *Clear and Present Danger*, Harley Jones said, "Do we get a 'Get Out of Jail Card'?"

Despite the tension, the President chuckled. "We should all be so lucky."

The connection broke and the two men stared at each other.

"Jesus," said Browner, "what was that?"

Jones stood up wearily and nodded to the door. "Teddy, let's go for a walk. I think we need some help from the dark side. I'm going to make a call, and you're going to meet a woman with *chutzpah*. Let's hope she can help."

10:00 A.M.

The drone of the ancient M113 armored personnel carrier had almost lulled Private Miller to sleep, despite the lurchings of Alan Coster, the asshole incompetent driver. Private Miller had been up since midnight. Blearily he looked at his watch, then realized that he couldn't read the liquid crystal display in the semi-dark of the APC. He was too tired to press the button that would light the display and tried to shift a bit to get into a slightly more comfortable position. The excitement of the midnight alert had transformed into a mind-numbing fatigue. He envied the other squad members who were somehow able to sleep.

It had been exciting then and especially weird with this "Hand" guy playing tunes on 960. The troops were raring to kick ass on the terrorists in Boston. The officers and senior NCOs, especially the First Sergeant, were not happy. While the officers talked about target discrimination, the First Sergeant said something that Miller still couldn't fathom, something about "swim with the fish in the sea." Asshole Coster said it was something from Chairman Mao's little red book, but Miller didn't know who Chairman Mao was. Miller had asked Sergeant Grace, the armorer, what the First Sergeant had meant. Sergeant Grace had replied, "All gooks look alike." Miller shook his head. It made him uncomfortable when the leaders didn't have their act together. Suddenly the APC lurched to a halt, spilling the men who were unbuckled onto the deck. The ramp dropped with a squeal and Miller blinked at the bright sunlight. He looked at his watch. Ten past ten.

His APC was the second in a patrol of two vehicles. The streets were busy with cars, but traffic was lighter than normal, perhaps because it was Saturday. There were a few pedestrians gawking at the unusual sight of military vehicles in an American city. Sergeant Gomez, sitting opposite Miller, was the squad leader. Gomez blinked, wondering about orders, then unbuckled and stepped out.

Miller got up stiffly and followed Sergeant Gomez out of the APC. Just as Miller's foot hit the ground, he heard a roar and watched with horror as Sergeant Gomez's face disappeared. He fumbled his rifle up only to see a scarred, thin, black man pointing a sawed off shotgun at his chest from only a yard away. His last recollection of that moment was the flash of fire from the barrel of the gun.

Although it felt like hours, it must have been only minutes before he regained consciousness. His chest ached as though he had been run over by a truck. He rolled to his side and the pellets from the shotgun rolled off his flak jacket and onto the ground. He groaned and tried to rise, but could only get up on one elbow. Something smelled horrible. It was a sweet burnt meat and gasoline smell that nauseated him. He could feel heat on his face from the APC. Slowly, because it hurt, he turned his head. In the distance, he could hear screaming. Then it was right next to him. A face and behind it a burning back. Then the screaming stopped.

Private Miller staggered upright, avoiding touching the APC by using his rifle as a crutch. He looked around through his tears. Dimly, he saw civilians. Horrified, pointing, useless civilians.

Miller wanted to collapse and cry. Instead, he wiped his tears on his sleeve. No one in the crowd seemed dangerous so he turned to the APC. As he looked at the man who had screamed, he wondered who it was. It didn't look like anyone he knew, but that must be because of the burning. He knew everyone in the squad. Anyway, he had screamed, so at least he must be alive. Miller put his rifle down and started to pull the man out, trying to remember what one was supposed to do with burns.

10:41 A.M.
Office of The Secretary of Homeland Security
Washington, D.C.

Melody Jane Harmony sat behind her desk. Its massive surface was not cluttered. Only one object rested on it: a yellow pad of paper. Susan Page, the Deputy Director, sat across from her. Unlike other executive offices, there was no conference table. You were either the Secretary, or you worked for her, and that was made clear with this arrangement.

Melody Jane had several of her computer screens projected on the wall, as well as two fifty-inch television screens. One television was on

CNN while the other was on Fox News. Jerry Price was on the speakerphone.

"It's unbelievable. I've seen it myself," he said. "The glass went everywhere. A few people were in the basement or the bathrooms. They're alive ... no windows there. There's blood everywhere." He sobbed, "My sister was there. I got her a job at the fusion center. I couldn't even recognize her. They could only identify her by her name tag."

Susan Page leaned towards the phone. "Go home Jerry. But first, have your deputy contact me. OK? Did you hear me?"

He gathered himself for a moment, replied with a broken "Yes," and hung up.

"Why did you do that?" snapped Melody Jane.

Susan Page paused. How to explain this to Melody Jane? Unlike Melody Jane, Susan had done military service. After law school she had served for five years in the Buffalo prosecutor's office—a nice start for any litigation-oriented law career. When 9/11 happened, like her grandfather sixty years earlier, she had joined the Marine Corps and gone to Officer Candidate's School. OCS was followed by the twenty-six week Officer's Basic School where all Marine Corps Officers were trained as infantry officers. Shortly thereafter, she had been assigned to the Judge Advocate Corps and sent to the Naval Justice School. When she learned that she was assigned to Iraq she expected a boring tour doing Legal Assistance, but at least she'd be helping.

On her second day in-country she was in a convoy towards Nasiriyah. She was in the third truck in the convoy. The convoy commander, a very young-looking second lieutenant, was in the first vehicle. Just south of Nasiriyah an improvised explosive device detonated, flipping his Humvee completely over. She had run up to the vehicle only to confirm that the lieutenant, his driver and the radioman were all dead. The IED had only been the beginning of an intense ambush. Captain Susan Page had directed the vehicles to move out of the kill zone and form a circle as the road had been destroyed. She had rallied the Marines, organized a defense and then called in both artillery and air support. For her action she had been awarded the Combat Action Ribbon and the Bronze Star with Combat V. For getting a small piece of shrapnel from a mortar shell lodged in her ass, she'd been awarded a Purple Heart. The wound had led to more than a few good-humored "get it in the ass" jokes. Overall, compared to some of the action, it was not a big thing, but she had been quite a celebrity for a few weeks with the men and women of the 15th Marine Expeditionary Unit. Later in her tour she had seen battle fatigue in its many forms, particularly PTSD, post-traumatic stress disorder. Jerry Price wouldn't be functioning for a while.

Ever wary of crossing her boss, she replied, "He's going into shock, just as though he'd been through the explosion himself. Very soon he's going to feel guilty for not having been there. Then he'll need medication and therapy. We need someone who is completely functional."

Melody Jane stared for a moment, then relented to Susan Page's judgment.

"We need to activate the EOC in Framingham," Melody Jane said firmly.

"With the fusion center destroyed, we don't have any intelligence to feed it."

Melody Jane pursed her lips. "We'll get some intelligence. I have someone in the headquarters of this CTU abomination."

Susan Page looked at the televisions for a moment and then the computer screens. "Are you sure you want to intervene? Perhaps it would be better to assist."

Melody Jane rocked back in her chair and looked at the ceiling for a moment. Then she leaned forward. "This FBI-CIA CTU abomination was concocted to undermine Homeland Security." Susan Page couldn't tell whether "Homeland Security" meant the organization or the concept. Melody Jane continued, "My sources tell me that people, people in high places, are after me. But, she waved a finger at Susan Page, "I know how to get back. The nation must be defended. We can use this situation to our advantage to strengthen Homeland Security. We just need to get things organized so that everyone knows who they're working for."

Melody Jane sighed and took another drink from her ubiquitous Diet Coke. She wrinkled her lips and reached into her mini-fridge for another.

"Harley Jones is a cowboy," Melody Jane went on. "He's running a disordered mess. I hear he's going to try and bring the Army in. That is simply not possible. It is not legal. I've already issued orders to the Secret Service to mobilize as many men as possible. A few people are going to have to get along with smaller security details for a few days. And the agents working on counterfeiting will find that their cases will be there when they return. All together I have forty-five hundred agents. I don't need them all. Maybe a thousand will do the job."

Melody Jane got up and began to pace. "Things should be ready by this evening. I've got a plane lined up to get to Logan Airport and the Secret Service will have a helicopter there for me." She smiled. "I'll descend like an American eagle, and the cameras will be running." She turned to face Susan Page. "This will be a pivotal moment in American Internal Security. One cohesive force to protect the American people."

Susan Page was beginning to worry seriously. With the resources she could muster, Melody Jane Harmony might actually be able to take over, and the mess in Boston didn't look like a place for amateurs.

11:15 A.M.
Patrick Henry Johnston

Patrick Henry Johnston was fixed to the television news, just as he had been during the war with Iraq, but this was different. This was just up the street and it stank. Something was going on. Now he understood how his parents had worried about communism in the days of Joe McCarthy. Lots of smoke from Tail Gunner Joe, but the atom bomb secret had been stolen. Something was going on, and it wasn't what it seemed. Pamela Clark, the original painted bitch, was babbling about some action over on the Common. Damn, that was close by. Only six blocks up Marlborough and over to Beacon, an easy walk. Still, for some reason he couldn't explain, he decided to drive. That way, he told himself, he could check out the whole area. It was the smell of danger, however, that prompted him to throw his 6mm Remington varmint gun into its case and carry it out to the Nissan Pathfinder. The Colt Python went into the pocket of his long baggy duck hunting coat. That was for up-close-and-personal varmints.

Patrick Henry Johnston started up the Nissan and moved carefully over to Beacon Street. The traffic was light and almost nothing was coming down from the hill. Carefully he moved up towards the Common. As he crossed Charles Street, which bisected the Common, he could see a gaggle of armored vehicles down to the right, halfway through the park blocking the street. He was distracted by the activity. A motorcycle roaring by him up Beacon Hill caught his attention. Stupid, he thought, there were always cops around by the State House at the top of the Hill. Up ahead, he saw two soldiers step out from between the cars to block the motorcyclist. Suddenly, without warning, one of them flipped up his rifle and sprayed the motorcyclist. He flopped off the slow-moving bike like a disconnected puppet as the motorcycle slowly canted to the right, doomed to crash into the parked cars.

Johnston slammed on the brakes and spun the front wheel. The Nissan stopped, perpendicular to the roadway, exactly in the center. Johnston was transfixed, staring at the body in the road as the two soldiers watched him. One spoke briefly to the other, and Johnston realized what was coming next. Without hesitation he stepped on the gas and was slammed back as the Nissan leapt like a horse out of the starting gate. Perhaps that rapid action saved him, he thought later; but at that moment a sound like hail reverberated though the Nissan and the windshield fractured into interconnected spider webs with bullet holes in the center. With a scream he kept his foot down and weaved the truck back and forth while he tried to punch out the windshield to get a clear view. Another hail of lead passed through the machine and he jerked the steering wheel to the left as bullets went through his two right tires. With a speed which surprised him, the Nissan rolled onto its side and slid down the street in a shower of sparks.

Silent now, his right knee bruised from slamming into the gearshift, Johnston fumbled with the safety belt that held him suspended in the air. Finally, the belt released him and he dropped down to the right side of the truck. Quickly, smelling the gas, he kicked out the windshield. Before crawling out, he grabbed the rifle case. He was going to blow those fucks away.

As he crawled out through the glass, he realized that the Nissan would shield him from the soldiers up the hill. The others, down on Charles Street, might be a problem. He ripped open the rifle case and tore the top off the twenty-round box that he always kept in the case. He tried to listen for the running feet of the soldiers up the hill as he jammed five rounds into the magazine of the bolt action rife, but all he could hear was the rear wheel of his Pathfinder spinning uselessly in the air.

Private John Miller

Miller was talking to Captain Polasky when the first burst of gunfire echoed over the Common. Up the hill, he could see two soldiers in familiar camouflage, too far away to identify. Captain Polasky stood, indecisive, staring. Private Miller, veteran of one contact with the terrorists, knew exactly what to do. He clambered up on top of the M113, swung the .50 caliber in the direction of the shooting and pulled back the massive cocking lever. He was never, ever again going to be caught unprepared.

Hassan Bucheri

Hassan Bucheri's hands were shaking slightly as he watched through the shaded windows of 25 Beacon Street. He and Sergeant Besso were on the second level of the building that housed the Unitarian Universalist Association. Sergeant Besso was the commander of the Somalian unit. Tall, thin, and scarred, Besso looked like a tribal warrior. Perhaps he was, but he was well trained after fighting in the Somalian guerrilla war for twelve years.

Bucheri smiled. "God is on our side, providing us with such a perfect location." Typically, Besso didn't reply. Like any good leader, he was worried about his men and the mission for today. Nonetheless, it was funny. God obviously had a sense of humor. On the balcony a sign had the message: United States of America – U.N. - We Believe - Canada. Yes indeed, smiled Bucheri, We Believe.

Bucheri's location gave him a good, but not excellent, view of his ambush zone. The trees in the Common were a bit of an obstruction. He could easily see along Beacon Street where his two Somalians had shot a motorcyclist and then a civilian vehicle. He had captured that on video tape since he had been unwilling to call Pamela Clark. She might have lost her greed, been sated by her victories. Certainly her telephone lines would be tapped by now. A video tape delivered anonymously would be best.

Now, on Charles Street, he could see four of the National Guard armored personnel carriers. One of the troops had climbed up onto one of the carriers and prepared the machine gun. It was time to warn his two Somalians off. The video tape of troops killing civilians would be front page material; there was no reason to lose his troops. Just as he turned to Sergeant Besso, a new sound rolled across the Common. A very sharp high crack. A rifle, certainly, but different. He could see one of his Somalians leaning over the body of another. The first now ran forward and vaulted the rail and slid down the hill into the park. Now he would surely be out of sight of whoever had shot his companion. Bucheri gripped the binoculars feverishly but couldn't control his excitement. He leaned forward and braced himself on the window sill. From the corner of his field of view, he saw movement. A slight shift brought a figure with a telescopic rifle into view. The figure dropped to a kneeling position as he brought the rifle to his shoulder, pointing it at the fleeing Somalian. That peculiar crack came rolling again across the Common just after the flash from the rifle. A quick swing of the binoculars confirmed Bucheri's fears: his second man was down.

With the thump of a heavy machine gun, Bucheri swiveled to watch the National Guard group. The officer was yelling at the gunner, as the gunner blazed at the shooter's last position. Over the deep crumping of the heavy machine gun, Bucheri could hear the crack of the high-powered rifle once again and the officer flopped forward.

Allah be praised. It had started. Even better than he had planned. It was surely the will of God. The Americans were fighting each other on the Boston Common. This was a scene that he wished he could savor, but it was time go. It was time for Santa to give out more gifts: Bucheri giggled at his thought. The image of him delivering bombs to Americans from Santa's sleigh was too much. But the continued hammering of the heavy machine gun sobered him as he raced down the back steps. Getting hit now would be a stroke of evil luck. The machine gun continued to send its half-inch bullets slicing through the cars and houses along Beacon Street as Bucheri raced up Spruce Street to find his car.

* * *

Private John Miller stopped shooting when the belt for his 50 ran out. He continued to grip the butterfly trigger as he searched for the demons that had attacked them.

Meanwhile, Patrick Henry Johnston carefully placed his rifle in a trash can behind a Chestnut Street house, just off the Common. He would be back tonight. He forced himself to control his breathing as he walked down Chestnut. Slowly, slowly, he told himself. Blend in with the terrain. He gripped the .357 Colt Python in his pocket, hoping he wouldn't need it. There were better tools for the job.

Usually, Johnston would have had a picture taken with his kill. Obviously, that wouldn't be possible this time, but he had gotten a good look at the man through his 16-power scope. The face was the blackest black. And the scars on the cheeks—strange.

Thirty minutes later, Special Agent Tim Blackwell was standing near to Johnston's second victim. Next to him, Private John Miller looked very ill, white with a sheen of sweat on his face.

Blackwell sensed confusion in the soldier. "Isn't he from your company?"

Continuing to stare at the face, Private Miller answered quietly, "No sir."

Captain Thorn, Miller's company commander, was standing on the other side of Miller. He turned towards Blackwell. "The private is correct, sir. This man isn't one of ours."

Blackwell shook his head. Company C was the advanced party for the battalion. They should have been the only troops in the area. Something about Miller's stare had caught his attention.

Captain Thorn put his arm around Private Miller's shoulders. "Don't take it too hard Miller. Soldiers die in combat. There are worse deaths than dying for your country."

Miller shook off the Captain's grip. Almost crying, he screamed, "He isn't any goddamn soldier."

The Captain was dumbstruck. Blackwell stepped over, "What do you mean?"

Miller pointed at the body. "This is the guy that shot Sergeant Gomez and me."

Blackwell stared for a moment and then ran for his car.

11:20 A.M.
JFK Federal Building

Jones was just hanging up the phone as Ted Browner, Nadia Nikolsky, and Jeannie Kawai filed into his office. As they took chairs, Jones couldn't help but notice Nikolsky's appearance. Today she wore a well-tailored cream-colored suit which emphasized her complexion and her small gold earrings. Those clothes couldn't have come from Russia, he thought to himself. Nikolsky sat gracefully but allowed her skirt to ride up somewhat higher on her thighs than Jones would have expected. Her eyes were locked on his but not in amusement. There was something there that he couldn't quite follow.

"I've just been speaking with one of our agents. You already know about the bombing this morning, I presume?"

Nikolsky nodded. It had, of course, been on Pirate Radio, Bucheri's first method of reaching the public. Shortly after that WXTV had shown a video narrated by Pamela Clark. Nikolsky was intrigued by the detail that Clark could provide. It suggested that she had been well briefed by someone involved with the bombing.

"There has now been some sniping on the National Guard as well as on civilians. What does all of this suggest to you?" Jones asked.

Nikolsky hesitated, collecting herself. "First, our records on the man Bucheri indicate that he does not commit random acts of terror. He is a chess player. You must also realize that he comes from a different society. Here, in America, the police are not hated as they are in other societies. In Israel the Palestinians look upon the police as the enemy. Any bombing of the police would be viewed with great support there and many other places. The police are despised."

She paused again, "You cannot consider that this attack on the police was a propaganda move. It might be or it might not be. Can you guess what he is thinking, or is he guessing what you are thinking that he is thinking? It is like our Russian dolls within dolls. You are, as you say, 'caught between the rock and the creek.' I think that the strike against the police was a tactical move, to paralyze them. It will probably be part of several moves, as in any good chess game."

"Why would he want to paralyze the police?" Browner asked. "The police don't seem to have been much of a problem for him so far."

For a moment, Nikolsky looked tired as she closed her eyes and rubbed the bridge of her nose. "I have been trying to be polite. I think that you do not realize the bigness of the problem that you have." She straightened up in her chair. "We have indicators that his group is very large. We also know that they come from many countries." Browner nodded, as this confirmed some of the CIA's intelligence.

She continued, "It does not take a large group just to bomb the police station. They have been doing other things too, the gassings you have seen. My superiors believe that Bucheri wants to destroy the structure of the city, perhaps the city itself."

Browner snorted. "How can he destroy the city?"

Nikolsky shrugged. "I am speaking for my superiors in that statement. Myself, I think that Bucheri is playing propaganda very hard." She raised her eyebrows slightly while looking at Jones. "*Very* hard. He is a master of the propaganda."

She paused, waiting for her words to sink in. "Remember Beirut. His attack was the beginning of the end of any military presence there. The Marines left and soon was the end."

Jones nodded, watching Nikolsky closely. He waited for a moment, and then asked, "Is there anything else you can tell us?"

She shook her head slightly and stood up. Jones shook her hand again, as did Browner, and then Jeannie escorted her out.

As the door closed, Jones sighed. "Well?"

Browner leaned forward like a conspirator. "You know what I think?"

Jones blinked, waiting.

Browner continued tensely, "I think the FIS is here to kill Bucheri. If Bucheri gets captured and he was trained in the Soviet Union, they're going to be in more trouble than any of us can imagine. Most people don't see any difference between the old Soviet Union and Russia now. Once the media get a hold of this, the Russians won't cooperate for the next century. Massive—I mean *massive*—embarrassment. They've got to kill him, and she's the front man to find out what we know."

Jones sighed again. "It's possible. We're certainly telling her what we know about what's happened. I can't see that as much of security breach. Bucheri himself is getting everything on the news anyhow. What choice do we have? If her information's any good, what does it matter if the Russians kill him?"

Browner bristled. "Jesus, Harley, I wish you wouldn't pull this devil's advocate crap on me. First, I think this propaganda thing is a smoke screen." He raised his hand to stop Jones from interjecting. "And, no, I cannot explain this new media crap. Maybe that's a smoke screen too."

There was knock on the door and then it opened. Jeannie Kawai put her head in. "Nikolsky is making a call from one of the payphones downstairs. I've asked Liz to try and tap it." The door closed quietly behind her.

Browner shook his head. "Where was I? Yah. Smoke screens. Second, it sure as hell does matter if they kill Bucheri. We need to question him and find out who's behind all this."

"You don't believe in Nikolsky's Iran or Iraq?"

"Iraq is just leaderless. Maybe Iran. They've got enough crazies there, but this kind of thing takes big money. You know, it feels like a lure—it's close enough to pull you in but it isn't the real thing." He sighed and slumped in his chair. "Then again, they've got lots of money." He finished by shaking his head. "What a mess."

Jones nodded sympathetically. "You guys just don't have enough assets on the ground over there. The NSA has become such a powerhouse with its satellites that they've got the glitz. These politicians just won't believe that our problems need to be solved by people, not by machines."

The two men sat in silence for a moment, then Browner rose. "I'll leave you to your misery."

Jones smiled faintly, "And you to yours." As the door closed, Jones slouched down in his chair and closed his eyes.

12:02 P.M.
His Master's Voice

Pamela Clark fumbled with her key as she tried to insert it into her apartment lock. She was literally shaking with rage. Here she was working on the story of a lifetime and there was a massive leak from the apartment above hers. Apparently it would soon cascade down on her closet, soaking her clothes. She had considered ignoring the call from the building manager, whom she had never met, but despite all the pressure that she could apply, he had refused to go into her apartment. She simply had too much invested in her wardrobe to ignore the call.

The key slid in and she twisted the lock violently. The door slammed back as she burst through. Surprisingly, it didn't hit the wall, but closed quietly behind her. She spun around, terrified, to see a man just slightly taller than she was, wearing a suit and a life-like Ronald Reagan mask. The man remained immobile, his gloved hands holding a submachine gun. A familiar voice spoke behind her.

"You knew that I would come for you."

She spun again to face a similarly dressed man, but this one wore a Clinton mask. His hands were also gloved but empty. Somehow, his very presence was more intimidating than that of the other man.

"The Hand?"

He bowed slightly.

"Why are you here?" she asked.

He took her arm and led her towards her bedroom. "We must talk my dear."

She was thrilled but terrified at what was to come. As they stepped through the door, she was surprised to see that her bed had been pushed against the wall. Her lamps had been arranged behind one chair to illuminate another. There were two video cameras mounted on tripods, each facing one of the chairs.

He gestured towards the well-illuminated chair. He would be in shadow. "Your script is there," he said confidently. "Please sit. I have a busy schedule today and so do you."

Pamela Clark bridled for a moment but realized that this was the chance of a lifetime. No western journalist had ever interviewed Osama bin Laden, Carlos the Jackal, or any other major terrorist, and the Hand would eclipse them all like the sun would overwhelm a faint morning star. The Hand would be news for a decade whether he lived or died: a legend. There was a place for her in the legend, she realized—both making it and being part of it.

She picked up the script and sat down. She glanced at the page and noticed that only her part was written in. She shrugged. She would edit the sequence any way she wanted.

She heard a tiny hum as the cameras started up. The masked man sat down in the shadows across from her. "Are you ready?"

She nodded, then looked quickly to her script. "Are you the person called The Hand that Wields the Sword?"

The masked face nodded. "Indeed I am. I come to you, Pamela and the people of Boston, as an enlightener—an educator, if you will," he finished in his smooth, articulate tone.

Quickly, Pamela looked at her script. "Educator? Would you please explain?"

"First, let me explain this mask. I wear the face of one of your great deceivers. You Americans love your images. I felt you would be more likely to listen to this face than to my own." The smooth voice became more angry now. "Listen to me, Americans, I have come from farther than the far side of the moon, another world, a land of poverty, of despair, pain and suffering that you cannot imagine. I have taken it upon myself to introduce you to the misery of being homeless, the fear of the unknown, the pain of loss. Yes, within the next day the people of Boston will learn what it is like to be one with the Third World, where death wears red, white and blue, where angels drop Rockeye bombs, where Satan sucks our life from beneath the soil and gives us filthy water to drink while our children die in the sun." The masked man halted, and seemed to be reining himself in.

He resumed in a more urbane voice, "Yes indeed folks, that's the way it's going down, right here in the good old U. S. of A."

The masked figure leaned back and spread his hands out, palms upward. "Why travel when you can have all the thrills of a foreign land at home?"

Pamela Clark sat mesmerized, then looked at her script for a moment. "You have been using music to reach the public. Why is that?"

The masked figure was motionless for a moment, apparently surprised by the question. "Poetry is dead, reading is a lost skill, television is a blank wall. Music is the last form of American self-expression. I will speak to you in your own words. Perhaps you will understand me then. Listen carefully: the truth surrounds you."

146

Pamela Clark looked at her script, then shook her head slightly as though she couldn't believe what she was reading, "What are your plans for the future?"

In a near-perfect imitation of Arnold Schwarzenegger's voice as the Terminator the figure said, "I'll be back."

Somehow, it wasn't funny at all to Pamela Clark. He seemed to mean it quite sincerely. She paused again, then looked at her script.

Just then, a large rumble passed through the building.

To Pamela Clark's horror, the figure reached over to his mask and pulled the rubber into a parody of a smile.

"It begins," he said after releasing the mask.

Spontaneously, Pamela Clark left the script and asked the question that she knew had to be asked.

"When will it end?"

This time, in a near-perfect imitation of Gary Cooper's voice from *High Noon*, the masked figure replied, "Sunday, High Noon."

12:17 P.M.
25 Beacon Street

Sergeant Besso looked through the upper-story windows of 25 Beacon Street. He stood well back from the window, careful so that no one could see him from the outside. He was a careful man, patient and meticulous, having learned many lessons in the harsh Somalian desert. Attention to detail was the most important. Weapons were always scrupulously cleaned, ambushes carefully laid out, infiltrations thoughtfully planned. He was uncomfortable now, despite The Fox's detailed planning. This wasn't his desert and things were not as predictable. He sighed and shifted his weight minutely so that his legs would not become cramped. As his eyes roamed constantly, his mind played. He thought of himself as a hawk, about to swoop on his prey, but the other side of his mind told him that he was a vulture. A slight smile tugged the corner of his mouth, then disappeared as he thought of the two men that he had lost today. It wasn't that he suddenly minded losing men—he had always minded that. It was the unpredictability of it all. Shooting at a few civilians shouldn't have been dangerous, but this time one of them had pulled a sniper rifle out of his truck and killed his people. He shook his head. This operation was a madhouse. Only the money made it worthwhile. Already there was a stream of refugees, of cars packed with clothes, children and valuables. Anxious men driving, children silent, women staring fixedly ahead. If it hadn't been for the cars, it would have been a familiar scene. The wealth here defied the imagination.

The radio crackled.

"Station Leader, Station Three."

Besso answered, "Station Three, this is Leader, speak."

"The one we want is coming past me now. He is going in your direction."

Besso nodded to himself. "I understand, Station Three. Stay where you are until you hear from me." Besso rotated the dial quickly from channel 33 to 35 on the CB radio. "Taxi One, this is Leader."

No response. Impatiently Sergeant Besso waited. Whoever the Taxi team was, they were slow.

* * *

Inspector Anmar Habib jerked upright at hearing his call sign, Taxi One. He fumbled for his cellular phone, ignoring the CB Radio over which the call had come. "Calm, calm," he told himself and stopped to inhale deeply. "Start the engine first," he finally decided. This diesel truck was a real whore. Fortunately, the engine coughed to life immediately. Then he found the cellular phone and punched the preset button for his team leader, Taxi Three. This had not been part of the instructions provided to his team at the briefing by The Fox, but the entire Syrian team had two missions: the mission for The Fox, and the mission to report on the mission. To some, this might have seemed Byzantine, but it was typical for Syrian Security, watchers to watch the watchers. It didn't matter who was in power; agents with experience were always needed. The Fox thought he was getting freelancers, but that was not the case.

Ignoring radio procedure and using the cellular phone just as though it was secure, his control answered with a sharp nasal, "Yes?"

Anmar shrugged and decided to follow the other man's lead. "I have been called."

"Carry out your mission, but keep this line open. Do you understand?" Anmar grimaced at the implication that he was stupid. Wisely, he decided not to reply. He picked up the CB radio microphone.

"Leader, this is Taxi One."

Sergeant Besso fumed at the delay. This was the problem with working with other teams. You never knew how much you would have to compensate for their incompetence. The delay might just have killed this mission.

"Taxi One. Start along your route at fastest possible speed without getting stopped. You are one minute late."

Anmar jerked at the implied rebuke. What did this idiot expect? What was so important about delivering an empty gasoline truck anyhow? They had even vented the system for seven minutes exactly as instructed after pouring the gasoline into the sewers. It seemed quite silly but one never knew when The Fox might be watching. With a man known in the intelligence community as "The Butcher" one didn't take chances. Angry, Anmar jerked through the gears, pushing the truck up Beacon Street towards the Common.

* * *

Sergeant Besso was beside himself with rage. Taxi One, the whore of a goat fucker, was late. The mayor's black limousine was already parked and the door was open. Two motorcycles had preceded him and he was followed by a car filled with armed officers. They were already deploying in front of the State House. Several had binoculars and one had a telescopic rifle. At any moment they would spot him as he observed them from the balcony. Curse that flea bitten failure.

"Taxi One. Go at fastest speed you idiot. You are late. They are here." Sergeant Besso, despite his disgust at Taxi One, finished with "*Allahu Akbar.*" Martyrs deserved it.

Anmar shrugged at the communication, stepped on the accelerator and pressed the air horn as he bullied his way through the Massachusetts Avenue intersection on a red light. Horns blared but no one wanted to argue with a big tanker truck. Behind him, Anmar could see the lights of a police car come on, but it was caught in traffic. Anyhow, his Uzi sub machine gun could deal with these poorly armed American policemen. Fuck them. They were already on the run. Anmar thrilled as he raced up the hill, the powerful engine quickly taking him through the gears with the light load of an empty tank.

Besso could see the truck now, moving rapidly up the hill. He swung back and saw two people get out of the limousine. Two of the police were pointing excitedly down the road toward the truck, but Besso couldn't hear what they were saying. Would they be able to save the mayor?

Anmar saw the limousine and police at the top of the hill. From the map, he knew that this was the State House. His instructions were that he should roar by at maximum speed. He was to be a diversion to a sniping. He resisted the temptation to honk. His orders were explicit: roar through, then abandon the truck at Joy Street and escape on the back of a motorcycle.

A star appeared in his windshield. It took Anmar a moment to recognize that he was being shot at. He ducked as low as possible as several more stars appeared in front of him. He was glad now that they had drained the gasoline.

Sergeant Besso, looking on, was thrilled. This was more exciting than dog racing. He took his model airplane control and held it out before him so he could watch as the truck roared toward the State House.

Anmar shrieked and jerked the wheel as a high-velocity bullet penetrated the truck body and his thigh. The truck curved slightly to the right and rammed a section of cars before coming to a stop.

Damn. Besso kicked the wall in rage. Thirty meters short. It would have to do. He pressed the button on the homemade detonator and ducked behind the wall. A relay closed on a 12-volt battery and powered a standard General Motors ignition coil to charge and collapse. In a millisecond, the ignition coil had triggered a Champion spark plug inside the tanker. The ten thousand gallons of gasoline-air mixture was less than optimal for a military fuel-air explosive, but it was sufficient. It exploded instantly with the power of five hundred pounds of dynamite.

The blast blew out windows for a block around the Common, but the effect by the State House was much more dramatic. Both the mayor's limousine and the accompanying police car were rolled over and shattered. Their gas tanks, ruptured by the overpressure, sprayed flaming gasoline over the steps. This presented no danger to the mayor and his escorts: they were already dead from the initial shock wave that had dashed them against walls and steps as though they had been shot from a giant cannon.

In the State House, the governor was saved only because he was in his interior restroom, washing his hands in preparation for a meeting with the mayor. After he staggered to his feet and opened the bathroom door, he found that glass shards from the shattered windows had already killed the lieutenant governor and his secretary. Their pooling blood shocked him into immobility. His press secretary found him, minutes later, still staring at the lieutenant governor and the woman who had been his mistress for five years.

* * *

Sergeant Besso's survival was nothing short of a miracle. He dragged himself from the wreckage of the second floor and staggered, dazed, into the street. Slowly, shaking his head, he wiped the blood from his eyes. His scalp wound was drying up now, he realized, as he slowly recovered his wits and started walking carefully towards his rally point. *Allahu Akbar*.

In the distance, other explosions could be heard. Four other trucks, similarly prepared and driven by unwitting Syrians, were exploding in Boston. Only the team leader, Taxi Three, was alive. He had disobeyed orders, left his truck and gone into a Dairy Queen for a hot fudge sundae.

CHAPTER 17: SHOCK WAVES

JFK Federal Building

Harley Jones lay in his cot trying to grasp the significance of the killings. What was their message? What could be done? Would there be more? The string of questions went on endlessly, but fatigue pressed him into another region—the half-asleep, half-awake state that he remembered from Vietnam.

It was spring, just months after the Tet Offensive of 1968, and he had been lying exactly as he was now, flat on his back, facing up towards the triple canopy of the lush Cambodian jungle. The sounds of the street faded to the hum of the jungle. He closed his eyes, still listening for searchers, never quite sleeping. Malcolm X was on radio watch, listening to the static and hoping for a mission abort. Night Hawk was slightly downstream, protecting his night vision with dark sunglasses, watching for enemy patrols. The terrain was so thick that the only possible approach was up the creek. So, they were up the creek, maybe in more ways than one. Jones smiled. These sensor-planting missions were much better than snatches or cheap tricks, like the time that they had substituted booby-trapped mortar rounds for real ones right in the crates. The shock-detonated C4 would blow a mortar crew to hell. It was supposed to make other mortar crews lose confidence in their ammunition. To Jones, it was risky business. More psych games devised by the clever little boys working for the Puzzle Palace, the Pentagon. He twitched slightly in his semi-sleep. Assholes. They should come out in this shit. Maybe they would feel as out of place as he did.

He had wanted to be a helicopter pilot and get his excitement without too much sweat, but he had failed the physical. Could he help it if the blue green was greener than blue? It had looked blue—or was it green? The Army gave him his second choice, but like everything in the Army, there were catches. Oh sure kid, Special Forces, the thinking man's specialty, sign here. Oops! Did we forget to mention Airborne Training? Gee, you thought that was hard? Yes! He had. But it was trivial compared to Ranger training. That was when Harley Jones had learned to rely on his mind. The sheer agony of endless patrols, semi-starvation and sleep deprivation should have stopped him. He knew then that he had an ordinary body. He just couldn't do what some of the others could, but he could control his mind and through that, his body.

The last climb through the Georgia foothills—or was it the patrol through the Everglades?—he had disconnected his mind from his body. He could have quit, but then he would have been assigned to the paratroops. Yes indeed, the *baaaad ass* paratroops. The shock troops of God, destined to do His work and send the little yellow Reds to Hell. So much cannon fodder. Not him. Special Forces were valuable. They wouldn't be squandered. Something crawled over his face, but his mind commanded his body to ignore it, and it did. If it was going to bite him, it would already have done so. His body screamed that it wanted to swat the critter, but his mind ruled. Yes, that was the lesson. He wasn't the fastest, and he wasn't the strongest, but he could make it.

Special Forces training was a breeze after Ranger School. It was harder academically, but he could handle that. The physical hurdles were past. He trained with weights and ran three miles every other day, but he knew: his strength was in his mind. Jones burned the midnight oil so that he could get his first choice specialty, Intelligence. That would keep him out of the bush. Then there was language training at Monterey. No one did better than Harley Jones. His lips twitched slightly. Major Bear, the executive officer, known as Eager Beaver Bear, had read his file when he checked in to staging in Da Nang. Jones remembered standing at attention in front of the Major's desk, surprised at the spit shine on the Major's boots.

"Outstanding Jones, we need a man like you in Recon. You'll be better than a wiretap." The Major could hardly contain himself. "You can crawl in there and listen to them. You can interrogate prisoners on the spot. Damn!" He slapped his forehead lightly with the palm of his hand. "The possibilities are endless." So Harley Jones went to Recon, where they ran five miles for fun. The last man on every run, Jones hated it, and they hated him—the weak link.

The creature finally dropped off Jones's face. He heard water rippling slightly louder than usual and concentrated on the sound as he wandered further through memory. He had been the first on the team to bring a silenced weapon, a .22 Colt Woodsman. Staff Sergeant Gomez, the team leader, had laughed. "Shit, I've seen guys in the Barrio shot with 22s and not even know they've been hit. Jones, you've got the brains of a piss ant."

Two days later they were deep in Cambodia being pursued by a large enemy patrol. They had crawled off at right angles to the patrol, but two flankers had practically stepped on them. Jones had killed them both, using all ten shots in the Woodsman, without alerting the main body of the patrol. The slide of the Woodsman whipping back and forth had sounded hardly louder than the wind slapping leaves. Later, Gomez had leaned over and whispered in his ear, "Jones, you're a wimp, but you're a smart wimp. Keep the pistol." Jones still hadn't stopped shaking.

The water was too loud. Jones pushed Malcolm X with his foot and turned his head. Night Hawk was backing up rapidly, crouched with his CAR, the short version of the M-16, pointed downstream. Malcolm X pushed Gomez, who jolted awake. Silently, Night Hawk hand-signaled: *enemy coming up the stream*. Gomez was just reaching for Lieutenant Riley, the new green Lieutenant, when the booby-trapped Claymore mine went off, lashing the downstream kill zone with steel balls. Gomez jerked Lieutenant Riley completely to his feet. Riley was still wearing all his gear, as they all did. They moved up the swiftly flowing stream as quickly as they could, pursued by the shrieks of the wounded and the sounds of AK-47 fire as the enemy responded to an imaginary ambush.

Twenty minutes later, they were trapped. The squad from what must have been the Ninety-First Division of the North Vietnamese Army had pursued them ferociously and they hadn't had time to scramble up the walls of their valley. Now they were caught in a steep rock canyon box. A waterfall tumbled from the top, filling the air with a sharp cool mist. The moss on the steep rock walls was a brilliant emerald green and impossibly slippery.

"We're fucked!" Gomez yelled over the roar of the fall. Jones and the rest nodded. Malcolm X had been killed just a few minutes before. For just a fraction of a second he had slipped into the stream bed and the NVA had opened up. Not only was he dead, the radio that he was carrying was lost, probably destroyed in the hail of bullets. He had disappeared in the torrent, just vanished.

Jones grabbed Gomez and yelled so that he could hear.

"Look, maybe we can hit them from two sides. The Hawk and I will take the subway," he said gesturing to the stream.

There was no time for a debate. Gomez nodded his head, and Jones and Night Hawk started shedding gear nonessential for a quick firefight. Down went the rucksack with food, batteries, first aid kit, canteens, and all the other supporting tools of the trade. They both strapped their rifles to their backs and lay facing downstream at the edge of the torrent. At Gomez's instance, Night Hawk lay in front. Jones lay behind, holding onto the Hawk's boot. Then Gomez pushed them sideways into the stream and they were gone into the cold, blue hardness.

Within seconds Jones lost his grip as they were flung about in the roaring water. A giant hammer hit Jones in the back hard enough to crack his M-16. Enough! A few more seconds and he would be dead. He thrust for the shore and received a smashing blow to the ribs, but his head was above the water now. He grabbed a sharp boulder and was swung in towards the shore by the flood. Gasping, he came up looking for trouble, thankful to be alive.

He recognized the area: it was about 100 meters downstream from the falls, around several sharp bends. He reached for his M-16, but it was gone, torn away in one of the underwater crashes. He reached for his pistol, and was relieved to find it still in its holster. Carefully, he checked it. It looked OK. He pulled back the slide and let the water out, then test-fired one shot downstream, knowing that it could not be heard above the torrent. Nine shots left.

Steadying his shaking body on the canyon walls, he looked carefully around the bend. There they were; only three of the NVA from the squad were left. Presumably they had sent a messenger back to the main body. Firing carefully to cover each other's movements, they scrambled nimbly from one rock cover to another. In one part of his mind, Jones admired their professionalism. Exhausted, he lifted the pistol, but he couldn't stop trembling long enough to aim at the men fifty feet away.

"Fuck this," Jones said to himself. Balancing gingerly, he walked carefully through the rocks, praying that Gomez and Riley wouldn't shoot him from the other direction. He moved up behind the last man, stepped on his back with one foot and shot him three times in the head. He looked up then as the NVA team leader turned towards him. The soldier stared at Jones for only a moment, his black eyes burning with hate, before he swiveled and sprayed the rest of his magazine at Jones. In that moment before the team leader moved, Jones was transfixed by those eyes, as a cobra's prey is hypnotized by his sway. That instant remained forever burned into his memory.

* * *

Jeannie Kawai entered the room carefully. Assistant Director Jones had left word that he was to be woken up after only an hour, so that was what would happen; but he really needed more rest, she thought. Then again, as she felt her own fatigue, they all did. She walked over quietly to wake him.

Ted Browner was right behind her with a fresh cup of coffee and the class papers of Bucheri that someone had managed to scrounge from the Harvard thesis archives. Jeannie leaned over to wake Jones just as an explosion rattled the windows.

* * *

The 175s were firing too close. Someone had bungled the fire mission and they would all be blown to hell. The next rounds would do it. Jones jerked awake and there they were, the eyes, cold, black and filled with hate. They had found him. The hands were reaching for his throat.

* * *

Browner jumped back in astonishment as Jones shrieked and seized Jeannie Kawai by the throat. In a second they had rolled off the cot onto the floor.

* * *

There was a burning pain on his back, rough hands, then the cool of linoleum on his face. He was back now, many years later, in the JFK Federal Building. He shook his head briefly and sat up as Jeannie Kawai scrambled away on hands and knees.

"What happened?" he stammered.

"Ms. Kawai and I came in to wake you up. There was a boom outside and you leapt up and started choking her. I poured hot coffee on you and then pulled you back." Browner paused. "You must be hell on wheels on a first date."

Jeannie Kawai, now standing disheveled against the wall, snarled at Browner's attempt at humor. She started for the door.

"Wait!" Browner said. He turned to Jones. "We'll give you a few minutes to ... wash your face. Then I'll be back with the stuff from Harvard."

Just outside the door, Browner caught up with Jeannie Kawai. He put his hand on her shoulder and pulled her around.

"You're a witness. He's losing it."

Jeannie stared at Browner for a moment, one hand massaging her neck, before she spun around and stalked away.

As was his nature, Browner's eyes followed her buttocks, but his mind was trying to make sense out of what he had seen.

CHAPTER 18: SECONDARY EXPLOSIONS

1:00 P.M.
JFK Federal Building

"Quiet please." Harley Jones spoke in a voice somewhat harsher than the CTU was accustomed to. The noise died away quickly as he scanned the assembled group leaders seated around the table. Jeannie Kawai sat at the far end of the conference table, the scarf around her neck incongruous in the unusually hot April air.

Jones gestured to a man seated to his left and the man rose to his feet. For all of his five foot six inches, he was very impressive indeed, thought Ted Browner. His Marine green uniform was immaculately tailored and five rows of ribbons decorated his chest. Above the ribbons he wore two sets of wings—very unusual. The first set were those of a master parachutist while the second were those of a naval aviator, or, in this case, a Marine aviator. "Ladies, this is General Thomas Bradley. He has been assigned to us by order of the President. As you know, the use of military personnel in the territorial United States is quite restricted, but the General has considerable latitude in this situation." Almost as an afterthought, Jones turned towards the General. "Thank you, General." Then he turned back to the rest of the team. "The General is on the team one hundred percent. Are there any questions?" Ted Browner had plenty but decided to keep quiet. The General sat down in a proper military manner, but those three stars and burning green eyes kept Browner from even considering a smile. The others seem to be similarly affected.

Jones waited for the room to quiet down. "News is coming in rapidly." He raised a sheaf of papers in his hand. "So I'll give it to you as coherently as I can. Feel free to interrupt if it's important to what I'm discussing, but let's keep the minor details out for now." He paused to let the message sink in.

"First, most recently, we have had four, no, five car bombings in the last hour. The locations seem random with the exception of one, directly in front of the State House. That was too well timed to have been anything other than deliberate targeting. The Mayor and Police Commissioner were killed in that attack as well as an unknown number of others. The governor is apparently OK but we can't establish communications directly with him. We'll discuss the political implications of this in a moment. The explosives used in the attempt may help us."

Jones noticed Jeannie Kawai's hand. "Yes, Jeannie."

She started rather quietly, "I don't know whether this is important, but they weren't really car bombs."

Jones was irritated by the apparent triviality, but decided to let her go on. "Yes?"

"The one up the hill, by the State House, is the only one I've seen. But the radio reports that we've intercepted on the others indicate that they were the same." She paused. Jones nodded. "They were empty gasoline tanker trucks. It looks like they were emptied and a little air was allowed inside. Usually they are flushed with nitrogen gas and kept sealed."

"Fuel-air explosives," the General commented.

Jeannie nodded.

Jones watched, then shrugged his shoulders slightly. "So?"

Jeannie answered strongly now. "Where's the gasoline?"

George Alvarez groaned and slammed the palm of his hand into his forehead. "God Almighty. Gasoline in the sewers. Just like Mexico but there it was sewer gas. Whole streets were blown up, hundreds of casualties. That stuff..."

Jones cut him off with a raised hand. "Good, we have something to warn the Boston P.D. about, but let's get on with stopping these people. What's the motive? Why are they using this method? What do they want? Where are they and who are they?"

After a moment's silence, George Alvarez started. "The use of tankers as car bombs falls in line with their usage of field expedient or stolen weapons. I just wonder whether—"

The ringing of the phone interrupted him. It could only be for Jones, and it had to be important to get through the reception staff filtering. Jones grimaced at the interruption.

"Assistant Director Jones here."

The voice on the other end was clear despite the heavy accent. "My name is not important. You may call me ... Taxi Three. I am one of the group that has been destroying your city. I have something you want."

Jones paused, stunned, and turned on the telephone speaker. The voice continued. "Are you there?"

Jones gathered himself. "Yes," he said, and then he pointed to George Alvarez and mouthed the word "trace."

As Alvarez was getting up the voice continued. "Don't bother tracing. I'll be gone. I have pictures."

"What kind of pictures?"

"Telephoto pictures of the various teams training. I think you may find them very useful."

158

"What do you want in return?" Jones inhaled, waiting for the punch line.

"Three hundred thousand dollars in two hours."

"Impossible! I need more time."

"Mr. Jones. Do not play games with me. I know of your experience with the Hostage Rescue Team. Secondly, you have no choice. You have no time. Your city will burn before your eyes; perhaps my material is already too late, but you must try."

Jones sighed, allowing the sound to be heard over the phone. "All right. Where do you want to meet."

"I will call you on the payphone downstairs in the building lobby. Two hours. The last four numbers are 7737. I must go now. My time is running out."

"Wait! Can you authenticate yourself somehow?" Jones asked.

The voice said, "The leader is Bucheri. Will that do?"

Jones nodded. "Yes."

The voice answered, silkier than before, "You are out of time Mr. Jones, but I'll give you a present."

Jones paused, not knowing whether to speak.

"Mr. Jones, you are one of the targets. Watch your back." The receiver clicked loudly.

Harley Jones, Assistant Director of the FBI, flopped into his chair, ignoring the staff that watched him keenly. Ted Browner watched through narrowed eyes, then flashed a knowing look at Jeannie Kawai. Jeannie caught the look but held her face expressionless. As she looked back at Harley Jones he stared up at the ceiling. It was only a moment, but it seemed an eternity to her, before George Alvarez burst into the room.

"Payphone in Copley Place. We'll never get him."

Slowly Jones swiveled his eyes to George Alvarez. "George, play the tape please."

A murmur rose as the team settled in to handle a new piece of information. Ted Browner left the room quietly, his movement followed by two pairs of eyes. Jeannie Kawai's eyes held concern; those of Harley Jones betrayed nothing at all.

* * *

The Director of the Central Intelligence Agency was startled by the ring on his special line. This line bypassed all secretaries and the number was known to only a few.

"Yes?"

"Sir. Things are a bit strange here." He recognized the voice of Ted Browner, one of those being groomed for a higher position.

"Go ahead."

"I think Jones is falling apart. I need to know more about him. It may become necessary for us to distance ourselves from the CTU."

The Director nodded. "I have a dossier on Jones. Obviously I can't send it to you. It would be best if we kept this whole thing on a 'need to know' basis. Would you like me to give you a summary?"

"Yes sir"

"Well, in short, Jones went to Harvard and was doing well, but quit in 1966 to join the Army. He ended up in Special Forces for a tour in 1968. Silver Star, several wounds. He transferred into Army Criminal Investigations where he did undercover work in Saigon and Da Nang. Oh, and I forgot to mention—he spoke Vietnamese. Anyhow, apparently he did well. Odd, there is no printout of the commendation, but he got a Distinguished Service Medal for the tour in 1970.

"He left the Army then, finished at Harvard and went directly into the FBI. He did some work in California having to do with the Vietnamese there. Then ... hmm, he became active in following potential internal terrorist groups, Weathermen and such, until 1978. Then he transferred to the Hostage Rescue Team. There his duties become somewhat murky. It appears he was initially a negotiator, then perhaps a shooter. Eventually he became Special Agent in Charge. After that he was on various assignments. He was in Israel for three years. It's not clear what he did. He was also a liaison to DEA in Colombia. After 9/11 he was assigned to the combined New York Police-FBI anti-terrorist team. Since then he has been forming what is now the CTU."

There was a pause on the line. "I need to know anything that might suggest instability. Maybe he's having flashbacks. He's definitely weird."

The Director nodded. "Weird, but effective."

"So far," Browner conceded.

"Perhaps he's a bit of a maverick—I'll have someone look into it. Anything else?"

"No sir. Do you want me to keep in touch on this?"

To Browner, it seemed that the Director's voice purred. "Oh, definitely."

* * *

When Browner returned he found Jeannie Kawai in the conference room watching what appeared to be Bill Clinton on television. Browner started to speak until he heard the voice, which he recognized from telephone taps, and the voice of Pamela Clark.

When the tape was done, Browner sat back and said, "When was it aired?"

"One o'clock," Jeannie replied, still watching the frozen masked figure on the screen.

"Any conclusions?"

Jeannie grimaced slightly. "Plenty, everybody's got one. Some people think he's nuts, some think he's faking it. Some think he's faking faking." She shook her head, her long hair waving. "Nikolsky laughed. She called it propaganda."

Jeannie turned from the screen to face Browner. "You know, Ted, I don't trust Nikolsky."

Browner smiled. "Of course not. She's a Russki and a spook."

Jeannie shook her head again. "It's more than that. I can't quite put my finger on it, but there's something about her."

Browner smiled. "Sure it isn't jealousy? She's a mighty fine-looking woman."

"I'm sure."

Browner shrugged and left the room.

Jeannie settled back in her chair. It wasn't jealousy, she *was* sure of that. There was just something wrong about her, and there was the predatory way she looked at men.

1:33 P.M.

The exchange had gone smoothly, but Jones's hands were shaking as he looked at the grainy photographs. The subway car had pulled into Government Center and he had climbed off to be met by two of Tim Blackwell's people as well as two uniformed officers from the Boston Police Department. All of them had looked around warily, despite the almost empty station. It was eerie for this time of day, but Boston was running scared. Within minutes they were back in the conference room.

"I recognize some of these people," said Jones pointing to one photograph. "These are Japanese Red Army Faction people. The other images are too small."

Ted Browner looked up. "Our photo reconnaissance teams have all sorts of enhancement techniques. They are absolutely amazing. We can fly them down to Langley and get them back in another three hours."

Jones shook his head. "You don't seem to realize, we don't have five hours for that sort of thing. We need facts now. These guys are kicking our shins damn hard right now and I know they're going to move higher soon."

The General looked up from the photos. "I can get them to Langley in twenty minutes."

Both Jones and Browner stared at him.

"I have a high resolution digital processing unit in one of my communication vans outside right now. Another is ten minutes away from Langley." He looked directly at Jones. "Shall I do it?"

Jones nodded. "Please, ASAP."

As Soon As Possible suited the General just fine. He stepped out the door and handed the photos and negatives to an aide. In a moment he was back. "What are we going to do with the enhanced images?"

"We have people who have been looking at terrorist faces for years at the Bureau," said Jones, turning to Browner, "and I'll bet you've got a few too. We'll use high resolution file transfer to share the images. Within an hour we'll have names and images to give to the local police."

Tim Blackwell grimaced. "Mr. Jones, I don't think you can expect much help from them. They're brain dead with the Commissioner blown up. Most of the Superintendents and Deputy Superintendents are taking a real low profile from what I hear. They think they've been targeted."

Jones looked distant for a moment, and then his eyes squinted slightly as a cunning expression came onto his face. "What about that man Yeager, their SWAT team man? Is he back at work?"

Blackwell looked surprised. "Yes sir. He's a real tough cookie. He was back in the office two hours after we saw him last night, screaming for blood, but he's only a Deputy Superintendent."

"Ex-military isn't he? Most of these SWAT types are."

"Yes he is, ex-Marine," Blackwell replied.

"Get him in here now and get me the Deputy Mayor on the line."

Blackwell hesitated. "Sir, the Deputy Mayor is on holiday in Bermuda and, well, appears reluctant to be involved in this situation."

Jones stared at Blackwell briefly, coldly, as though he himself was the absent Deputy Mayor. "You tell that ...*man*... that he is about to be extradited as an accessory to murder. We believe that he divulged the meeting between the governor and the mayor. If he doesn't cooperate he can meet the reporters at the airport in handcuffs."

Blackwell nodded soberly and left the room. The General, Jones and Browner, the only ones left, watched him leave. Browner turned to face Jones. "I'm no lawyer, but that holds about as much water as a sieve."

Jones turned his hard eyes on Browner. "You're right, Mr. Browner, and I don't give a flying fuck. That man is going to give me what I want or I'm going to destroy him, one way or the other. Is that clear?"

The General and Browner exchanged glances. There was only one answer to that question and Browner gave it. "Yes sir."

Ted Browner had an image of Jones, tied to the stake like Joan of Arc, but in Browner's version, Jones himself had just thrown a match into the kindling. General Thomas Bradley thought that working with Jones was going to be interesting. Harley Jones wondered what pieces the photographs would provide to the blistering puzzle of Hassan Bucheri.

1:37 P.M.
WXTV Studios

Pamela Clark stood up and unbuttoned her microphone. She was almost shaking with the pleasure of the experience.

"Watch it," she snapped as a technician bumped against her while cleaning the set.

She could feel the power coursing through her veins, the energy. This was better than cocaine, sex—anything that she had ever experienced.

Mostly due to the short time, she had decided to play the tapes unedited. They were piped simultaneously to CBS headquarters. Then she had been interviewed again. Bucheri and his silent partner had actually left immediately after the interview, but she had said that she had continued the interview untaped for another half-hour. She claimed that she could not do direct quotes from that conversation but that she could give impressions on the man and his mission. There was no way that Bucheri could contradict her. If he did, it would just elicit more interest. Perfect. Rather than have someone local interview her, CBS had called in Katie Kane again and they had gone with a remote linkage. It was beautiful. She had suggested the topic areas and off they went. This was the way the pros worked. You scratch my back and I'll scratch yours.

As she walked back to her desk, Pamela couldn't help but notice the admiring glances from her co-workers. She nodded and chatted briefly, playing the celebrity, as was her right. She glanced at the boss's office door, wondering how her name would look there instead. She shook her head, this was silly, she would get an office upstairs, away from the lower-level workers. She didn't want to be the Director of News anyhow; she was a star level reporter now. She sat down carefully after smoothing her skirt. She'd probably be co-anchor on the evening news now too. She sighed and tilted back her chair just so.

For just a moment she allowed herself to think back. In grammar school, she'd always been the teacher's pet. Others had despised her, calling her a "suck up," but she hadn't cared. Erase the board, have work done on time, tattle on the spit baller, whatever it took. In high school, it had been different. Sucking up to teachers got you very little. She'd been much more circumspect about it then. The real target was the jocks. At age sixteen she'd found out what a powerful lever her body could be on a horny football player. Using it as bait, she'd gone to the prom that spring on his arm. After he graduated, she had men from the junior college take her to the next prom. She'd had to work harder on them though; they weren't as easily impressed, but once she became known as a "hot piece" things had gone well. The best thing about high school was the yearbook. She'd worked like a dog on it every year and by her last year, she was editor. Magically, her friends had shown up prominently in the major pictures throughout the book. When the journalism teacher had asked her about "balance" afterwards, she had been genuinely surprised. That was when she realized that adults often didn't know how things were done. Somewhere in their youth they had stayed young and immature. From that time on, no one had ever been able to influence her. She had learned, certainly; but she was never influenced. She had her own standards to meet.

A ringing phone woke her from her reverie. It was too bad that she had talked the boss into firing Jeremy so soon. She would have enjoyed flashing her new success to him. "Smoking dope in the van." What a great line to feed the boss—he was such a knee-jerk anti-doper since his kid had overdosed. He hadn't even called Jeremy in to explain. One more annoyance out of the way.

Pamela closed her eyes for a moment, imagining herself as the co-anchor of the News at Six tonight. What outfit would look best, she wondered.

2:00 P.M.

Jones turned off the radio as soon as it was apparent that there was no new message for him from Bucheri via Radio 960. He shrugged as Jessica Williams stood up to leave.

"I'm sorry. Nothing to work with."

Jessica turned as one figure then another appeared in the doorway. She didn't turn back, but almost whispered to Jones, "Look who's coming to dinner."

Jones looked up absently, then straightened in his chair. For a moment he just stared, but then thought better of it and stood up.

"What brings you here, Jay?"

A man stepped in, followed by a woman. The man was tall and balding, becoming fat. He wore a slightly seedy brown cotton sweater with elbow patches, despite the heat. The woman was small and slim, perhaps in her late-thirties. Her off-white linen suit, narrow briefcase, and designer glasses marked her as a professional.

"I'm still with HRT. Thought you'd need a psychologist." He turned to introduce the woman. "This is Loraine Hawthorne, she's new to Behavioral Science. I'm showing her around."

Jones paused for only a moment. "This isn't a good time for on-the-job training, Jay."

Jay Schwartz paused before replying, "There's no need to be hostile."

Jones squinted. "Schwartz, I've had quite enough psychology to last me a lifetime. I didn't invite you to this party."

"Harley, you can't hold me responsible for Tom Coyle. Psychology isn't an exact science and there wasn't sufficient data."

Jones rose deliberately from his chair. "Schwartz, you're right. It was my call. My mistake was listening to you. You and Tom Coyle. Now I choose when I listen to you people, and it isn't often."

Jay Schwartz straightened up. Apparently he wasn't so meek, despite his demeanor, Jessica Williams noted. She also noted a slight shift in Loraine Hawthorne. "Harley. I'm with the HRT, not under the CTU. I've come with the team and I intend to do my part."

Jones nodded. "Schwartz, you can stay, but let one thing be understood. This is not the HRT of the old days when you greased me out. This shit pile is mine. I'm the king here and what I say goes. If you put one single banana peel on my path during this assignment, I'll disappear you and your protégé from the face of the earth. This mission is too important for meddling. Am I being clear?"

Schwartz nodded slightly, his face a mottled red.

"Now please wait outside."

When they had gone and the door was closed, Jones turned to Jessica Williams. "Find them some dark place away from me and allow them access to the data."

"Meetings?"

Jones shrugged. "They'll have to be allowed in."

Jessica Williams tilted her head and looked Jones directly in the eye. "Did he really get you dumped from the HRT?"

Jones sat down heavily and looked up at her. "Yes and no. Mostly I did it to myself, but he greased the skids, even after he blew the call on the mission that got Tom Coyle killed."

"Is he competent?"

Jones sighed. "Are any of them?" He turned back to his reading. As Jessica Williams reached the door he raised his head. "Jessica, please assign Jeannie Kawai as a liaison to them. She's to have complete access to all their work. I don't want to meet with them unless there is an important discovery. Jeannie sees me as she feels the need. Clear?"

Jessica Williams nodded. "Sure, but why her?"

Someone else might have bridled at this challenge to his authority, but Williams and Jones had worked together long enough to understand each other completely.

Jones pursed his lips. "Several reasons. First, she has a minor in psychology. Second, she looks like a wimp, and, third, she isn't. Good enough?"

"You're the boss," Jessica replied, "but you're sure giving them a hard time."

Jones looked at her for just a moment, then turned back to his computer screen.

Outside in the hallway, Jessica Williams led Schwartz and Hawthorne in search of John Woods, who was responsible for space allocation. Jay Schwartz stepped up beside her as they walked.

"Ms. Williams, are you a friend of Mr. Jones?"

Jessica stopped and turned to face him, ignoring the woman. "Mr. Schwartz. All of the CTU have the highest respect for Assistant Director Jones. It would be well for you to keep that in mind. Keep in mind too that we are in the middle of what is, without a doubt, the largest police operation ever undertaken in the United States." She looked him directly in the eyes and leaned in. "Don't get in our way."

Schwartz didn't back off at all. "Your loyalty is admirable, but not in question. Has he talked at all about Bucheri's music? The material coming out of that pirate station?"

Surprised, Jessica pulled back. "Why?"

Schwartz smiled faintly, "It's for him—for Jones. We've got it figured. You remember the line in the first piece, 'two cool shorts, standing side by side'?" Jessica shook her head. "That's them," Schwartz continued excitedly. "Jones is the fuel-injected Stingray and Bucheri is the 413. Get it?" Jessica shook her head again. "Jones has a Stingray. This is a competition between the two of them. A race."

"Who wins the race?" Jessica asked.

"The Stingray," Schwartz replied, puzzled.

Jessica sighed in relief. "Thank God. We're safe, then."

Schwartz's face turned red but the woman, Loraine Hawthorne, answered coolly, "Don't expect a one-to-one correlation."

Jessica turned to her. "So you believe what you want to believe?"

Loraine Hawthorne inclined her head slightly towards Jessica. "Did Harley Jones tell you that he and Bucheri went to Harvard together?"

Jessica stepped back. "You mean they knew each other?"

Loraine Hawthorne cocked her head. "I didn't say that."

Jessica Williams threw up her hands. "Jesus people, get a life!" She left them standing in the hallway as she went out for some air. Still, as she stepped out into the hot Boston afternoon, she couldn't help but wonder.

2:17 P.M.

Jeannie rapped sharply on Jones's door and, uncharacteristically, walked immediately in. Ted Browner followed closely behind. Jeannie placed a small recorder on Jones's desk top and pressed the play button. Two voices could be heard speaking Russian.

Jones looked up and shrugged. "Nikolsky and her boss, so?"

Jeannie nodded grimly. "Listen carefully to the man."

Jones listened and then paled. "No!"

Jeannie nodded. "I'm almost positive, and so is Ted. We're transmitting copies to the labs for voice ID and Langley for translation."

"Bucheri," said Jones, stunned. "She works for Bucheri. What the hell is going on?"

Ted shook his head. "We haven't got it figured out. We're keeping her compartmentalized so she doesn't know what we're doing. The only thing I can figure is that she is here to influence us. It just doesn't make sense—she's a powerful asset, too powerful to be used for something like that."

Jeannie suddenly reached under her jacket and had a compact automatic pistol in her hand. Jones was surprised by the hard set of her face. "I'll get her," she said and started down the hallway. Both men pulled out their weapons too and followed her downstairs to the cubicle that Nikolsky had been assigned. The telephone was still off the hook, but Nadia Nikolsky was gone.

Browner shook his head. "That's the last we'll see of her."

A perplexed look passed over Jeannie Kawai's face. Browner missed it but Harley Jones didn't. He raised his eyebrows in inquiry, but she simply shook her head and stalked away.

Browner shook his head and left the room. Jones leaned against the wall, stunned. What the hell was happening? He sagged down into Nikosky's chair and picked up the receiver absently. For some obscure reason, he put it to his ear. Surprisingly, he could hear breathing at the other end.

167

"Jones?" the speaker at the other end said.

"Bucheri?" Jones replied.

"So we meet at last," Bucheri said.

"You could have called anytime," Jones replied. It took just a moment for him to realize the implications of what he had said. He quickly but gently placed the handset on the table and stepped out towards the door. Just as he reached the door, he heard a high-pitched whistle through the phone followed by a small explosion. He didn't stop until he was safely around the corner, then he looked back carefully. The bottom of the handset was intact, but the top portion, the earpiece, was shattered. Jones stepped outside again, bracing his back against the wall. Then slowly, very slowly, he slid down the wall as feet pounded through the corridor.

Fifteen minutes later Jones was in his office, sitting in his chair. Jeannie Kawai, clearly concerned about his welfare, was standing by his side, a hand on his shoulder, while a paramedic looked into his ears for damage. Ted Browner was pacing.

The paramedic stood up. "Nothing I can see. The ringing should go away in a few hours." He placed his tools in his bag and left.

As soon as the door closed Browner said, with just a hint of sarcasm, "Enough to ruin your whole day."

Jeannie Kawai shook her head, unamused. Jones didn't respond at all. His eyes had a glassy look which distressed both Browner and Kawai. Browner stopped his pacing and turned to face Jones.

"Harley, you in there?" Browner waved his hands in front of Jones.

Jones focused and looked up at him, an angry expression on his face. He jerked upright, sending his chair flying backwards. Jeannie Kawai leapt aside. Jones walked around his table and grabbed another chair. With a display of strength that surprised Browner, he flipped the chair upside-down one-handed. On the bottom was a small shiny object. Everyone recognized it: a bug. A battery powered microphone with a low-powered FM transmitter.

"*She* sat here," Jones snarled.

"My God," said Jeannie Kawai. "That's how Nikolsky was warned."

Jones swung the chair upright and placed it out in the hall. "Let forensics go over it. We'll probably have more wherever she's been."

Browner shook his head. "Jesus, we've been had bad."

Jones seemed to be recovering. "Well, maybe we'll have a more even playing field now. Do a damage assessment," he said to Browner. They had to find out what had been said in the vicinity of microphones.

Browner was still shaking his head. "Boy, like a friend of mine used to say, 'Bend over, I'll drive.'"

Jeannie Kawai and Browner smiled slightly as Jones said, "Damn near blows your mind."

Kawai smiled and marveled a bit at Jones. It was a special man who could make jokes only minutes after an attempt on his life.

2:45 P.M.

Eddy Yeager shook his head. This was too weird to be true. Last night almost half of his Arrest and Apprehension Team gets blown away and now he's the Police Commissioner. It was like the Peter Principle to the maximum, but it wasn't funny at all. He put down the telephone receiver thoughtfully. The Deputy Mayor's voice was still clear in his ears.

Assistant Director Jones, the only other man in the room, was watching him. He raised his eyebrows momentarily. "So now you believe me? You are the Commissioner."

"Temporary Commissioner," Yeager shot back.

Jones nodded. "Like winning the lottery, but you've got thousands of police officers reporting to you."

"What about the Superintendents? One of them should have been appointed. Will I get their cooperation?"

Jones leaned back in his chair and folded his hands across his stomach. "Commissioner Yeager, let me explain some of the facts of life in Boston today. First, your police department has lost its headquarters and communication network. Several of your officers have been attacked and killed on the street, others have been maimed. In short, your force is in shock. Now, the Chief Superintendent and the Superintendents of Operations and Internal Affairs have died in the Headquarters explosion. The others are keeping a low profile or not in town. Either they're scared or in shock. Maybe they're just political animals who don't want to be around when it hits the fan—and it will hit the fan, Commissioner Yeager, for all of us. The only way to come out half clean is to win this battle, because Hassan Bucheri is playing us like a violin. He knows us inside out.

"The only way we can win is to change the rules, and that won't make friends. The hindsighters are going to have a field day on us, but we can win. We can take this asshole out. We must take him out, because if we don't, he'll be back with hundreds more like him, savaging every major American city. It will be Pandora's box. You're a serviceman, you know what it means to sacrifice for your country. This may be the ultimate sacrifice. There won't be many medals handed out later, but we can save hundreds, maybe thousands of lives. Are you up for it?"

Eddy Yeager had heard a lot of pep talks in his time, and this was one of the most subtle. He smiled slightly. Reverse psychology, patriotism, motherhood and apple pie—it had everything. There was a lot to this Jones. Maybe he could pull Boston through. Anyhow, he had a debt to pay, and Eddy Yeager always paid his debts.

"Assistant Director Jones, you can expect complete cooperation from the Boston Police Department."

Jones smiled, as though he had always known that Yeager would make the right decision. He stood up and held out his hand. They both shook silently. There was little to say about their compact. They were both totally committed, each for his own reasons.

Jones indicated the door. "Let's get the General. I think it's time to call in the cavalry."

* * *

General Bradley recoiled. "The 82nd Airborne? Mr. Jones, are you joking? Congress will go nuts. This isn't like calling in the National Guard."

Ted Browner sat back and smiled to himself. This was priceless. Jones had just put on the expression he used just before he flamed someone.

"General Bradley, in case I haven't been absolutely clear in my enunciation, I said 'a battalion of Military Police from the 82nd Airborne.' If you will recall your history, three battalions were sent to St. Croix when looting broke out after the hurricane of 1989. I think that our situation is much more serious. Now, I believe that your superior, General Power, the Chairman of the Joint Chiefs of Staff, ordered you to provide me with all the support I requested, did he not?"

General Bradley had flushed a deep red and started to sputter a reply when Jones overrode him. "Of course, if you feel that you cannot carry out the orders of your superior then I would be delighted to assist you by asking General Power to send someone who is capable of command in this situation. I had expected that a man with recent command experience could handle this, but if I'm wrong, now is the time to rectify it. Please note, however, that the support of the military is critical at this juncture and any loss in command continuity will provide us with a serious setback which will be duly noted."

General Thomas Bradley, holder of the Navy Cross and Distinguished Service Medal, was absolutely furious. Jones had boxed him neatly by stating that the military support was critical and following that with his comment about loss of command continuity. Jones was, in

170

fact, right. By the time a new man could be found, briefed and transported, it would be too late, and anyhow, Bradley knew that he was the right man for the job. He also knew what Jones meant by "duly noted." If things went to hell, the military would get the blame. Bitterly, Bradley had to agree. This situation couldn't be resolved without some military support. Damn, but he hated to be corralled like that.

Jones started again, driving the last nails into the coffin into which they would all climb. "General, we have the CIA," he nodded to Ted Browner, "we have the FBI, and we have the Boston police." He nodded towards the new Commissioner, Eddy Yeager. "Do we have the Armed Forces of the United States?"

Once again, there was only one answer, and General Bradley gave it: "Yes sir."

Satisfied, Jones leaned forward and gave a thin-lipped smile. "All right, now listen carefully. We're going to play hard ball here and a lot of people are going to get pissed off. A few are going to get hurt. That's inevitable and you might as well reconcile yourselves to it. We've just begun to fight back, and we haven't seen Bucheri's last trick yet either. I intend to shift the balance of power from him to us, and here's how we're going to do it."

CHAPTER 19: DOG DAY AFTERNOON

3:00 P.M.
Copley Place

Hassan Bucheri leaned back in his chair, admiring the view to the east from their room on the fourteenth floor. Copley Place was a complex including the Copley Hotel, a very large shopping mall, and business offices. Their other room on the twenty-eighth floor had an excellent view to the west. Bucheri took a sip from his drink, a Havana Club Cuban rum and Coke, ignoring the disturbed look of Dr. Kamal.

"Why worry Ali? Alcohol will not affect me. It is appropriate that I should drink this beverage. Do you know what the Americans call it?"

Ali Kamal shook his head, not wanting to antagonize Bucheri. He was chagrined that Bucheri had caught him grimacing.

"They call it a *Cuba Libra*, a 'free Cuba.' Tomorrow, from this room, I will drink another *Cuba Libra* and watch Boston burn. Perhaps you'll join me then." Bucheri turned back to his drink, not really caring what Kamal thought. The view really was magnificent.

Now was the time to manipulate the truth a little. Then again, what was the truth? What did the Germans say? "One man's meat is another man's poison." Yes, that was it. Well one man's truth is another man's lie. Was it John Fitzgerald Kennedy, potentially the last great American president, who had said, "Where there's smoke, there must be a smoke machine"? It was too bad he wasn't matching wits with him—that was a bright man. Harley Jones was an enigma—bright perhaps, but confined by the laws and officials of a decadent society. Great societies were led by great men. That was the only way to achieve excellence. Hitler, Stalin, Churchill, Roosevelt, Mao: all of these were men who led despite the inertia of their societies. Any might have led their nations to a greatness like that of the Roman Empire, given the right opportunity. If Hitler hadn't been so greedy, if China hadn't been so poor ... well, the list went on. Bucheri took another sip. Perhaps he could have been a great leader, like Menachem Begin in Israel, terrorist turned statesman. He smiled slightly. It was just a question of time and place. His smile widened as the cellular phone by his side rang. It was his time and place now. Like Patton, Rommel, Halsey, and the other greats of modern warfare, his name would go down in the history books.

JFK Federal Building

The room was very dark. The blinds had been closed almost completely. He sat directly between her and the window, silhouetted. Pamela Clark jerked slightly in the hard chair as the stop button snapped on the digital recorder. She was uncomfortable but still confident. The man opposite her didn't look like much. Only his eyes were a giveaway. They seemed to burn through her. For a moment, he said nothing; then he leaned forward over his desk, his eyes unblinking. Pamela tensed, expecting a blow, despite the six feet of space and the desk that separated them.

"Ms. Clark, you've been a very bad girl."

She straightened up. "I have every right to protect my sources. It's in the Constitution." Or at least she thought it was, somewhere there, written in gold.

The man continued to keep his eyes on her, glittering in the darkness. "Ms. Clark, you had prior knowledge of events that led to the death of over fifty persons. *Prior knowledge*. This recording indicates that you are working with a foreign agency. Have you any idea what the espionage laws of this country say about that?"

Pamela Clark sat, stunned to silence. *Espionage?*

The man continued to stare at her. Before she could formulate a reply, he continued.

"The man with whom you are collaborating is called Hassan Bucheri, and he is the agent of a foreign power. You certainly noticed his accent," he added sarcastically. "It isn't exactly Beacon Hill."

Pamela Clark had turned an ashen white, but she didn't give in. She had one last card to play. "You can't use those recordings. Those taps probably weren't even legal."

He shook his head slowly, while keeping his eyes directly on her, as though scolding a child. "My dear Ms. Clark, entirely different rules govern questions of national security, as surely you must know." Pamela didn't know, but she couldn't help nodding. It sounded all too plausible.

Jones smiled faintly. "You've heard of 'rendition' haven't you, Ms. Clark?" At that moment, Pamela was transported, feeling the cold of an Egyptian prison, hearing the screams, feeling the electrodes attached to her nipples. Somehow Jones knew. He paused, stalking her with his eyes.

"Those recordings, you see, Ms. Clark—they might not be used as evidence. They might somehow slip into the public domain. I wonder how the families of those victims, particularly the parents of the children, are going to feel when they listen to the tapes? 60 Minutes would love to get hold of them. Lara Lanigan would have you for lunch. I don't think the networks will be interested in you then. Do you? I would guess that there are going to be about two dozen law firms filing suits against you, and poor you, suddenly unemployed, and your face known all over the country as the 'woman who sacrificed the children for a story.' I'd be surprised if you survived a year in this country, with all the righteous crazies with guns."

He leaned back now, apparently enjoying a private vision. "I would find that very interesting. Pamela Clark, making the news rather than reporting it." Jones rocked forward. "I'm exaggerating, of course. You won't even last a year. I'll see to that. I can be a powerful enemy, Ms. Clark, believe me. You've crossed the wrong people on this. You're so far out of your depth that you can't even see the surface."

Pamela Clark broke like a dry stick. She leaned forward and put her face into her hands, sobbing. Harley Jones settled back in his chair, waiting for the next step.

In the darkened room, a peasant woman sobbed. A smashed bowl of Nuck Mam, the ever-present Vietnamese fish sauce, lay on the floor, the odor saturating the air. The Phoenix Program, assassination of suspected Viet Cong by the CIA, had begun. Sergeant Tran slapped the woman hard, demanding to know where her brother was. The blow knocked her down onto her husband's body. She screamed and recoiled from the bullet-riddled corpse, then fell upon it weeping, her hands and face covered with blood. Racked breathing and more sobbing, shuddering, another slap and more crying. She'd have to be taken away for interrogation. That was unfortunate, because it would leave time for the local Viet Cong Battalion, the 132nd, to reorganize. Jones was disgusted. Tran was terrorizing her so much that she couldn't answer. Tran was really too brutal for this work. It required some finesse. He'd seen others do it, but the Phoenix Program was not his project. He was just here to find out about Viet Cong drug smuggling to American troops. Dope was a double-edged weapon. It destroyed the troops and made money for the V.C.

A double-edged weapon. Pamela Clark raised her head, still sniffling. "What do you want, Mr. Jones?" He could still smell the Nuck Mam.

Lobby,
JFK Federal Building

"He's well and truly off the deep end, sir. I mean, really. He wants us to control the press, at least the radio and television. We're going to take over their news broadcasts."

"Mr. Browner. That's nothing new. We've been doing that for years. You shouldn't be shocked."

"But sir, you don't quite understand what he wants. We don't just influence the news, we're going to have a news blackout. All over the Boston area. He has printed up an order on official stationery citing an FCC regulation that's only applicable in times of national emergency—at least that's what he says. This isn't a declared emergency and anyway, I think he's faking it, but it's Saturday and no one can check."

There was a pause at the other end. "Yes, I see what you mean. Doing this sort of thing in the continental U.S. would seem to exceed all our mandates. What are you planning to do?"

Ted Browner was stunned. The Director had hit the ball back into his court. He was also certain to be taping this. Ted decided to give it one last try. "I was hoping you could provide some guidance, sir. We seem to be getting in a little deep."

The Director's voice was warm and confident. "Ted, you're with the CTU now and you'll have to live by their rules. Perhaps Mr. Jones has something special arranged with the congressional oversight committees. Please do keep me informed on anything extraordinary. The Agency is behind you one hundred percent." The click of the receiver cracked like a bullet overhead. Enraged, Ted Browner slammed the phone down and smashed the heel of his hand against the plastic side of the telephone stall. The plastic sheared away and slid along the marble floor.

"The Agency is behind you one hundred percent," he mimicked and smashed another piece. "Please keep me informed," he mimicked again but stopped himself from hitting the plastic this time, as someone entered the lobby, looking curiously at the broken stall and then at Browner.

The shrinks, he thought. There's a weapon that will take that wind out of Jones's sails. But how to use them to maximum advantage? That was the question. Browner paused as he reached the stairs. Of course, if Jones were thrown out, as second in command, responsibility might fall on him, Mr. Theodore Browner, formerly of the CIA.

As he walked slowly up the steps, Teddy Browner had a lot to think about.

3:30 P.M.

"Ted, I'm going to give you the news assignment. I think you have the creativity to convince the various stations that they should fall in line. I have a list in order of priority. How many men do you have available now?"

Ted Browner groaned inwardly. The muzzling of the news: the worst possible assignment for backlash when the dust settled. He'd be lucky to get an Agency job counting poppy plants in Thailand after this was over. Then again, if Jones pulled off some of the stunts he was planning, maybe this would be one of the better assignments when scalps were taken. He maintained a straight face. "One hundred and twenty on loan from Langley plus the thirty on permanent assignment to the CTU. All armed to the teeth, but some of these boys are off desks and haven't done field work in years. Most of our assets are overseas."

Jones nodded tiredly. "Get the Langley people assembled. You'll only need about thirty, so pick the most persuasive of the lot. Commissioner Yeager will provide a uniformed police escort for each person. Betty has prepared letters at reception. I want all the stations putting out nothing stronger than Barry Manilow by six o'clock. Have you seen the briefs I prepared?"

Browner hadn't been up to his desk yet. "No, I've—"

Jones cut him off with a "stop" hand gesture. "In short, the message is 'Stay in your homes, send only women out, and then only for essentials. The Red Sox game are canceled.'"

"Jesus," Browner burst out uncharacteristically, "Only women? My God! That's —un-American."

A wide smile beamed from Jones like a ray of sunshine, transforming him. He nodded vigorously. "That's exactly right, Browner, and that's how we're going to get this asshole Bucheri."

Browner stood immobile. Shocked again, just when he thought himself beyond it.

Jones jumped up from behind his desk and put his arm around Browner's shoulders. "Don't worry Ted, they won't shoot the messenger, at least not immediately. I've also gotten you some help, someone with some real clout." Jones reached over and pressed a button on his phone. "Send her in."

Browner turned, guided by Jones's surprisingly strong arm, to face the door. The last thing he needed was some FBI watch bitch. Browner stepped back when she entered. "Pamela Clark," he said in an awed tone as she came up him.

"Happy to make your acquaintance, Mr. Browner," she said with a trace of irony and a sideways glance at the smiling Jones.

Jones nodded to her. "Thanks Ms. Clark, that's all for now. Mr. Browner will be right out."

As the door closed, Jones released Ted Browner and faced him, "And Ted…"

Browner blinked, stunned by the turn of events. "Yes?"

"With all these assets, I don't see how you can miss, but if anyone gets truculent, I want you to pull their plug. Got it?"

Ted Browner was starting to seize mentally, "Plug? How?"

Jones's mood changed in a flash. "Use your goddamn initiative Browner, but I don't want a squeak of disruption coming over the air from now until the 'All Clear' sounds in Boston. Got it?"

Browner didn't, but he turned to leave. He'd figure something out. Just before closing the door he remembered something and turned back.

"What about Pirate 960 ? They're offshore out of my reach."

Jones closed his eyes and nodded tiredly.

4:03 P.M.

"I don't understand why we aren't meeting with Harley," Jay Schwartz said with a pained expression.

Jeannie repeated herself. "Dr. Schwartz, I'm just following orders as I'm sure you will." She paused for a moment, holding his attention with her eyes. "Assistant Director Jones is extremely busy now, as you know. He has everybody from the Boston Fire Department to a Marine Corps General on his mind. I'm sure you can understand."

Schwartz changed to a mildly whining tone. "What's the difference between you briefing him and me?"

Jeannie sighed. "Really, Dr. Schwartz. Can we get on with it? It's not my decision. Now, what about the music?"

Schwartz leaned back and glanced at his associate, Loraine Hawthorne. "How does he look? Is he concentrating? Is he having trouble making decisions?"

Jeannie stood up. "I'll report that you have no conclusions."

Schwartz looked up in surprise, then raised his hands in a placating gesture, "Music. Well, we think it's an attempt to manipulate Jones. Somehow, Bucheri is linked to Jones. If a person has listened to a lot of music during a time of stress, that music has the ability to take them back to their feelings, even many years later. All of the Vietnam veterans have very strong ties to the music that they spent hours and hours listening to during very trying times in their lives. Often a given song will be linked to a friend who liked it very much and died. Music is a powerful mood-altering tool if properly used."

Jeannie pursed her lips. "I don't see it. For one thing, Mr. Jones doesn't listen to the radio while he's working. I think this is an attack on the people of Boston—perhaps on the same people you're thinking of, the veterans, but probably on everyone. Bucheri seems to have some pretty powerful ways of communicating his general message of 'get out of Boston.'"

Schwartz shook his head. "You don't understand the power that Bucheri is searching for. You really don't have the full story."

Loraine Hawthorne nodded. Jeannie Kawai shrugged. "Well look, who's to say that Bucheri isn't playing the music mostly for himself? He's roughly the same age as Mr. Jones. Isn't it likely that the music has meaning for him too? Anyhow, what is it that I don't know about Bucheri?"

Schwartz leaned back in his chair and glanced at Loraine Hawthorne briefly. "You know that we have direct links to Behavioral Science at Quantico and the Agency files."

Jeannie nodded.

"Well, we've gotten a more detailed history on Bucheri. My guess is that someone leaned on the Mossad, but we have no 'need to know.' Anyhow, that's what we're basing our assessment on."

Jeannie leaned forward, her brow wrinkled slightly. "Files on Bucheri? Could I see them please?"

Schwartz placed a hand on a thick folder. "I'm sorry, these are the property of Behavioral Science. They aren't even graded for classification yet."

Jeannie could barely contain herself. "Let me get this straight. We're in the middle of a combat zone and you're telling me that I can't see the material?"

Jay nodded sympathetically. "It's a difficult situation, but considering the possible linkages that may exist between Bucheri and Assistant Director Jones, it's better that this material stay with a trained psychologist."

Jeannie could feel her shoulders tightening up. Her hands were already clamped like claws over the ends of the armrests on her chair. Fortunately, they were hidden underneath the table. She took a deep breath and let it out very slowly, silently. Maybe the psychologists were playing games with her too.

"Perhaps you could tell me what you've concluded from this work."

Schwartz paused. "Well, it won't make much sense unless you've seen the file."

Jeannie nodded, not trusting herself to speak. Surely Schwartz could see that he had just torpedoed himself. After a long pause, Schwartz slid the file over to her. "You can read it here. Then I'll explain what it means."

Twenty minutes later, Jeannie Kawai looked up from the folder. "Nice life. His family has been severely hammered."

Schwartz shook his head. "You've missed the point. Bucheri's ideals were formed when he was young. The training in Moscow is especially important. They didn't waste their time there. He's a communist through and through."

Jeannie shrugged. "So was Boris Yeltsin."

Schwartz gave her a shocked look. Jeannie continued, "Look. Lots of people lose their ideologies. They think, they learn, they change. Maybe he did believe in communism once, but I doubt that it's important now. I think that his family is the key. They've all been destroyed by Israel one way or the other. He has to hate that country. What about 'transference'?"

Schwartz waved his hand in a deprecating manner. "A simplistic theory that has never held water."

Jeannie persisted. "Well, he hates Israel and can't do anything directly to get back at it, so he shifts his hate to something that he can reach—the United States, Israel's big brother. It makes sense to me."

Schwartz looked dismissive. "That's complete amateur rubbish."

Jeannie stood up. "Maybe, but Mr. Jones will have to see this file so he can make up his own mind."

Schwartz leaned across the table and placed his hand flat over the file folder. He looked directly into Jeannie Kawai's eyes and said, "I told you, no."

Jeannie leaned forward so that her nose was inches from Schwartz's. "Sorry," she said as she placed the knuckle from her middle finger over the top of Schwartz's hand and slowly put her full weight on it. For one, then two seconds, Schwartz did not move as his eyes watered, then he jerked back his hand.

Jeannie Kawai held his eyes for a long moment, then picked up the folder and left the room.

* * *

Thirty minutes later, Harley Jones nodded. "I agree, it's revenge. That changes things dramatically."

Jeannie cocked her head.

"It means that there will be no real demands. So there can be no concessions, no way to delay him. He's out to make us look like fools. I don't see any real agenda. This family history is very sad. It's too bad that we don't know who he was really close to. It might help."

179

Jeannie inclined her head in agreement. "There is very little hard information in the file. His father was a village head man. He was probably a very wise man. He sent his son to Harvard. That must have been a great sacrifice."

Jones leaned back in his chair, folded his hands together and looked up towards the ceiling. "There's something here. I just can't put my finger on it."

Jeannie Kawai waited in silence for a minute, then left quietly. Jones was still in the same position.

4:15 P.M.
Harvard Bridge

Private John Miller ducked back into the M113 armored personnel carrier as the Band-Aid, the medic's M113, wove its way back into Boston carrying the second sniper victim. A clang against the armored side confirmed his good judgment. Miller should have been toughened by what had happened this morning, but it hadn't happened yet. Right now, he was just confused and touchy. He was oddly comforted by hearing Captain Thorn talking on the battalion net.

"What do you mean, Cambridge jurisdiction? A sniper just took out two civilians. Are we going to take him out or not?"

Miller turned his head to watch as Captain Thorn plugged his ears to hear over the engine rumble. "Say again?"

Captain Thorn's face turned a livid red and he stood bolt upright. He was saved by his helmet as his head hit the roof of the M113. He sat down abruptly without having lost his grip on the handset of the radio.

"What do you mean 'aggressive stance'? Look asshole, I've lost ten men today. I'm either going in to kick ass or we're getting out of here." Another bullet clanged against the side of the command M113, distinctive for all its antennae. "Hey, did you hear that? We're taking fire. Now, can we return fire?"

"Yes, I already told you that, Major, it's on the Cambridge side." There was a pause as the radio man handed Captain Thorn another handset from the company net. "Hold one."

He took the other handset and listened briefly before replying, "Roger that, stand by."

He picked up the battalion net handset. "Look, we've got him located. We picked up a muzzle flash. Can we hit him with the fifties?"

Once again, he paused and listened with a pinched expression on his face. "I told you it's in Cambridge. Yes, that's affirmative, Cambridge, and negative, we cannot cross the bridge except on foot. All the civilians abandoned their vehicles. It's totally blocked. We have to go on foot, and I want to use the fifties for suppressive fire."

Private Miller liked the idea of using the fifties. The .50 caliber bullet would knock down some of those stone and brick walls quick enough. Someone would be in a hurt locker real soon. Now they'd kick some ass.

Captain Thorn jumped up and was saved by his helmet again. "Fuck," he yelled and threw down the handset. "Cambridge. Fucking Cambridge."

* * *

Dieter Schmidt put down his 7x50 Bushnell binoculars and turned to the man next to him. "Hans. *Raus*. It's going to get hot here soon."

Hans withdrew his eye carefully from the 16 power Weaver scope. Fondly, he stroked the stock of the 700 Remington bolt action rifle. "A very nice weapon, I think. Not as good as the Heckler and Koch, but for this lightweight work, good enough."

Schmidt nodded as they packed up the rifle in its modified guitar case along with a powerful spotting telescope, much more powerful than the 7x50 binoculars, and the small bags of lead shot that Hans had used to hold up the forearm and base of the rifle stock. The table in the office had served quite nicely as a shooting bench. They had cut a section out of the office window and moved well back in the room to minimize the number of people that might see the muzzle flash. Sound escape was reduced to a minimum by the walls of the room and the remaining glass in the window. The entire room acted like a silencer. For further insurance they had stacked books on either side of the hole that had been made in the window. Their visible arc was only about seven degrees. For watchers four hundred meters away, their flash could be seen over only fifty meters. You couldn't do much better than that and still get a decent view of the end of the bridge.

Two minutes later, they were ready. Dieter raised the small radio to his mouth. "Unit One moving from Task Three to Task Four. Have there been any calls from our friend?"

The reply came crystal clear over the Motorola 1610 unit. "Station One, no call is coming."

Dieter shrugged. Poor English, but the message was clear. No change in plans from The Fox. He checked his watch. 16:23. In twenty hours he'd be a rich man. Or dead, he cautioned himself. A man couldn't get too cocky in this business.

As they closed the door and left the building, Dieter couldn't help but smile. Classic military tactics, just as The Fox had predicted. A few rounds through the windshields of the people in front. Then they panic and abandon their cars. A few more rounds through the windshields of the drivers at the far end of the bridge and they were running screaming down the streets. And there it was: an instant one hundred car roadblock complete with panicked civilians, frightened police and frustrated soldiers. The Harvard Bridge, a major traffic artery, clogged by one sniper team with fifteen minutes work. A few wounded civilians for authenticity, and on to the next job. Dieter liked it. No unnecessary killing but maximum impact. This was the equivalent of what the United States Armed Forces called a "surgical strike," only they did theirs with F117 stealth bombers costing fifty million each. Yes indeed, as The Fox had said, this was the poor man's surgical strike, and it was shaping up nicely from Dieter Schmidt's point of view. And Dieter Schmidt knew terror when he saw it.

5:30 P.M.
JFK Federal Building

Harley Jones had fallen asleep with his head on his arms. Like everyone in the CTU, he had been working constantly for almost two days. While others had been able to take three- and four-hour naps, he was lucky to get two, and it was getting to him. He didn't even wake up when Jeannie Kawai knocked.

Jones was surrounded by reams of papers, both handwritten messages and computer printouts. His computer terminal blinked an icon warning that urgent email was waiting. What had sounded like a printer from outside the office was instead his snoring.

"Harley."

Louder: "Harley Jones."

Still no response. She stepped forward and pounded her tiny hand on the table like her brothers had taught her, hammer fist. Jones jolted upright.

"Wha'?" he said with a bleary look, eyes gummy.

At that moment, Jeannie felt very sorry for him. A lonely man pushed to his maximum. But it only took a moment for intelligence to come into his eyes.

"Hi Jeannie. Not getting too close?"

She smiled—what else could one do? "No, sir."

"You can call me Harley when we're alone. All the girls I strangle do."

She smiled again, more deeply.

Jones straightened up and rubbed his eyes. "Look Jeannie, I'm sorry. Sorrier than I can say." He put his hands down and looked into her eyes. "I had hoped that..." He paused. "Well," he smiled helplessly, "I just wanted..." He shrugged.

Jeannie sat down opposite him. She took his hand and looked into his eyes. There was a tortured look there that touched her.

"Harley," she said, liking the sound of his name, "what happened?"

He took a deep breath. "I was having a dream, a very bad dream. You woke me up just when someone was trying to kill me."

Jeannie's eyes opened wide. "My Lord. Do you have dreams like that often?"

Jones hesitated and pulled his hands back to rub his face again. "Yes, no—well, it depends. When the stress picks up, so do the dreams, but nothing like the, ah, incident with you, has ever happened."

"Do you feel like you're losing control?"

Jones hesitated. Jeannie waited patiently, her calm permeating the room, her eyes locked on his.

"Only in my dreams."

She continued to look at him steadfastly.

Finally Jones gave in. "I haven't been this way forever. It started fifteen years ago, when I was in charge of the Hostage Rescue Team. I had a friend, a good friend, and I made a mistake. It cost him his life." He shuddered. "Sometimes I can hear that shot, echoing, just echoing."

She took his hand again in both of hers. He tingled slightly at her touch, dry and warm.

"So you worry that you'll do it again?"

"I don't know. That's what..." he paused, knowing that he couldn't mention the psychiatrist, "a friend says."

"You're very close to your CTU members now. They look on you as much more than a leader."

Jones nodded. "I've done it again, the cardinal sin. I've gotten too close to my people. I just can't help it. They're my family. They're all I've got."

Jeannie cocked her head. "No friends outside of work? Relatives? Girlfriends?"

"My folks are in San Diego. Once a year is enough for all of us. My father never forgave me for becoming an enlisted man. He's a retired admiral. As for girlfriends, not for a while. There's no time."

Jeannie nodded. She knew about people who became married to their work. Her father had explained to her that the battles that were waged in every organization were between those who fought for a place in the organization and those who fought for the organization, the professionals. It was, as her father described it, a basic battle between good and evil. He attributed the global decline of American business to the replacement of professionals by professional managers. He would point with great vehemence to the automobile industry as an example while he grumbled about bean counters trying to supervise engineers. Jeannie had seen it in the Bureau. The climbers and the doers. Harley Jones was a doer.

"Harley, there's more to life than your work. You can do other things, enrich your life, and still do your job—do it well."

Jones sighed and looked down at her hands on his. "I know. I kind of got drawn in." He raised his eyes to hers. "What would you recommend, Dr. Kawai?"

Jeannie blushed and pulled her hands back, then laughed. "That's not what I meant."

Jones smiled. "I know, and thanks for listening." He watched her for a moment and then his tone changed. "Now, what brings you in?"

Jeannie hesitated as she shifted mental gears. "Mr. Alvarez sent me in with some news. A chemical truck was driven into Fresh Water Pond in Cambridge."

Jones closed his eyes tiredly. "My God, he's trying to poison us out. What was the truck carrying?"

Jeannie sighed. "Old transformers from the power company."

Jones looked puzzled. "So?"

"They're filled with transformer oils with PCBs, polychlorinated benzenes. They're super carcinogens. That's the bad news."

Jones looked hopeful. "So what's the good news?"

Jeannie leaned forward intensely. "You aren't going to believe this, but Mr. Blackwell checked. Fresh Water Pond doesn't feed Boston. It doesn't feed anything. It's just a park. So when this goes on the news, we can tell people that…"

Jones held up his hand, "Let me get this straight. These PCBs are deadly but they won't affect the Boston drinking water?"

Jeannie nodded. "Right."

Jones's face took on a hard aspect. "Get to Browner and have him squelch the news of this. This is not, repeat *not*, to be put on the news."

Jeannie looked horrified. "You can't suppress news like this. Some people might go down to the pond."

184

Jones said, "Look, Jeannie, you're the forensic chemist. You get on the phone to the Cambridge Police and tell them to keep people out of the park. Maybe we'll have a few mutant ducks next year, but we'll try and limit the damage. But, I repeat, under no circumstances will this get on the air. Now wipe that expression off your face and get into motion."

Jeannie stared briefly at Jones, but he ignored her as he turned to his computer terminal. Shrugging, she left the room. Jones had the six o'clock news meeting with the CTU heads to prepare for. At least the news broadcast should be tame, despite the reality.

6:10 P.M.

Harley Jones hit the remote control button and the six o'clock local news was replaced by blackness. He settled back with a satisfied expression on his face.

"Well folks, I guess that's a wrap."

Most of the CTU leadership, General Bradley, and Commissioner Yeager were still staring at the blank screen, incredulous. Ted Browner caught Jeannie Kawai's eye and gave her a slow insiders' wink. Jessica Williams spoke first.

"But there's no news. I mean, no news of anything that's going on, the snipings, the killing of the mayor, nothing. It's impossible. And Pamela Clark says not one thing about this. That's unbelievable! All she mentions is the State of Emergency and that ridiculous suggestion that only women should go out."

She looked around. Most of the faces had the same questioning expression. Finally, she fixated on Ted Browner.

"OK, Teddy. What has the Agency done now?"

Browner's expression of mild amusement changed to one of total neutrality at the mention of the Central Intelligence Agency.

"I no longer work for the Agency. I'm with the CTU, Jessica. We all float or sink with the CTU." He looked at her meaningfully and paused so that she and all the others would get his point. "Perhaps you should ask our leader," he added, gesturing towards Harley Jones who had maintained a pleased expression throughout the interchange.

Jones raised his hand in his characteristic "stop" gesture and then held it out, palm up, indicating that Ted Browner should do the explaining. Browner scowled his displeasure but pulled out his notebook.

"As of approximately sixteen-thirty hours today, the CTU has begun a program of news suppression in the immediate Boston area. All local news is approved by us and network news is subject to censorship. We can't keep news from being called out to the networks, but we can keep it from being broadcast here, and that's what we are doing. I'm doing this strictly under orders, and I still don't understand quite why."

Jones nodded, "It's very simple folks. The man we are dealing with is a terrorist. People can't be terrorized if they don't know what to be terrorized about. This man is using the news to create an emotional atmosphere in the city. I don't know the reason, but he's going to exploit it soon. As I've told you before, this man doesn't do anything thoughtlessly. He's been like a stage manager, setting the mood for a crashing final scene. I've just turned off his lights. It's as simple as that."

Jessica Williams flared up. "It's not as simple as that. We are blocking the people's Constitutional rights as well as God knows how many laws."

Jones's face had turned hard and his eyes glittered as he rose to his feet. "We're all together now, so I'll say it one last time. We are fighting a master. You've all read the file on Bucheri and now you've all seen his handiwork. We have not once, I repeat, *not once* stopped him at anything. The body count is now above one hundred and he's been playing with kid gloves so far, setting us up. I don't know what he's trying to do, but he's already blocked all the major traffic arteries with sniping and acts of terror. He's going for a body count in the thousands, I'm certain of it. Panic has already set in. National Guard troops have killed civilians and civilian sniping has started in South Boston. We have to put a damper on the situation. I've just done it. And folks, if you think that is the limit of what I will do to protect the American people, you're wrong. We're at war here, and I will not lose. There is no time to go to Congress, the President, or the courts. The battle will be fought in the streets of Boston tonight and tomorrow. We must win this battle and win it decisively or we will relive this again in every major city in this country. If, as a byproduct of our tactics, we draw some heat, so be it. I'm prepared for that. I am not prepared to lose. If you don't have the stomach for it, submit your resignation by 7:00 p.m. I expect enthusiastic compliance with my orders and nothing but your very best. If you can't do that, get out."

Jones sat down abruptly, his normally white face a mottled red. Nothing was said. He looked at his watch.

"Intelligence briefing here at 7:00 p.m. Be here or be gone."

Dr. Kamal was out on a mission, so Hassan Bucheri was talking to himself or perhaps the television. It wasn't really talking. It was more like a restrained scream, restrained just enough to avoid being overheard in the hallway.

"That painted whore." He kicked the couch. "That ungrateful bitch!" He flung aside a chair. "I'll peel her skin off inch by inch." Finally, still trembling, but satisfied with his tirade. The sound of his own voice apparently comforted him, and the act of speaking seemed to clarify his thoughts.

"She's of no importance. Someone got to her. Her manager? No! None of the stations gave any news of our attacks. Who? The mayor? No. He's dead. What a brilliant stroke that was. If only we could have gotten the governor too. Brilliant, Bucheri—they don't call you The Fox for nothing. So who? Who has the most to gain. The governor? No, a political milquetoast. Someone powerful. The President? Perhaps. A man of considerable will but bad advisors. No, his advisors would not let him. Who, who, who? Jones! That cursed son of a camel thief. A thousand dicks up his ass. That's who did this. Damn him to the lowest chambers of hell."

Hassan straddled the last remaining upright chair, resting his forearms on the top of the back rest and settling his chin on his forearms. He didn't bother to think about how Jones had shut off the news; it didn't matter. What really mattered was the next step. He stared, unseeing, through the window. After several minutes, he shook his head briefly and began pacing. For just a moment, as he passed the table in his suite, the newspaper caught his eye. Like a fish hooked on a line, he approached the table and began feverishly to read, a smile growing on his face. Finally, he was satisfied.

He walked over to his briefcase and opened it. On one side, his 9mm MAC-10 with integrated silencer rested in spring clips. Next to it, also in spring clips, was his major weapon, the cell phone. He picked up the device and dialed.

* * *

Patrick Henry Johnston turned off the television set in disgust. There wasn't a bit of news. He'd switched between all the news channels and gotten nothing but mush. Someone was controlling the press. The Hand of Allah or whatever it was called must have threatened all the stations, and the wimps must have caved in like the limp dicks that they were. Well, there was only one way to find out what was going on.

Patrick dressed carefully, as he would for any hunt. To match the terrain, he wore sneakers, blue jeans, and an olive drab field jacket, despite the heat. The floppy pockets would carry ammunition and the bulk of the jacket would conceal the Colt Python .357 in his hunting shoulder holster. Finally, he checked his wallet. There it was, his American Express Card. "Never leave home without it," he said with a smile as he closed the door.

* * *

Faneuil Hall Marketplace, just off Government Center, was very quiet as Harley Jones and Ted Browner entered. They looked down the almost empty corridor when a voice said from behind them, "Not very alert, are we?"

They both turned to see a slim woman of indeterminate age right behind them. She had long red-brown hair pulled back in a ponytail and wore a short leather jacket with tight designer jeans. She was shorter than Jones—about five foot six, thought Browner. She moved with feline grace as she reached up and hugged Harley Jones. "How's my *goy toy?*" she said softly. Jones hesitated only a moment and wrapped his arms around her, pulling her up off her feet. She wrapped her legs around him and they rocked for a moment, reliving something from their past. Browner was stunned by intensity from both of them in that brief moment. Then Roz dropped down and said, "Wassup?"

Harley Jones said, "Roz, this is Teddy Browner, of the CIA."

Browner extended his hand and received a brief strong handshake. She nodded and seemed to catalog him in an instant.

Harley Jones looked around and apparently decided that they should stay where they were. "We've got a problem here."

Roz nodded. "Good observation, *Tembel*. You're *dafook*."

"Oh, Roz," Jones said as he smiled faintly, "don't hold back."

Roz cocked her head slightly as she looked at Jones, and Teddy Browner realized that Roz never held back. The foreign words sounded Yiddish, and Browner remembered that Jones had spent some years in Israel. Was 'Roz' short for 'Rosaline'?

"Thanks for coming up," Jones said.

"Hell," Roz grinned. "A free flight with Air America. What more could a girl ask for?"

Jones couldn't help himself. He grinned too. "Did you bring some friends?"

Roz nodded and held up five fingers. "But," she said, "no toys." She shrugged, "Didn't know what might be called for, and, anyhow, airlines are annoying about machined steel and plastique."

Jones gestured towards Browner. "Teddy's going to open the candy store, or you can get into HRT stuff if it's needed—but I think subtlety is more in line."

She looked at them both. "I don't know what you want done, but I want a No Penalty Clause in our contract." She looked hard at them both. Of course, there would be no contract, but a commitment in the clandestine world between allies was sacred.

"Of course," said Jones.

"All right," she said. "Let's talk. I owe you, Harley Jones, but I think that this is going to more than pay off the debt, don't you?"

"We'll be seriously in your debt once all this is over," he replied.

Roz snorted. "Who's this '*we*,' white boy? You guys or your country?"

Jones hesitated. "Well, us white boys for sure, and the President, but maybe not a whole lot of people in between."

Roz rolled her eyes. "Great." She waved her hands in the air, witch-like. "I sense an ugly ambiance." She put her hands down and looked straight at Jones. "So tell me what you want."

Jones looked at Browner and gestured with his head towards the door. "You don't want to hear this. Just give Roz anything she asks for."

Browner gave a minute shrug. "That bad?" he said then left to wait outside.

"Damn, Harley," exclaimed Roz, "what do you want, *exactly*?"

"That's the problem, Roz. I don't know, *exactly*."

7:00 P.M.
JFK Federal Building

A number of heated debates had taken place, shrill voices echoing through the normally quiet corridors. There were some flushed faces present now, but everyone was back in the conference room.

At exactly 7:00 p.m. Jones rotated in his chair, the only swivel chair in the room, and ran his eyes over the group, slowly nodding his head as he established eye contact with each of them. Finally, he nodded to Ted Browner.

"Mr. Browner, please begin the briefing."

189

Ted Browner leaned forward to consult his notes on the conference table.

"As the updates show, things have deteriorated significantly in the last six hours. All the major traffic routes are blocked. Just thirty minutes ago they did a really cute one and blocked the Sumner and Callahan tunnels. That may affect you, General Bradley."

The General leaned forward, his stars glittering in the conference room light. "Why?"

Browner answered, "Because that was your best route to Logan Airport. Highway 93 and the Charlestown Bridge are just as jammed as the Harvard, Longfellow and Charles River Dam crossings. It's a nightmare out there."

"Damn it!" the General growled. "Is this guy telepathic? That's where my troops are coming in. A whole battalion by midnight. We've secured the entire perimeter, but we never thought to secure the route."

Jones interrupted. "Mr. Browner, you said they did something 'cute.' What was that?"

"Well, as best we can tell, they've actually done two things. They've blocked both tunnels in the same way. They pushed over a couple of propane trucks and then opened the valves on them because they're double-walled and didn't crack. To make matters worse, they've dropped a truckload of chlorine gas cylinders next to the propane truck. Then they opened the valves on those, too. Unfortunately, neither gas seems to be clearing out."

Jeannie Kawai interrupted. "Chlorine gas is much heavier than air, so it would tend to settle in the tunnel. It was used as a poison gas in World War I. It's not a nerve agent, just a blistering agent, so it shouldn't be any trouble to put protective gear on and work on the wreck."

Browner looked at her for a moment longer than necessary. "Unfortunately, as was pointed out to me, we can't move any equipment in to clear out the wreck. The slightest spark and the tunnels are history. Those propane trucks were tipped over so that if they were scraped or winched it would create a spark. This guy's miles ahead of us."

Jones had leaned back. "Maybe not. Ms. Kawai, what happens when water comes in contact with chlorine gas?"

Jeannie looked startled. "Why, it gets absorbed into the water and eventually becomes hydrochloric acid."

Jones was still leaning back, but watching her intently. "So if we turn on the sprinklers, it goes down the drain, right?"

Jeannie hesitated, then smiled and nodded back. "Right."

"OK, one problem handled. What about the propane? Is there any cute way to get rid of that?"

No one had a reply at first, then General Bradley spoke softly. "Propane isn't a very powerful explosive, and the tunnel is big. If one truck blows, it probably won't affect the other."

He looked around. No one contradicted him.

"Well, the airport has foam firefighting equipment as well as sealed breathing systems. Let them go in as close as they can, shut the valve on the truck and foam the equipment. Then we can attach a cable from a vehicle as far away as possible, winch the truck upright and pull it out. My engineer vehicles have winches that can do the job easily. We can get the Logan fire trucks to foam the site. That will minimize the chance of a spark."

Alvarez voiced the concern that everyone was feeling. "What if something ignites the propane?"

The General shrugged. "Then we start on the other tunnel."

There was a moment of silence as everyone thought about what would happen to the men in the tunnel. Then Jeannie Kawai raised a final point. "All of that's fine, but what about the residual propane?"

The General replied with another shrug, "There are lots of places to get a big fan. All the movie studios use them, wind tunnels, even rental agencies have them with heaters for drying out rooms. We just load a whole bunch on some flatbed trucks. It'll be the biggest blow job in history."

Only Ted Browner chuckled with the General, although several others were clearly trying to control themselves.

Jones nodded to General Bradley. "OK, so you're on it."

The General nodded to one of his aides, a colonel, and the man left the room. The General turned back to Browner. "Yes sir. We're also in the process of collecting some aviation assets—transport helicopters primarily—but waiting for them would damage our timetable. The assets might come in handy for some other work though." He looked intently at Jones for a moment. Jones nodded. Clearly there was some contingency that they were planning for.

"All right. That's covered. Proceed please Mr. Browner."

They were interrupted by a loud, "Director Jones!" at the door.

The room fell silent as Jones looked at Jay Schwartz, the psychologist. Tiredly he swiveled in his chair, gesturing to the other personnel present.

"Ladies, Gentlemen. This is Dr. Schwartz, the psychologist assigned to the Hostage Rescue Team." He turned to Dr. Schwartz. "Yes?"

Dr. Schwartz, clearly put off, answered strongly, "Yes. I believe that it is essential that we study Bucheri's psychology. The music that he has been playing may be a very valuable clue as to what's driving him."

Jones sighed and leaned back. After a brief pause, he turned to the personnel in the room. "OK. CTU section leaders only. General, please assign a representative. Mr. Browner, I'll represent you. Please carry on with your duties."

Dr. Schwartz flushed red as the majority of persons left the room. Jones leaned forward and said, "Well?"

Dr. Schwartz flushed even more but started in a strong voice, "Dr. Hawthorne and I believe that we have been able to get a solid understanding of Bucheri from his record and the trail of clues he's giving us. We believe that the first song he played was a direct challenge to Assistant Director Jones. The lyrics mention a race between a Corvette Stingray and another car. Director Jones has a Corvette Stingray."

Some murmurs from the group interrupted Dr. Schwartz for a moment. He looked pleased.

"We believe that his choice of *Light my Fire* had sexual overtones, perhaps directly towards Director Jones. *Strangers in the Night* is clearly an expression of loneliness. *One in Five...*"

Jones sat up, exasperated. "Jesus H. Christ, Jay. Where do you get this drivel? I can't believe this crap. Did you read transcripts of those tunes?"

Dr. Schwartz paled and nodded. Jones shook his head in disgust.

"You can't work out of context like that. I'm not going to sing these for you here but I'm going to give you the message so thoroughly that you won't need to bother us again."

Jones rocked back in his chair and stared at Dr. Schwartz for a moment. "To start with. That Beach Boys song, the first one, is about the start of a race. That's it, 'two cool shorts standing side by side.' It's just coincidence that I happen to own a Corvette. Now, the second tune was *Light my Fire*. Have you looked out the window? The BosGas tower is burning. The third and fourth tunes, *Strangers in the Night* and *One to Five* were meant to scare the people of Boston. Did you catch the key words—the refrain in *One to Five*?"

Dr. Schwartz shook his head.

Jones sneered just slightly. "'No one gets out alive.' Now it doesn't take a lot to figure out how that's going to hit a million people in Boston. Then he plays Dire Straits' *Ride Across the River*: just what words do you think are going to stick in the minds of the listeners?"

Jones paused just long enough for Schwartz to open his mouth before overriding him. "It says, in essence, that he's 'a dog of war and doesn't care who the killing is for.'"

"Is that really subtle or what? Now let me go on to reveal the rest of the obvious so we can stop wasting our time. The next song played was

Bad Moon Rising." He paused for a moment to catch his breath. "That is replete with unsubtle messages like 'don't go out tonight' and 'the end is coming soon,' not to be outdone by 'hope you're prepared to die.'"

"Now," Jones suddenly dropped his pitch to a conversational level, laced with menace, "Do we all need PhDs in psychology, Dr. Schwartz? That wouldn't seem to be enough to prevent us from screwing things up, would it?"

Dr. Schwartz jumped to his feet. "You've lost all perspective. You're not fit to command this operation." He started for the door, closely followed by his colleague.

"Stop right there," Jones called out.

Despite himself, Dr. Schwartz stopped and turned to face Jones. Jones held up a thick stack of papers. "You haven't even read Bucheri's essays from Harvard, have you?"

Dr. Schwartz sputtered as Jones stepped across to him. Jones thrust them into his hands. "Don't come back until you've got your homework done." Jones turned to the rest of the room's occupants. "All right, people, back to work."

Jones flopped back into his seat as the CTU members filed past. Jessica Williams was last. She stopped before leaving and closed the door.

"Bit harsh weren't you, Harley?"

Jones looked up, a bleak expression on his face. "I don't need a goddamn shrink running around now. At least, not one that's more interested in me than the job."

Jessica Williams narrowed her eyes and nodded slowly. "Was there anything in those papers?"

Jones smiled faintly. "No. College bullshit. But it will keep Schwartz off my back for a while. I don't like that twit one little bit. I talked to him a lot in the old days, before I found out what a politician he is. He wanted to have the HRT Special Agent in Charge be a psychologist. Jesus!"

"So he's a threat?"

Jones looked up at her and nodded.

CHAPTER 20: SATURDAY EVENING

8:15 P.M.
JFK Federal Building

Harley Jones watched from his window as the MH-6 Little Bird helicopter landed smoothly in the small available space between City Hall and the JFK Federal Building. Around the perimeter of the large plaza area and on the rooftops, Jones could see troops facing outward searching for threats: snipers, machine guns, shoulder-launched SAMs. These were paratroops from the ready battalion of the 82nd Airborne Division, just one of General Bradley's important contributions— contributions that would cause enormous trouble later when the accounting came. Under pressure from Bradley, Jones had decided that more firepower might be essential. Logan Airport was now closed to civilian traffic. This would cause a major uproar in itself. And sitting in one of the hangars across the bay at Logan were three teams, the FBI Hostage Rescue Team and the Special Forces Rescue Unit, code-named Delta Force, and a company of Army Rangers. Jones was comfortable with the HRT—he had been part of that team. He had even been their leader for a time before starting the fledgling CTU. The Delta Force was another matter. He didn't have enough experienced high quality troops, real shooters, so he needed Delta, but they were a wild card. In theory, they couldn't even be deployed in the U.S., and what's more, even though they could be used for rescues, their reputation indicated that they might be more inclined to shoot first. Even worse, there were the Rangers. These were the Army's shock troops, commandos, and they might be very dangerous to civilians. Jones shook his head. They just didn't have enough people trained for this sort of thing.

An alert military policeman with neatly pressed Army Combat Uniform (ACU) and an M-4 carbine stepped out of the helicopter, followed by a husky man wearing a rumpled ACU. This was the man Jones was expecting: Colonel Shaw, the commander of the Military Police battalion. He had been on the first flight in with the staging team, out in front, where a commander should be. The husky man looked directly at him, even though Jones knew he was invisible behind the glass. Perhaps that was a good sign.

* * *

They met in a small conference room, but this would be the last time. Things were getting crowded. Aides and subordinate commanders were standing against the walls as Jones entered. The husky man followed him in, slipping past the door just before it closed. From his name tag, Jones knew who he was, but the face was the giveaway. A hundred fights, a thousand arrests, ten thousand lies all showed in that savaged face. Like a torpedo, the man honed in on Jones. He walked boldly up, obviously expecting others to move aside, stopped and saluted.

"Colonel Shaw, sir, reporting with the first elements of the 18th Military Police Battalion, 82nd Airborne."

Jones shook hands with the Colonel. "You've met General Bradley?"

Colonel Shaw nodded. "Yes sir, downstairs. I met the Commissioner there too." He nodded toward Commissioner Yeager.

Someone called, "A-ten-hut!" and all the military people locked into a state of attention. General Bradley entered the room.

"At ease people, Assistant Director Jones is in charge here. We go by his rules." He turned to look at Jones.

Jones acknowledged the look. "Gentlemen, ladies, we're in a combat zone so we will dispense with the usual saluting both inside and out. It might make you a target for snipers."

Several officers laughed, but stopped immediately when they saw how serious Jones was. "We've lost thirteen military personnel, seventy-two police officers, as well as fifty-eight civilians. People, this isn't a joke. If you treat it as one, I'll have you looking out through the bars of Leavenworth Prison. Now get it together."

The room quieted considerably. Jones gestured towards the few remaining seats. "Take a seat if you can find one. We'll keep this meeting short and then break into smaller working groups."

After the last person was seated, Jones remained standing, pacing in the restricted space.

"First, we now have photographs and identifications of a number of the terrorists. They are being mass-produced as we speak and will be ready for distribution in an hour." He looked at Commissioner Yeager, who nodded that this was correct.

"Now, here's where you and your people come in Colonel." Jones nodded towards Colonel Shaw, who leaned forward with an intent expression. "The Boston P.D. has had its communication network seriously damaged. We're also short of manpower. We're going to pair up two Boston police officers with two MPs. The MPs have brought their own communication network, which will be augmented by one Signal Corps company. There are some specialized electronic warfare units coming in also."

General Bradley cleared his throat. "Yes sir. The special units are already in place, as you instructed. They will be ready to go on line at midnight. What you've requested is rather unusual, but they think it will work. So does Ms. Martin of the CTU."

Taking her cue, Liz Martin stood up. "Hello. Since I'm not wearing a name tag, my name is Liz Martin. I work directly for George Alvarez, the CTU Head of Electronic Surveillance. What we are attempting is a bit unusual, but in keeping with the nature of the meeting, I'll keep it short. I would like the commanders of the involved units all to meet in room 312 later for a more detailed discussion. For the rest of you, here it is. At eleven o'clock, we're going to cut all land line phone service in the City of Boston, the downtown, except for 0, the operator, and 911. All other calls will receive an automated message telling them that service is down. The news at eleven o'clock will report that the service was cut by the terrorists."

An officer at the back broke in. "You said 'land lines'—any reason why only land lines?"

"Yes. We are leaving the cellular phones operating for two reasons. The first is that we couldn't block them out without shutting down a much larger area. The second can perhaps be best explained by Captain Knight."

Captain Knight had been slouching against the wall. A very thin, tall man with horn-rimmed glasses, he spoke in a high, excited voice. "The idea is really kind of cool. It's never been done before, but we've got the equipment, so it ought to work. Our inter-modal frequency-hopping..." He stopped as eyes started to glaze over. "Well, our radio-direction-finding people are going to try to triangulate every call made on either a Citizens Band radio or a cellular phone. Our computers are really fast, I mean like *now*, you wouldn't believe it, and our listeners, you know, electronic surveillance—well these guys are going to snatch the signal and send it to AT&T. They're going to send it out to FBI agents all over the country waiting with recorders and listening. With a digital multiplexer we should be able to—"

Commissioner Yeager interrupted. "Wait. Cut the gobbledygook. You mean you're going to tap every call and know where it came from."

Captain Knight look startled. "Sure, that's what I just said. And with the—"

Liz Martin spoke up this time. "Thank you, Captain." She smiled at him and he returned to his position against the wall. "The FBI will be providing two resources. The first is listeners. We have several thousand agents across the country waiting for calls to be shunted to them via the AT&T link. If any of them have a call about which they are suspicious,

196

they will call us and play back the recording. If it looks interesting, we will use the start time of the transmission and send it to Data Processing." She nodded at Jessica Williams, who raised her hand. "They will use the start time of the message to get the approximate address provided by the radio direction units and give it to the Central Police Command Unit, the Headquarters of Commissioner Yeager and Colonel Shaw."

There were murmurs from the group. Someone called from the back. "Is this legal?"

Jones smiled in his direction. "Call me Monday for an advisory on that."

The group laughed uneasily. Jones's face turned hard again. "General Bradley will advise the military personnel immediately after this meeting on my feelings. As the senior person, I set the policy. You people implement it.

"Now, to get on with it. This isn't going to be easy. We haven't worked together before and there will be no time for a honeymoon. My people have been without sleep for two days now. Don't expect any yourselves. You all know the mission: Find these bastards and arrest them. Note the word 'arrest' —that's why Commissioner Yeager is the senior police officer, understood?" He looked at Colonel Shaw, who nodded. "If they offer resistance, we will still attempt to capture them. We need them immediately to interrogate—the CIA will be doing that— and we need them for trial. Obviously, it may not always be possible, but I expect you to keep your people on a very short leash.

"Now, one final warning. The leader of this attack, Hassan Bucheri, is one clever son of a bitch. He had people out in National Guard Uniforms earlier today. Snipers. Keep that in mind when you brief your people. He might pull something fast, so all movement must be controlled. Remember, this isn't the U. S. of A. anymore, it's a war zone, and we must control the turf. Right now that means controlling movement. I have a plan called Blackjack. It will be activated at 2300 hours —that's 11:00 p.m. for you civilians. Be prepared and use your brains. Remember the old infantry saying, 'it all depends on the terrain'—so adapt and make it happen."

Jones stood up, signaling the end of the meeting, and left the room. General Bradley's senior aide, a Brigadier General, caught up to Jones in the hallway. A tall thin man, well over six foot six inches, his chest was at Jones's eye height. Jones couldn't help noticing his Judge Advocate insignia. He was an army lawyer. "Given the looseness of the chain of evidence, Director Jones, the phone taps, military forces and so on, do you really think that you can convict these people if you capture them?"

Jones, realizing that everything he said would go directly to General Bradley, looked the Brigadier directly in the eye. "Read my lips, General. This is a police operation under the command of the Joint Task Force Counter-Terrorist Unit. We do not shoot people because it is inconvenient to try them. Are you reading me?"

The Brigadier straightened up to his full six foot six inches of height, towering over Jones. "Loud and clear."

8:31 P.M.
Logan Airport
Helipad 2

Melody Jane Harmony walked towards the descending helicopter, noting its size. It certainly wasn't very big. A flash of the landing lights revealed a slim woman in black combat gear and weapons harness, clipboard in hand, her red hair tied back in a ponytail pulled through the back of her black FBI baseball hat. She had a clipboard in her hand and Melody Jane concluded that the woman was in charge of the helicopter flights. Melody Jane's entourage of seven followed her across the tarmac. The group included her makeup artist, her communications manager, her personal Secret Service security man, Steve Wyckoff, and four other Secret Service upper management people that she had selected to run her four teams. The stony expressions on the faces of the Secret Service agents were, she supposed, just professional.

The woman wore ear protectors but took them off as Melody moved up next to her. Melody Jane leaned in against the wind blast from the helicopter. "I have my own helicopter here somewhere. Can you tell me where it is?"

The woman pointed off to the left. Melody Jane's white Secret Service helicopter was being pushed into a hangar. "We need to keep the helipads clear for the military machines when they come in."

Melody Jane was furious. "I'm the Secretary of Homeland Security and that's my helicopter."

The woman seemed completely unconcerned, though she did hold her hand out to be shaken. "Hi. I'm Willamena Peters. Just call me Willy Peter. All the guys do. You can't fly your helicopter over Boston. Only this one flies." She gestured to the small helicopter with the blades still spinning. "No more 9/11s, ya know ... aircraft make such a mess when they hit a building. The airspace is restricted. There are certain flight paths, radio codes and all that. Right now, this is it. You don't want to fuck around with the paratroops on the rooftops out there. They aren't

198

too bright and they have Stingers—you know, missiles that are smarter than the paratroops—they love a hot body, Infra Red seekers on 'em." The woman smiled at her joke.

Melody Jane almost stamped her feet. "I need to get out there. I'm in charge!"

The woman calling herself Willy Peter said, "No problem. Mr. Jones mentioned you, I think." She looked at her clipboard. "Yep. VIP." She looked up. "Who do you want to go with you?"

Melody Jane gestured. "I need them all."

The woman shrugged. "Only two of you this time. I'll take you over personally or you won't get through the cordon. It's pretty tight. They've taken some sniper fire. Sure you want to go? Look at the Little Bird— there, on the door."

In the near dark it was hard to see, but there appeared to be three bullet holes in the window of the passenger area. Roz-call-me-Willy smiled faintly as she recalled the laughter of the helicopter crew when she had pasted the realistic decals on.

Melody Jane swallowed hard. This wasn't quite the safe bunker she had expected. Still, she had her duty to do. "I'll take Steve for the first run. The rest can get relayed."

Melody Jane climbed into the first of the four available seats so that her security man had to climb around her. The red-haired woman held out her hand and yelled over the roar of the blades, "Your bag ma'am. All gear must be secured as we'll be doing some maneuvers to avoid sniper fire." Melody Jane shook her head. The woman signaled to the pilot and the blades started to slow down as the engines were shut down. The woman leaned over. "You can hold your bag and sit here all night or have me secure it and get on your way."

Melody Jane flushed with fury but thrust the bag out. The woman took it and climbed gracefully into the seat behind Melody Jane. The rotors spooled up and the helicopter took off. The woman handed Melody Jane a headset and, as the helicopter zigzagged through the streets of Boston at heights of not much more than ten feet, showed her the blocked bridges and jammed highways. Melody Jane was surprised at how few people there were on the streets—even the police were curiously absent. It was a thrilling ride. Melody Jane decided to get a helicopter like this.

Finally, after what seemed far too short a time, the helicopter flared and settled down in a small darkened plaza. The woman had already taken the headset and was standing on the skid as it touched ground. She reached across and quickly unbuckled Melody Jane then pulled her out and started her at a run across the plaza. The was a brief thunderclap and a flash of white; they both staggered but kept running into the building.

Inside the building the woman handed Melody Jane's bag to her and turned to the Secret Service agent. "M84," she said, referring to the stun grenade that had just gone off. "Screws up the sniper's night vision device ... we hope."

"Christ," the agent said. "Is it really that hot here?"

The woman grimaced. "We lost over a hundred cops in a second. I'd call it 'hot.'"

Then she turned to Melody Jane. "Ma'am, you look a bit disheveled, and we have a press interview set up for you. I'll take you to your ready room where you can compose yourself before the tour and the interview. If you like, I have some stress pills here." She took out a small white bottle and shook out two tablets. "Vitamins —but they seriously help," she said as she tossed one her mouth, threw back her head and swallowed.

Melody Jane shook her head. "I have my own medication." She dug in her bag and pulled out a small red-tinted prescription bottle. The woman started to say something but Melody Jane ignored her and dry-swallowed her own pill. Then she pulled a Diet Coke from her bag, unscrewed the cap and chugged a bit, ending up with a small belch. "Sorry." She looked around at the gray corridors. "I'll wait for my makeup girl. Now where do I go?"

The woman called Willy Peter shrugged and started down the corridor with Melody Jane and her security man, Steve, following. She sighed and glanced at her watch. Things never went according to plan.

9:02 P.M.
Washington Street, Roxbury

Dieter Schmidt wasn't happy about the new orders. The Fox hadn't explained the change in plans, but it had to be because of the lack of news. Well, he thought, as von Clausewitz said, they were in the fog of war.

Fortunately, a theatrical supply store was close by (though perhaps, Dieter thought to himself, "fortunately'" was not the word). The Fox even had the address. With their stolen props and their own equipment, it might work. It was simple—a little paint on black jump suits, a few badges and a lot of fast motion. Or so he hoped.

Their two Chevrolet sedans, freshly stolen, did not look like standard police issue. Details. Haste screwed up details and details could kill. The paint on Hans's jumper had smeared slightly. Chris looked more tense than usual. Dieter leaned forward and patted him on the shoulder, "No sweat. Just don't talk. Your accent might give us away."

Chris nodded seriously. They made a right and then a left. "A real ghetto," Dieter said. "They're doing to the blacks what we did to the Jews seventy years ago. They're just slower about it."

Hans smiled quietly to himself. Dieter had always been embarrassed about his father having been in the Waffen SS. Silly. All of this group had been *Stasi*, East German Secret Police. Now they were out in the cold. Just the winds of time. Dieter was too serious, but he was a good leader. Hans cocked his Uzi and pointed it at the car roof for safety as their target came into sight. The rest followed his lead. Chris, the driver, checked the rearview mirror. "OK." Their second car was right behind them.

They slowed to twenty miles per hour, then, as planned, pulled into the curb rapidly but quietly. A young black man—they were all black in this neighborhood—jumped up from the steps on which he had been sitting and started to run. A lookout? A brief ripping sound erupted from Chris's Heckler and Koch, the only silenced submachine gun in the group, and the man tumbled forward into a crumpled bloody heap. Screams could be heard from down the street, but nothing indicated that they had been seriously compromised. Hans ran over to the man and rolled him over with his toe. Chris could see a pistol in his belt, not that it mattered. He still might be an innocent. A lot of people carried guns in this neighborhood. It was the American way.

Kurt Boerekart took the lead down the stairs. A massive steel door awaited them at the bottom of the steps, a large X painted on the front. They had arrived. This was the headquarters of the notorious X-Men of Roxbury. Drug dealers, thieves, murderers—they were the best known in all of Boston. Unfortunately, they had mounted their doors with the hinges on the outside. This meant that the door would resist battering, because the door opened outward. That was deliberate. While the police battered the front door, they would disappear like rats down several bolt holes. This, however, was not going to be a normal police operation. Chris, with his silenced weapon to the peep hole, waited while Kurt set his briefcase on the steps and started pulling out blocks of C-4, plastic explosive. This was one of the few imports allowed by The Fox, and now they were going to get the payoff. Kurt shaped the white-doughy plastic explosive around all three exposed hinges, then put a whole four-pound block over the other edge of the door, right at waist level, where a large bolt could be seen by flashing a light through the crack. Still no sign of activity on the inside.

The other carload was supposed to be protecting the team from attack from the street, but somehow they missed the woman. Perhaps she came down the stairs leading from the upper apartments.

"What you boys doing down there? I live here. Don't y'all do nothing here, ya' hear?"

Dieter swung around, startled out of his intense concentration on the activities at the door. It was a large, older black woman in a cotton dress and light sweater.

Dieter peered at her, his eyes yellow behind his shatter-proof shooting glasses. "Beat it, bitch."

The woman looked shocked and started to reply, then turned and walked rapidly away down the street. As she strode past, one of the other men appeared from the shadows, his face almost invisible in the shadow thrown by the street lights on his black-billed cap. His submachine gun moved slightly towards her. With a final "Well, I never," she moved on down the street, shaking her head.

Dieter turned back to Kurt. The detonation chord connecting the explosives could be clearly seen, white against the darkness of the door. The explosion of one mound of C-4 would be carried almost instantaneously to the others by the detonation chord. Dieter nodded and there was the brief flare of a match. Sixty seconds.

All of the men in the stairway walked quickly but carefully out to the street and then crouched down behind their car. The other team members took cover. Dieter, Kurt, Chris, and Hans all turned on the mini maglight flashlights taped to their weapons. The shock wave might break all the light bulbs as well as all the ear drums of anyone inside. Each of them then placed his weapon carefully on the ground and put on the gas mask that had been dangling around his neck. In a few seconds, there was a tremendous crack from the high-velocity C-4 explosion. A large piece of metal flew out the stairwell and cartwheeled down the street. As it rattled to a stop, Dieter stood up.

"Let's go."

Chris and Kurt, the first entry team pair, ran in. Kurt stumbled slightly over the body of someone who had been right behind the door, which had now completely vanished. There might have been several people; it was impossible to tell in the small spotlight of the mini maglight. They moved forward quickly. In the first doorway they saw only a small room with several mattresses. Before they reached the second room, two men had stumbled out of it into the corridor. Kurt and Chris fired simultaneously, the roar of Kurt's Uzi deafening in the confined space. The men slid to the floor, leaving bloody smears on the wall. The door to the second room slammed shut just as they reached it, and a shotgun blast ripped through the thin planking. Instinctively, all four of them emptied their magazines into the room. Chris fired through the door, but the rest fired right through the walls. The military 9mm hard ball ammunition penetrated the thin walls like a hot knife through butter.

Everyone paused a moment as they changed magazines. "Ready!" Chris yelled, his voice muffled by the gas mask.

"Go," Kurt acknowledged. Chris fired a short burst at the door latch then kicked it. The door flew open and they both stepped through the doorway and moved to either side. Again the snapping sound of Kurt's unsilenced Uzi echoed down the hallway. Dieter and Hans were working their way further into the building, searching for more X-Men.

"Clear!" rang out Chris's muffled voice; another "Clear" came from Kurt.

"Team Leader, here!" called Kurt.

Hans kept his position, covering the hallway as Dieter inched backwards. He reached another doorway; the lights were still on in this room. There were two tables. One had several clear plastic bags filled with white powder, the other held stacks of money with more bundles lying on the floor. Behind the second table, a small thin man lay on the ground, his body riddled with bullets, a shotgun still clutched in his hand.

Dieter lifted his gas mask and tested the air. Most of the dust had settled. He gestured to Kurt and Chris. "Go check out the rest of the place," he said. "Two minutes." He pulled a large garbage bag from one of his pockets and started stuffing the cash into it. He heard Hans move up behind him.

"Glad Bags?"

"Extra tough so you don't spill your garbage," Dieter replied. He looked at Hans, who was shaking his head.

"Really?" Hans asked. "Garbage bags for robberies. This country has something for everything."

"Exactly," Dieter replied as he tossed another Glad bag at Hans. "Get the drugs."

"What for?" asked Hans. "We don't need them."

"It's part of the deal. Anyhow, the Americans have a saying for this."

"Yah?" said Hans with an eyebrow raised.

"'Waste not, want not.' Now, get the drugs. We have only one minute left. *Schnell.*"

Ten minutes later they were out of Roxbury, riding down Washington Street towards Interstate 95. Dieter slapped Hans on the knee as he was struggling in the back of the car to get out of his jumpsuit.

"Well, that's it comrade. We're rich and we just got our Christmas bonus. Don't you love capitalism?"

Kurt turned from the front seat. "Are we really done?"

Dieter laughed. "That's it for us. Three days of leisurely driving to Mexico for you and Chris. Hans and I will be dropped off soon to take another way."

Caught up in the gaiety, Kurt laughed too. "Still no 'need to know,' eh *Mein Fuehrer?*"

"Exactly, my friend. We will dump our weapons and split the drug money at the Holiday Inn rally point in..." he checked his watch, "less than an hour. Then my life as a policeman ends."

"Terrorist you mean," corrected Chris from behind the wheel.

Dieter looked at Hans, his oldest friend, and shrugged. "I guess it's just a question of viewpoint."

9:17 P.M.

Melody Jane had finished her Diet Coke and had asked for another. The makeup girl was done with her face and hair. The Xanax was working well. The grenade had really shocked her, but she felt steady now with Steve outside the door. She belched slightly and waved her hands to fan herself. The room was very hot; they'd been drying out a spill and had only taken out the heater when she came in. The humidity was oppressive.

Harley Jones watched from his office. The web cam image was a bit low in resolution so he couldn't make out any details. The sound quality was poor too. "Roz, what do you think?"

She stood behind him, her hand resting comfortably on his shoulder. "I don't know what that Xanax will do. I should have thrown it out when I went through her bag."

Jones turned his head. "What the hell? It's show time." He paused. "Good luck."

She laughed. "Me. Good luck? Hell. You're going to be here with your *schmeckel* in a wringer when this goes south. I'm going to vanish and you and your friends are going to owe me and my friends—big time. Hope you'll be around to pay up."

Jones nodded. "Duly acknowledged."

"Shit, Harley," she said quietly, "This whole thing could go so badly."

Harley Jones just shrugged.

Moments later, they saw movement in the room and a burst of static came through.

Roz checked her watch.

* * *

Pamela Clark entered the room with her camera man. "Good afternoon Madam Secretary." She held out her hand. "I'm Pamela Clark and I'm here to do an interview before you tour the site and take command. We're doing this now because I think you'll be very busy later and the public should know a bit more about you."

Melody Jane smiled. Pamela Clark motioned to the camera man to set up and then she proceeded to place Melody Jane in the best light. Then, since there was only one camera, she placed herself so that it would view over her shoulder. The camera man set up two small but bright lights. Pamela turned to the makeup girl. "We'll need some privacy here. The room is small and it's going to get really hot with the lights." The girl left with a slightly peevish expression.

Pamela settled in and touched her hand briefly to her ear to check the tiny speaker there. The camera man attached the microphone to Melody Jane's blouse and stepped back to his camera, making final adjustments. Pamela stood up and checked the camera field of view. It was perfect, completely focused on the Secretary and missing Pamela herself. It was already recording. She indicated with a slight movement of her head that the camera man should leave. He baulked for a moment but an angry stare got him moving. Pamela sat down.

Pamela smiled. "So how are you feeling? I understand you were shot at on the way in?"

Melody Jane replied, "Actually I'm feeling fine. It was a bit disconcerting but my people got me out of the kill zone safely." She paused for a moment. "Xanax. I took a Xanax."

Pamela Clark leaned forward. "We can edit that out later if you like, Madam Secretary."

"Oh I'm feeling fine, rowdy even. I'm in charge." Melody Jane gave a big smile.

In his office Harley Jones said to Roz, "What did you give her?"

"Do you really want to know?" Roz asked.

Jones paused. "Since you don't exist ... why worry?"

"Roofies," she answered. When Jones squinted at her she added, "Rohypnol, the date rape drug...often induces amnesia. Perfect, eh?" She glanced at her watch. Just over forty minutes. I don't know what the Xanax will do. She chugged the bottle of Diet Coke I doctored, then we gave her some more in the second bottle. It's hard to tell what the right dosage is. This could be wild."

"Christ," Jones said. "I figured you'd giver her Valium or something like that. Just to get her out of the way for a day or two."

Roz pursed her lips. "You're a wimp. Valium won't do jack unless we give it IV and that wasn't so easy to set up. This is the best we could come up with on short notice. Ride with the tide, Jones. This should be fun."

Jones shook his head. "Christ Roz, you're hard."

Roz chuckled and waved expansively, gesturing to all of Boston. "Shit Harley, look who's talking."

She turned to the screen. "Let's watch The Late Show."

Back in the small conference room, Pamela could sense that Melody Jane was more than comfortable—she was intoxicated on something. It wasn't alcohol but ... something. She sensed a unique opportunity to get out from underneath the dark cloud that Harley Jones had put over her. He had promised that a good performance would eliminate her from his "black book."

"Madam Secretary," Pamela started.

"Oh, call me Melody, just between us."

That brought Pamela up sharply. This was out of character.

"Ok, Melody, briefly, how did you come to be Secretary of Homeland Security?"

"Well, when that idiot Spencer got diagnosed with pancreatic cancer, he quit. The President needed someone strong and that's why I am here. I'm in charge. Soon the FBI and CIA will be part of Homeland too. That's why I'm in charge."

Pamela paused. Melody Jane Harmony had just thrown herself into a minefield and even a local news reporter could see that. "What are your qualifications for the position?"

Melody wrinkled her face. "It's a question of character. I'm the kind of person that takes charge. I know how to run a tight ship ... really tight. Everyone works for me and they know it. I don't take any back talk."

Pamela smiled encouragingly. "Can you give an example?"

Melody Jane slapped her palm down on her knee. "Damn right. The Director of the Secret Service told me that he wasn't sure it was wise to send Secret Service people into Boston. I fired him. Just this afternoon. Then his deputy tried to block me. I fired his ass too. These people need to follow orders whether they like them or not."

Pamela nodded. "Like storm troopers."

Melody nodded back. "That's right. I love those uniforms too—a fashion statement. Now those people, the SS—they knew how to throw a party."

Pamela flushed slightly, this was getting outrageous. What was this woman on? "Party?"

Melody smiled sweetly. "Auschwitz, Dachau—you know. Problem solvers. Just what we need here."

Pamela almost groaned. This was going beyond bad, but she couldn't stop. "You're serious? Problem solvers?"

Melody nodded. "The usual suspects, 'cept not Jews... well, not most. Spics and niggers mostly. Fucking weak ass liberal scum too. But, mostly, we need to round up a lot of Muslims. They're infiltrating with everything from school food to Sharia law. It's un-American, and it can't be tolerated."

Pamela felt a little sick. Melody leaned forward and patted her on the knee, then left her hand there. "Pamela. Do you like a strong woman?"

Melody Jane dropped down on her knees in front of Pamela and put one hand on either knee. Pamela immediately regretted wearing a short skirt.

Melody Jane looked up into Pamela's eyes. "I can show you a good time … something you'll never forget."

Pamela tensed as Melody Jane's hands inched slowly up. It was only a minute, but it seemed hours before the woman called Willy Peter came in with the Secret Service man, Steve, in tow. "Steve," she said, "Pamela called me. It seems that the Secretary has had an adverse reaction to her medication."

Melody Jane remained on her knees, but snapped her head around. "Fuck off, bitch. She's mine."

Steve was confused. This particular situation wasn't in the playbook. Then he shrugged. Maybe a trip back to D.C. was in order. Things could be kept quiet there and the Secretary could sleep off whatever was happening. A trip to the hospital was possible too; Washington was only an hour away and Boston was not secure.

Steve squatted down by Melody Jane and put his arm around her. "Come on, Melody, let's go home. These people don't understand how important you are."

Melody Jane scrunched up her face and began to cry. With surprising gentleness, Steve picked her up carried her out of the room.

Pamela absently turned off the camera and turned to speak to the woman called Willy Peter, but she was gone.

10:00 P.M.

Muhammad Wasfi, the leader of the Abu Nidal Strike Force for Palestinian Freedom, waved to the rest of the team in the apartment building as he leaned against the car. It was all clear. Adnan Al-Tahir, brash but trustworthy, and Isa Khalifa, the thief of passports, were first. Carefully they put their workout bags in the trunk of the stolen Ford Escape and sat in the front seat. Next came Khalid Al-Suffarini, tall and arrogant in his position as second in command. Finally, menacing in his strength and karate skills, came Atif Jabir.

Muhammad took the wheel as Isa took up the map. This was their second sniping mission. Adnan would be the sniper, while Khalid was the spotter. The rest would act as lookouts. Their new mission was to block Route 93 south by Quincy. The jam on 93 in the center of Boston was being cleared up. They would move to the Bates overpass so that they could shoot at the vehicles as they moved directly towards them or directly away—that was the easiest type of shot. Even then, it would require many shots from Adnan. None of the team was a great shot. They preferred close work with Kalashnikovs, but they had their orders. Their controller had been very specific: "Do exactly what you are told. This will be the ultimate strike for freedom. You must be prepared to pay the ultimate price." They were prepared, although they would have preferred to go back to Libya as heroes. They had discussed this properly, in a forthright session of self-assessment. Only Khalid had been sparse in his self-criticism. Such doubt was unbecoming for a man who had spent seven years with the Abu Nidal organization. Still, he was intelligent and resourceful.

The car started immediately as Muhammad crossed the hot wire to the starter wire. Carefully, looking both left and right, he pulled away from the curb.

Washington Street

Detectives Andrews and Maloney were moving down Washington Street towards the downtown area. They had just left the Roxbury crime scene.

"Jesus," Andrews said. "I've never seen anything like that. And that door, completely blown off."

"Scary," Maloney agreed; "and those people claiming it was us. That whole place is going to get messy real soon now. Did you see the way they looked at us? Man, I wouldn't want to be the riot squad when these people get going. They are maximally pissed."

Andrews nodded, not taking his eyes off the traffic. Like any well-trained policeman, his eyes were always roving.

"Yep. Sure are. What do you think—did we do that?"

Maloney reflected for a moment. "No. Not officially, anyhow. Hell, everyone's been called up. No one could get away for something like that."

The radio squawked briefly. Maloney shook his head. "Damn, I hope they get us back on the air soon. This is creepy, not being able to call for backup. Do you think this thing at eleven is going to make any difference?"

Andrews shrugged. He'd seen too many things go wrong to believe in any rapid improvements. "'Blackjack.' Isn't that just like the Army. Have you ever seen the Army do anything right? Shit. We'll be getting the blackjack is my guess—Whoa!"

Andrews had swiveled his head around to watch a car going in the opposite direction. Carefully checking the traffic he swung their own car in a U-turn.

"Possible stolen car," Andrews said excitedly.

"Shit, Andrews, how can you know?"

"Maloney, look at it. It's just like mine. One was on the hot sheet today, just like mine."

Andrews pulled up directly behind the Ford and turned on the blue lights hidden behind the grill. When the car didn't slow, he brought out the blue flasher and put it on the roof. The car pulled over slowly to the curb. Its occupants looked agitated.

"Kids," Maloney muttered. "Be careful. Damn, we can't call in the plates."

Andrews stepped out of the car and placed his badge so that it showed by his belt. Maloney did the same. The streets were oddly quiet for Saturday night. It had been a long time since Andrews or Maloney had pulled anyone over, but they remembered what to do. They moved up on either side of the suspect car, although only Maloney had a flashlight.

The windows were all rolled down, and the driver, a young man with dark eyes, looked up at Andrews. Just then, the beam from Maloney's flashlight swung over the ignition. When Andrews saw the loose wires, he jumped back and pulled out his service weapon. Maloney did the same.

"Hot wired, Al. Hot damn—stolen. I knew it," Anderson called across to Maloney.

Keeping his pistol pointed at the driver he started the procedure.

"All right. One at a time. Driver first. Everyone keep your hands in sight."

Carefully, they let the occupants out of the car and lined them up in "the position": hands on the car, feet spread, leaning in. Andrews was about to undo the trunk, which was held closed by a wire, when one of the occupants seemed to levitate. Astonished, Andrews turned to face him and felt intense pain in his hand as his pistol flew into the air. In less than a second, the stocky man had launched a second devastating kick into his solar plexus, completely paralyzing him. Maloney, who had been intent on the trunk, swung to face the man but found that somehow he kept swinging, his arm pushed past his point of aim and up into the air. The man held Maloney's hands up, then swiveled and propelled Maloney away from him with a hip throw. Maloney, like any human in flight, reacted to save himself and released his pistol. Just as he landed he received a crushing kick to the ribs. He rolled to escape more punishment and scrambled to his feet, only to find himself facing his own pistol.

For just a moment, both men froze. Then an enormous explosion sounded to Maloney's right, along with a flash of flame. The man who had taken Maloney's pistol flew backwards as though he was a puppet whose master has jerked the wrong string. Everyone froze. Maloney looked to the right and saw a man in a dull long coat holding an enormous revolver. Maloney was transfixed, staring at the metal glinting in the streetlights.

"Get your pistol," the man said hoarsely.

Maloney scrambled and did what he was told, being careful not to point the weapon toward the stranger, whose revolver was locked on the former car occupants.

"Are you in control now?" the man asked.

Maloney gulped and nodded vigorously. "I guess so."

The man stared at Maloney for a moment. "Well, then put your weapon on these people."

Maloney nodded and turned to face the group. An idea had occurred to him. "OK. All of you lie down on the ground, face down, hands over your head." He'd seen it in a movie. He looked back, but his benefactor had vanished into the shadows of Boston.

Deep in the building's shadow, Patrick Henry Johnston put his Colt Python .357 magnum back into his shoulder holster. His hands were shaking now, he acknowledged, but he was a rock when it counted. He leaned against the building, breathing in the hot night air. Damn, it felt good to hunt.

10:20 P.M.
JFK Federal Building

Captain Paul Brooks knocked carefully at Assistant Director Jones's office door. He had held the job of liaison officer for the Boston Police Department for only an hour, but already he knew about Assistant Director Jones. Captain Brooks was forty-three years old and a hardened police veteran, but he knew that anyone so high up who was called "The Flame-Thrower" was to be handled gently. The latest rumor was that the nickname had been shortened to "Flame," and he wasn't certain whether the new name held some more subtle meaning.

"Yes?"

Captain Brooks stepped in but stayed close to the door. "Good news sir, we've captured some of them."

Jones's haggard face lit up. "Outstanding. Tell me more."

"Well, sir, it was kind of luck. Two detectives happened to stop their car. These detectives almost got themselves wasted—one of the terrorists just about ripped them apart with his hands, some sort of karate man. Anyhow, a civilian blew this guy away and then disappeared. The detectives are writing it up now. We have four of the five intact."

Jones nodded his approval. "Do we have photos of these people? Any ID?"

"No sir. They're all very quiet. We turned them over to Mr. Browner as you instructed."

A helicopter could be heard landing in the plaza.

"That should be Mr. Browner's people. They've set up shop over at Logan in one of the restrooms—or at least that's the story."

Jones's face took on a quizzical look. "The story?"

Captain Brooks's face assumed a totally neutral look. "Well, the story is that they wanted a place where it would be easy to wash down the blood."

Jones leaned back in his chair. "I think that's an exaggeration, Captain."

The Captain took this as his cue, and left hastily. Harley Jones leaned even farther back in his chair. "I hope it's an exaggeration," he said and closed his eyes. The smell of Nuck Mam was strong again.

CHAPTER 21: BLACKJACK

11:00 P.M.
Phase I. Checkpoint 7

Sergeant John McGeorge, Boston Police Department Patrol Division, looked at Staff Sergeant Jason Howard, Military Police Detachment of the 82nd Airborne. "What do you think?" he asked, waving at the intersection of Beacon Street and Massachusetts Avenue. Both of them knew that his gesture encompassed the whole of operation Blackjack.

Staff Sergeant Howard rubbed his chin and shook his head. "Damned if I know. Hell, this is your town. What do *you* think?"

Sergeant McGeorge leaned back against the MP Humvee—a sort of super jeep, he thought. "Well, since you ask…" They both smiled. "We've had plans for sectoring the city before, but only to cut off the escape of perpetrators. This idea of sealing up sectors and making everyone who wants to go from one to another go through a checkpoint—well, I don't know, it sounds like Northern Ireland."

Staff Sergeant Howard looked around at the intersection then turned back to Sergeant McGeorge. "Yeah, it does. But it worked there, didn't it?"

Sergeant McGeorge shrugged his shoulders. "No idea. But we sure need something here. Have you heard about what's been going on?"

Staff Sergeant Howard shook his head. "Not much, some sniping and all. We were too busy getting ready to come up here."

Sergeant McGeorge leaned towards him, while still watching the intersection. "Well, just last night, we lost over half of our Arrest—SWAT team to you—in an ambush. These assholes blew down a whole building on them. Sniping, yeah, we've got sniping, but everyone seems to think it's a build up for something else. I guess Blackjack is supposed to put a stopper on it."

Staff Sergeant Howard checked his watch and stood up. "Twenty-three hundred, time to go into action. What do you say?" Sergeant McGeorge nodded and blew his whistle.

From all four directions waiting units moved out to block the road—some were Boston Police Department, some were Military Police. All had their flashers running as they moved into a segmented chevron pattern. This required that all cars come to a stop, be checked, then slalom around one unit in one lane and then back into the original lane to get through the intersection. There were four men for each direction: two

212

policemen and two MPs. The police had their service weapons and one riot shotgun. The MPs each had a pistol and an M-4 automatic rifle. The two sergeants, the supervisors for this corner, watched as the first car pulled up. The policemen went to the driver's side while the MP moved up behind and to the rear, checking out the back of the car, his hand on his pistol. Directly behind the car, now that it had stopped, the other police officer stood with his riot gun ready. Off to the side, the other MP stood with his M-4 ready for quick action.

Sergeant McGeorge turned to Staff Sergeant Howard. "Well, it *looks* good," he said. They both knew that looks weren't worth much when the pressure was applied.

Howard nodded. "We'll get the procedure broken in overnight. Tomorrow we'll be smooth." He nodded towards another Humvee in the middle of the intersection. It mounted a .50 caliber machine gun. Another MP stood behind the large gun, ready to swivel in any direction. "We've got armor piercing in that. It should take out just about anything."

Sergeant McGeorge looked startled. "Armor piercing? Won't that go right through a house?"

Staff Sergeant Howard smiled. "Several. I see your point, but we've got to be able to stop anything short of a tank, right? I mean, it would be easy to load up a pickup truck with a few sand bags. We've got to punch through. Of course," he smiled even wider, "if those don't work, we've got some old LAAWs in the back of the Humvee."

"LAAWs?"

"Rockets—like bazookas but disposable. About 300 yards range. Don't know what they'd do to a car, but they can punch a hole in an armored personnel carrier, so you can guess. Man, I'd like to see that. That would make my day."

Staff Sergeant Howard and Sergeant McGeorge watched the questioning of the driver of the first vehicle, a single black male.

"Seems to be going a bit slowly," Howard noted, "And the guy on the shotgun looks like he's afraid of it."

Sergeant McGeorge hesitated a moment. "That's Craft. The other man is Green. They really shouldn't be out here. Last night there was a shooting incident. Craft may have shot a citizen. He's pretty shook up. He should be on a desk waiting for a shooting board, but everyone is out for Blackjack, absolutely everyone."

Staff Sergeant Howard watched Craft carefully. "Maybe we could find another place for him?"

Sergeant McGeorge looked towards the roof, where a sniper team waited. "You want to put him up there?"

Staff Sergeant Howard decided to change the subject and gestured towards the holding area off to the interior of the intersection. This was where suspicious people would be held and questioned. There was another Humvee there next to a table which was stacked with photographs of suspects. Several police officers chatted with a young tall Army lieutenant as the two sergeants walked up. Staff Sergeant Howard saluted.

"Does it work, sir?" he asked.

The lieutenant shrugged. "Sort of. It's a weak link. The digital camera is OK but the interface to the FAX in the Humvee is flakey. If it works, instant photo to the Command Information Center. They can send us blown-up photos too. A direct television link would be better." He paused for a moment. "We could use cell phone cameras too, as long as the cell phones work, but I'm not sure of the bandwidth."

Sergeant McGeorge stepped forward. "What happens when a lot of people start calling the—what do you call it—'Information Center'?"

The lieutenant hesitated. "Well, I guess it's busy."

Sergeant McGeorge's face took on a displeased look. The lieutenant added hastily, "Look, if you're in doubt, just arrest them and send them down to Central Receiving."

Sergeant McGeorge shook his head. "Well, Lieutenant, what really worries me is what if we have some serious trouble here? How quickly are we going to get help?" The lieutenant thought for a moment, then shrugged.

A voice from behind startled Sergeant McGeorge. "I'm Assistant Director Jones, Sergeant. What seems to be the problem?"

Sergeant McGeorge turned quickly to see an unimpressive man in a leather jacket. So this was the famous FBI counter terrorist. He sure didn't look like much. Sergeant McGeorge recognized the man standing next to Jones, Captain Brooks, as one of the pricks from Headquarters.

"Well, sir, I was just wondering who is going to support us if things get ugly here. If the bad guys can be wearing uniforms, it gets complicated. I mean, if our support has to go through every check point and be checked, won't it take damn near forever for them to get here?"

Sergeant McGeorge was pleased to see that he seemed to have scored a point. Assistant Director Jones turned to Captain Brooks. "Any comment?"

Captain Brooks looked Sergeant McGeorge directly in the eye. "You seem to have something there, *Sergeant*."

Sergeant McGeorge returned the look coolly. He was a professional police officer and didn't have to crawl for any goddamn captain who should have been blown up with Headquarters.

Captain Brooks seemed startled when Jones interrupted: "Captain Brooks, I want to see you in my office." Jones pointed to a nearby Humvee with the canvas top up.

Moments later, Sergeant McGeorge had the pleasure of seeing the face of Captain Brooks turn to a pale white as Assistant Director Jones pointed his finger repeatedly at Captain Brooks from his position in the driver's seat. Sergeant McGeorge couldn't hear what was being said, but the angry tone came through the soft top of the Humvee.

Staff Sergeant Howard leaned over to Sergeant McGeorge. "They call this guy Jones 'The Flame'—now I know why."

Sergeant McGeorge nodded and turned to Howard. "Yeah, well maybe we need a little flame around here. Some of these people need to get lit up."

12:00 A.M.
Pirate Radio 960

"Well folks, this is Big Al keeping you company in the midnight hour. Whooo-eeee, are we having exciting times or what? This Hand dude is strictly baaad. You want to know what he's got for you this midnight? Maybe it's a sermon! After all, it's Sunday now. Time to talk to the Lord. I always do. Ahhh, just scratching my crotch, oooohhh. Anyhow, looks like The Hand has got a great midnight message for you folks still in town. Me? I'm safe on the high seas. Big Al on Pirate 960 with the word from The Hand. Credence Clearwater doing Graveyard Train."

Credence started singing about graveyards and boxes made of bone.

* * *

Harley Jones shook his head and snapped off his radio.

* * *

Patrick Henry Johnston looked up from cleaning his pistol. This was the third time and he couldn't seem to get it clean enough. He heard the song too, but could only remember something about crying out a name.

* * *

215

Commissioner Eddy Yeager rubbed his aching neck while watching the traffic on Mass Avenue after hearing something about midnight.

* * *

Pamela Clark lay in her bed wondering what Hassan Bucheri looked like, what he would feel like.

* * *

Private John Miller slept on the floor of the command APC but Perez, the radio watch, tapped his fingers in time to Radio 960. He heard about thirty people turned to stone.

* * *

All across Boston, listeners thought about being number thirty-one.

12:05 A.M.
JFK Federal Building

The new briefing room was the largest in the JFK Building. Some of the chairs were empty since this was only a scheduled news update, but every section was represented. The room was full of dark police uniforms and camouflage military uniforms, and sprinkled with assorted suits and a few haggard workers in shirt sleeves or dresses.

Harley Jones started the meeting.

"First, I need to mention that, yes, indeed the Secretary of Homeland Security was here."

The room quieted completely. "She seems to have had an adverse reaction to the flight over in the Little Bird." Jones smiled slightly. "It seems that she was given the scenic tour and a bit of a roller coaster ride." There were a few laughs. "So, she appears to be out of the picture. I think we must proceed as before." He looked around the room for any disagreement. When there was none, he continued.

"I've been out on the streets. Phase I of Blackjack is underway. As expected, there are a few rough spots, but it looks like it will work if Bostonians can stay home tomorrow. We won't know until then if they really got the message. Captain Brooks will now report for the Boston P.D."

Captain Brooks stood up, looking clean and fresh compared to the rumpled Harley Jones.

"As Assistant Director Jones mentioned, we are working very hard now to smooth out any problems with Phase I. So far things are going well in the sectored zone, which is Boston proper. Something interesting has happened in Roxbury, however, which may cause us serious problems."

Jones looked up with interest.

"It appears that there was a raid on the headquarters of the X-Men." A stir went through the policemen in the crowd.

"For those of you who don't know them, the X-Men are a very powerful black gang operating out of Roxbury. To summarize what appears to have happened, white men in police uniforms shot the place up and killed everyone present, including one bystander. Then they cleaned the place out. We can only speculate, but our intelligence and forensics indicate that large amounts of illicit drugs were there. This makes it likely that there was considerable cash. These people don't take MasterCard."

There was only the slightest laughter from the group. Harley Jones looked up unsmilingly at Captain Brooks, who continued quickly.

"All of this is unfortunate, because, of course, these weren't our people. The perpetrators were wearing police uniforms and the people of Roxbury are holding us responsible. Our units in the area have been stoned and there has been one shooting incident. A thirteen-year-old male was shot by one of our officers. He did have a firearm, but that doesn't seem to matter. In short, we have a powder keg there and the fuse is burning. Tomorrow is going to be very touchy. We may have to pull personnel from Blackjack to handle the situation."

Captain Brooks looked down at Jones, who was shading his eyes and shaking his head.

"Is that all?" Jones asked with a pained tone.

"Yes sir," Captain Brooks answered and took his seat.

"Anyone want to comment?" Jones asked.

From close by, Ted Browner spoke up. "It looks like Bucheri's hand to me."

Jones nodded. "Can you think of anything else that he might do? Something that we should prepare for?"

No one spoke up, although there were some murmurs.

Jones waited, then continued, "OK. Bucheri may have played another card, but we're still in the game. Mr. Browner?"

Ted Browner stood up. "The Boston Police Department captured most of one cell of this organization." He nodded to the Boston P.D. liaison officer. "A well-done to your detectives."

He turned and spoke to the group. "The terrorists are undergoing interrogation now, but so far it appears that they know very little that is useful to us. They are highly compartmentalized. As we suspected, they get their instructions by telephone. We may cut that off, although they can still use cellular phones in Boston and the whole phone network outside of the downtown Boston area. Many of you aren't familiar with intelligence work, so I'll simply say that we often work with partial information and guess from there. That's what we're doing here. Phase II of Blackjack should, I repeat, *should* seriously hamper their communication."

Ted Browner sat down and looked across to Harley Jones. Jones rose slowly. "The gentleman to my right is George Alvarez. He is going to be running Phase II. He'll brief you on anything you need to know. See him after this briefing for details. I'm going to get a few hours of sleep. Mr. Browner is the second in command, so please see him until 0400 this morning, when I'll be back at work."

George Alvarez rose at Jones's nod. "Phase II has already begun. We're working one exchange at a time and breaking it in as we go. Right now, a third of the downtown has been shut down with no problems. Cellular traffic is light and we're handling it. Triangulation by the radio-direction-finding units seems to be working well. We're calibrating it now." He looked around and then sat down.

Harley Jones started, as though he had been sleeping, and stood up. "That's it until the 2:00 a.m. briefing by Mr. Browner."

Jones walked quickly out of the room, heading for his office and the waiting cot. Just as he stepped into the elevator, George Alvarez slipped in behind him.

"Tired?"

Jones raised his eyebrows. "Dead. I'm too old for this."

Alvarez walked down to his office with him. Jones stepped in and Alvarez followed.

"Well, George, what is it?"

"Harley, as your former second-in-command, I've got to say it."

"What?"

"Look. I heard about the last briefing and the questions about 'is it legal?'"

Jones sat on his cot but continued to watch Alvarez. "So?"

"Well, that Judge Advocate General, he's been on my case too. You know, he's right. There will be so many holes in the chain of evidence, so much tainted fruit that the ACLU and every other group will go absolutely nuts. We'll never get a conviction. We've got illegal taps, coerced confessions for sure, no telling what the Agency is doing to those guys, and the military presence. My God, Harley, there's going to be hell to pay. Oh, Jesus, did I forget our relationship with the press? Christ, you're going to come out of this looking like a cross between Goebbels and Saddam Hussein."

Jones nodded tiredly. "I know, George, the courts will be a problem, but we can't just blow these people away. We arrested Noriega and brought him back. You can't tell me that was *legal*? There has to be a way. This isn't 'Nam. We can't do things like that here."

George Alvarez nodded. "I know how you feel, Harley, but that's that way everyone else does it. The SAS, GSG-9, all these guys just go in and blow the bad guys away."

Jones stood up; the conversation was irritating him. "I know George. You remember Munich. Nine hostages and four terrorists. All shot up by the Germans. They didn't have the right people there. You know the difference here?"

Alvarez shook his head.

"Here, they've got a million hostages." Jones stared at Alvarez, his eyes unblinking. Alvarez was about to reply, to express his sympathy for Jones's situation, when Jones pushed past him.

Jones felt the walls closing in, the pressure building. He had to get some fresh air before going to sleep. The JFK Building had become a mad ant hole, with black and camouflaged ants pouring in and out of the entrance. Outside, it was different. The fresh night air was cleaner, mild and warm. After he moved away from the machine gun positions guarding the entrance, the atmosphere was less tense. The paratroops were alert, but more relaxed now that they had drawn no fire. A few recognized him and nodded; most ignored him—one of the suits, no danger to them.

As he walked around to the back of the building towards the vehicle park a boom box played and the strains of a familiar song drifted across the heat waves.

He recognized the Rolling Stones' version of "Satisfaction."

An off-duty male paratrooper was leaning against the wall, talking to a female MP comfortably ensconced between his extended arms.

Jones couldn't help but smile, thinking that maybe someone was going to get some "girly action," despite what the song said.

The woman's teeth flashed, but her words were lost over the music.

They ignored Jones as he passed by, an invisible civilian. Farther across the vehicle park, a match flared just as the engine coughed to life on an M113 armored personnel carrier.

The song said something about being a man and smoking the right brand. The diesel fumes from the M113 were taking Jones back, way back.

Like the song said, he was on a losing streak.

Jones shook his head. He sure as hell was. It was time to get to bed.

Slowly he ambled back through the plaza, trying to soak up the warm night. On the steps he saw a familiar silhouette.

"Jeannie, hi! Out soaking up the rays?"

He was rewarded by a flash of white teeth. "Tired?" he asked as he sat down by her.

"Dead. I'm so tired I'm afraid I won't be able to sleep."

Jones nodded slowly. "Really something isn't it?" He gestured generally towards the machine gun nest and the paratroop sentries.

Jeannie shook her head. "I never thought I'd see something like this in America. It's so ... alien."

Jones sighed and leaned back, resting his elbows on the step. "I have, a bit during the sixties, but it wasn't really like this. Everyone, students and soldiers, they all thought it was joke. This has a bad feeling to it. There's a terrible loss of control here, a sense of things gone berserk— and, what's worse, this could just be the beginning. This could spread all across the country. Bucheri is a genius. I'll give him that."

"He's like a *wu shu* master using *pa kau* techniques. Have you ever heard about that?"

"You mean like karate."

"Yes. *Wu Shu* are the Chinese fighting arts. They have many styles, styles based on imitating animals, tiger, bear, crane, and so on. One of the hardest styles to learn is *pa kau*. It's a circular style. Whenever your opponent attacks, you deflect and move to the side. The harder he attacks, the closer inside you get. It's really neat to watch."

"Are you a karate person?"

Jeannie laughed, a surprisingly low chuckle in the night. "No. I used to like doing the forms, the *kata*. They're like dancing, really challenging, but I couldn't stand the sparring. I couldn't bear to hurt anyone. My brothers used to laugh at me and call me the eel, because I was so evasive, but the thought of hurting someone is just so ... repugnant. I eventually quit. I think my father understood."

"What did he think of you joining the Bureau?"

She paused, wondering how much she could tell him. "He wasn't pleased, but that's a long story." She sighed. "He did make me promise to always be armed. He even gave me a pistol. One that he carried in Vietnam."

Jones tried to imagine Jeannie carrying a huge .45 caliber automatic. "A forty-five?"

"Oh my, no. A 32 Walther PPK. A James Bond gun. Tiny, just like me."

"And do you always go armed?"

Jeannie's tone turned serious. "Absolutely. I promised. Usually a Glock 26. Only 10 rounds but small … like me." She smiled faintly.

Jones turned to look at her, looking for where she might have a pistol concealed. "Always?"

"Always." The teeth flashed again. "I enjoyed the pistol training, but that was all a game. I'm not sure I could shoot someone. It's just too ugly to think about." She paused for a moment and her tone again turned serious. "You were in Vietnam weren't you?"

Jones nodded in the darkness.

"How did it feel?"

"To kill someone?"

He could see her nod against the stars.

"Well, at the time, you're so scared that you don't feel much of anything. Most of the guys, I don't think it bothered them too much. For them, it was losing their buddies that really hurt. With me, it was different."

"Why?"

"Well, I saw most of my action with a recon team deep in the boonies. I was the intelligence man and, even worse, I had training in Vietnamese, so I had to go through enemy documents looking for anything useful. That was a real bummer."

"Papers. Why?"

"We were looking for anything that might tell us what units we were facing, how many casualties they took and anything, just anything that might be useful. The scraps of information we would paste together. For example, if a wife wrote that there wasn't much rice, the intel guys in Saigon could connect that with bomb assessment damage information on bridges to conclude that they were having an effect on the economy in that region. That wasn't the bad part. It was the pictures of the wives and kids, sad letters, promises. It made them into people. Before, they were just the enemy, depersonalized. It was a definite downer."

They sat for a moment, enjoying the warm night, before Jones stood up. "I'm going to get some sleep. You should do the same. Final exam tomorrow."

Jeannie looked up. "OK, Boss. In a minute. Sleep tight."

Jones smiled. "Tight? Sleep of the dead. Good night."

From his bench on the other side of the plaza, Ted Browner watched Jones walk into the building. He stubbed his cigarette out and considered joining Jeannie Kawai on the steps. She really was a fox, but the problem of Harley Jones swirled around in his mind. Jones was an enigma to Browner. Jones was either incredibly naïve or a master deceiver.

Ted Browner considered himself a man of integrity and experience. He had been heavily involved with two large operations during the Iraq war while controlling one of the largest networks in the area. He had always heeded the government adage, CYAP: Cover Your Ass with Paper. It didn't mean you couldn't do a good job. You just did it the government way. It was the way things were done. There was a certain rightness to it. It was a game of rich complexity with the rewards of power and position.

Jones was ignoring all the rules. Could he possibly be this naïve? He was going to get crucified later. Or was he so smart that he could make new rules? Perhaps he would play the ultimate risk game, the media game, by trying to become a media hero, a Schwartzkopf, immune to criticism. And then there was General Bradley. No one became a three-star general without knowing how to play the game. Was he really going to take orders from Jones? And Yeager, from prince to King for a Day. Would Jones protect Yeager? Could he protect Yeager? Yeager had military experience, but he was a cop to the bone. How would he handle it if shooting started and the Rangers were called in to his city? It would be like turning piranhas loose in a public swimming pool.

Browner lit another cigarette, the match flaring in the night. Just when he thought he had quit. He squinted across the plaza. Jeannie Kawai was still there. Where did she fit in? There was some sort of chemistry between her and Jones. Browner could see it, even if they couldn't. He tracked her with his eyes as she walked into the building. Jeannie Kawai could be a serious troublemaker. He sighed—so could Jessica Williams. He wondered if Jeannie Kawai knew that Jessica Williams was Jones's old flame. He sighed. Maybe Jessica Williams was the clue to understanding Jones. She probably knew him better than anyone.

Browner stubbed out his cigarette harshly. The interrogation teams. What a bunch of creeps. Anxious to try out their drugs and devices. God, what a ghoulish crew, right up from the basement. Still, they had to find out what these guys knew. The trouble was, most of the Agency techniques were designed to be used over days, even weeks, especially sensory deprivation. There just wasn't enough time. They had to have answers quickly. How would the interrogation teams respond to the pressure that Browner would have to put on them? Would it be back to electric shock with pain intensifiers? Browner shuddered. Sometimes Agency work really sucked.

CHAPTER 22: SUNDAY

1:32 A.M.
City Hall

Jessica Williams, head of the CTU data analysis section, had taken over the tax assessors' office. Cables snaked out through the partially closed door to link with the local area network. Her section labored at desks and counters out in the main area. Jessica looked with disgust at the blue smoke cloud that hung in the small room.

"George, I thought you quit."

George Alvarez, head of the electronic surveillance section of the CTU, nodded his head. "Uh huh," he said, and took a deep drag as he watched the screen. Captain Knight sat despondently next to Jessica Williams.

Jessica leaned back in her chair. "Harley isn't going to like this."

Captain Knight perked up slightly as he watched the outline of Jessica Williams's breasts through the semi-shear fabric of her blouse. Jessica seemed oblivious to his stare as she concentrated on the screen. George Alvarez noticed Knight's fascination and shrugged. If Knight's attentions were unwanted, he'd be lucky to escape with his extremities intact. Jessica Williams had a nice body and knew it, but she hadn't gotten to be a section head by lying down for anyone, not even Harley Jones. Yes indeed, George thought, in a male-oriented fraternity like the FBI, the women survivors were tough with a capital "T."

Knight coughed nervously. "Well, everything's working. It's just not fast enough."

Jessica turned towards Knight and caught the direction of his gaze before he could shift his eyes.

"Captain Knight, 'sort of working' may make it in the Army, but we're playing in the big time here." She crossed her legs, letting her dress ride up slightly. She was playing him like a trout on the line.

"I suspect that General Bradley feels the same way," Knight responded.

Jessica got tired of the game. "Look, Knight," she snapped, "it doesn't matter what goddamn General Bradley thinks, what matters is that people are going to be dying in the streets tomorrow if Jones is right, and he usually is. This 'just not fast enough' isn't going to make it." She paused. "Right?"

He nodded tiredly. George Alvarez sat down with a squeak in a tired swivel chair.

"Look, let's go through this again. Just the highlights. Correct me if I'm wrong. First, the radio direction finding is working, but it only gives coordinates, not an address, right? So that takes about five minutes?"

Knight nodded slowly again, closing his eyes briefly. "So, to speed it up, we're waiting to find out what calls to figure out the addresses on."

"Right." George nodded in agreement. "So all the people across the country that are listening to the taps, they call when they hear something funny. Liz Martin says we're getting about a call every minute."

Jessica Williams cocked her head towards George. "That's way too many. It's past one o'clock. There can't be that much going on. They've got to filter it better."

George shrugged his shoulders as pained expression crossed his face. "Look, these people aren't trained for this. Even pros don't have to react immediately to a tap. They sit and talk to each other about what it means, get together and compare notes. Usually they've spent weeks, even months learning the people they've tapped."

Jessica wrinkled her nose. "Come on George, they're passing the buck out there. You can't tell me that sixty calls an hour are all really suspicious at one o'clock in the morning. Give me a break."

Captain Knight interrupted: "Actually, that's not bad. There are over a hundred calls a minute going out just on these cellulars. It's amazing. They're doing a pretty good job, getting it down to one percent."

Jessica raised her hands and locked her fingers behind her neck, further emphasizing her breasts. The tension was so palpable that no one noticed.

"Look, like I said, this just isn't making it. George gets a call a minute. The conversations are usually at least five minutes long. So he has to decide which ones to drop almost immediately. Then, when he finds one he likes, we try to backtrack through time, but with almost a hundred calls per minute, that's over one per second. Knight gets them in his computer, but George's people don't have their time accurate to a second, maybe not even to the exact minute, so basically, we have to check out about a hundred addresses and we don't even start that for about an hour, because that's the time it takes to go through all the calculations and cross checks."

George looked at them both. "And it's only," he looked at his watch, "one thirty. Wait 'til eight this morning."

George Alvarez and Jessica Williams looked at each other and said simultaneously, "Harley isn't going to like this."

2:30 A.M.
JFK Federal Building

The meeting was held in the large conference room. Not surprisingly, the few participants clustered together around the table, as though seeking warmth. In addition to the CTU section leaders, General Bradley, Jeannie Kawai, and Commissioner Yeager had been invited by Ted Browner. In theory, at the round table there were no superior positions, but it was clear where power was concentrated. Ted Browner had seated General Bradley to his right with Commissioner Yeager to Bradley's right. On Browner's left sat Charley Montresor, also a CIA man and now head of the CTU intelligence section. On Montresor's left sat Jeannie Kawai. Next to her were the two psychologists, Jay Schwartz and Loraine Hawthorne. Across the table, seemingly in random order sat Jessica Williams, head of Data Processing, George Alvarez, head of Electronic Surveillance, and John Woods, head of the section called Support, which handled everything from administrative records to equipment acquisition. Ted Browner sat in two capacities, head of the CTU Operations division and second in command. The overall arrangement had been a quick compromise of power sharing between the FBI and the CIA during the formation the previous month. Some of the arrangements were still a bit rough, with FBI people angry over having been bumped downwards and almost everyone unhappy that Browner, a CIA man, should head Operations, since most of the operations would be in the United States, an area of operation forbidden by law to the CIA.

Despite the hour and his fatigue, Browner looked impeccable, his blue power suit carefully matched with a white shirt and maroon tie. General Bradley and Commissioner Yeager both looked tired but alert, curious about the unexpected meeting. Jeannie Kawai's face was still slightly puffy. She had been awakened for the meeting and was clearly both surprised and apprehensive as she scanned the faces of the others.

Jessica Williams and George Alvarez were clearly exhausted. Within minutes of sitting, Alvarez's head had started nodding. Williams, by his side, kept him awake with her sharp elbow while watching Browner through fatigue-darkened eyes. John Woods was not as tired as Williams and Alvarez, although he had worked just as hard getting equipment and men into place. John was a long distance runner and in remarkably good shape. A few naps had kept him going while others had dropped. Jay Schwartz and Loraine Hawthorne still looked quite fresh and were clearly excited about being at an important meeting.

Browner leaned forward and put his elbows on the table. "I've called you all here because we have a problem."

John Woods snorted. "Jesus, no kidding Ted—half of Roxbury is trying to kill the police and the other half has gone on a looting spree."

Ted Browner didn't like the informality encouraged by Harley Jones, but he had to live with it. He straightened up. "I wasn't referring to Roxbury. I had something more important in mind."

More important than Roxbury? Now he had their attention.

"I'm referring to Harley Jones. I believe that he has become unstable."

All of the FBI team members bristled, but Jessica Williams was on her feet before Browner had finished his last word. Her finger quivered as she pointed it at him, but her voice was low, steady and menacing.

"Listen, Browner, you may not like his style, but he's the best. You haven't worked for him before but I'll tell you straight out, he's a master. You're not even in his league."

With those words she settled slowly back into her seat, her eyes never leaving Browner's face.

Browner smiled condescendingly. "Jessica, I can understand your reasons for personal loyalty to—"

Jessica bolted to her feet again and leaned across the table, holding her weight on her arms. Even the great view of cleavage didn't distract from the ice in her words. "Fuck you Browner. That's your problem, you think loyalty is a friendship, you-scratch-my-back kind of thing. That's exactly why you aren't in Harley's league. He's a good leader, not a good player, that's why you read him wrong."

Browner's face hardened as he stood up, facing Jessica. "Sit down. You'd better hear this."

Reluctantly, she sat down. George Alvarez patted her on the arm, but she jerked away, still staring at Browner.

Browner looked at Jeannie Kawai who was trying to appear as small as possible. Startled, Jeannie looked back at Browner, realizing why he was looking at her.

"Tell them how Jones attacked you." He sat down, giving her the floor. She didn't move.

"Well, it really wasn't a big thing, I guess. He was sleeping and I walked in to brief him. When I leaned over to wake him up he started choking me. I guess that's it."

"There's more to it," Browner interjected. "He screamed when he grabbed you, didn't he?"

Jeannie nodded. "Yes, but he apologized later."

Browner waved dismissively. "What did he scream?"

Jeannie breathed in deeply. "'No'—he just kept screaming 'No.'"

George Alvarez stood up. "Jeannie, you said it was no big deal. Was he really choking you?"

Before she could reply, Ted Browner reached across and pulled off the scarf from her neck.

"Look at those bruises. Jones wasn't trying to make out with her. He's going off the deep end. Ask her how she felt just after it happened."

Jessica Williams was squinting at the bruises around Jeannie's neck. Both Commissioner Yeager and General Bradley had their eyes fixed in the same place.

Jeannie cleared her throat nervously. "Well, when I woke him and he grabbed me he was really strong and incredibly intense. He was staring in my eyes as he was choking me. Then Mr. Browner threw some hot coffee on him and he seemed to wake up, kind of. He just stopped, relaxed kind of. Really, it's no big thing. Maybe he was having a bad dream."

Jessica Williams cringed slightly, hoping her concern didn't show on her face.

"Delayed stress syndrome, PTSD," diagnosed Jay Schwartz, adding, "Maybe," after a slight delay. Loraine Hawthorne nodded.

Commissioner Yeager, also a combat veteran, nodded, "Maybe. But does it affect his work? So far he's been right on. We'll just have to watch him carefully, see if starts to crack."

"My God man!" exploded Browner. "You want a borderline psycho running this operation?"

Dr. Schwartz leaned forward. "Harley Jones is a brilliant man. No one can deny that, but he hasn't been at his best for years."

George Alvarez straightened in his chair, now fully awake. "How do you know? You knew him over seven years ago when he was in HRT, correct?"

Dr. Schwartz twisted his head oddly then realigned it to face George Alvarez. "Yes. I was referring to his HRT experience. I was forced to remove him."

George Alvarez raised his eyebrows. "*You* removed him?"

"Ahem, well…" Schwartz started.

"Wait!" interjected Jessica Williams. "Let's get this absolutely correct. Didn't Jones go into a depression after his best friend was killed on an assignment, and didn't you recommend to Jones that he send his friend into the very position that got him killed?"

Dr. Schwartz moved his head back. "That's got nothing to do with this. That was a professional judgment, as was my *recommendation* that Jones be transferred."

"Well," said Jessica Williams, with a slight sneer, "your professional judgment was off in both cases it seems."

At this point General Bradley seemed to take over the meeting. The personality that had dominated ten thousand Marines through Afghanistan radiated from him.

"I think we all agree that the decisions made by Mr. Jones have been exemplary to date. He seems to have a feeling for this Bucheri man. Like any good combat leader, we have to give him his head."

He slapped his palms down on the table and stood up, signaling the end of the meeting. Commissioner Yeager, also a former Marine, seemed to follow his lead, as though still under the command of this powerful presence. The rest rose and filed quietly out, leaving Ted Browner still sitting next to Yeager and Bradley. Jeannie Kawai glanced back anxiously as she closed the door behind her.

Bradley gazed down at Browner. "You're new to this level of operation, aren't you Mr. Browner?"

Browner looked up from his frustrated reverie. "Yes, so?"

Bradley smiled down. "We may be successful against this threat, or we may not. I believe Mr. Jones's methods are the only way, but many very hard questions will be asked later and some very nasty fingers will be pointed. You've made your point with respect to Mr. Jones's state of mind. Perhaps it's best to leave it at that, for the record, if you catch my meaning."

Browner looked quizzical for a moment; then, as the light dawned, he nodded. "Yes, General, I catch your meaning."

* * *

The paratroops at the door snapped to attention as General Bradley passed by their checkpoint on his way out of the building. He needed to think, and the Federal Building was a madhouse, even at this hour. He walked to the center of the plaza and looked up to the stars—looking, but not seeing. "Jones." The name echoed through his mind. After twenty-seven years in commands all over the world, General Bradley had learned to evaluate men and women under stress. The mishandling of the aftermath of the Iraq invasion had been a monumental FUBAR, Fucked Up Beyond All Recognition. Afghanistan wasn't much better in hindsight.

Now, it looked like another clusterfuck, and it was true that Jones didn't seem quite sound—there was a tension in him that wasn't quite right. Second, he wasn't at all convinced that this was a job for a policeman, FBI or not. This wasn't a bunch of religious nuts trapped in

Waco, Texas. Bradley cringed mentally at the thought of Waco. Well, he couldn't hold Jones responsible for that, anyhow. Jones just didn't have the perspective for a military-type assault. This called for a military viewpoint. The General stopped and put his hands on his hips, looking up at the night sky. Perspective. Perspective.

On second thought, maybe Jones did have the perspective, since he had both military and Hostage Rescue Team experience. The General shook his head and resumed his stroll around the plaza, ignoring the sentries as they snapped to attention and saluted. Damn. He liked Jones. Jones was a no-nonsense guy who had called them all right so far. Still, General Bradley hadn't won his campaigns without knowing about defense in depth. He stopped his tour of the plaza by City Hall, reflecting as he watched the people inside working furiously on their computers.

3:10 A.M.
Copley Place

Hassan Bucheri hung up the cellular phone with a firm click and turned to Dr. Ali Kamal.

"That should do it. That man was an incredible pest. This should let all of those in leadership know that they are not untouchable. Let them surround themselves with guards and quiver in their basements."

Ali Kamal nodded, as he knew he should. "Do you think that this will change things—the tactics I mean?"

Bucheri stopped for a moment. "Yes, almost certainly. Jones is what the Americans call a 'loose cannon.' Anyone replacing him would have to be more ... responsible."

"He has outwitted you then?"

Bucheri almost flared but contained himself.

"I have been developing this plan for almost ten years. It is part of my study of Americans. Jones has taken ... unexpected measures. They cannot possibly be legal. Any new commander must necessarily consider what has been done and how this might affect his career. That will be the end of this ... this abrogation of American law."

Ali Kamal was rubbing his eyes, wishing he could wear his glasses rather than these wretched contact lenses. He looked blearily at Bucheri, wanting to change the subject. "This Cobra that you have released, he will be effective?"

Bucheri smiled hugely at some private joke. "Yes, the Cobra is the best. Jones won't stand a chance."

Nadia Nikolsky

The click on the receiver galvanized Nadia. At age forty-five, Nadia Nikolsky was a striking woman, her Slavic features were nicely emphasized by flowing hair, now glossy jet black. At five foot eight inches with slim hips, she could pass for a boy if she had to, but tonight, that wouldn't be necessary. The Boston police had women on the force. She moved over to her closet and opened it. There they were, three military uniforms, one nurse's uniform, and one police uniform. The rest of the closet was filled with civilian clothes for all occasions. Nadia watched herself in the full-length mirror as she dressed, her leg and stomach muscles rippling as she moved. Nadia had never been with the FIS; she probably could have gone in later, but she was too caught up in her athletics. Thousands of hours had gone into training, first as a runner, and then later with the Spetsnaz, the Russian Special Forces. As she moved through the various layers to the top echelon of the Spetsnaz, her training continued. She continued to run and do the long jump in competition, but that was only her cover for leaving the country. At any time, she might receive orders to slip away from the competition and carry out a mission. It was on one of these missions that she had met the man currently calling himself The Fox. She thanked her personal gods for that meeting.

She had been unemployed then, like many Russian soldiers. She spent most of her time sitting in an apartment in St. Petersburg with her aunt, occasionally coaching high school track, until a single phone call two months ago. Now wealth awaited her. Only a single killing too—what luck. A tough one certainly, but only one. What a break.

Spetsnaz officers had always been reluctant to accept women. She had proven them wrong in Chechnya. As a woman, she could pass unmolested through the most dangerous part of the country, using the language skills required of a first-level Spetsnaz operative, including English. She laughed as she thought of the grammatical errors that she had made for Jones and his FBI clowns. Fourteen times she had gone in alone and killed, all for the reward of coaching high school track. She could still remember the filth of some of the men she had had to sleep with, disgusting, degrading. Killing some of them had been a pleasure. A wire, a knife, even bare hands. She had suffered for acceptance and reward. Damn them, damn them all. She was on her own again. Alone and dangerous.

She knew the building, the personnel, the procedures. Jones, the fool, didn't have a chance. She smiled to herself in the mirror as she did up the top buttons on the uniform blouse. Cobra. An appropriate code name, but she would have preferred Panther. It would have matched her dark eyes, her black hair, her heart.

Commissioner Yeager

Commissioner Yeager was startled by the salute from the woman officer as she passed him in the hallway. It wasn't that officers couldn't salute, it was just that they didn't normally. A nice sharp military salute. He only took vague note of her appearance as she went by: black hair, good-looking for sure—but he did notice her sidearm. Most women went for the small pistols which fit into their hands nicely. This woman was tall—not big, but tall—and the revolver was a 41. An old-time man killer, but it was out of favor now and non-regulation. Another time he would have stopped her; only .38 caliber revolvers and 9mm Glocks were allowed. All the officers these days wanted high-capacity 9mm automatics so that they could have eighteen friends in the palm of their hands. He frowned thoughtfully as he stopped at the front desk of the JFK Building.

Nadia Nikolsky

Nadia was almost giggling. It was so easy. The Fox had been right about the briefcase. Everyone she had asked had believed that she had documents for Harley Jones. It was pathetic, they weren't even wearing identity badges inside. Her uniform was her ticket in, and it would be her ticket out.

After she stepped off the elevator on the third floor, Nadia slipped into the women's restroom and carefully placed her briefcase on the wash basin. She flipped up the lid, removed the silencer and placed it on the next wash basin. She was just about to close the lid when another woman walked in. Nadia froze, hoping the woman would ignore the briefcase and the silencer, but one look in the mirror told her that the woman understood immediately what these tools were. Nadia sprang backwards thrusting out her right leg violently in a vicious side kick. The kick missed the woman but connected with the door, slamming it shut loudly despite its hydraulic damper.

The woman stepped inside Nadia's kick and was behind her now. To Nadia's astonishment the woman grabbed her by the hair and swept her left leg from under her, sending her flying down hard on the tiles. Despite years of judo training, the fall knocked the wind out of Nadia. The other woman turned to run, but Nadia swiveled and scissored the woman's legs out from underneath her. This irritating woman still had fight in her as she fell to the ground and turned to claw Nadia. That was her last mistake. Nadia grabbed the woman's outstretched hand rather than avoiding it and brought her own leg high up in the air. Then once, twice, three times she brought the heel of her boot down hard on the woman's head until finally there was a sickening thud.

Breathing hard now, gasping for air, Nadia scrambled up, pulling out the .41 caliber revolver in case someone had heard the struggle. She forced herself to calm her breathing. Her hearing was animal-sensitive. There was no alarm. Quickly now, she screwed the silencer onto the threaded barrel of the gun. The .41 fired a subsonic round, so there would be no high-velocity crack. A small amount of gas would escape from between the cylinder and the barrel, but that couldn't be avoided. She couldn't go to a .22 caliber—they were not good enough killers, and none of the larger automatics silenced well enough. The .41 was the best. With a grunt, she gave the silencer one last twist; then, keeping the revolver in her right hand, she closed the briefcase and picked it up with her other hand.

Carefully, she opened the door, exposing only her eye. One direction was clear. Quickly, but still quietly, she opened the door and looked in the other direction. Still clear. More confidently now, she walked down the familiar corridor. The whole reason for infiltrating the building had been to find out where Jones's office was. All else was secondary. As she reached the corner, Nadia squatted briefly and put the briefcase down, followed by her hat. She rose slowly and moved to the corner. Then, exposing an absolute minimum of her face, she looked very slowly around the corner.

Just as slowly, she moved back. Damn, there was a guard there, a soldier, and he looked alert with a rifle in his hands. Normally, with sights on the pistol, she could easily have killed him at fifty feet, but the sights had been ground off so that the barrel could be threaded. The pistol was an unfamiliar shooter, too.

Just then, Nadia heard the bell of the elevator. Someone was getting off at this floor.

Time was running out. Hastily, Nadia put her hat on and picked up the briefcase. She held the pistol in her right hand and rested the briefcase like a tray on it as she started towards the soldier. Immediately he noticed her then seemed to relax. With one hand still on the pistol grip of his M-4 he held up his hand in a "stop" gesture. Nadia kept going. Now the fifty foot distance was down to forty. The solider looked puzzled at the lack of response. Under other circumstances, he would have shouted "Halt," but part of his orders required that he keep things quiet so that the Assistant Director could get some sleep. Finally, when she was at thirty feet, he made his decision and started to raise the rifle to a firing position. No one could misunderstand that.

Thirty feet was close enough for Nadia. She had already cocked the big revolver. The first shot sounded no louder than someone slamming a book shut. Slightly off, the large bullet caught the soldier in the shoulder, spinning him around. Nadia ran up lightly, now holding her briefcase by her side with her left hand, her revolver in her right. The soldier was sagging against the wall, still holding his rifle weakly in one hand. Nadia put down her briefcase carefully and grabbed hold of the rifle with her left hand. Calmly, she put the silencer against the soldier's head, moved to one side so that the bullet would land somewhere down the hallway, and pulled the trigger. The soldier slumped to the floor.

Gently, she put the rifle on the body. She ignored the smear of blood and brains on the wall. From the direction of the elevator, she heard steps.

Commissioner Yeager

Commissioner Yeager had decided to ask at the reception desk about the woman officer that had saluted him. The desk had informed him that she was a messenger from the temporary police Command Post across the plaza in City Hall. But two things were wrong with this. The first was that he probably would have noticed her there before. He always tried to remember the faces, even if he couldn't remember the names of his officers. The second thing was the time. At the midnight briefing everyone had been told that Jones was going to sleep until 4:00 a.m., but it was barely 3:30 now. It was just ... odd.

He had decided to go up to Jones's office to find out what was going on. He stepped off the elevator and walked down the corridor. Just as he turned the corner, he saw the soldier dead, his blood smeared in a ghastly streak along the wall. He saw the woman officer reaching for Jones's door. Her head snapped up, trapping him in her dark eyes. He reached for his service weapon.

Nadia cursed to herself as she swiveled to meet this new threat. Her first shot missed; she could see the hole in the wall slightly to Yeager's left. Her second shot fired just as his weapon cleared leather. Her pistol bucked as the massive bullet left on its assigned mission. Less than a tenth of a second later, the police general spun like a child's top and fell to the floor, face down. The halls were silent.

It was time. Nadia flipped open the revolver cylinder with a practiced motion and ejected the spent and unspent rounds. They gave a small tinkle as they hit the floor. In less than three seconds she had reloaded with the speed-loader. With another practiced motion, a sideways flick of the wrist, the revolver cylinder snicked into place. Ready.

Cu Chi

Time passed, but the smell of the diesel remained in Harley Jones's nostrils as he lay on his cot. Diesel for running the M113, diesel for burning the shitters—the half barrels that everyone crapped in, diesel for washing down the tracks, diesel for everything. He was at Cu Chi, the base camp for the 25th Infantry Division. They called themselves the Tropic Lightning Division and had been based in Hawaii before the war. It was February 1969, raining and crappy. The Viet Cong sappers, the Dac Cong, had crawled from their tunnels the night before and blown up fourteen CH-47 Chinook helicopters. Rumor had it that General Williamson's ass was in a frying pan. General Williamson was commander of the 25th and every one of his officers was trying to find a way to turn defeat into victory. Jones had been sent to Cu Chi a week earlier, following a dope trail that led to a whorehouse run by the Korean officers' wives. Located just outside the gates of Cu Chi, it was typical Asian subtlety: a tea house which was really a whorehouse which was really a dope distribution center. Would CID, the Army Criminal Investigation Division, do anything? Could they do anything without getting burned for upsetting American allies, the Koreans? A typical Vietnam-style layered corruption scandal. Jones groaned as he lay on his bunk. What about what he had done, posing as an officer? Would that get him burned? Was the evidence valid? Did anyone give a flying fuck?

The screen door on the hooch slammed and someone shouted "ten hut." Like everyone else, Jones scrambled to a position of attention. Cu Chi was a hornet's nest after last night's fiasco. There was no telling what this was, but Jones knew it didn't concern him. He was just an investigator from CID.

"Jones?"

What the hell? "Here, sir." Jones kept staring rigidly forward, willing this voice and the person behind it to disappear.

Someone wearing a tiger striped uniform stepped in front of him. Jones kept his eyes looking straight forward, into the man's chest. A tiger striped camouflage pattern could spell a number of things, a soldier from the Vietnamese Army, or maybe an advisor to the ARVNs. Then again, it could be Special Forces.

"We meet again, Jones," the voice said.

Jones looked down at the man's boots, still shiny despite the rain. It was Major Bear, "Eager Beaver Bear." A Special Forces officer who had carefully avoided going into the bush despite claiming to be a fantastic tracker, a full-blooded Sioux.

"Do you remember me, Jones?" said the boots.

"Yes sir! You assigned me to Recon when I checked in at Da Nang."

The voice warmed with anticipation. "Well, Jones, I haven't forgotten you and your linguistic skills."

Jones groaned silently. Learning Vietnamese for Special Forces had been a waste of his time, but it had been useful for getting him into CID, where Vietnamese speakers were rare. Finally, he had gotten out of Recon and away from all the cowboys that despised him, away from the danger of ambush, away from the bugs, the rot, the pain. Jones could sense that something unpleasant was coming. Eager Beaver would do anything to advance his career.

"I'm with CID now, sir. I'm out of Special Forces. I'm not even assigned to this base. I'm in the middle of an investigation."

Major Bear positively purred.

"Jones, you wouldn't be trying to crap out on me would you?"

Jones raised his head and looked up into Major Bear's eyes. "Major, I don't work for you or anyone on this base."

Major Bear's grin widened. "You are aware, aren't you, Sergeant Jones, that anyone on a base can be co-opted if the base is under attack?"

Jones shook his head, glaring at Major Bear. Major Bear's grin changed to a thin-lipped expression of displeasure. "Jones, if this were the old Army, I'd have your ass for 'silent contempt.'"

Jones continued to glare at the Major. They stared at each other until Major Bear finally said, "Jones, you're going into the tunnels."

And so it was. Sergeant Harley Jones, who suffered from low-level claustrophobia, found himself in an M113, bouncing over the bomb craters towards the infamous Ho Bo Woods. Sergeant Randy Ellis of the 1st Engineer Battalion Tunnel Rat Team was briefing him with great enthusiasm. The rest of his squad, all distinctive for their small size, tried to relax as the armored personnel carrier rocked towards the objective. He had seen the patch on their chests. It read *Non Gratum Anus Rodentum* and showed a rat holding a pistol and a flashlight. When he asked Ellis about it, Ellis answered, "Hey, not worth a rat's ass." Jones shook his head.

Ellis continued with his briefing as the M113 lurched over another obstacle. "Some grunts saw a V.C. run over a hill. They followed him and he'd disappeared. One of them was smart enough to keep the rest away from the tracks. They followed the tracks to a covered hole. The smart thing was, their platoon sergeant pulled them off, so the gooks don't know we're onto them. We're going to jump into their hole and kill 'em. I love it." He smiled and waved towards the rest of his squad. "We all do." Jones looked at the rest of the team. They seemed frightened.

Just then, the M113 shuddered to a stop and the back ramp squealed down. Jones shook his head. This was not the stealth that he had learned at Ranger School and practiced in Recon. This had all the subtlety of a mailed fist. A bullet twanged into the interior of the M113 and ricocheted several times before coming to rest in a carton of C rations. The driver screamed at them and they ran out and took cover in a bomb crater.

Jones yelled at Ellis, "I thought this area was secure."

Ellis shrugged. "They've always got a few tunnels interconnecting to spider holes that protect any entrance. If they knew that we were on to them, they'd just abandon this section. Then we'd have more trouble finding them."

Jones shook his head. He didn't want to find anybody. "Why am I here?"

Ellis looked surprised. "Didn't they tell you?"

Jones shook his head.

Ellis smiled. "We're going to catch us a gook, then you're going to interrogate him."

Jones pointed over towards the Kit Carson scout assigned to the team. The Vietnamese was looking back at him. "Oh, Pham. We don't trust him. We don't trust any of the *Chieu Hois*. Once a red, always a red."

Jones wasn't going to tell Ellis that Special Forces had been using the *Chieu Hois*, ex Viet Cong, for years with great success. Instead he asked, "Have you ever done this before?"

Ellis shrugged. "Naw, we just kill 'em. You know, it's dark down there. You use a knife and, well, it ain't really classy."

Jones felt his throat constrict. "Why are we questioning this gook that we catch?"

Ellis gave him a disdainful look. "So we can find out where the sappers are. The General wants them dug out."

"How are we going to catch a gook?" Jones asked.

Ellis smiled faintly. "We were told that you knew how to catch gooks. That's your job."

Later they had worked out a plan that almost made sense—almost. Jones put black camouflage paint over his face while Ellis listed the hazards.

"Well, there's the step-and-a-half, you know about those?" Jones cringed: he knew about the bamboo viper that was so toxic that its victims supposedly died in a step and a half. Ellis continued, "Well, they rig those up so they'll fall on you. Just freeze. Don't piss it off. Then whisper, don't shout." Jones nodded.

Ellis looked at Jones closely. "Hey, you OK?"

Jones shook his head. "No, but go on." The sweat was dripping down his face and his t-shirt was soaked.

Ellis shrugged and continued, "Well, there's all sorts of annoying shit like fire ants, big mothers, and these chiggers that get under your skin and itch like hell, but don't worry about them, it's the gooks that'll get ya. If it ain't booby traps, well, sometimes they build false walls and stab you through the wall with a spear. A guy over in C Company got it that way, but he didn't die. Anyhow, sometimes they get you when you go through the trapdoors. They let the first guy get halfway through then strangle him with a wire. Blocks the tunnel, real bitch to get the dude out. Anyway, the scariest things are the water traps—sometimes the rats hang around those. You know what those are for?"

Jones shook his head. Ellis looked disgusted. "Shit man, you don't know shit. They're to keep out gas and smoke. We throw in CS to force 'em out, or smoke to find out where the other tunnel exits are and it all gets stopped by these traps, see, like a U trap in your sink. These gooks are smart."

His hand waved over the blasted terrain. "You see, up here, these are only the first-level tunnels. Some grunts come across these and blast them. Man, they haven't done jack shit. These things go down three levels. The traps keep the gas out. You have to swim through the trap and hope it isn't a dead end. Man, that'll give you a rush. But when you get somewhere, well, you wouldn't believe some of the shit they have down there. I once saw a hospital with a generator." He shook his head at the memory.

Then he looked up at Jones. "You ready?"

Jones said, "Never, but orders are orders."

Ellis nodded, "Ain't that the truth. Now, that 22 of yours, be cool and keep it on safe. I'll start at point and we'll go as fast as we can. If I ask you for your weapon, or I fire six, you give me yours, got it?"

Jones nodded. Ellis continued, "Now, they shouldn't have any booby traps 'cause we're not chasing anyone. If someone calls out in gook, you answer them, OK?" Jones nodded again.

Minutes later, with a speed that terrified Jones, they were crawling through the tunnel. Normally the tunnel rats would use flashlights, but today they were imitating the Cong, so there would be no lights. As Jones wriggled behind Ellis his skin tingled with the heat and moisture.

The hot air clawed at his lungs, draining his strength. Even at one hundred and forty pounds Jones felt too big for the tunnels.

Six men including Jones had entered the tunnel. To keep track of their path, the last man unreeled a small roll of communication wire. Jones couldn't help but think about Hansel and Gretel having their trail eaten. At the first branch, perhaps fifteen meters along, Ellis turned and whispered, "branch right." Jones passed the word back. The last man would hand the com wire reel to the next man and then stay at this branch, defending the escape route with knife and revolver. Twenty minutes later, Ellis was still leading. They had passed two other branches and left men there, so they were down to only three men. Ellis turned back in and whispered in an excited tone.

"There—up ahead. Can you smell them?"

The third man, Watson, crawled up partially over Jones. Jones found the closeness terrifying. Watson whispered hoarsely, "Yeah, and something else. Paraffin oil maybe?"

Somehow, Jones knew that Ellis was nodding in the dark. Ellis started crawling again. Jones followed him by keeping in touch with his boot. Again Ellis stopped. Jones moved up and again Watson moved up partially over Jones.

"I smell something different," whispered Ellis. Jones could smell it too. Over the stench of incredibly stale sweat and Nuck Mam, there was something else, something having to do with machinery that he couldn't quite name.

Ellis whispered again, "I can feel a small breeze. Watson, you stay at the hole, but get turned around and ready to go. Jones and I will go in."

"Got it," whispered Watson, even more hoarsely than before.

Ellis moved on only about five more meters when suddenly his feet disappeared. Jones recoiled but suddenly there was a dim light ahead. Hesitantly, Jones moved forward into the light. He crawled into the cavern and then stood up, awed by the five-meter-high ceiling that was dimly visible in the flickering lamps. Watson moved out behind them and got ready to dive back in, the com wire reel in his hand. He gave three tugs and got two back before whispering, "Secure," in the muffled dampness of the cavern.

Ellis smiled, his teeth gleaming in the dim light. "I'm going to turn on the light. Cover one eye." All of them covered one eye to try and preserve their night vision when the flashlight came on, but Jones forgot and lowered his hand when he saw where they were.

"Jesus Christ," he said softly. There were three disassembled 105 howitzers along with stacks of stored weapons against the cavern wall. It was inconceivable to Jones that the Viet Cong could have disassembled the artillery pieces and moved them into the caves. Even Ellis seemed stunned.

"Fucking unreal," was his quiet response.

From the far side of the cavern they both heard the hiss of cloth against the hard clay of the earth. Ellis was starting to point his revolver in that direction when an AK-47 fired from the other end of the cavern, filling the air with green tracers. Just before ducking, Jones had seen the Viet Cong's face: a tiny woman with long hair, she couldn't have been over sixteen. Ellis fired six shots into the dimness, and Jones could hear her changing magazines. Faint cries of Vietnamese were coming from the tunnel at the far end of the cavern.

Ellis grabbed him. "They've shot my light. We've got to cut fuck. Let's go."

Watson had already disappeared up the hole. Ellis was right behind him and Jones brought up the rear, ramming his head into Ellis's ass at the tunnel mouth.

"Give us cover fire," he hissed. "Use the fucking 22."

Another fusillade of green tracer fire swept over their heads. Jones fired twice in their direction then followed Ellis into the tunnel. Darkness clawed at him while sweat oozed from his body as they scrambled ahead. Pain from his knees and elbows burned through Jones. Ellis and his tunnel rats had pads. Just before they reached the first curve Jones caught up to Ellis. Since he couldn't move forward, he dropped onto his back and looked back to see something blocking the dim light from the cavern. In desperation, he fired three rounds from his .22, the *phut* from the silencer making the shots sound ineffectual. Ellis moved ahead and grabbed Jones, dragging him around the bend. Jones was almost around when an AK-47 fired down the tunnel with an enormous thunder and flash of light. He felt something like a bear trap slam on his foot.

"Shit," he cried. "I'm hit."

"Where?" Ellis called back.

"In my foot," Jones answered, his voice tight with the pain.

"Keep crawling, we can't turn around," Ellis called back. "You don't need your foot, man—gut it out."

And so it went for an eternity. Jones would fire back whenever he stopped behind Ellis. Once Ellis fired over Jones, having somehow loaded his .38 revolver. No one else fired at them during the long crawl back, but they were there. Jones could hear them. But then he realized why they weren't firing. They knew he was wounded. They were talking about taking a prisoner. He called to Ellis,

"They want me. They want a prisoner."

"Fuck 'em." Ellis answered. "Tell them you're only a sergeant. Maybe they'll throw you back?"

Jones giggled despite the pain burning up his leg. He giggled at the absurdity of it as Ellis moved a little ahead. Then a strong hand grabbed his ankle.

* * *

Harley Jones woke in a sweat. The room was pitch black and something was wrong. No, there was light, a slim slice of light from underneath the door, broken by two dark shadows: someone's feet. He listened and then heard it—the door latch. It was being opened very quietly, very slowly. Would the CTU people open the door that way? Then he remembered Jeannie Kawai. Yes, she would be careful. He sat up, clad only in his underwear. The door swung open quietly. His cot was on the side of the room, out of view behind the door when it was opened. The door swung toward him; he heard the click of a hammer being cocked and a long silencer appeared.

He roared a primeval call of combat and fear as he kicked the door, knocking the gun out of the assassin's hand. In a single move, the assassin closed the door and dove for the gun. In the briefest flash of light as she had closed the door, Jones had seen her outline. A woman. Jones moved on bare feet away from the cot to the desk which faced the office door. Listening, listening, trying to still his breathing, he found his Glock on the chair and slowly eased it out of its holster. He remained there, knowing that time was on his side. Then again, he thought, she's probably better at this. A better shot, better reactions. Jones gritted his teeth. He needed an edge. Then it came to him: muzzle flashes. Slowly, ever so slowly, he picked up his agenda book with his left hand and threw it against the door.

Nothing. Jones felt his face flushing in fear. Well, there was another way. He would provide the muzzle flash. Holding his Glock as far out from his side as he could, he pulled the trigger. Immediately he saw her in his peripheral vision. She was within inches of him, gun hand back, other hand forward, feeling like a blind man towards the corner that he had fired into. She was already swiveling the cannon in her hands as he jumped at her, wrapping his arms around her. For just a moment, they were frozen as he squeezed her in a bear hug, trapping her arms and lifting her off the ground. He felt her back arch and then her whole body whipped forward. A lightning bolt lanced into his brain and he almost lost consciousness from her forehead smash. As his grip loosened, the second smash came directly on his nose, breaking it with a snap he heard more through his skull than his ears. Distantly, he felt himself losing his grip and falling back on the desk. There was a flash of light and the roar of a gun.

4:30 A.M.
JFK Federal Building

General Bradley leaned over, disregarding the blood still trickling down the face. "How is he?"

The Army surgeon looked up. "He'll be all right, but we'll need to work on his nose later. Should be fit for full duty in a week."

Bradley straightened up. "He needs to be fully operational in two hours. Am I right Mr. Jones?"

Jones nodded weakly.

General Bradley turned to the doctor. "Give him something for the pain and don't worry about his nose. We've got bigger problems than that."

Almost as an afterthought the General added, "And doctor, for Mr. Jones, nothing that will affect his thinking, understood?"

The doctor nodded, walked over to a portable cabinet and filled a syringe. "Toradol," he explained to no one in particular, "as good as morphine but non-addictive. We'll have you feeling ... well, OK. Real soon now."

Jones signaled for General Bradley to lean closer to him. The General complied and Jones whispered hoarsely in his ear, "I've had it with this shit. We'll need better security at the front. We'll use Bureau people. It won't be so easy to BS them. And, while you're at it, send a SEAL team out to the pirate radio station. I'm really tired of their broadcasts." Jones seemed to slump a bit. "We'll pay the bill later."

General Bradley knew what Jones meant. There would be a lot of bills for this operation, and he was happy that final responsibility would fall on Jones's shoulders and not his. Congress and the press were going to go absolutely berserk when they found out what had been done. The Supreme Court would probably spontaneously combust. He smiled a bit. Shutting down the pirate radio station was the last thing that they could do but hadn't done yet. It had become a symbol of their attempt to live within the law, the last fruit in the bowl. Jones was pulling out all the stops. Shutting it down would be illegal as hell, but then so much of what they were doing was outrageously illegal anyhow. It was too bad that he hadn't put the SEALs on alert. Well, Bradley sighed to himself, there were a lot of lessons to be learned from this miserable experience.

Jones winced as the doctor injected him, but the doctor had already turned to his next patient before Jones could complain. The General waited patiently while the doctor looked at the enormous bruise on Commissioner Yeager's right side.

"How do you feel?" the doctor asked as Yeager flinched from a prodding finger.

"Terrible. Like I was kicked by a horse."

The doctor looked up impatiently. "Can you be somewhat more specific? I've never seen anyone who has been shot at close range while wearing a bulletproof vest." The doctor was actually lying, just a bit. He had seen plenty of men who had been injured while wearing flak jackets, but he wanted Yeager to talk.

Yeager looked down at himself. "Well, doctor, it feels kind of like it looks. I get sharp pains when I move."

"Any feeling of pressure?"

Yeager thought for a moment. "No."

"Trouble breathing? Spitting blood?" asked the doctor as he continued prodding.

Yeager looked slightly squeamish. "No."

The doctor straightened up. "OK. We'll take you for X-rays now. Almost certainly you have some broken ribs. We'll check for internal bleeding. If the fractures are severe then bleeding is very likely. You should get a nice two-week holiday out of this."

Commissioner Yeager grimaced as the doctor took one last gentle prod. "Doctor, the same treatment for me as Mr. Jones. We've got work to do."

The doctor looked at the General then back at Yeager. "You know, this isn't a Rocky movie. I'm sure you can be replaced. If you've got internal bleeding we'll have to operate."

Yeager eyed the doctor, a full Army Colonel, steadily. "Colonel, so that you can understand the situation, we're right in the middle of an assault. You don't change commanders then."

The doctor shrugged. "It's your ass, Commissioner, but if you have severe internal bleeding, you're going to be one very sick man before noon today."

Yeager nodded. "If I start splitting blood, we'll do lunch, OK?"

The doctor couldn't help a small smile. "Roger that." Then the doctor straightened up. "Oh, I almost forgot. Your wife's outside. She almost shot me to get in here. A formidable woman."

Eddy smiled. "Formidable?" Barbara, normally cheerful and friendly, became a tigress when either he or their daughter was threatened. Eddy could imagine her standing on her toes, leaning into the doctor's face as she fondled her pistol. "Formidable," yes indeed. That's my woman. Woman! Eddy straightened abruptly, then stopped as a blaze of pain flashed along his right side.

"Doctor, what about the woman I shot?" Yeager asked.

"Oh yes, what a foul temper that one had. Cursed in several languages. Anyhow, your bullet went into her leg and broke her femur. She was in considerable pain when Mr. Browner's medics took her away, but she was in no danger. Otherwise I wouldn't have released her."

Commissioner Yeager and General Bradley exchanged meaningful glances.

The doctor had his own question. "Commissioner, your bulletproof jacket. I've never seen one like it. Very light. What's it called?"

Yeager smiled weakly, as though his mouth was the only part of him that didn't hurt. "Second Chance."

The doctor smiled faintly. "Very appropriate. You're lucky that it was a glancing shot."

Commissioner Yeager nodded, but his mind was already wondering what Browner's interrogation team was doing to Nadia Nikolsky. Like his swimming coach used to say, "No pain, no gain."

Nadia Nikolsky

There was blackness, and time had passed, she knew. Lots of time—an eternity since her capture, months, maybe years. Her memories were vague now that so much time had passed. The injection—she remembered that there had been an injection. Where had it been? Her arm? No, Yes, Maybe. It was so confusing. She felt as though she were floating in the darkness. Was this sensory deprivation? She had heard of sensory deprivation once, but no mention of pain had been made, and she was in pain—pain beyond belief. She couldn't sleep, hadn't slept forever. She was floating in hell, her burnt skin was peeling off but she couldn't touch it, there was nothing to touch, nothing to smell, nothing to hear. Now she was freezing, bone deep freezing; she would be dead within minutes, she knew. She wanted to curl up, but she couldn't move, although nothing was holding her. It was infuriating to be so helpless. Nadia had always been in control. Now she was in hell—the hell of her Orthodox grandmother—and she had no control. Nadia wept but could feel no tears. Nadia screamed and screamed and screamed, but there was no sound in hell.

CHAPTER 23: SUNDAY DAWN

Private John Miller

The rap of metal on the combat locked door bored through Private Miller's sleep as he lay on the floor of the command M113 armored personnel carrier. They had pulled off to the side on Brookline Avenue with the Band-Aid, the medic's APC, around 2:00 a.m. Now, even though it was dim inside the APC, Miller knew that it was morning. He raised his head up blearily. Perez, the radio watch, sat slumped over the radio. The Captain was curled on his sleeping bag in the front next to Hardy, the driver. Miller groaned, feeling like an old man, as he got up. He gave Perez a shove to wake him up as he moved past him to the door. The Captain would toast Perez if he caught him sleeping on radio watch.

The hammering was driving Miller crazy, like an unremitting hangover headache. Before unlocking the door, he looked out the rear gun port. It was one of the medics. Miller unbolted the door. As the door was opening, he could hear the medic babbling in a high-pitched voice.

"Hey man, did you hear the explosion? Hey man, ka-boom. Hey man, did you hear the explosion?"

Miller could hear the Captain unzipping his sleeping bag. He knew the Captain wasn't going to put up with any half-baked report.

"Look man, calm down. When was the explosion and where was it?"

The medic, a short fat man with a cherubic face, looked stunned for a moment, then pointed down the street.

"There man, just now, like right down the street."

The Captain pushed past Miller and stepped onto the street, rubbing his eyes. He turned in the direction the medic was gesturing and tensed like a pointing bird dog. Miller followed his gaze. He caught only a glimpse of a gray dusty dirt cloud about three blocks down the street, because the Captain pushed him back into the vehicle with "Saddle up, Miller, get on the fifty."

Miller climbed up through the hatch and cocked the .50 caliber machine gun as Hardy, the driver, spun the APC on its tracks. Down in the APC, Miller could hear the Captain trying to call someone on the net.

The Captain must have been whipping Hardy like a tired horse, Miller reflected as the APC shrieked down the streets, its treads clattering on the Boston pavement.

Hiro Yamoto

Hiro Yamoto sucked air through his teeth in an expression of disgust. There wasn't enough Semtex, the Czechoslovakian fast blasting explosive, to properly set off the ammonium nitrate. Even then, it would have worked, but the water main was at least two feet lower than he had been told. Well, instead of a geyser, there was now a flood welling out of the ten foot crater he had blasted. It would have to do. There was one more water main to destroy and they would be done. Years of training, mental and physical, would be rewarded—not, as he wished, with a new Japanese order, but at least with a resounding personal success.

His observation post on the roof alerted him with two whistle blasts. He looked down the street to the North, but he couldn't see well through the dust cloud. Something was coming. It looked vaguely like a truck. Three blasts on his whistle and his team moved to their ambush positions. One group of four moved behind a large step van that they had used to block the road. This would also be their escape vehicle. It held the rest of their ammonium nitrate and Semtex. His other group of three moved behind the parked cars on one side, about fifty feet up the street. It would be a classic L-shaped ambush, with either group capable of firing relatively freely without fear of hitting the other. He ran and joined his best friend "Tiny" Takahashi behind a silver BMW. Tiny was a monster for a Japanese at two hundred and ten pounds of solid muscle and bone. Tiny held a sawed off shotgun with an extended magazine, a souvenir from the Boston gun shop, Spiders. The menacing weapon looked like a toy in his hands. Hiro pulled out his Colt 45—another great "man stopper," the salesman had told him. If ever anyone needed a man stopper, it would be now, he thought.

As the vehicle got closer, its sound changed in pitch and it slowed down. It wasn't a truck, Hiro was certain of that. The vehicle had slowed down considerably now. He didn't dare look in case he was seen. An ambush depended on complete surprise. A drop of sweat rolled down his face. He shook his head to send it flying. It was almost time. He cocked the pistol and tasted the metal of the whistle in his mouth. He could feel everything around him, hear his pulse in his ears. This was the awareness, the battle fever that he had read about. Since his cause, a revolutionary Japan, had died, he had been a *ronin*, a *samurai* without a master. Now, for the first time, he was *samurai*, and he would serve his master or die. It was a wonderful feeling.

Hiro waited until the vehicle was right next to the BMW. It was moving at a crawl now. One sharp blast on the whistle and he rose to battle.

Private John Miller

Over the engine whine, Private Miller heard the whistle to his right. He snapped his head over to see two men rising up behind a car. Orientals by the look of them; but Miller didn't pause to think. He started to swivel the fifty as the big guy fired. Miller's right hand burst into flaming pain, and he dropped back through the hatch into the APC.

"Ambush right, ambush right!" he screamed. Before the Captain could give an order, Hardy slammed on the brakes and slammed the APC into reverse. The sudden movement threw Perez, Captain Thorn, and Miller to the deck. The APC gears shrieked as Hardy backed in reverse as fast as the APC could go. Miller pulled himself up by his left hand. "I'm hit," he said. The captain looked at him in the dim night and nodded. "There were two of them, at least, maybe more, just to the right of us. No uniforms. Gooks." He had heard his father use the word "gook." It seemed to refer to all Asians.

The captain swung towards Hardy,

"Hardy, can you see them? Chinese. At least two on the right."

Hardy turned his face slightly, to be heard better.

"Yes sir. There's four really. Hiding behind two cars about thirty meters down. They've just got small arms. Shall we go get 'em?" Against the civilian vehicles where the ambushers were hiding the M113 could be used as a gigantic battering ram. They would be crushed.

"Do it."

Hiro was aghast. It was some sort of armored car. There was only one way to get it, with the Semtex explosive in the step van. He turned to the others. "Give me covering fire. I'm going for the Semtex."

Hardy yelled, "Hey! Gook in the open. Running for the van. About fifty meters dead ahead."

The Captain looked at Perez, but Perez's eyes were wide with fear. His hand was rigidly gripping the fold-down table holding the radio.

Miller flexed his right hand. He could move it, even though it hurt like hell. The Captain was about to climb up, but Miller pushed in front: "I'll get it." He climbed out without looking down. Grunting with pain, he levered himself to a position behind the butterfly triggers. There the gook was, just behind the van in the middle of the street, trying to get in. Miller decided to ignore the machine gun sites as the hornet sound of buckshot flew past his head. He levered the gun slightly to the right and gave a burst to the group at the right, just to keep their heads down. Then he loosed a long burst at the van, walking the tracers from right to left.

Normally, modern high explosives like C-4 or Semtex will not respond to impact. Ammonium nitrate is even less explosive. Blasting caps, however, are very sensitive to impact. One armor piercing round punched through the side of the step van as though it was made of paper. The impact caused the bullet to tumble and deviate slightly from its course. The spinning bullet hit a box of blasting caps which was resting on the Semtex. In less than a thousandth of a second, the Semtex was exploding. In less than a hundredth of a second, the Semtex had started the two hundred pounds of ammonium nitrate blasting.

Hiro's ammonium nitrate was quite high grade, having been purchased from a chemical company, and it exploded efficiently. The first explosion, the one had that blasted the crater, had been relatively contained because most of the explosive was underground. It had been placed underground by the simple expedient of opening a manhole cover and placing the ammonium nitrate down into the drainage sewer. One of the team had then dropped down and placed the Semtex, blasting caps, and fuse. That explosion had been what is called "tamped" in the demolition business: it was contained. The second explosion was not tamped or contained in any way. The shock wave killed the four team members behind the truck and Hiro Yamato instantly.

Private Miller, eighty meters away, was hit by the shock wave less than half a second later. For just a moment, he felt incredible pain as the overpressure ruptured his ear drums, then he felt nothing. The same shock wave rolled over cars parked on both sides of the street as it moved outward. Windows were blown inwards for three blocks in each direction down the street. It would later be determined that over two hundred injuries and five civilian deaths were caused by those glass shards.

Roughly ten seconds after the explosion, Tiny Takahashi, the last survivor of the unit, discovered that he had been pinned at the legs by the silver BMW when it had rolled over. At the same time, the survivors in the APC were recovering from the overpressure of the blast. Captain Thorn touched his face and found blood flowing from his nose as he pulled himself upright. Private Miller had dropped down into the APC. It took only one look to know that he was dead. Captain Thorn turned to Hardy and tried to tell him to drop the ramp, but either he couldn't talk, or Hardy couldn't hear. In his present confused state, the Captain couldn't tell which. Finally, Hardy seemed to understand and the ramp started to drop. Captain Thorn knew that he should hear a whine, but he didn't. As the light filled the interior, he picked up an M-4 rifle and stumbled down the ramp. Shaking his head, he tried to orient himself. Then he realized that the APC had been facing the enemy.

Captain Thorn was beyond wondering what type of weapon the enemy had used to devastate the APC crew. If he had been more coherent, he would have realized that there was no hole in the vehicle. Then again, if he had been more coherent, he would have realized that he should lock and load his rifle. He thought of neither, as he shuffled down the center of the street. He could only gape at the ruin, which was unlike any he had ever seen. He was in another world, surreal, with automobiles on their backs, their wheels spinning, shattered store fronts, and bodies in the street—even occasional body parts.

As he walked down the street, he recovered somewhat and started looking to the left and right. A wrecked vehicle in the road caused him to change course along the right side. There he came across a curious sight: a huge oriental man, probably Japanese, according to his facial structure, pinned by an overturned BMW. Something ironic, Captain Thorn thought dimly, something funny about a Jap being pinned by a German BMW. Then, abruptly, it wasn't funny. This was one of them. Carefully now, holding his unloaded rifle at his hip, he moved towards the man.

Tiny Takahashi was enraged by this trick of fate that had left him trapped, at the mercy of his enemy, to face the final ignominy: capture. He closed his eyes briefly to compose himself for his final act, to make Hiro proud of him. He could see the soldier, grinding rocks and dust beneath his boots as he came closer.

Tiny reached under his shirt and pulled out his knife, the *tanto*, admiring the curve of the blade for the last time. The knife was a gift from Hiro. The soldier croaked something that could have been almost anything; the man's voice was so hoarse. It was unfortunate that he would have to do this like a woman, across his throat, but it was better this way, more reliable. He couldn't take the chance that he might pass out. He had no friend to swing the big blade and do him the final honor of *seppuku*.

* * *

Captain Thorn yelled, "Stop!" but he was ignored by the Japanese. He thought of shooting, but the man was clearly trapped. With a smooth motion, the man brought up his blade in both his hands and stabbed himself in throat, then he jerked the blade to the side, cutting a jugular vein as well as the carotid artery. A jet of red blood shot up into the air. Captain Thorn stared as the man carefully placed the blade on his chest and folded his hands, shaking only slightly. Thorn continued to stare as the man bled to death, not more than five feet from him. When the bleeding stopped, Captain Thorn slipped down to a sitting position, resting his back against the iron railing, still watching the man.

When Hardy found him a few minutes later, Captain Thorn looked up and said, "You won't believe who we're fighting." Hardy ignored the Captain's words as he helped him back to the APC. Miller, Perez, and now the Captain—they were all wrecked.

Hassan Bucheri

Hassan Bucheri woke as always, instantly awake, listening. Hearing nothing, sensing nothing, he pulled his pistol from underneath his pillow and moved to the large picture window. There, he breathed deeply and looked down on Boston, his town. Dr. Ali Kamal came out from his bedroom and paused, but Bucheri continued to watch the city. Dr. Kamal wasn't surprised by the weapon; Bucheri was always armed, even in his pajamas.

Dr. Kamal moved up next to Bucheri. Together they looked over Boston. Finally, Kamal asked, "What do you see?"

Bucheri pulled up a chair and turned back to the view. "I see a refugee camp."

"A refugee camp?"

Bucheri nodded, rocking back and forth. "I see women cooking, cooking on kerosene stoves, children playing in the dust, men talking in the coffee shop."

Dr. Kamal was wide awake now. "Yes?"

"It's sunrise and out of the sunrise comes a whisper." He paused, breathing harder. "The whisper, it turns to a shriek, and then a flash and a roar." He rocked back, eyes clenched shut, then jumped to his feet pressing his face and hands against the cool glass.

"I see flames, Ali, flames, beautiful flames. I see the vengeance of God, Allah in all his glory. These Christians believe in an eye for an eye. Let them reap what they have sown. My mother burned before my eyes. Today they will live her pain, my pain, a thousand times over."

He turned to Kamal, tears running down his face. "I cannot let them forget us. A hundred mothers, a thousand sons, they watch us die on television and change the channel." He grabbed Kamal's shirt front and pulled him to his feet with a shocking strength that tore the shirt. "These Americans, these weak children of the dollar, these ... voyeurs." Terrified, Kamal tried to retreat, but Bucheri pulled him close, his breath hot and stale. "They will live a nightmare today, my nightmare, a hell on earth, and my dear friend Ali, they will never, never forget."

Harley Jones

Harley Jones was speed-reading the night action reports when he heard a light rap on the door.

"Come in."

Jeannie Kawai opened the door just slightly and put her head in. "Breakfast?"

Jones hesitated for a moment. His mouth tasted like the inside of a garbage can. Still, it was going to be a long day.

"Sure. Come on in." He even managed a weak smile. Jones was not a morning person, and this was one of the worst in memory.

Jeannie sat across from him at the big table. She looked bedraggled too, Jones thought; although her clothes were still tidy, her hair was uncharacteristically disordered. Jeannie caught his glance.

"I'm a mess."

Jones hesitated. "Yes, but a beautiful mess. Do you always look this good in the morning?"

Jeannie blushed and then Jones realized the implication of his question. *Damn,* he thought, *I've got to watch it.*

Jeannie relieved the tension with a smile and raised eyebrows. Then she held up the bag in her hand.

"Here we go. Just what every red-blooded American wants for breakfast. Egg McMuffin, coffee, fries, and ketchup. I think I've even got a piece of carrot cake in here."

Jones groaned aloud. "God, is that what America is all about?" Even still, he reached greedily for the Egg McMuffin. "What is this? It smells good."

Jeannie smiled quizzically. "You really don't know?"

As Jones munched hungrily he said between mouthfuls, "Nope, I don't do mornings."

Jones swallowed the last of the Egg McMuffin. "Hey, that's not bad." He settled back and picked up the steaming Styrofoam coffee cup. He looked at the wall clock and decided to take a short break. "Jeannie, tell me more about yourself."

Jeannie wiped her lips daintily. "Well, there's really not much to say. Most of it's in my file. I grew up in Hawaii on the Big Island. It was great."

"Surf City for you?"

"No, my father ran a karate dojo. In fact, he's one of the more famous karate instructors in the islands."

Jones tipped forward in his chair and held up his hand in his characteristic "Stop" gesture. "Let me guess. He learned it from his father and so on and so on."

Jeannie gave a short laugh, surprisingly low in tone, "No, it's not that easy. My father was actually in the Army during the Vietnam War. He stayed there with the Army for three years after the war ended. That's where he started, by learning Tae Kwon Do—Korean style karate with a lot of kicks. Then he came back to Hawaii and studied with Jian Men Liu, a Chinese Kung Fu master. He thought the Tae Kwon Do kicks were good, but the Tae Kwon Do people didn't have good hand techniques. You see, the Koreans believe that hands should not be damaged—they're for working—so they developed fabulous kicks. Flying kicks to knock men off of horses, powerful kicks to break wooden armor—well, it just goes on and on. Anyhow, to make a long story short, Father merged the Korean kicks with the Chinese hand techniques to make an integrated style. It's really quite effective. Someone from his school always places well in the All Island competitions, and there's a lot of karate in Hawaii."

"So, I guess I'm lucky you didn't break my head."

Jeannie gave the same low laugh, then straightened up. "Actually, my father would be very disappointed in me, but really, my brothers are great fighters. They've opened up a school in Honolulu that's doing well. I never liked to fight. I dance."

"Dance?"

"Jazz ballet. Lots of fun and great exercise. But, Father didn't approve." Jeannie wished she could tell him more about her father, but she would have to know Jones much better before she would risk telling him how her family felt about the FBI.

Perhaps her tone suggested something, because Jones decided to change the subject. "Where did you go to school?"

"The University of Hawaii. They have a great oceanography program, which attracted me, but I sort of drifted into chemistry. I don't regret it now. I got a PhD in analytical chemistry doing microscopy. I applied to the Bureau and here I am, doing some field time before I go back to the labs."

"Well, they can't complain about you not getting some experience here."

Jeannie nodded, then turned serious. Hesitantly, she said, "Mmm, Harley, did you hear about the palace revolt?"

Jones cocked his head and looked quizzically at her.

Jeannie rushed ahead. "Look, I don't want to be the bearer of bad tidings, but Browner tried last night to have you replaced. He

252

even had Dr. Schwartz there. They implied that you've gone off the deep end."

Jones looked at her with a slight smile on his face. "What do you think?"

Jeannie looked uncomfortable. "Well, I think you're doing the job well, really well, but…" She began to reach up towards her neck, but stopped herself. "Well, you have done some weird things."

Jones's smile remained in place. "But you aren't afraid of me now?"

Jeannie smiled shyly. "No, but you sure scared the hell out of me yesterday. I think you scared Ted too."

Jones's face took on a curious expression. "So you don't think that this was just a power play?"

Jeannie shrugged. "I wasn't there for the whole thing—all of us FBI people and Charley Montresor left first. Then a few minutes later Bradley, Yeager, and Browner came out. I didn't know what was going on until it started. Browner brought me in because of the ... incident." She gestured towards her neck. "Jessica and George were behind you all the way. General Bradley and Commissioner Yeager seemed to be fence-sitting. I couldn't tell about the intelligence guy, Charley Montresor. He seemed as surprised as everyone else. My best guess is that it was just Ted. If he was really scheming, you would think that he would have worked on Montresor. He's CIA too."

Jones rubbed his chin thoughtfully. "Jessica would stand up for me, she's great, and so would George. Well, Ted probably thinks he's doing the right thing." He looked up to her and smiled. "Don't worry about Ted Browner. I can handle him."

They smiled at each other over some unstated understanding and settled down to finish their breakfast. As they finished Jeannie jammed the refuse into a bag. "I'll take this down to the ladies' room garbage can or your office will have a Mc-roma."

Jeannie left and Jones sat down to scan the stack of papers when he heard Jeannie walking back down the hallway. Something about her steps, slow and hesitant warned him. When she appeared in the doorway her complexion had gone sickly white.

Jones jumped up. "What? What is it?"

Jeannie turned, tears coming to her eyes and looked down the hallway: "In the ladies' room."

Jones charged past her and down the hall, but he slowed before pushing the door open. Her tone had told him there was no rush. Jeannie moved up behind him as he moved into the room. First he saw the feet, then the whole body. He dropped to his knees by her head.

"Oh, Jessica, you poor baby. That bitch got you. I'm so sorry, Jessie baby, so sorry."

He gently picked her head up and put it on his legs, stroking her hair, clumsily trying to straighten out the tangles. Slowly he rocked back and forth.

"Oh, Jesus baby, I'm so sorry," he repeated again and again as the tears formed in his eyes.

Jeannie watched for several minutes and then knelt down beside him. "She was special to you?"

Jones looked up his voice choked. "Yes. In the past. Very special."

Jeannie put her hand on his arm. "Well then, we should cover her up, shouldn't we?"

Jones nodded. Jeannie took off her sweater and gave it to him. She watched as he carefully covered her face. She stood up gracefully and put her hand on his shoulder. "We should get some people to take care of her now."

He nodded, but didn't move. She waited for a moment, then squeezed his shoulder. "Harley, you can't help her now. She would want you back on the case, wouldn't she? She was like that wasn't she, Harley?"

He nodded and stood up reluctantly, putting Jessica's head down gently on the tiles.

"She was so good, so special."

Jeannie gently pulled him around so that he faced her. "Harley, later, I want you to tell me all about Jessica. Where she came from, what she did, who she was. Everything, so that we can remember her. Will you do that?" He nodded and started to buckle as the tears flowed down his face.

She wrapped her arms around him, holding him upright. Then he wrapped his arms around her as his body shook, the sobs coming from deep inside. Jeannie held him fiercely, caught up in his grief, crying herself as she grieved for him. It felt so sad, so very sad, but so very good to hold him like this. It was so sad, she cried some more.

Slowly, gently, he disentangled himself from her embrace. He held her at arm's length, searching her eyes. Then he pulled her to him and kissed her gently on the lips. Then he wiped the tears from his eyes with his sleeves before pushing past her and walking out the door.

She waited a moment, then followed him down to his office. Before she reached the door, she heard his voice.

"Blackwell, Jones here. Jessica's in room 310. She's dead. Please take good care of her."

7:30 A.M.
JFK Federal Building

The eight o'clock meeting of the CTU leaders, support group commanders and immediate deputies had been moved forward at the request of Commissioner Yeager. Harley Jones was the last to arrive. Except for the tape across his nose and the facial swelling, he looked pretty normal, thought Ted Browner. Jones remained standing and spoke with a slight sad smile.

"I've had kind of a rough night."

There were some small smiles of appreciation and most nodded their heads. Browner noted that Jones's hands were trembling slightly.

"My gut tells me that today is the big one. Commissioner Yeager has some vital information which even I haven't heard, so we'll get right on with news, then go to assessment and finally to any operational changes." Jones sat down with a wince, despite his efforts to be gentle. Commissioner Yeager rose.

"Two things have happened since we last met. First, without going into details, the situation in Roxbury is going from bad to worse very quickly. It's beginning to look like we might have an L.A.-type problem. You remember what happened when the verdict on Rodney King came out—the community erupted. The people of Roxbury think that the police are killing wantonly on the streets. I'm sorry to say that we still do not have a clear picture of what happened at the X-Men headquarters. It was definitely not authorized by the police department. We are almost certain that it is none of our people. Everyone who isn't sick is on duty. That in itself is causing problems. They're all exhausted. To top it off, our communications are still out. In the downtown Boston area it's not too bad because we can use the Army network. Roxbury is another story. Communications are useless; even the land lines are down because we turned them off. Our people are getting trapped by the gangs in Roxbury and they have to fight their way out because they can't call for help. I've had three officers killed over the night. One of them was a female who was also raped."

Yeager paused, a flicker of fear passing over his face as he thought of his wife, Barbara, patrolling in Roxbury. "We are patrolling in convoys of three cars, four officers to a car. Obviously, we can't cover much area, so basically it's a free-for-all in there. I cannot allow this to continue. I've asked for assistance from surrounding areas, but I'm only getting a few units because they think this may spread. I'm going to have to pull some of my people off the downtown checkpoints."

Commissioner Yeager looked down to see Harley Jones rubbing his forehead as though he was trying to make a headache disappear. The Commissioner paused for a moment, then continued, "The second problem is water. The downtown area is fed by two water mains. At approximately six thirty this morning a guerrilla team cut one of these mains. They were apprehended by the Army, so I think I'll pass on to General Bradley for more details."

General Bradley took off his reading glasses and stood up; apparently he was going to do this from memory.

"To be quite correct, it was not an Army unit involved, it was the National Guard, which does not normally fall under Army control in peace time. It should have been federalized, but that's another story. Since there is no one here from the Guard, I will tell you what I know." He paused for a moment to organize his thoughts.

"Two Guard armored personnel carriers were parked on Brookline Street. At about six thirty there was an explosion on Brookline south of their position by about three city blocks. The senior man, a Captain Thorn, took one of the vehicles down to investigate. As he approached the site, their vehicle received heavy fire from two directions. They withdrew and then started in again, using the heavy machine gun for suppressive fire. Apparently the suppressive fire set off a large cache of explosives. From the wreckage we deduce that the explosives were in some type of truck parked near the site of the first explosion. None of the enemy was captured." The General stopped. "Questions?"

Harley Jones looked up. "Why wasn't anyone captured? Usually someone is wounded."

The General nodded, understanding the need for prisoners and information. "Mr. Jones, you must realize that the situation here is very odd. The explosion killed all but one of the enemy. That one man was trapped by an overturned automobile."

Jones was beginning to look angry. He stared at the General and raised his eyebrows in a query.

The General understood. "Sir, the man committed suicide right in front of Captain Thorn. With a knife, he cut his own throat. Captain Thorn has been severely shocked by the incident. Perhaps it was aggravated by exposure to the overpressure of the explosion. We had to MEDEVAC him for psychiatric observation."

Jones nodded tiredly. "So what can we conclude from this incident?"

The General sat down as Jones looked around the room for comments. Charley Montresor, the CIA man who was the head of CTU intelligence, spoke first.

"We've had a little time to think about this because we monitored the radio transmissions. One thing that General Bradley left out was that all of the terrorists in this instance were Asians, possibly Japanese. We can conclude that the rest of the explosive was to be used elsewhere by the same group. Our best estimate is that they were going to go for the other water main. That would then deprive all of the downtown of water. This would make the downtown uninhabitable in one to two days in this weather. We believe that this is the objective."

Charley Montresor sat down abruptly and pushed his thin wire rimmed glasses up on his nose. Unlike Ted Browner, Charley Montresor looked uncomfortable in a suit. His tie was slightly askew and his shirt collar was biting into his neck, giving his face a red tinge.

Jones stared at Montresor for a long moment. Montresor's face began to get redder. Jones cocked his head to the side. "So you think they're shutting off the water to force people out?"

Montresor nodded.

"Well then why didn't they just turn off the power? Anyone with a little plastic explosive can do that."

Montresor cleared his throat before answering. "We thought about that. Basically, it's easier to reroute power. Cutting off water is more permanent."

Jones's face didn't change. "I'm not so certain about the motive. What else did you conclude?"

Montresor looked startled. "I don't know what you mean."

"Well, what about the rest of the explosives, those that blew up?"

Montresor looked uncomfortable now. "Well, er, we didn't discuss that."

Jones inspected Montresor as though he were an abstract painting, then he said, "The remainder of the explosives were to be used to destroy the rest of the water system, weren't they?"

Montresor hesitated. "Probably."

Jones settled back in his chair, looking toward the ceiling.

"That tells me that we have to protect the system and, what's more, that we've probably been lucky and wiped out the team that was supposed to do the job." He leaned forward to look at Montresor. "Agreed?"

Montresor had pulled himself together a bit. "Yes sir. We'll get the layout of the city water system and look for weak points."

Jones turned to Commissioner Yeager. "Eddy, since none of the other city services is represented here, I'll have to ask you to look into the repair."

Commissioner Yeager shifted uncomfortably in his seat. "I'm not certain how to get that done. Frankly, without phones I don't think we have a chance to get a good-sized crew together. Even if we knew who to get, we would have to send a unit for each man. Under normal circumstances, maybe it wouldn't take too long, but I've got my doubts that we can get this thing fixed with our city people. If things start to get at all rough, they'll vanish in a flash. After all, they're civilians. There might be another way."

Jones had a questioning look on his face. "Like what?"

"Army engineers. There's a heavy construction unit at Fort Devens, forty-five miles from here."

General Bradley nodded.

Jones looked from one to the other. "OK, I want you two to get together on this. Eddy, I want you to push the city end as far as possible. Get people who know what's going on—maps, diagrams, dimensions, supplies, all that sort of thing. And then hold onto them in case we have another bombing." He turned to General Bradley.

"Same to you. Overkill. More people, more equipment than we should need under any reasonable scenario. I just hope they can get here soon."

General Bradley looked mildly pleased. "Actually, I don't think there will be a serious problem. I placed all the units in the area in a maximum readiness stance. All units should have their personnel on base and their equipment loaded up. I warned them that I'd have some hides if they weren't ready for anything."

Jones smiled strongly for the first time that morning. "Damn, it's good to get some good news." He turned to Commissioner Yeager. "And Commissioner..." He paused. "Turn off the water. Let's let him think he's won another round."

A general clamor started around the table, but Ted Browner's voice overrode them. "Jesus, Harley, you can't do that. Half the people in town will be in their cars before noon if you do that. It will be panic. The roads will be totally jammed. Bucheri will have won."

Jones waited patiently for Browner to finish. "Yes, Ted, that could happen, but you and your favorite news person are going to get on the news and say something that's going to keep everybody in their homes."

Ted Browner settled back in his chair and cursed himself for having grabbed so firmly onto the nasty end of the stick. What could he possibly say that would keep people in their homes, and then, what would happen to him if he did say it? Ted Browner had the uneasy feeling that he was setting himself up for a political gang rape.

7:45 A.M.
Sergeant Besso

The Fox had been very specific about everything—the car, the clothes, even the sunglasses. Sergeant Besso wasn't certain who they were posing as, but it certainly was a dangerous game, only two men working from a car. And the use of a Mac 10 submachine gun was silly. He could have done much better with an AK-47 or an M-16. Even a semi-automatic hunting gun would have been more effective in the long run. This was all so strange. Indiscriminate killing bothered Besso and this was worse than he had imagined—women and children. Still, he had his own family to think of. This was his last assignment. With his fee he would be the richest man in his village—possibly the whole country, he thought. What a joke: the richest man in Somalia.

Yes, if a few Americans had to die, so be it. He tapped Abdul on the shoulder and the car started forward.

Abdul was a rotten driver. Even Besso could see that, and Besso had never been in an automobile before this assignment. Abdul claimed to be expert because his uncle drove a taxi in Addis Ababa. But it didn't matter that Abdul was a rotten driver, because Besso couldn't drive at all. The automobile was a twenty-year-old four-door Ford sedan whose original blue paint had faded to dullness. The car had been where The Fox had said it would be. The only surprise was a slogan on the side. Had The Fox put this on, or some vandals? If Besso had been able to read English, he would have known that it spelled out "Remember the X-Men," but that message would have meant nothing to him.

Abdul pulled onto Broadway and they rolled past Cardinal Cushing High School in their low-slung Ford. As they neared the Cathedral, Sergeant Besso pulled back the cocking lever on the Mac 10 and rolled down the window on the left side. As predicted, the people from the seven o'clock mass were emptying out onto the front steps and the spacious lawn. The Fox had said that this was an attempt to start a holy war. Besso could understand that. The one true religion was worth fighting for. If only these were Jews. They were fiends, Satan's helpers on earth. He almost told Abdul this, but decided not to disturb him. Abdul was a nervous man and wouldn't handle distraction well.

When they rolled up opposite the church, Abdul slowed as they had rehearsed. Besso slid across the seat and sighted the weapon. Then, in a professional manner, he began to traverse the weapon from left to right, squeezing off five round bursts. Suddenly, the car jerked and began weaving.

Sergeant Besso almost never shouted at his troops, but this was too much. "Stop that you fool!"

Besso didn't turn but he could hear an odd slapping sound. With a cyclic rate of six hundred rounds per minute, the MAC 10 ejected a veritable torrent of hot spent casings out its right side. Abdul was trying to escape the hot shell casings from the MAC 10. Two of the hot casings had gone down the back of his shirt.

Besso fired another burst. One casing went down the front of Abdul's shirt. This he could reach. He looked down just for a moment and then was slammed into the steering wheel. Besso was thrown against the back of the front seat and then down. He shook his head and pushed himself up. When he reached window level he looked out. Abdul, the King of Fools, had driven into an oncoming car.

"Abdul, get out," he yelled as he threw open the back door. Abdul didn't answer. The MAC 10 was empty, so he threw it down. His pistol had been knocked out of its holster. He was about to search for it when he saw the crowd running towards him. There was no choice. He ran. Up the middle of Broadway, he ran right down the center line as cars swerved away. As he ran, he glanced back over his shoulder. Now he knew why cars were swerving: there was a large mob of young men closing on him. Sergeant Besso sped up, but a lifetime of poor diet could not be compensated for. He was already gasping and knew that he couldn't last another minute. There was no way that he could escape. He slowed abruptly then turned around, his hands upraised to surrender. Perhaps his money would buy him out of the criminal system. He had heard that it worked that way in America.

The expressions on the faces of the crowd as they approached told him that he would never make it to jail. Sergeant Besso was a black man caught murdering whites in South Boston. He had only minutes to live, all of them painful.

8:15 A.M.
Commissioner Yeager

Even from five thousand feet, Yeager could see the pool of emergency vehicle lights as his helicopter lifted off from City Hall. South Boston was its own sort of tinder box, strongly Catholic, adamantly white, the scene of several extremely violent attacks on innocent blacks. The reports had been fragmentary: drive-by shooting, multiple deaths, two black perpetrators, something about the X-Men. His men on the scene were frightened, the mob was incredibly large, and there was no manpower. Yeager felt the stomach rise that comes with a quick drop in altitude; even his pilot was rattled.

The helicopter steadied over the church lawn. Even before he had unbuckled, Captain Frank Graham was opening the helicopter door. When Eddy Yeager had been a sergeant he had worked for Frank Graham. Graham was a veteran of the streets, not office politicking, and Yeager respected him. Commissioners would normally not go to crime scenes. Frank's call had been personal and urgent.

Yeager had to shout to be heard over the slowing blades of the helicopter. "What's happening, Frank?"

"I'm glad you're here, Eddy. Congratulations on your promotion."

Yeager had to laugh. Frank was the King of Sarcasm.

Captain Graham went on. "Eddy, it's like this. These people heard about that thing with the X-Men in Roxbury. Now, all of a sudden, we've got eleven dead and seven wounded badly here in South Boston. Half these folks blame us for getting Roxbury in a stew, the other half just wants to kill blacks. This is bad. I mean really bad. You better do something quick, and I don't know what."

Commissioner Yeager nodded; it was what he had both feared and expected. "Show me the shooters' bodies."

The bodies were under a tarp with only their boots sticking out. As Captain Graham was about to peel back the tarp, he said, "These guys don't look too good."

Commissioner Yeager raised his hand, staring at the boots. They were identical, very worn on both the bottoms and the top. The tops were particularly odd; they looked as though they had been rubbed with coarse sandpaper. Yeager nodded to Captain Graham, who uncovered the bodies.

Both men were very lean. Yeager leaned forward and opened the mouth of one. He recoiled slightly at the damage, but there was enough to see.

"Frank, come here."

Captain Graham leaned over.

"Frank, have you ever seen dental work like that?"

Captain Graham looked in, puzzled. Finally he pulled back. "No. I'm no dentist, but if someone did that to my teeth, I'd sue him."

Commissioner Yeager turned to Captain Graham. "I think these men are part of the terrorist outfit that's been shooting us up. They sure aren't from Roxbury."

Captain Graham nodded. "I guess. You gonna tell them?" He gestured with a motion of his head towards the crowd.

261

Commissioner Yeager grimaced but nodded. Captain Graham helped him up onto the hood of a patrol unit and handed him a bull horn. The Commissioner turned to face the crowd and raised the bull horn.

"I'm Commissioner Yeager. May I have your attention please?"

The police line was barely holding back the mob, only twenty feet away. The cries from the crowd were hostile and threatening. One man in front screamed, "Fuck you asshole. You let the niggers in."

Yeager paused for a moment when the heckler threw a bible at him. Even through his bulletproof vest, it felt as if he had been shot again. Yeager folded up, unable to move. Dimly he could hear the crowd roar. He turned painfully to Captain Graham.

"It's too late. Start using gas and move into the church. I'll send some people to get you out. Get me to my chopper."

As the chopper rose over the crowd, he was thankful that people didn't go armed to church in South Boston, because many would be going for their guns soon. South Boston would soon be run by the mob. The only question was, what would the mob do?

Eddy Yeager looked out over Boston, his town, as the helicopter leveled out. The dark plume from the BosGas tower was drifting over the downtown, pointing a finger towards Roxbury. With the police communications net down, it was a nightmare. Where was Barbara? Was she out on the streets? Images of the raped policewoman went through his mind; her body had been a crumpled rag in the FAX picture. Eddy was torn as never before. He couldn't send anyone looking for Barbara; she was just another one of the troops. He couldn't show anything that would be interpreted as favoritism. When he had been a Deputy Superintendent, a lifetime ago (could it have been only two days?), he would have asked one of his patrolmen to find out. Now he was frozen, paralyzed by his position, unable to ask.

He sighed and flipped the microphone on. "Charley. Fly me over District Three. I want to see what's going on."

8:45 A.M.
JFK Federal Building

Harley Jones was incredulous. "They what?"

Commissioner Yeager was trying to be patient, but the pain in his chest was intense. "They shot up a crowd coming out of church. Lots of women and children. South Boston is in an uproar. I'm afraid they're going to march on Roxbury. It's just ... unthinkable what will happen then."

262

Jones leaned forward and put his hands on the table. "Tell me again how you know that they are part of the Bucheri outfit."

"The boots and the dental work. Their other clothes could have been bought here, but you know, people are real fussy about their shoes. These guys kept their Army boots. They were weird cheap ones. I've never seen any like them. They'd seen a lot of desert, is my bet."

Jones leaned back, apparently satisfied. "OK, we'll do a post-mortem if we ever get the bodies out. Now what do you want to do about South Boston?"

Yeager leaned back, his face pale. "I don't have any choice. I've got to saturate the area. Disperse the mob. They'll be looting, everything, the whole nine yards."

Jones shook his head. "Look, we need you in the downtown. Let's look at the map."

Jones walked over to the large city map taped to the wall of his office. General Bradley, the only other person in the room, followed. The General took in the situation at a glance.

"Look, it's easy. South Boston is isolated, just like downtown Boston. You can use the same tactics against them that Bucheri is using on us. There aren't more than what, five, seven ways in and out of South Boston. It's a peninsula. Just place your men here, here, and here," he said as he jabbed the map.

Yeager shook his head. "Look, this isn't an armored division; these guys can go on foot through the rail yards. They aren't limited to roads."

Jones had been listening to the exchange between the men as he examined the map. He turned to Commissioner Yeager.

"Eddy. Trust me. These are Americans. They aren't going to walk that far. If you block it up tight, only a few will get across. I'm going to talk to the General about the railway yard, because that is a potential hole. You run roadblocks and don't let anything through but emergency traffic. You'll have to make them serious blocks, at least fifty men and maybe some heavy machinery in the middle. Form a mobile reserve—hell, you know what to do."

Commissioner Yeager nodded. He did know what to do, and how to do it. He just didn't want to. "OK. We'll still be short of men in the downtown. Now I'll need ... maybe three hundred more."

Jones grimaced. "I agree. Bucheri's bleeding us. Something's going to happen soon. He's like a goddamn puppet master, and you know who we are."

9:00 A.M.
The Westin Hotel, Copley Place

Dr. Kamal was watching the television as Hassan Bucheri paced the central room of the suite. In some senses, their roles had become reversed. Now it was Kamal who urged patience and Bucheri who worried. Kamal found this slightly amusing and was relaxing as much as one reasonably could when trapped with a tiger.

Bucheri tried the tap again. "Look. Still water pressure. Those 'superior' Japanese have failed despite their extravagant fees and promises. So much for Japanese perfection."

With an uncharacteristic gesture, Kamal cut off Bucheri and turned back to the television. He adjusted the volume so that he could hear the news bulletin that was coming on. Pamela Clark's voice was as strident as ever.

"...water will be off for at least twenty-four hours. Residents in the affected area are reminded that they have large reservoirs of water in their hot water tanks. Toilets should not be..." Kamal cut off the sound and stood up. He walked over to Bucheri, who still looked perplexed, and kissed him on both cheeks.

"My friend, you've done it. They can't possibly survive without water. This was the last barrier. Your plan can not fail now. I congratulate you."

Bucheri shook himself free, then smiled. "Why yes, of course. How foolish of me. The hotel must have its own reservoir because it is so tall. That's the water that we have been using. Allah has been with us through this campaign. We cannot fail now."

Bucheri walked over to the window and opened the drapes, allowing the bright sunlight in. He looked down towards the street. "Traffic is still jammed. It will make no difference. We can fall back on the contingency supply plan if necessary."

Kamal moved up beside him. "Indeed, as you say. America is a rich country. It will supply us with all we need. Shall I bring the telephone?"

Bucheri took another sip of the rum and Coke drink in his hand. It seemed to Kamal that it had become a permanent part of his arm. "No. I'll wait until noon."

He swiveled to face Kamal. "Did you see *High Noon* with Gary Cooper? Fantastic movie. Typical American egotistical fantasy. One good man facing several bad men. The good man wins. Well, this time, we're the good men and we're going to make it happen right at high noon. It's the American way."

A pleading note entered Kamal's voice, "Hassan, couldn't you give the order now. It seems more ... sensible."

Bucheri took another sip and started a more sedate pacing in front of the window. Occasionally he would look out to admire the view of Boston. Then, he stopped and faced Kamal again.

"No, high noon. You see Ali, timing is everything. In love, business, politics and, for us, in war."

Kamal shook his head and then took off his glasses. Bucheri pointed with his drink at Kamal and said, a hint of menace in his voice, "And Ali, keep the damn glasses off."

JFK Federal Building

Captain Knight knocked hesitantly on Assistant Director Jones's door frame. The door was always open now. Jones looked up from the stack of reports with a harried expression.

Captain Knight cleared his throat. "Well if you're too busy, sir..."

Jones gestured towards a chair. "It's Knight isn't it? No, please sit down. I know you wouldn't be here if it wasn't important."

Captain Knight swallowed. "Well, yes sir. I've been talking to some of my friends at Fort Huachuca, the Electronic Warfare School—" Seeing Jones's expression he hastened to add, "On a secure channel. They told me about something that we could probably use."

Jones looked expectant. Excited now, Captain Knight stood up and continued, "It's something the CIA doesn't have. It's used by NSA, the National Security Agency." Jones knew about NSA. They specialized in electronic surveillance and had a huge establishment—some said bigger than the CIA—with a very low profile. As far as he knew, none of their equipment had ever been used in the continental United States. It wasn't even discussed in FBI briefings.

"Well," Captain Knight went on, "they've got electronics that they use in satellites or planes, I don't know. No one outside NSA really knows, but anyhow, they can pick up telephone and radio transmissions. Lots of them at once."

Jones cocked his head. "So? We're actually recording every conversation."

Captain Knight started bouncing slowly on the balls of his feet and talking faster. "Yes, but you know about the time lag problem and all of that. Like we have to wait for someone to call us back, and then we can't synchronize quickly or accurately with the start of the conversation. There's that and most of the people don't know what to listen for. Well, here's the cool part: these NSA electronics are hooked up to a computer. They digitize all the speech—like put it in computer readable format, and then they only record when they hit a key word."

"What?" Jones interrupted.

"Well, they wait for key words to come up in the conversation. Like if they were listening for doper communications they might listen for words like 'shipment' or 'production' or the name of someone, like 'Escobar.' Anyhow, what I'm trying to say is that these guys, I mean computers, they listen to *everything*, and they are fast, like *now*, so that means that we could get exactly synchronized."

Jones stood frozen for just a moment before picking up the phone. "Get me Mr. Browner and General Bradley immediately."

* * *

Ten minutes later Captain Knight had just finished repeating the description of the equipment and its capabilities for Ted Browner and General Bradley. Jones turned to them.

"What do you think?"

Both men paused briefly, then Browner spoke up. "We've gotten intercepts from NSA, of course, but they don't work for us. How are we going to get their cooperation and how can we get it quickly? If your intuition is correct, things are going to be happening soon."

Jones replied, "Don't worry about whether they'll help. I'll talk to a friend. You're right about the time, but we won't know until we try. If they've got anything on the East Coast it could be here in an hour or two."

General Bradley had been thinking as he watched. "If they use anything like the AWACS communication system we should be able to pipe it directly into my command vehicle. What worries me is that we don't have any recognition phrase or word. This isn't going to work worth a damn if we don't have that."

Ted Browner shook his head in disgust. "We've been interrogating everyone we can. The Fox, Bucheri, has been keeping his operations completely compartmentalized. There are no common denominators that we know of. The Fox tends to use euphemisms like 'make contact' for sniping or 'cook' for blow up. I'm afraid there's just nothing we can count on."

The men sat in silence until Captain Knight said hesitantly, "Well what about 'Fox'? He always calls himself that, doesn't he?"

Jeannie Kawai knocked tentatively at the door. Harley Jones looked up.

Jeannie paused.

"I know you aren't real big on these radio broadcasts from the pirate station, but they're announcing that the last one will be coming up in a moment. Liz told me. She's recording it but you might want to listen."

Jones nodded and turned on his radio. Maybe the last broadcast would have something really useful.

"Hey folks, this is Big Al, and you know, my thing is really dragging, but we're coming up with the last piece from the Cool Hand his-self. Yes indeed. We've had some greats this morning, *This Is the End* from the Doors, *Round the Bend* from Credence Clearwater ... pretty cool stuff, and enough to make you blow out of here. I don't think I'm going to invite this guy to supper. Nope, I wouldn't do him with your thing. Talk about anti-so-ci-e-tal, my God, he makes Jack the Ripper look good, and it isn't often that we get to talk about sponsors that way. What the hell, he paid his bill. So now, my lovelies, the last tune on his list. Let me know when you have this one figured out—*American Pie* by Don McLean."

Harley Jones leaned back to listen as Don McLean reminded him how the music used to make him smile.

Hassan Bucheri thought about a woman from Harvard and smiled even as he remembered the day the music died.

Yes, indeed, today the music would die for Boston and all of America.

It would be bye, bye, American Pie...

* * *

Captain Thorn lay in a tent, waiting for a non-priority MEDEVAC, thinking about the men that had died, wondering whether it was over for him and Company C.

He was thinking about the good old boys drinking whiskey and rye...

Singing that this would be the day that they would die...

* * *

Private Miller's mother couldn't stop crying and she didn't know why.

* * *

Barbara Yeager wasn't laughing as she pulled out her Glock 9mm. The three young black men laughed at her— "Little white cop cunt," they called at her. Then the one in the middle threw the radio he was carrying directly at her. It was surreal; the music kept playing as it flew by. She danced aside but they kept coming.

She might be out of luck, this day that the music died...

* * *

It was Sunday, and in the Greater Boston Area, people turned to the Good Book for comfort.

And like Don McLean, they sang dirges in the dark...

* * *

Harley Jones squinted, apparently lost in thought, almost transfixed.

Fire, fire, the devil's friend, there was something about Bucheri and fire...

Harley Jones looked at his hands; they weren't clenched, they were shaking slightly. Angels born in Hell and flames climbing into the night. It was Satan laughing with delight... It was Bucheri.

"I wonder what he looks like?" said Jeannie Kawai to herself.

As the children screamed in the streets...

Harley Jones looked up. "He's leaving today, and he's laughing at us."

Jones paused for a moment, then stood up. "Let's make Schwartz earn his pay." He gestured towards Jeannie. "Come on. I want to see what our resident shrink thinks about this."

Moments later they were down in the basement looking for the office assigned to the two psychologists.

"Room seven," said Jeannie. "Over there."

Jones pushed in the door, then stopped abruptly. Jeannie barely avoided colliding with him by stepping just to his side. Jay Schwartz was standing nude from the waist down, his trousers gathered around his ankles. He was facing away from them but swiveled around when they entered. Loraine Hawthorne was on her knees before him. She had a surprised look on her face, but Jeannie saw shock, fear, even hate passing across the face of Dr. Jay Schwartz.

"Well, I see you're keeping on top of things, Jay," said Jones. Jeannie looked at Jones's face, not surprised to find a wolfish expression that matched his tone.

"Ethical to the end."

268

Jones paused for effect. "Would you like Ms. Kawai and me to keep this quiet for you Jay?"

Schwartz nodded with an open mouth.

"You'll be leaving us soon, I understand," said Jones.

Schwartz clamped his mouth shut angrily but nodded.

Jones turned and left, Jeannie trailing behind. "Wait," she said as she caught him by the elevator.

"If I didn't know it was impossible, I'd say you weren't really surprised."

Jones nodded slightly. "Schwartz is a creature of habit. Excitement gets him horny. He also likes to hit on women that come to him for training. He got squeezed out of Penn State for hitting on his students." Jones stepped into the elevator. "Two can play at damned near any game."

10:30 A.M.
Checkpoint 7

Sergeant John McGeorge was startled when Harley Jones spoke behind him.

"How's it going, Sergeant?"

When McGeorge turned around, he was even more startled by Jones's appearance. There had been rumors that something had gone on at the Suit House (as it was called now), but no one believed the one rumor that said there had been a hit attempt on Jones. It was preposterous. Well, maybe not, thought McGeorge now. Maybe not. He certainly didn't get that whacked nose shaving this morning. Jones seemed to be waiting for a reply.

McGeorge turned to the intersection. "Well, sir, as you can see, it's a zoo." There were cars backed up all the way to the next checkpoint in both directions.

"If you want to slow these perps down, you've done a great job, sir."

Jones looked both ways. "Look. I've got a convoy of heavy equipment coming in. Heavy long stuff. What should I do to get it here ASAP?"

McGeorge pursed his lips for a moment. "Well, sir, you just about have to bring them across this bridge." He pointed down towards the Harvard Bridge, since Jones was not a native Bostonian. "It's the only one that has even a single lane open. The Cambridge side is clear. They haven't had any trouble yet. Now, if we were to act as traffic cops instead

269

of road blocks, we could probably get some of these main roads clear in half an hour."

Jones looked south on Beacon. "How long to get me a clear road down to Brookline Avenue?"

Sergeant McGeorge raised his eyebrows. "So that's where the bomb was. OK, about forty minutes. You want me to start now?"

Jones nodded. "Please. Call me on the military net when it's clear. My call sign is Flame."

Sergeant McGeorge, despite the fatigue of twenty-four hours of continuous duty, couldn't help himself. He convulsed in laughter. When he had recovered, Jones was waiting patiently. "What's so funny?"

"Your call sign."

Jones looked surprised. "What about it?"

"Well, your nickname used to be 'the Flame-Thrower.' Then it got shortened to 'the Flame.' Someone handing out call signs has a sense of humor."

Jones nodded, too tired to be amused. "Just tell me my route is clear. OK?"

Sergeant McGeorge straightened up, but couldn't erase his smile. "Yes sir, Mr. Jones."

Jones's voice took on a tone of impatience. "Anything else to report?"

McGeorge lost his smile and his brow furrowed slightly. "Well, yes sir, something odd. We've come across two cars with cans, big cans, of gasoline in their trunks. They had only one person in them, the driver. Neither had ID so we sent them downtown. It isn't often you find a car with a trunk full of gasoline. Otherwise," he looked over the jam, "everything is normal, FUBAR."

It was Jones's turn to be surprised. "FUBAR?"

"Fucked Up Beyond All Recognition."

Jones smiled tiredly. "Ain't that the truth?"

11:15 A.M.
JFK Federal Building

Jones sat with the usual small working group—General Bradley, Commissioner Yeager, and Ted Browner.

"I've been out on a little tour. Things are a mess transportation-wise, but that may work to our advantage later. Right now, I've opened up a channel for the engineers over the Harvard Bridge. This checkpoint system may be working as much for Bucheri as for us. I just can't tell.

Checkpoint seven picked up some people carrying large amounts of gasoline. They're down at Central Receiving waiting for questioning along with everyone else we've picked up. I can't help but believe that we've got a lot more dolphins than tuna in this net; still, this gasoline thing has me worried. There's just something about it that I can't put my finger on. Any ideas?"

Jones looked around the table, but there were no comments. Jones turned to Commissioner Yeager. "Why don't you put those people to the top of the list for interrogation? Squeeze them a bit and let's see what comes out."

Commissioner Yeager was writing in a notepad. "Checkpoint Seven?"

"Right."

Jones waited until Commissioner Yeager stopped writing, "Now, I know you gentlemen have been making contingency plans, but I want to be sure that you're ready to move your manpower. I have the HRT prepared to come in by chopper directly to the Haymarket. We have a total group of eighty and two choppers so it will take us four runs, about an hour, to get them all from Logan. How about you General?"

"Well, to start with, we've got a lot more birds, and Director, if you have some rooftop entries to do, I think we should have Delta Force do them. They're well-trained to drop a large group into a small area."

Jones nodded. "OK, but I want them held in reserve for something special."

The General nodded. "Agreed. We have available both the ready reaction platoon and the ready reaction company from the 82nd Airborne. The ready platoon can land anywhere in five minutes; we keep the engines turning on those birds, and they're loaded. The ready company, minus one platoon, can land anywhere within fifteen minutes—less, with luck. They're resting on the strip beside their birds. My MPs are deployed along with the Commissioner's men."

Yeager blinked in agreement.

The General continued. "The MPs have their own transportation, mostly Humvee and pickups. No heavy stuff. I'm worried about that. These National Guard people have armored personnel carriers with .50 caliber machine guns but they're ... very tired. I don't trust them."

"So how are you going to get your people around?" Jones asked.

"Well, everything seems to be close by here; I figure they'll just have to jog in. Hell, they're light infantry and fit as a fiddle. Should be no problem. We're going to use the Common as our LZ. We can land the whole company there. I should also mention that we have a company of Rangers."

Jones grimaced slightly.

The General caught the expression. "Is that a problem, Mr. Jones?"

Jones looked thoughtful for a moment. "I'm worried about the Rangers. My understanding is that these are special assault troops. They usually rehearse a mission in detail and then go in for a quick violent hit. Am I correct?"

The General looked annoyed. "Yes, that is the essence of their mission. They are raiders, but they have very good leaders and they are absolutely the best assault troops the Army has. You couldn't ask for better."

Jones's face had turned a bit hard. "General, I know they're the best. So do they. That's what worries me. People don't join the Rangers to stand by and watch shooting. They want to be part of it. From my point of view, that of a policeman, the Rangers may just be too willing to tango."

The General looked disgusted. "Mr. Jones, you're talking about them like they're rabid dogs."

Jones replied, "No General, they're not like rabid dogs. They're like highly trained, very spirited, Doberman guard dogs. I wouldn't take my Doberman guard dog to a domestic dispute; someone would get shredded."

The General shook his head. "Sir, you're exaggerating. I've worked with these boys. They're good. Very good, very versatile. You'll be pleased if you decide to use them."

Jones nodded but kept his expression neutral.

11:45 P.M.
JFK Federal Building.

Captain Knight knocked on the door frame again. This time it was a much more confident knock. Jones looked up.

"Yes?"

"Sir. The ELINT aircraft is on station now. We've gotten a link and we're getting a download now. It's a miracle. There was one at Andrews getting one of its engines replaced. We got it just as they were about to fly south."

"What type of signal are you looking for?"

"They're going to watch only the cellular phone frequencies. It may be hard because they'll get stuff from all over the Boston area, but the reception should be best for the downtown. They trained the computer using recordings of Mr. Bucheri's voice and then they're generally going to look for the word 'fox.'"

Jones stood up and started to pace. "You mean, they're actually going to try and recognize a voice?"

"Yes sir. They said they would try. Hell, excuse me sir. I mean, we really don't know what they can do. It's kind of scary. Anyhow, they're somewhere up there listening now."

Jones was fascinated and wanted to go to the command vehicle parked in the plaza, but there were other things that needed to be done.

"Thanks Captain. Call me when something solid comes through."

CHAPTER 24: SUNDAY: HIGH NOON

12:05 P.M.
Westin Hotel, Copley Place

Hassan Bucheri and Dr. Ali Kamal stood at their room window looking down.

"The traffic is starting to move. Excellent. That will help. We'll be able to get more material into the area." Bucheri looked to Kamal for confirmation.

Kamal, realizing his role, nodded. "Yes. Everything seems to be working as you planned. So you will give the order now?"

Bucheri looked at his watch again, the third time in the last five minutes. "Absolutely, my friend. It's high noon. Time for the shoot-out at the O.K. Corral?"

Kamal hesitated and then decided to be brave. "Hassan, Friday night, you asked me why I thought you were a Muslim or even a Palestinian. What are you? Why are you here? My motives are clear, but yours are mysterious. Soon we will be parting ways, and yet I feel I hardly know you."

Bucheri paused and took a sip of his drink as he watched Kamal. Kamal squirmed slightly but held eye contact. Bucheri said,

"All right, my friend. I'll tell you why I am here."

Ali gave an inward sigh of relief and nodded. "Please. I would deem it a great honor."

"You know of the partitioning of Palestine by the United Nations in 1947?"

"Yes, the great betrayal."

Bucheri nodded. "Some call it that. It was an attempt by the United Nations members to soothe their consciences about the Jews. Part of Palestine would go to the Jews and part to the Palestinians who had lived there for over a thousand years. My family lived in Jaffa. We were successful growers of fruit, mostly oranges. We Palestinians refused to accept the U.N. mandate, so the Jews took it upon themselves to throw us out, frighten us or kill us."

Ali Kamal nodded—this was part of modern Arab lore.

Bucheri continued. "In 1948, two Stern Gang terrorists, Zionist extremists, came into town disguised as Arabs. They were driving a truck filled with dynamite which was covered with oranges. They detonated the dynamite and killed over one hundred people, mostly Arabs. Early in that year the Jews started terrorizing the Arabs, trying to panic us, so that they could claim as much territory as possible before the British left on May 15. They believed that regular Arab armies would pour into Palestine then and throw them into the sea. Their tactics were primarily those of terror. They would mount loudspeakers and harangue Arab villages, then use mortars or rocket bombardments for the final push. Thousands of Arabs panicked after the massacres in Deir Yassin and Kolonia, small isolated villages. In all, perhaps three-quarters of a million fled. The Hagana, the Jewish defense force, moved into Jaffa on May 14, 1948. Looters from Tel Aviv cleaned out the town and thousands of Jews moved in immediately. Of an Arab population of seventy-five thousand, there were only three thousand left. Ali, by 1953 a third of Israel's Jewish population was living on land taken from us. One of my aunts was killed in Jaffa when her family tried to escape by sea. They overturned their boats when Jewish snipers opened fire. And Ali, do you know how I have learned these statistics?"

Ali shook his head.

Bucheri threw his head back and laughed. "From the Jews. They are just beginning to admit to their atrocities. Just a few years ago..." He closed his eyes for a moment. "Yes, in *Hadashot*, one of their daily newspapers, they reported that five hundred men, women, and children were killed in Dweima on October 28, 1948. And Ali, the best part—they were killed by a regular Israeli army unit. Isn't it unbelievable what these people do? And they have an incredible grip on the propaganda machinery in America, especially the movies. Movies like *Exodus*, all about the heroic defense against massive Arab legions—pure propaganda, a myth. Even the Jewish historians are admitting it now, men like Simha Flapam and Benny Morris. Unfortunately, it's too late. They have gone way beyond the myth now with their moves into the occupied territories. They are a greedy people, eating the land and the cultures that lie before them. Even their own truths don't slow them. Only the Americans can stop them."

Bucheri looked at Kamal, but Kamal had nothing to say. Bucheri stood up. "Are you going out?" Kamal asked.

Bucheri looked up as he picked up his briefcase, his constant companion. "Yes. I'll be down at Legal Seafood on Level 2 of the shopping galleries. You know the place?"

Kamal did not. He spent most of his time in the room as his instructions from Bucheri required. "I'll be able to find you."

Bucheri shook his head. "No, you stay here and watch the news. If anything comes up, call me using your portable phone. And Ali?"

"Yes."

"Set the alarm system while I'm gone."

"I always do."

Bucheri paused at the door to look through the spy hole. After sticking his head out very quickly he turned back to Dr. Kamal. "Ali, do you want anything?"

"No, thank you," Ali gestured towards the room service breakfast. "I'm fine."

The door closed silently and Ali went to set the alarms. Bucheri was adamant about them.

12:13 P.M.
Command Vehicle 2

Captain Knight was jerked upright from his small seat in the cramped communication van by the cry from the Sergeant on the console.

"Data, Data. Holy Shit. Another one."

Captain Knight looked over the Sergeant's shoulder. This was the second positive contact in … he looked carefully over the time hash, two minutes. The Sergeant pointed mutely. Now a third one was starting. Knight took out his notepad and started writing down the exact time of transmission. Two minutes later they were still coming off. He leaned over to the Sergeant.

"Let me know if they stop and get me a continuous printout."

The Sergeant nodded as Captain Knight moved over to his radio. He pressed the talk button and waited a moment for the cipher unit to wind up.

"Bishop Three, Bishop Three, this is Six."

"Six this is Three, go ahead."

"I have some times for you."

"Shoot Six."

"Twelve zero five and three three seconds. Say again, twelve zero five and three three. Say back please."

"Roger that, Twelve zero five minutes and thirty-three seconds."

And the process went on.

12:22 P.M.
JFK Federal Building

Jones had the working group ready when Captain Knight ran in, breathless, printouts crinkled in his hand. Jones gestured to a seat next to him. Captain Knight ignored the chair and started spreading the printouts next to Jones. The others leaned over.

"We've actually gotten ten intercepts. I don't know whether they triggered on voice ID or word recognition. The program doesn't tell us, but here's the cool part." Knight gestured down the right hand column. "Look, they all originate from the same coordinates. This has got to be him. Bang, bang, bang, one call right after the other. And they're all nearly identical, as best we can tell from the transmission time. It's a code probably, but they're the same."

Jones leaned back in his chair and rubbed his chin. "He's sending out orders to his teams. They must all be doing the same thing."

Jones looked at General Bradley for confirmation. The General pursed his lips before replying, "Maybe. Code words. That's fast too."

Jones stared intently at the General for a moment, actually seeing nothing. "I doubt it. The time linkage is too close. Anyway, we'll know in about half an hour when we get to listen to the tapes." He looked up at Captain Knight for confirmation.

Knight nodded but added, "Sir, it will save time if I just listen to them. I know what you're looking for. If I have to copy them onto another format in the Communication Vehicle and all that, well, add another thirty minutes."

Jones nodded his approval. "Check the voice ID as best you can. Now, these coordinates, where are they?"

Captain Knight unfolded a large map of Boston then overlaid a clear plastic sheet with thin grid lines drawn on it. He carefully lined up two registration marks on the map with two similar marks on the overlay sheet, then taped the sheets together with clear tape.

"The blue circles are the location of the originator. All the readings from our triangulation units place it within this area." His finger drew a small circle.

Jones leaned over, deliberately pushing Captain Knight out of the way of the bright light from the desk lamp.

"Intersection of Huntington and Dartmouth, close enough. Tim, what's there?"

Tim Blackwell, the head of the local FBI office, looked more closely. "Library, Trinity Church, Copley Square. That's not exactly a small target."

Commissioner Yeager sat down after a glance. "He won't be in the library or the church. He can't stay there long or use a portable phone from there. If he is using this as a base, then he's in one of the hotels there, the Marriott or the Westin. If he's just hanging around, well, he picked a great place. There must be over a hundred shops and dining facilities."

Jones leaned back and closed his eyes. For just a moment, the others thought he might have fallen asleep. Then his eyes opened slowly, almost reptilian. A predatory smile crept onto his face.

"He's there. In one of the hotels. Probably the Westin. That's his base."

Commissioner Yeager snorted. "How do you know that?"

Jones turned the predatory smile on Yeager. "I saw everything on Bucheri. Everything. Every report, every picture, every rumor. He likes to command from close by and he likes luxury. I've also read about Boston."

Commissioner Yeager shook his head. "We've got plenty of luxurious hotels in the downtown."

Jones smiled again. "But only one that claims to be New England's tallest building. I read the advertisement. I'll bet he has several suites on different floors, all high and all facing in different directions. It lets him see everywhere."

Commissioner Yeager nodded, "That makes sense, sort of, but there are other hotels—the Bostonian, the Marriott Long Wharf—that are even farther downtown and also high. He can't see over Beacon Hill from where he is."

Jones put his palms on the table. "Yes, but maybe there's something he knows that we don't. Some reason that he doesn't want to be at that end of town. The fact remains, he's in Copley Square somewhere. Now, Tim, I want you and Commissioner Yeager to get together and seal that area up tighter than a submarine. The General can provide extra manpower from the MPs. Then I want you both to start a search, a smart search, for Bucheri. Use your detectives, pump the staff, everything. And," he paused for effect, "do it now and don't give him any warning. I know that seems impossible, but do it. If we get him, everything collapses."

Jones turned to Ted Browner and stabbed a finger in his direction. "Get the HRT here now. Everybody. Move them into Copley Square and have them ready." He turned to General Bradley. Bradley stood at attention, leaning forward slightly, a tiger ready to leap. "Get Delta Force ready to be airborne on five minutes' notice."

The General was gone almost instantly. Jones watched the doorway for a moment after he had left.

"Fast isn't he?" commented Ted Browner.

Jones watched the door, seeing nothing for a moment, before turning back. "There's more."

Yeager couldn't quite stifle the groan that escaped. Jones swiveled to face him. "Stop everything."

Yeager was confused. "Everything?"

Jones nodded. "All traffic except those engineer trucks, if they aren't already in position." He turned to face Ted Browner. "Ted, pull the plugs on the cellular phones. Shut down any cellular centers that might pick up signals from the area. You gentlemen get the picture?"

Yeager nodded. Ted Browner replied, "Total shutdown."

"Right," Jones replied. "If anyone wants to go anywhere, they walk. If anyone wants to talk, they can't. Now we'll see how foxy Bucheri's people are."

1:17 P.M.
JFK Federal Building

Jones had moved to the Command Post in the cafeteria of the Federal Building. Cables snaked out the double doors to the command vehicles parked in the plaza of Government Center. Paratroops in two sand-bagged emplacements guarded the entrance. The presence of the M-60 machine guns spoke volumes. The tension from the command center had rippled through the troops; they were wire taut.

Jones paced. From computer consoles to radio operators and then back to the situation map tacked to the wall, he paced. He sat down briefly at the center table that he used as his desk. He picked a donut from the Dunkin Donuts box, took a bite, wrinkled his nose in disgust and then finished eating it in quick nervous pieces.

Jeannie moved up next to him and shook her finger reprovingly. Under other circumstances, he would have laughed. The best he could manage now was a tired smile. He gestured for her to sit. He was about to speak when a radio operator waved to him and called, "Director Jones."

Jones motioned for Jeannie to follow him and trotted over the tangle of discarded printouts, food boxes and computer cables that decorated the floor. "What?"

The operator handed him a handset, "Sir, it's Checkpoint Seven. The senior man insists on talking to you."

Jones picked up the handset and keyed it to talk. "Jones here." With his finger, he pointed to the speaker, indicating to the operator that he should also turn on the speaker.

The voice came through free of static. "Sergeant McGeorge here, sir. I've got something interesting."

Jones thought for a moment. Probably no one above McGeorge had been willing to consider this important. "Go ahead."

"You remember the gasoline that we found in a vehicle?" Jeannie Kawai jerked upright at the mention of gasoline. Jones threw her a questioning look but kept on with the conversation.

"Yes."

Jeannie Kawai had closed her eyes and was pressing her fingers against her forehead, just above her nose, as though she had a severe sinus headache.

"We found two guys carrying gasoline this time. All the alarms went off in my head."

They all went off in Jones's head too. "We'll send someone for them right away."

After a brief burst of static, Sergeant McGeorge's voice came through. "Well, sir, I don't think that's really necessary. Anyhow, we've got the word to block everything rolling anyhow. You'd have to fly."

Damn, Jones thought, "it wasn't necessary." Maybe they'd gotten trigger-happy and killed them. Jones turned to the radio operator. "Is this secure?"

"Yes sir, it's a cipher set. Only you and the other end can hear. It's just static to anybody else." Jones nodded.

"Sergeant McGeorge. This system is secure, it's scrambled. Why don't you tell me what happened."

There was a moment's silence before Sergeant McGeorge responded, "Well, sir, it was kind of accidental." Jones groaned to himself. "The team searching one of the men found a firearm on one of these boys and well, one of our patrolmen sort of went nuts. I'm sorry sir; he really shouldn't have been on the street. He pulled out his weapon and emptied it into the guy, saying, 'I knew it, I knew it.' It's a long story on him, sir. Anyhow, the other guy started talking, and I mean talking a lot. My man Craft, that's the shooter, scared the hell out of him."

Jones sighed with relief. "Well, what did he say?"

"Well sir, the important part is that he and his group are moving up to Foster Street to start fires with this gasoline of theirs. He thinks that a number of other groups are going to do the same thing. All of them starting at 2:00 p.m. I mean this guy will tell you anything you want to know, but that's what they're going to do. You going to send someone to pick him up?"

Jones nodded slowly to himself as absentmindedly he handed the handset back to the radio operator.

Jeannie Kawai turned pale and gripped Jones's arm, "My God! His mother. She was burned in an air raid."

"Son of a bitch," he said very slowly and distinctly. Those nearby, including Commissioner Yeager, stopped what they were doing to stare. Then he said it again, yelling, "SON OF A BITCH! HE'S REALLY GOING TO DO IT."

Commissioner Yeager asked, "Do what?"

Jones slammed his fist into the table. "He's going to burn Boston. It wasn't rhetoric. He's really going to burn Boston. That's why he's cut off the water."

Jones slammed his fist on the table. "That son of a bitch, he even told us, twice. Yesterday with *Light My Fire* and today with *American Pie. Jumping Jack Flash* my ass. That's him, 'the Devil's only friend.'" The others looked bewildered. Jones saw their confusion, paused, and then ignored them as he kicked over a folding chair. "Jesus H. Christ!" Then something else clicked in his mind. He looked around frantically. "Where's Bradley?"

A lieutenant jumped up. "Sir, General Bradley's in Command Vehicle Two."

Jones jabbed a finger at the lieutenant. "Get his ass over here now."

She turned to pick up a phone but froze as Jones yelled, "No! You. Get him NOW!" She sprinted out through the obstacle course of chairs, tables, cables, and soda cans.

Moments later, she came running back, breathing hard. Jones held up his hand. "Now look at me." She stopped, transfixed. "Find Liz Martin or Ted Browner. Tell them that the news must go out instantly. The news is, 'Stay in your homes until notified. Do not go out for any reason.' Is that clear?"

She nodded. He made her repeat it. Just as she finished, the General ran in.

"She told me. Burning," he gasped.

"Right," Jones replied. "Now listen you two." He gestured to General Bradley and Commissioner Yeager as they gathered by him to look at the map. "He's going to start at least one fire here." His finger landed on Foster Street. "The team that we got, or got part of, though there would be others. My guess is … ten. There were ten calls. Now, if they're like the Japanese team, then eight to ten people. That's a lot of arsonists. If they know what they're doing, and Bucheri is goddamn thorough, they could light this whole place up. My guess is that they'll try and light a line of fires like this." With his finger, he traced a line roughly following the waterfront.

Yeager asked, "Why?"

281

"So that he can get a wall of fire going. The wind is from the sea, the east, during the day. That will drive the fire westward. If it forms a wall, it will be impossible to fight."

General Bradley nodded. "Kind of like being outflanked. You can only do an attack from the front, and the rest moves by and flanks you."

Jones looked up from the map. "That's right, close enough." He paused for a moment, looking into the distance but seeing nothing. Then he snapped his fingers sharply. "Probably right on. It even sounds like a military tactic. This is very Russian, massive strength to the front. Damn that son of a bitch. What's more, I'll bet he has boats for his attack teams to escape to the east."

Jones turned to Yeager. "Two things. First, alert your boats to start patrolling this area."

"Right," Yeager replied. "I'll get the Coast Guard too. They've got some boats there. What's two?"

"Two," Jones said, "is get the firemen there. Every fucking fireman in fifty miles with every piece of equipment that rolls. Now, that means you're going to have to have communication lanes, entrance routes, assembly areas. If you need the Common, we'll move the Army into the Haymarket."

Jones checked to see whether General Bradley was going to fight over the loss of terrain, but Bradley's eyes were fixed on the map. He looked up. "Most of the bridges are jammed."

Jones jabbed a finger at him. "That's your job. Use the engineers and their equipment. Throw those cars into the river if you have to. Give Colonel Shaw, the MP commander, *carte blanche* on that problem."

He tuned to Commissioner Yeager. "I'm sorry Eddy. A lot of people are going to be pissed, but we have to have those communication lines free."

Commissioner Yeager looked uncomfortable. Jones stabbed him impatiently with his eyes. "Well, what is it?"

"Well, I can handle all the police problems, but I'm not the Fire Commissioner."

Jones clenched his teeth in exasperation. "Jesus H. Christ! How often do I have to explain it to you people? You have to make it happen. Take your goddamn helicopter and pick him up. Go up to five thousand feet and tell him to come through or you're going to push his ass out. We don't have the goddamn mayor, the goddamn assistant mayor. Hell, we don't even have a janitor, Eddy. You've got to make it happen."

Eddy Yeager stared at Jones for a moment then decided that he'd find a way to convince the Fire Commissioner.

Yeager seemed about to go, but Jones gestured for him to wait.

"All right General," Jones said, turning to Bradley. "Now we'll see how good your people really are. Deploy the ready company along this area. Their job is to keep everyone off the street, period—everyone. They should apprehend anyone suspicious and call in some MPs to take them away. They are to absolutely lock down that zone. They are authorized to fire their weapons in self-defense and in protection of the firemen. They can use lower levels of force to motivate the poor innocents of Boston, but they must keep people off the streets. Can you control them?"

General Bradley looked insulted. "Yes *sir*," he replied, with a very heavy emphasis on the 'sir.'

Jones flared. "Don't give me any insolent shit, General. We're turning the wolves loose in a chicken ranch. Your people aren't trained for this and they're armed to the teeth. I want you to bring in your Rangers and break them up into groups suitable for sniper suppression and you damn well better keep a rein on them, because they're going to get to play hardball today. Do you know what happened to Yeager's team?"

General Bradley shook his head.

"Eighty percent losses from one damn sniper," Jones replied.

General Bradley looked to Commissioner Yeager for confirmation. Yeager closed his eyes and nodded sadly. General Bradley paled. "How—" he started, but Jones cut him off. "A trap."

1:32 P.M.
JFK Federal Building

Commissioner Yeager moved up next to Harley Jones in the command center. "I just thought of something."

Bradley and Jones turned to him. "We haven't got any water," Yeager said.

Harley Jones literally screamed, "Shit!" Then he calmed slightly. "What do you mean, no water? I thought the goddamn engineers fixed it."

Commissioner Yeager nodded. "They're finished now."

Jones put his hands on his hips and jutted his chin forward. "So what's the problem?"

General Bradley interrupted. "The engineers say that water isn't like electricity. It takes a while to build up pressure."

Jones closed his eyes as though praying. "All right, how long?"

"Two hours to full pressure," Yeager replied.

Jones was clearly having trouble controlling himself. Finally, he spoke in a barely restrained voice.

"General, you kick ass on whoever you have to get us pressure. Eddy, you tell those firemen that they'd better keep those fires out if they have to piss on them. They can pump from the harbor for all I care, but if this town burns, so do they."

Rigidly, barely in control, Jones walked outside to get some air.

1:48 P.M.

Jalil Ferahian closed the door as Musa came into the rented apartment. It was time. There had been too many delays, and only four of his seven men had made it to the rendezvous. It wasn't a tragedy but it didn't look good either.

Musa apologized. "I had to leave my gasoline container. There are police and soldiers everywhere."

Jalil decided to display some leadership. He smiled. "Do not worry Musa. We have our alternative plan, do we not?"

Musa nodded. Jalil reached into the box and handed to each man a six-foot length of clear plastic tubing. "Have no fear. This is Tygon. It will not be melted by the gasoline. What is the one thing you must remember?"

They answered in unison. "Do not swallow the gasoline."

Jalil paused for a moment. "Except Musa, we know he is a fire breather."

The others laughed, relieved to shed some tension. Jalil continued, "The automobiles all have gasoline. Any house will have a container of some kind, a pot, a jar, something like that. Remember also that burning cars will provide a considerable annoyance to soldiers. A single shot, or a stab into the gas tank. You all have your knives?"

They all reached for their knives. Musa, always the individual, showed an ice pick for gas tanks as well as a knife.

Jalil could not keep from smiling at Musa. "We see that Musa will stick the American eagle in the rear with his ice pick and then cut his throat when he turns around. Musa is clearly a man meant for paradise."

Jalil kept smiling despite his slip of the tongue. Today any mention of paradise suggested death. Death might be acceptable, but failure was not. There was the Long Road to remember.

"Now. Matches?"

They moved smoothly, putting away their knives and pulling out packs of safety matches. Satisfied, Jalil continued with the inspection.

"Cigarettes?"

Each man showed his hard pack of Marlboro cigarettes.

"Now, is there anyone who does not remember how to make the long fuse? Put the burning cigarette so that it ignites the match book when it burns down. Ten minutes for a full cigarette."

Everyone nodded. Under other circumstances, they would have been bored, but the promise of imminent action had an energizing effect. They were riveted to his every word.

"Finally, what are the three rules?"

Jalil held up one finger.

"Use lots of fuel," the group chorused.

Jalil held up a second finger.

"Start on wood."

Jalil nodded encouragement and held up three fingers.

"Start on a wall."

Jalil pointed a finger. "Salwa. Why?"

"So that the fire can climb."

Jalil was pleased; they had learned their lessons well. He continued, "Magdi. Alternative sources of fuel."

Magdi hesitated a moment. "Ah … natural gas for the stove, cleaning solvent, medicinal alcohol." He hesitated a moment longer. Jalil nodded that this was sufficient. It was not the time to rattle confidences.

"Pistols." Everyone pulled out their pistols.

"Rifles." Musa and Salwa turned around and tapped their backs. Under their sweatshirts each gave a metallic clack. Musa had an American Ruger Mini 14 with a folding stock. Salwa had an Egyptian folding stock AK-47. They turned to face him.

Jalil quickly scanned the men. They all had earphones plugged in.

"Radio check."

Each man in turn tapped the microphone hidden somewhere under his sweater. Jalil had his pinned right up by his collarbone so that he could talk simply by turning his head. The others nodded that they had heard the short transmission.

Jalil checked his watch: 13:55. There was still time to review the tactics. "Now, we can no longer work in teams of three or four. We must go as teams of two. One man provides fire support for the other. We are more likely to be successful at burning the block if we start fires in different buildings. If any team gets in trouble, they call the other team, but keep the radio talk down. The Americans locked into our transmissions before and we all know what happened then." They all nodded. Every one of them had lost family at the Long Road.

Jalil motioned them all to their knees. "A brief prayer my friends, for our success."

Each prayed for a moment, in his own way. Then Jalil stood up, and the rest followed. He put out his hands, and Musa, then Salwa and Magdi, put theirs on top of his. "For the Long Road," said Jalil.

"My wife on the Long Road," said Salwa.

"My wife and my two sons," said Magdi with tears in his eyes.

"Revenge for my brother on the Long Road," said Musa fiercely.

"My mother, my wife, my daughters," said Jalil, his voice catching as he remembered them.

All of this team had belonged to the Army of the Province of Kuwait after the liberation. They had been allowed by Saddam to bring their families into the liberated territories. There was only one road from Kuwait City to Baghdad, and their families had all been on that road when the American helicopter gunships had machine-gunned the convoys. Those left alive were destroyed by the cluster bombs dropped by screaming fighter bombers. Jalil had seen it from a distance and had run over a kilometer to find his family. His oldest daughter was recognizable only by her dress. Jalil had come for payback.

2:30 P.M.

Harley Jones sprinted across Charter Street, followed by Major Page, the Ranger company commander. Just when he thought they would get across without trouble, a single round snapped through the air between them. Jones ducked between two cars, puffing loudly.

"Jesus! That was close."

Major Page wasn't even breathing hard. "Naw. I had at least a meter clearance, so you musta had the same," he drawled.

"What's the situation?"

Major Page smiled slowly, then spoke with a soft southern accent that contrasted sharply with the command voice Jones had seen him use minutes before. "Well, fucked up, but not bad at all really. We didn't exchange cipher codes with the Airborne. So we can't talk to them." He winked at the Airborne private that they had joined behind the car. "But you never could talk to these folks anyhow. So we just yell. It seems to work. They've been doing a good job of spotting where the fire's coming from, but my boys are a bit uncomfortable, if you catch my meaning, about having them do suppression fire. 'Cause of the radios—we can't shut 'em off, ya know, 'cease fire' and all that. Other than that, we're doing real good. And the closer we get, the better we do. These bad guys don't shoot real good and our body armor is ace."

Jones waited patiently then started. "Look Major, I don't have time for a goddamn jaw and a pull at the jug. Now have you got the situation under control or not?"

The Major looked startled. "Well of course, Mr. Jones. Rangers lead the way."

A burst of automatic weapons fire followed by the sharp crack of several concussion grenades rolled down from the direction of the sniping. The Major looked at the radio operator who had followed them across the street. The radio operator had the intent look of someone listening. He blinked twice, then said,

"Clear, sir. One enemy KIA, one friendly wounded. They're taking him to the aid station later. It's no biggie."

The operator looked pleased, as did the Major.

Jones stared at the Major. "Well?"

"Sir?"

"The wounded. Was it a civilian?"

The Major looked startled at the thought. The radio operator smiled and shook his head. "It was Webber, sir. He fell on the steps and broke his arm."

The Major turned to Jones. "Webber is … special. He's clumsy but he's the strongest man in the company."

Jones replied. "Accidents will happen, Major Page. Try not to add to the civilian body count. Got it?"

The Major nodded, unsmiling this time. "Roger that."

Moments later the Major watched Jones receive a radio message and then run back up the street. Something big was happening somewhere. Just before receiving the message, a sniper round had shattered on the wall behind Jones, barely missing him. Jones hadn't even blinked. Well, Major Page thought, Jones had nerve.

3:00 P.M.

Jones's stomach lurched as the helicopter dropped in a dizzying spiral. The pilot had warned him. They had to take a steep descent to avoid being seen from any of the Westin Hotel rooms. As Jones looked across to the Marriott Hotel, he couldn't help but wonder who was watching them from those dark windows. At least they wouldn't be using a cellular phone. Damn! Jones slammed his palm against his thigh. He hoped that Blackwell had shut down the hotel internal switchboard. He ground his teeth. There were so many things that could go wrong. They had to capture Bucheri, find out who had sent him, and then try him. Maybe they would find something to try him for that had a death penalty.

The helicopter settled with a distinct thud and lifted off as soon as he was out of the rotor zone. Jones ducked instinctively but looked around despite the rotor wash. Black-clad troops were occupying the roof, their balaclavas pulled down, short murderous submachine guns slung on their chests. Some had ropes over their shoulders. All of them watched him with a relaxed alertness that reminded Jones of Doberman Pinschers.

Ted Browner grabbed his arm. "Delta. Bradley brought them."

Jones turned to Browner with his brows knitted in a questioning expression. "Delta? Why?"

Browner shrugged. "General Bradley said he wanted to secure the roof. You know, he doesn't exactly sit and fetch for me, if you catch my meaning." Jones could see how a Marine Corps lieutenant general might be a bit hard to control.

They moved into the penthouse machinery room where all the hotel cooling equipment was running. Browner turned to Jones. He had to yell to be heard over the roar of the compressors. "We think we've found him. The staff noted one man who seemed to have several suites. We've been scoping all three of these rooms. No sound in any room but one, 2807. We haven't drilled any holes for a fiber optic visual yet. I wanted to wait for permission. You know, there's some risk in that."

Jones nodded. Even though the pin hole required for the fiber optic was small, it wasn't invisible. If someone happened to see the drill bit come through, or notice the small amount of dust from the floor, or even hear the drill ... well, the shit would hit the fan. A man came up to Jones, silent against the hiss of the compressors. He tapped Jones on the shoulder. Jones couldn't help himself—he jumped slightly as he spun around.

"Roger! Damn, good to see you." Roger Chan, the HRT Commander, was a protégé of Jones's and a long-time friend from his HRT days. "So they finally promoted you to your level of incompetence."

Chan smiled slightly. "With your assistance, yes."

Jones knew the procedure as a former HRT Commander, but he couldn't stop himself from asking the questions. Roger Chan wasn't surprised.

"Is the floor cleared?" Jones asked.

Browner nodded.

"What entry point?"

"The door. The walls have structural steel."

"Balcony?"

"None."

Jones sighed. "OK."

They moved down the stairwell quietly past the first HRT sentry. He nodded to Roger Chan. Jones didn't recognize him. "New guy?" he asked.

"Yes," Chan said. "From San Antonio, speaks Spanish. We're getting more and more incidents with Spanish speakers, so we've modified the team composition."

"What's Delta doing here?" Jones asked.

Chan looked startled. "I thought they were here on your orders. A captain came by and said that Delta was here to assist."

Jones looked puzzled. "I didn't order them in. That must have been General Bradley."

Chan shrugged. "We gave them our frequency. They've been a help since we want to crash all three rooms at once. They've taken over all the connecting corridors and stairwells. It's saved us a lot of manpower."

Jones paused for a moment, squinted at nothing, then said, "Are you ready?"

Again Chan shrugged. "We're ready to go but we have no visual on any of the rooms in the suite. It's a damn quiet hotel so we couldn't use the electric. We've used a hand drill to the gyprock layer, but since you were coming, I waited. The carpets in these rooms are very dark, so he might notice. I prefer to take a look. Hell, he's trapped. We can always wait him out. There are no hostages. Why take a chance?"

Jones thought for a moment. They had stopped at the 28th floor and were standing in the stairwell so that no noise would escape down the corridor to room 2807. The problem was one of entry. If the entry were smooth, then Bucheri would be unable to respond quickly enough to escape and would probably be killed or captured. It took only seconds, however, to run into a room and bar the door, especially if one had prepared wedges or braces—even a chair would do in a pinch. Give Bucheri five minutes and who knew what he could do? He could have several hundred pounds of explosive in there. With that he could blow a huge hole in the building. He might blow out a window and rappel down the building sides, or blow out a wall and try to escape that way. The list of possibilities was large for a trained soldier with a big budget. Despite what Chan had said, time was not on their side. Bucheri needed to be stopped and, preferably, questioned as soon as possible to minimize any future damage.

Jones gently pushed Roger Chan against the stairwell wall and leaned his palm against his chest, much as a football coach might talk to a player whose undivided attention he must have.

"What's right behind the door?"

"The door goes down a corridor into the suite. Bathroom on one side, closet on the other."

"OK. Use the eye just by the door. Look for any bar blocking the way. If it looks good, go in there immediately. How are you going to open it?"

Chan smiled. "Well, we could use the key, but he might have pennied it, so we'll blow it."

Jones smiled back. Chan was referring to the use of a penny in the door jamb. It would act as a tiny, almost invisible, door wedge. Plastic explosive could be directed fairly carefully to cut the hinges and locks simultaneously.

Jones asked, "Have you checked your charges?"

Chan nodded. "Yeah, we owe the hotel for a few doors on the eleventh floor. They were really pissed, but it works fine."

Jones looked into Chan's eyes. There wasn't much more to say.

"Do it."

* * *

Sergeants Jerry Moss and Steve Chambers pushed off as soon as they heard the command "Go" from First Sergeant Top Polanyi. Their anchors were only five feet apart—a little too close for comfort—so they rappelled almost side by side. Moss was the senior man of the two, but the whole show would really be run by Top Polanyi from the roof. He would also be watching their progress through a television which was feeding from a remote camera in the John Hancock building. As they passed the first window, Moss said, "Thirty-three."

Top Polanyi confirmed, "Thirty-three."

As they passed the next floor, the procedure continued: "Thirty-two." It would be very embarrassing if they broke into the wrong suite, Sergeant Moss thought. Typical Army fuck-up. He shrugged; typical Army maybe, but not typical Delta Force. They were the best. Sergeant Moss wasn't college educated, but he was a very bright man. There were no dummies in Delta. There was too much to learn, and one had to adapt.

Normally, Moss would have laughed at the "party line" that they were the best, but he'd worked with the British SAS and Germany's GSG-9. They had some outstanding troops, all of them, but the Americans had the best equipment and Sergeant Moss felt that equipment could make all the difference on Special Operations. Their rappelling gear was an example. The SAS had tried to have some of their people crash windows during the Iranian Embassy incident in '87. One of them had gotten strung upside down and almost burned in the fire that they accidentally started with their smoke and gas grenades. Delta had tested this new harness upside down and sideways. You never got hung up. Braking was automatic, all you had to do was squeeze to drop, and a single slap on the release button and you were completely free.

The plan was simple: swing through the window and kill the bad guy. Of course, it wasn't really that simple. These windows were very tough, so people couldn't accidentally break them and fall through. The second thing was the swing. If they swung out with six stories of line above them, their arc would be so long that they probably wouldn't be back for football season. The solutions seemed easy. To break the windows, he and Chambers would shoot them out with their weapons, 12 gauge Remington semi-automatic shotguns with eight-shot extended magazines. Nothing fancy there, except the barrel had been shortened to sixteen inches to get a wider pattern. Double-aught shot might not totally remove the window, but it would weaken it enough that he and Chambers should go through like a karate chop on Jell-O. The swing wasn't too tough either. They would just put a spike and a carabiner through the wall at the thirty-first floor. They would run their rappelling lines through that and they'd only have a two-floor, maybe twenty-foot length of line free to swing from. As for going through glass, that was the least of their worries. They both wore Nomex fire retarding woven hoods as well as very tough black combat suits. And to top it off, thought Moss, smiling to himself, our outfit is complemented with chic gloves and matching boots in leather. Yes indeed, thought Moss, some dude was going to get shot to shit by some very fashionable guys.

"Thirty-one," said Moss into his small throat microphone.

"Thirty-one," confirmed Top. "Install anchors."

"Affirmative," replied Moss.

The procedure went without a hitch, although Moss got a slight touch of vertigo and almost dropped his hammer when he looked down. "Jesus Christ," he muttered quietly. He'd never rappelled from this high before, not nearly. It was enough to slam your asshole shut real tight.

"Say again," said the Top.

"Nothing, Top," replied Moss. Top wouldn't say anything else, but the criticism would be there when the tapes were played back. No chatter allowed.

Moss looked at Chambers. Chambers, eyes hidden by the glass lenses in the hood, nodded back.

"Ready for last descent," said Moss.

Immediately Top replied, "Proceed."

"Thirty."

"Thirty confirmed," repeated the Top. Moss's heartbeat was picking up.

"Twenty-nine. Stopping."

"Twenty-nine confirmed. Understood stopping."

Sergeant Moss pulled his shotgun off his harness. This shotgun had only a pistol-type grip. It was nice, short and deadly. If he dropped it, it would go down all the way. There was no safety strap on this. He couldn't have it getting in the way if he wanted to dump it. He still had his .45 automatic Colt pistol for something up close and personal. If it got any closer than that, he'd just stomp the other guy to death. His pulse was pounding a tattoo in his ear. He looked over at Chambers. Chambers gave him the thumbs up signal. He was ready.

"Team One ready for entry." Moss was surprised that his voice croaked. He was ready to rock and roll.

"Team One, permission to enter. Execute. Execute. Execute."

It was up to him now. He started with the countdown.

"Three, two, one—go!" He and Chambers pushed out as they had hundreds of times before. Chambers was his wingman, and they had to be as precise as the Blue Angels in aerial maneuvers. On the out-swing it looked good—he could see Chambers just barely out of the corner of his eye. At the apex of swing, where they would get maximum spread, they both fired three times. Over forty .30 caliber steel balls smacked through the window. Things couldn't be perfect, and the firing had twisted Moss slightly so that he would hit the window sideways. He had tunnel vision now: he couldn't see Chambers; all his attention was focused on the glass. The inward swing seemed to last an eternity. Moss felt he was moving in slow motion as he curled up to hit the glass like a cannon ball.

* * *

Jones watched anxiously from the end of the corridor as the HRT lined up to move into the room, six men total. They had rehearsed in an identical suite three floors down and six seemed ideal, two for each of the rooms, although the acoustic sensor system indicated only one man pacing in the suite, a radio playing lightly in the background. The last man had stepped into place when the unthinkable happened. There was a tremendous "whump" sound and the door slammed outwards, ripping through the frame, followed by a wave of fire that washed over the first man in the entry team, setting him on fire.

The second and third men were knocked down by the blast, but the other three rushed forward and fell on their team mate, smothering the fire.

Jones and Roger Chan sprinted for the door. Jones yelled at Chan, "What happened?"

The flames were already dying down from the room blaze when they reached the doorway. Chan answered "Not us! No way. Bill still has the safety on his detonator box."

Jones looked around the corner into the room, over the carpet of flame on the floor. He was just in time to see a rope snake through the window and upwards.

Jones spun around and pushed Chan aside yelling, "Fucking Delta." Jones reached Ted Browner at the stairwell and shoved him in the direction of the up staircase. "Fucking Delta blew it."

Less than a minute later he was up on the roof sprinting towards a cluster of men in the center. A Delta trooper stepped tentatively in his way and was rewarded with a straight arm which sent him sprawling. The group was looking up as a Black Hawk helicopter descended onto the roof. Jones looked around the group, searching for the ranking officer, but they wore no insignia.

"Who's in charge here?" he yelled over the roar of the rotor wash. A huge man pushed him aside as the Black Hawk settled for only a few seconds. A body was placed aboard quickly and one man joined it. Then the helicopter lifted off with another rotor wash that flooded the area with roof dust.

The huge man turned to him. "How can I help you sir?"

Jones was furious. "Who's in charge here?"

The man eyed him coolly. "Who are you sir?"

Jones could feel his skin turning the livid purple color that he hated. "I'll tell you who I am. I'm Assistant Director of the FBI Harley Jones. I'm in charge of this entire operation." Trembling with anger, Jones pulled out his identification and thrust it in the man's face. The man stepped back and examined the ID critically. Then he stepped back coolly and saluted.

"Sir, I am First Sergeant Polanyi. The man in charge is Major Dell."

Jones tried to slow his speech. "Well, First Sergeant Polanyi, perhaps you could arrange an introduction to Major Dell for me sometime in the near future."

First Sergeant Polanyi was beginning to have a little trouble holding his temper too. "Sir, Major Dell was on the helicopter that just left with our wounded man. We also have one dead sir."

Jones leaned forward, his head barely reaching the First Sergeant's neck, and began jabbing his finger into the man's chest with each word. "Well, First Sergeant, maybe you can tell me just who authorized this assault of yours."

Now First Sergeant Polanyi became a bit uncomfortable. "Well, sir, I guess you did."

Immediately Jones lashed back, "I did no such goddamn thing First Sergeant. Now who authorized this colossal fuck up?"

First Sergeant Polanyi drew himself to attention. "Sir, I do not know, sir."

Jones felt a tap on his shoulder but ignored it. "Furthermore Sergeant, where is your KIA?"

"Sir, I believe that he was blown out of the room and fell."

Jones shook his head in disgust. Tired now, he said, "Well First Sergeant, why don't you take a search party and see if you can find him?"

Jones felt the tap again. He turned to find General Bradley in battle dress. First Sergeant Polanyi snapped to attention and saluted, then left to search for his missing man.

Bradley said, "They had orders."

Jones put his hands on his hips. "From whom?"

Bradley ignored the question. "This man had to die. Every two-bit terrorist in the world would have been hijacking planes trying to get him out of prison. It would have been intolerable."

Jones closed his eyes and clenched his fists. Slowly he opened his eyes. "We don't know who hired him. We don't know what else he's got lined up. We have no way to find his people. That terrorism excuse is bullshit. Now who ordered it?"

General Bradley refused to reply. Jones stared at him eye to eye for a minute. Neither man flinched. Finally Jones leaned in and jabbed his finger into the General's chest. "And what happens when they tell you to put Jews in the oven, Bradley, what then? Follow orders?"

Jones spun around and walked down towards the stairwell.

When Jones reached room 2807 the fire had completely died down. Chan came up to him.

"We don't know exactly what it was, something with gasoline for sure. It's real nasty in there. He had a Radio Shack alarm system hooked up. Those guys going through the window broke the electrical connection on one of the metallic tapes. If it's any comfort, we would have set off a sensor on the door. The same thing would have happened."

Jones walked over the burned carpet, which was spotted with both sticky and crunchy patches. Chan pointed to the body by the window. "Actually, we're lucky the body's still in here. It almost got blown out." Jones was stepping over to examine the body when something crunched loudly under his feet. He retreated carefully. Despite his training, he was just beginning to realize that this was a crime scene of sorts. There might be forensic evidence. He looked down and realized that he had crushed a pair of wire rimmed glasses. He looked briefly at the body and shrugged. Bucheri wasn't looking good today. The stink of burnt plastic carpet and flesh was appalling, yet, despite this, something held him in the room.

Jones turned to Chan. "Any wires between the sensor and the explosive device?"

Chan shook his head. "No. It was probably radio linked."

Jones raised his eyebrows. "Why wouldn't Bucheri just lay out wires? They're a lot safer as a trigger mechanism—not so subject to accidental discharge. Static is a real danger, especially with carpets."

Chan shrugged. "Convenience? These suitcases are plastic. The system would be operational instantly. The radio signal would go right through them. Maybe he wanted to have them available to leave anywhere. Sure would be quick to set up, and once you hid the detector, no one would know that the system was here. We'll never know."

Jones shook his head. "I guess you're right. We'll never know."

6:15 P.M.
Legal Seafood Restaurant,
Copley Plaza

"Table for six please." Jones smiled as the head waiter cringed. Perhaps it was the battle dress jacket that he had adopted to be less obvious to snipers. More likely, it was the two hard-faced HRT men with submachine guns standing behind him. Guaranteed to get you a table at your restaurant of choice. Of course, the restaurant was empty. He smiled to himself. He was finally going to get his Legal Seafood meal.

A server hurried over at a gesture from the head waiter. "Yes sir."

Jones turned to the radioman, who was clearly uncomfortable in his filthy battle dress. "Like fish, son?"

The young man, perhaps twenty years old, wrinkled his nose in disgust. "No thanks sir, I'm fine."

"Fries and a Coke?"

The radioman nodded. Jones raised his eyebrows to the waiter, who nodded. Jones sat with a tired thump. "Menu for me and please clear the rest of the table."

The waiter moved efficiently as Jones closed his eyes. Fires. He saw fires. They were dying down now. Sniper fire had been minimal when Yeager had picked him up in his helicopter for an overflight of South Boston and Roxbury.

"How's it going, Commissioner?" he had asked as soon as the headset was in place.

"Roxbury's the shits. They're really pissed off, but at least the cordon is working. No one from South Boston has gotten in. Roxbury should be contained by morning with the forces I have on hand. The neighboring cities have sent in over a thousand men. About goddamn time. We'll just flood the area, lock it down tight."

Jones looked down as the city rushed by below. "Communications?"

"We're doing OK. General Bradley got us a communications unit. With a strict radio protocol—you know, not much talk—we're doing all right."

"How about your wife?"

Yeager looked across surprised. "OK, I think. I've got some people watching out for her. She should rotate out at 6:00 p.m. I'll talk to her then. She had a scare but..." He shrugged.

Jones nodded as the helicopter banked steeply to take him back to Copley Plaza. He had to see that room again—feel it, feel Bucheri's presence one last time.

Jones looked into Yeager's exhausted eyes. "Do you think it's over?"

Jones saw Yeager breathe deeply, perhaps a sigh, then wince from his cracked ribs. "Probably. It's slowed way down. Hell, I don't know. With Bucheri dead and strict compartmentalization, it has to collapse, doesn't it?"

Jones turned back to watch the Copley Plaza tower approach, "Doesn't it?" ringing in his head. Did they have contingency plans? Had he countered Bucheri's people by cutting communications and blocking movement? How many were left? Now he asked himself the questions that he had wanted to ask Bucheri.

Jones looked up, surprised to see Ted Browner coming into the restaurant. Jones waved him to a seat and passed him the menu as the radioman gave the handset to Jones.

"Ciphered message?" Jones asked the man.

The radioman nodded.

"Jones here."

A voice came through clear but slightly tinny. "Major Page, 3rd Rangers here, sir."

"Go ahead, Major."

"It's looking real good, sir. We haven't had any sniper fire the last hour, since you left. That may have been the last group. The rest might be on the run, but they aren't shooting. Overall, we've killed forty-three bad guys and captured fifteen more. We lost five Rangers, four more wounded, and you know about those civilians."

Jones remembered. He had been with Page when one terrorist had detonated a gasoline bomb, destroying himself and a family of four. It had been the only time that he had seen Major Page lose his cool. Page's voice startled Jones back to the present. "The senior fire chief asked me to report on the fire status."

Jones nodded, bracing himself. "Go ahead."

"We're doing real well there too. All the fires are contained and the wind's dying down. The chiefs say it's under control as long as no more start. Even then, they've got three battalions in reserve and the roads are clear, so maybe we could even handle some more fires. I don't know."

Jones nodded, relieved. "OK. Anything else to report?"

"No, sir. Colonel Shaw is here with me. His people have now got the cipher code so he'll come up on this frequency in about ten seconds. Page, 3rd Rangers clear."

Jones wanted to say something to Page when a new voice came through. Jones recognized the gruff tones. "Colonel Shaw here, Mr. Jones. Permission to report?"

Jones smiled faintly. "Go ahead, Colonel Shaw."

"Sir, I'm pleased to report that my MPs and the Boston police have control over all of downtown Boston. The Airborne troops have been pulled back to the Boston Commons to stand in reserve. With your permission, I'll release most of the Rangers. This ...*situation*...seems to have collapsed. With your permission, we'll withdraw this evening and return control to civilian authority by midnight."

Jones felt a tired satisfaction. "That sounds excellent, Colonel. We are deeply in your debt. Please pass on my compliments to your troops."

There was a pause, then the brusque voice came through clearly, warmer than before. "Thank you, sir. Thank you very much. I'll pass the word."

Ted Browner put the menu down. "I've been talking to the Command Post. It looks like we're just about done in Boston. The water pressure is up. All the fires are under control. There were over a dozen, but we lost less than a city block." Browner paused for a moment.

"What do you think?" he asked.

Jones leaned back, his eyes drifting skywards. "I think I need to see the room again."

"I mean about the operation?"

Jones turned to the radio operator. "Stay here son. We'll be back in a few minutes." He gestured to the HRT bodyguards to hold their positions as he moved towards the elevator, Ted Browner in tow.

The elevator ride felt interminable for Browner. Jones waited calmly, totally silent, unusually still. When they got off, they moved down the corridor and past the guard. Jones stepped into the room and looked around carefully, then he stepped up to the shattered window, the warm breeze ruffling his hair. He looked down carefully, to avoid vertigo, then settled back and surveyed the darkening skyline. The body had been removed and the room had a blank aura, like an empty box. He could get no sense of Bucheri, the man or his mission. The broken window and the charred floor kept his secrets.

Browner coughed. Jones turned towards him, abruptly resuming the conversation. "What do you mean, 'the operation'?"

"Hell, Harley, we won. We got the bad guys. Terrorists *kaput*. Geez, you should be dancing. We even got Darth Vader. My God, it's a win for the home team."

Jones looked out through the broken window. In the distance he could see the smoke from the downtown fires. Off to the right, he could see the long pillar of smoke from the burning BosGas tower. Emergency vehicle lights blinked on all the main streets. Jones put a hand on Ted Browner's shoulder.

"You're right, Ted. Let's declare a victory and go home."

Browner started to reply, but stopped. Jones was watching the skyline again, seeing nothing.

Jones's fatigued mind was running freely over everything, looking for patterns, data, pictures, anything. He had the uneasy feeling that he had had when he first heard about the gasoline. The feeling of something missing—but he couldn't place it. Well, it would come to him. It had been a long three days and he was dead tired. He would be wanted in Washington tomorrow and it would be grueling as every cheap second-guesser tried to knock off him or the CTU. He leaned out of the window slightly and took a deep breath, but he couldn't escape the smell of gasoline. What was the line from Apocalypse Now? Then it came to him: Robert Duval in his cavalry hat, choppers flying overhead, saying,

"I love the smell of napalm in the morning. It smells like ... victory."

CHAPTER 25: MONDAY

Jeannie Kawai downshifted Harley Jones's old Corvette and bumped Jones from his reverie.

"Sorry," she said. "This is a lot different than my Miata."

Jones gave a slight smile. "American iron. Ya gotta buy American iron."

Jeannie reached through the open window and rapped her knuckles against the fiberglass body. She squinted her eyes and started with her best oriental accent, "Amelican plastic, numba ten. You bly Nippon, heh, allays ble happy."

Jones laughed quietly and turned to watch the Alexandria scenery go by outside as Jeannie drove him home. The day had been exhausting as he dictated preliminary reports and rearranged the CTU. Only the Military Police had remained in Boston an extra day, but they would be pulled out tonight. His hands had shaken all day. At his 4:00 p.m. meeting with the Director, Jones had fallen asleep while the Director had been explaining the slant he wanted on things. After waking him, the Director had emphatically insisted that Jones take the night off. Jones was amused. For some reason, the Director was embarrassed. Jones had been uncomfortable with the friendly handshake and had been happy to escape from the Director's office.

Jeannie had then insisted on driving him home, saying she would get a taxi back into town. Now, as they drove along, Jones played with the side view mirror on his door.

"Mr. Jones," Jeannie said in her best schoolmarm tone, "please stop playing with the mirror or your Plastic Pig will be plastic spare ribs."

Jones nodded absently and stared at the traffic ahead.

"Harley, that was brilliant, the thing with Ted," Jeannie said.

Jones started. "Huh?"

Jeannie smiled again. "Sending him undercover to the Middle East. Talk about a posting to Siberia."

Jones returned her smile. "Actually, it's not what it seems. It's inconvenient, of course, that his new assignment will make him unavailable for questioning, but it's absolutely essential that we have someone high up in the rank structure that speaks Arabic and understands the Arab mentality. And, of course, there is his priority assignment—to find out who Bucheri was working for."

Jeannie snorted in disbelief. "Right Harley, and what about all the captured types that were extradited to countries that already had death sentences for them? I noticed that the list includes most of those people who were questioned by the CIA interrogation teams."

Jones smiled and nodded his head slowly, his eyes almost closed. "That could be interpreted in different ways, but the fact remains that we are honoring extradition treaties already in place. Many of these people were very well known in their parts of the world. We will gain considerable face by having captured them and even more by returning them."

Jeannie shook her head in an expression of disbelief, her black hair swirling in the wind from the open window. "What about the Black Widow?"

Jones looked thoughtful. "Nikolsky? She'll go on trial, as she should. We've got her cold on evidence."

"What about her claims of torture?" Jeannie asked.

Jones squirmed slightly and loosened his seat belt. "You know, Jeannie, that wasn't the intent, really. The drug they gave her was simply supposed to enhance her time consciousness, to make time seem longer. They hadn't ever tried it on someone who was injured. If I had known that she was going to be in great pain, I never would have allowed it. It was pretty obvious that Bucheri had compartmentalization. We weren't going to learn anything from these people. I've seen this before. When you're dealing with professionals, time is against you." He looked at Jeannie and she could see the conviction in his expression.

"You know, I don't mind questioning someone, and I don't mind scaring them, but somewhere along an invisible line, you become evil. Jeannie, in the Nam I saw things that sadden me still. I was young then and got involved in some ugly stuff once. I feel dirty to this day. Sometimes I have dreams, bad dreams. Yet I don't believe that you can survive by being Mr. Nice Guy. Do you understand what I mean?"

She glanced at him and saw the intensity burning in his eyes. She nodded and he continued. "It's a broad gray line, nothing clear-cut—even hindsight can't tell. That's why the Bureau likes me. I get things done, but in the long run, I'm expendable. This appointment to Assistant Director is tokenism. All the other Assistant Directors have thousands of agents under them. I have only a hundred. If things go badly in the political arena, I can be discarded easily. The title, Assistant Director, will make it look good in the papers, but disruption to the Bureau will be minimal. The beat goes on."

"This doesn't bother you?" Jeannie asked.

Jones laughed slightly and shook his head. "Personally? No. It's the system. It's strangling America. We have politicians that only look towards re-election. They have no consciences. No one will tell us that we've got to pay off the debt, clean up the environment, work harder, save more, none of that. Jeannie," he paused, "it's the guys on the front lines, the soldiers, the cops, the teachers, all of us grunts that are holding our society together, the poor old farmers and mechanics who bust their asses every day doing their jobs. You see, some of us haven't gotten lost yet in the power trip. We produce something, a service, a product—but those guys, Jeannie, I've seen them, and it's a drug. They just lose it, all their morals, all their friends, family, they just lose it all. I swear, it's the saddest thing in Washington. It's people like you and me, who don't worry about how big our office is, the title on the door, the size of the desk: it's us. We're the ones that do the job. My job is the law. Beyond the law, I don't forget justice, but the law is the fabric that holds our society together."

Jones blinked for a moment, seeming to have lost his train of thought. "Like I said, it's the law that's critical. That's why I didn't give the Rangers free rein. It might have seemed like justice, but we must serve the law too. Those deportations, they serve both. And we'll get a little red in the face, maybe, about Nikolsky, but she'll have gone before the law. The whole country, the whole world, will see that we are a nation of laws."

Jones swallowed and looked mock-earnestly at Jeannie. "Anyhow, fuck 'em if they can't take a joke."

Jeannie laughed. "Jones, you're unbelievable. I suppose you have some excuse for the disappearance of the interrogation teams from the territorial United States."

Jones had to laugh with Jeannie—her love of life and laughter were infectious. "Well, I'm working on that."

Jeannie pulled open her blouse slightly and said into the gap, "Did you get all that?" to her imaginary microphone.

They both continued to laugh as she rolled into the driveway. With a short lurch, which got them laughing even harder, they stopped.

"Thanks Jeannie. I really appreciate the ride. I've got to admit, I am a little tired. Why don't you take the Plastic Pig and bring it to work tomorrow? I'll give you a ride to your place then."

Jeannie patted his knee. "Thanks Harley. Let's go in. I want to make sure you eat something and don't fall asleep in the kitchen sink. We all heard about your stunning performance with the Director."

Jones shrugged but smiled as they both climbed out of his Corvette. As she locked the doors he leaned on the roof and looked around the neighborhood.

"Something wrong?" she asked.

"No," he said, gazing around once more, "it looks just the same." He smiled at her and cocked his head slightly. "Maybe I'm different. I look around at this today," he waved expansively at the upper-middle class homes, "and I realize that it's not the outsides, the wood and stone, that we work for, it's the people. That's what we saved in Boston. Not the city, but the people." He sighed as he compulsively tested the door lock. "I just wish we could have been there sooner and better." He looked up into her eyes. "We were lucky, you know."

Jeannie nodded, more to comfort him than in agreement. Jones unlocked the house front door and ushered Jeannie through into the hallway. He took her lightweight summer coat and hung it up next to his own leather jacket. He led her out into the large combined living room-dining room area. There was a coolness there, a calm that flowed from the light walls and polished wood of the floor and table. At the far end of the room, a large stained glass painting almost filled the window. The end of the dining room section opened onto a very bright U-shaped kitchen.

They walked into the kitchen and Jones rummaged through the frozen dinners. "Nice, Harley, very nice. This woodwork is really unusual," Jeannie said as she ran her hands over the butcher block countertops. "Did you do it yourself?"

Jones stroked the counter, momentarily touching her hand. "Yes indeed. When I was with the HRT I had to stay near a phone, so this was what I did. I call it the Hostage Counter." Jones winked at her. "Get it?"

Jeannie groaned and shook her head. "No. I don't think I want to. Say Harley, how did you know that Melody J. Loony Tunes was going to come down and try and take over?" She leaned against the counter and folded her arms across her chest in a way that emphasized her cleavage. Jones couldn't tell if this was deliberate or accidental, but he tried not to look. She smiled enigmatically.

He looked down at the floor sheepishly. "Well, they say 'once a Marine, always a Marine.' Susan Page is a decorated Marine. I suspect she initially had conflicting loyalties, but she saw where things were going and did the right thing."

Jeannie wrinkled her forehead and was silent for a moment. "Oh!" she exclaimed. "General Bradley."

Jones nodded. "I don't know if they actually knew each other, but they served in Iraq at the same time. Anyhow, the Marines are a pretty tight-knit family."

Jeannie pursed her lips. "So he was leaking to Melody J?"

Jones's look darkened. "Schwartz. Got him through a cell phone intercept, because he was using the trigger words. She offered him a position."

"What's going to happen to him?"

Jones sighed. "Well, Melody J, as you call her, appears to be keeping a low profile. The President asked Susan Page to take over until the Secretary recovers from her seizure. Apparently she's thinking of resigning."

Jeannie raised her eyebrows. "Seizure?"

Jones shrugged.

Jeannie smiled broadly. "I guess I'll never know what really happened. I heard about a mysterious red-headed woman. Any idea what that's about?"

Jones shook his head slowly, but Jeannie couldn't tell whether it meant that he didn't know or wouldn't tell.

"Did you know that security cameras at Kennedy recorded a woman in a full burqa going to Amsterdam at 11:50 Saturday night?" she asked. "KLM 664 was non-stop; she'd be there in seven hours. Amsterdam would be a good place to disappear."

Jones nodded. "True, or just to climb on another plane. Once you're in the security zone of Schiphol Airport things are pretty casual."

Jeannie sighed dramatically. "Well, I guess we'd better move on. Why don't you show me the rest of your house? Let's see how the big people live."

Jones grimaced slightly. "I'm not really 'big people,' Jeannie." He pointed up the narrow staircase and Jeannie led the way. Jones stepped back two steps just to watch her move underneath her skirt. Damn, he thought, she is beautiful, smart, and funny. She could fry me like an egg. He shook his head. Fantasizing never got him anywhere.

Upstairs there were three bedrooms and a bathroom. One of the bedrooms was empty, the second was clearly a study. The third was Jones's bedroom. Jeannie stood in the doorway. "Charming" she said with a smile, gesturing to the barren room. Its only furniture was a single large bed, a night stand, and a lamp. The floor was littered with books. An art history book lay open with an empty Pepsi can resting on the *Toreador Fresco*, a man leaping over a charging bull. How appropriate, Jeannie thought. Leaping the bull. Jeannie pushed the can aside gently with her toe, a ballerina dancing in junk.

"A Renaissance Man, I see," she said with a soft smile as she stepped over a Far Side cartoon book. Jones opened his hand to explain but she had slipped out and moved on to the empty room. She put her head in and searched, laughing silently. "Lots of guests, I'll bet," she teased. But once again, before he could reply, she had stepped into another room, the study.

Jones caught up as she stared, transfixed at the wall of photos, memorabilia of a lifetime of government service. All of the pictures were uncaptioned: a display for a participant, not for visitors. She pointed to one. "My first Special Forces team. Deep reconnaissance," he said. She moved over the display, scanning, looking for something special. Two men in suits stood side by side, smiling. Jeannie pointed. "You're smiling. That's new." She turned to Jones. "Who's he?"

His hesitation was a warning to her. "Tom Coyle," he said, finally. She watched him intently, waiting. "He was a friend, a good friend. I let him down." He paused, his voice catching as he turned away. "He died."

She caught him as he started down the stairs. "Harley! Stop. What is it?" He turned around and she could see the tears forming in his eyes. "He died, Jeannie, and so many others. I let them down. I couldn't stop Bucheri. I couldn't even catch him. Oh Jeannie, I feel so bad."

Jeannie reached forward and pulled his head to her shoulder. She kissed his cheek and stroked his head. "Harley, you got him this time. The worst terrorist that we've ever had. Bucheri was brilliant and everything was against you."

He pulled his head back, his face wet with tears. "Jeannie, so many died, the people in the subway, the children, the —"

"Shhh! Harley." She held her finger to his lips. "Harley. You did everything a man could do, you were the best. You were … magnificent. Everyone is thankful for what you did. Your team trusts you, we love you."

Jones raised his head and looked into her eyes. Deeper than seeing, deeper than touching, for a long moment she was in his soul. Jeannie leaned forward and touched her lips to his.

CHAPTER 26: TUESDAY

1:12 A.M.

Harley Jones jerked awake, then relaxed as a long-forgotten feeling swept over him: warmth. Jeannie's leg slid over his, then her hair swept over his neck. It felt delicious. He reached up and trapped her in his arms. She stretched up and kissed him lightly, then slid off to sit on the side of the bed. Her hair was a waterfall over her back in the night, highlighting her smooth skin. Her small breasts swayed as she reached for the night stand. Briefly, she fumbled then put on a pair of granny-style glasses. She swung her head left and right to flip her hair over her shoulder. "I'm blind without them. Usually I wear contacts but not to sleep."

Jones reached up and stroked her face. "Glasses—you're full of surprises."

Jeannie smiled. "You weren't watching my eyes."

Jones flushed, invisible in the dark, but Jeannie touched his face and felt the warmth there. Her smile widened. She arched her back slightly as she leaned forward to kiss him.

Jones reached up and pulled her down slowly with a fierce strength that startled her. She tried to pull back, but was helpless in his iron grip. His lips brushed her ears. "Glasses. Bucheri doesn't wear glasses," he whispered. Paralyzed with fear at this change in Jones, she could barely force herself to shake her head. His grip slowly loosened. He whispered, "There were glasses in the hotel room. Bucheri isn't dead." Jeannie froze completely as Jones finished, "He's here, somewhere"

Jones rolled Jeannie over then slipped quietly to the floor. Jeannie rose up and saw him, a ghost in the moonlight, with his finger to his lips in a signal for silence. She followed him out of the bed, whisper quiet. She reached into her clothes for her pistol, but a quiet hand gestured that she shouldn't even cock it. Naked, she stood over him, guarding him, as he slipped on trousers. He stood by the door, the big Glock in his hand, as she pulled on his shirt—enough for the moment.

Together, they crept through the shadows of the spare room, study, then bathroom, the tile floor cold on their bare feet. He cupped his hands over her ears and whispered, "He's here. He'll come for me. I'm sorry. Stay close."

She gripped his wrist fiercely, then kissed him lightly. Together, they moved down the stairs, Jones facing down, Jeannie, facing backward with one hand on Jones's back for balance, reassurance. Jeannie could feel her senses tingling; the slightest creak of the stairs was a whip crack in the dark. Jones's sweat smelled of fear. Jeannie shuddered and moved slightly closer.

On the ground floor, there was a new smell. Jones crouched at the bottom of the stairs, scanning the dim living room; Jeannie stood on the last step looking up and trying to identify the smell. Jones stood up slowly and put his ear to Jeannie's lips. "Propane," she whispered. He nodded. She followed him as he stepped forward then spun at a movement. Only Jones's quick hand on her pistol, enfolding the descending hammer, kept her from shooting the mirror. Shaking, she rose from her shooter's crouch, eyeing the strange woman in the mirror: an apparition with naked, muscular legs and hateful eyes.

Jones moved to the basement stairwell and gestured that he would go down. Jeannie nodded and wrinkled her nose. The propane smell from the basement was intense. Jeannie waited a moment, then followed Jones into the darkness. Her shirt was wet with sweat, and even her feet were slippery on the painted steps. As she reached the bottom, she had to struggle to keep from vomiting. The atmosphere reeked of propane. With her fingers on his naked back, she followed Jones across the cool concrete. One basement window was open slightly. A garden hose was poking through the window, hissing quietly. Jones looked past it, out through the window. Then, quickly, urgently, he led Jeannie out of the basement.

At the top of the stairs, Jones shut the door gently and whispered in Jeannie's ear, "No matter what happens, don't shoot. We're in a bomb." She paused, realizing what the muzzle blast would do to them. Enunciating carefully, Jones went on, "The house is probably bugged. He'll detonate us immediately if he thinks we know what's going on." Jeannie nodded in the darkness, swaying with nausea.

Jones pulled her upstairs as the smell of gas began to take its toll on her shaky legs. "I'm going to be sick," she moaned.

"Later," he hissed as he led her into the empty spare bedroom. He pushed the door shut quietly and pointed to the window. Jeannie sagged to the floor, barely conscious. Jones padded to the window and opened it before coming back to kneel by her.

"He'll be watching the house from somewhere," he whispered hoarsely. "I'm betting he's on the north side, by my neighbor's barbecue. That's probably where he's getting the gas from. We've got to chance it here." Gently, he helped her to her feet.

Jones climbed out onto the garage roof first, and then half-pulled Jeannie through behind him. The cool night air brought some life back to her.

"I've dropped my weapon," she murmured. Jones ignored her as he helped to the roof edge.

"I'll lower you down. Then drop with your legs together, knees bent." He held her chin up and looked into her eyes. "Got it?"

For just a moment, Jeannie felt giddy, stupid, and timeless as she dropped, the baggy shirt billowing briefly before she landed.

It took all her control not to scream as she hit the ground. "Roses, that son of a bitch," went through her mind as she extracted her bleeding leg from the vines. A moment later Jones landed with a thud, just past the bushes. For a moment, he lay there. "He's laughing at me," she thought, until she saw his feeble movements. Quietly, feeling more stable now, she slipped up beside him.

"My ankle," he whispered. "We've got to get away from the house. Then I'll circle back and get him. If the house goes it will take out half the neighborhood."

As he said it, Jones became suddenly aware of the truth of his statement. The flying glass alone would kill anyone near a window. The neighbor's two boys, Eric and Rolfe, were sleeping under a window less than thirty feet away.

He turned to Jeannie. "We'll crawl down the hedge to the street. You go and find a phone. Get the HRT, not the locals."

"Why?" she whispered back.

"Any notice at all and this whole thing goes up. Bucheri will be gone. HRT can be quiet. Talk to Chan. He'll know what to do."

Jeannie nodded, but Jones had already started towards a small gap in the hedge, perhaps a dog's path. Within seconds he was through. He's surprisingly agile, Jeannie thought as she painfully worked her bleeding body through the bush.

* * *

Hassan Bucheri checked his watch as he took off his earphones. It was time. Jones and the woman would be almost asleep or almost awake. It didn't matter. He picked up the cell phone and pressed speed dial. The phone rang, and rang again. Bucheri frowned. Jones should have answered by now. Bucheri pulled up the earphone of his sound-actuated listening device. There it was. The phone was ringing in Jones's house. There could be no doubt. Why wasn't he answering?

Bucheri resisted the temptation to press the remote control airplane actuator he had rigged as a detonator, and straightened up in the seat. Should he drive by? No. He was safer a block away. Anything could set that propane off now. He stared intently at the house, a dim image in the light from the quarter moon.

Then a movement in the street caught his eye. He squinted, trying to focus. Cursing silently he brought his compact Nikon binoculars up to his eyes. The light-gathering power helped him make out the image the woman.

Damn! Bucheri slammed his hand into the steering wheel. Something had gone wrong. Jones was probably out too. He reached for the detonator, then hesitated. If Jones was truly gone, the detonation was a waste. He could always use the detonator another time. A fast cruise-by might tell him more.

* * *

Jeannie jerked like a startled deer at the sound of a car starting down the street. Jones whispered, "Just a neighbor. Now move out," but he gave her naked bottom a warm pat as he kissed her lips in a quick brush. Jeannie crouched and started to cross the street as Jones moved up behind the parked cars, trying to get in position to circle around the neighbor's house.

Something was wrong, very wrong, but Jeannie couldn't figure out what it was. Suddenly she knew. "Harley!" she screamed, as the car accelerated suddenly, the lights flipping into brilliant double suns. Jones stood transfixed like a deer in the headlights for a moment, then leapt to one side. He almost made it onto a car hood, but the onrushing vehicle caught his legs and threw him in a cartwheel right over the top of the car.

Bucheri ignored the woman and looked in his rearview mirror for Jones. Not seeing him, he calmly checked his side mirror. There he was, lying in the middle of the road. Carefully Bucheri shifted into reverse, checking the gear indicator on the dashboard of the unfamiliar rental car. Then, just as he had been taught in evasive driving school, he looked over his shoulder and accelerated straight back past Jones for twenty yards. He was going to get a good forward run at Jones and flatten him—pancake him. Bucheri indulged himself in a giggle. This was even better, more personal, than an explosion.

Bucheri stopped, shifted to neutral, and gunned the engine, relishing the moment. This was fantastic.

"Eat this," growled Bucheri as he stomped on the gas. The heavily muscled Mustang leapt forward, tires smoking.

"Damn," muttered Bucheri: the woman was standing over Jones; but he held his course. "Meddlesome bitch," he gritted. Suddenly, she raised a pistol and was firing, fingers of light blossoming towards him. Bucheri marveled briefly at the beauty of the scene in his headlights: a lioness, crouched, defending her mate.

2:45 A.M.

Harley Jones awoke to lights. Flashing lights, yellow, blue, red. The lights were so bright, so numerous, that they drowned out the sounds, sirens, engines. Slowly, he began to hear more. Voices, barked commands rang out, questions, children crying. He tried to move, but felt safe, warm. He looked up. His head was in Jeannie's lap. She held it between her hands, not letting him move.

"Lie still. The ambulance just arrived," she said quietly. Somehow, he had no trouble picking her voice up over the din.

"What happened?"

She paused for a moment. "I shot Bucheri. I missed. Your gun's too damn big."

Jones was fuzzy. "Dead?"

She shook her head, her long hair a shadow in the lights. "I wounded him. He crashed over there." She indicated the spot with a nod. Jones strained to look, but Jeannie held his head firm.

"Jeannie. My spine is fine, my leg just hurts like a bitch."

She nodded but didn't let him move.

Seconds later an ambulance team pried Jones gently away from Jeannie, careful not to come between her and the pistol at her side.

* * *

The paramedic later described the ride to the hospital that night as the most interesting in his entire career. A woman wearing nothing but a shirt and a pistol, a world famous FBI agent, and a world famous terrorist.

Bucheri was strapped down on the stretcher as well as being handcuffed to it. The wound in his right shoulder hardly seemed to trouble him at all. He turned to Jones beside him.

"You were lucky. Saved by a woman." He shook his head. "Unbelievable."

Jones didn't speak. The pain in his leg was increasing as the initial shock wore off. The leg itself didn't seem to be broken, but numerous broken blood vessels were bleeding into it, causing it to swell. Jones closed his eyes, then opened them again.

309

"How did you know?" Bucheri asked.

"The glasses," Jones answered tiredly; "they were on the carpet of the room after the explosion."

Bucheri shook his head, disgusted, seemingly oblivious to his wound. "Kamal was a careless man. Too bad." Bucheri sank back, more tired now. "It would have been perfect: Harley Jones blown up in his own house. No police officer would ever have slept a good night again."

Jones snorted. "Tough! You didn't win a thing, not in the long run."

Bucheri laughed lightly. "You don't think so? I brought an American city to its knees with Forty-Seven Ronin. In the oppressed world, they'll tell our story for centuries."

Jones turned his head to look at Bucheri. "Oppressed? Oppressed who? Who did you do this for?"

Bucheri settled back with a sigh. "That will remain my secret."

Jones snapped back, "Bucheri, you're a goddamn mercenary and always have been. You did this for money."

Bucheri looked over at Jones sadly. "You really don't understand do you? You're so naïve. Of course I make money when I do my job. So do you, Assistant Director Jones. You make just over a hundred and fifty thousand dollars a year, counting medical and pension. I have my own savings plan, that's all. What makes you so different from me? You killed people in Vietnam. You kill people in Boston. All for your country. I do the same. Are you upset that I don't have a population you can imprison, an economy you can subvert, a leader you can bomb in the middle of the night with your stealth bombers? No, you've done quite enough to me through your tools, the Israelis."

"What do you mean?" asked Jones.

"You've killed most of my family and friends, Jones. You meddling Americans traipse through the world spreading death like a foul pool of oil. Kurds, Iraqis, Palestinians, Salvadorians, Cubans, Iranians—how many have you killed with your largesse? At least the Soviets were consistent. But not you, oh no, not the bringers of freedom. First the SAVAK in Iran, then support Iraq against Iran, than go against Iraq and for the Kurds, then abandon the Kurds and support the Turks and Iraqis. You are the most manipulative people on earth. Can you imagine how many people you've killed with your actions?"

Jones lifted himself up, then dropped back to the stretcher. "Bullshit. We don't have a single colony. The Russians made colonies of all of Eastern Europe. We returned Germany to the Germans. We could have taken Cuba, but we left them alone. We even left Vietnam."

Bucheri smiled. "With friends like the United States, who needs enemies?"

"You mean Germany, Japan, South Korea? Some of the strongest economies in the world. We fought there, then built them up."

Bucheri nodded tiredly. "Maybe if the Palestinians could declare war on you, you could help them too."

"You've lost, you know," Jones said. "We stopped you cold. Boston was the end of it."

Bucheri turned slowly towards Jones. "You're a good man, Jones. If it hadn't been for you…" He paused, searching for words: "It would have been a magnificent victory." They locked eyes, and Bucheri said, "Remember the Terminator?"

Jones wrinkled his brow, questioning. Bucheri smiled. "I'll be back." He turned his face to the ambulance wall and closed his eyes.

Jones looked up at Jeannie. She smiled and shook her head. "Only in the reruns."

CHAPTER 27: WEDNESDAY

6:33
Walter Reed National Medical Center
Washington, DC

Jeannie Kawai stepped back as the door opened. The Director stepped out and said, "Special Agent Kawai, a pleasure to meet you." Jeannie shook his extended hand, at a loss for words. "Thank you," was all she could say; she cursed herself for being dumbstruck. Most agents never got to meet the Director, and here she was blowing the opportunity. The Director released her hand and smiled. "You should study the dress code. It's not what it was in the Hoover days, but we prefer that our agents follow it whenever possible." The Director was referring to her rather unconventional attire during the apprehension of Bucheri. She had been forced to stomp the potential scandal by agreeing to give a personal interview to the reporter who had taken a photograph of her standing in front of some headlights in only Harley Jones's shirt. She might as well have been wearing nothing at all. The Director winked and said, "You did well. I'm proud of you both." He nodded and then moved down the hallway to meet with his driver and bodyguard.

Shaking her head at the unusual meeting, Jeannie pushed into Harley Jones's room. Jones looked grim, but a broad smile spread across his face as he saw her. Jeannie's heart beat faster.

"Jeannie! Damn, it's good to see you. What's up?"

That was one of the things that Jeannie had come to appreciate about Harley Jones. Even when he had serious problems, he would ask about her situation first. She shrugged.

"The reporter is not going to put out that picture. He gave me the file. He had other ones anyhow, so I'll be plastered all over the Profiles section of the Post, but at least I won't look naked."

Jones nodded. "I knew you could pull it off. It's the way Washington usually works. Give a little, take a little."

"What happened with the Director?" Jeannie asked, remembering the grim expression Jones had been wearing when she entered the room.

Jones sighed and tried to settle himself more comfortably in the bed.

"OK?" Jeannie asked.

Jones nodded. "As long as I don't make a big move, it's fine. They sewed everything up great. I've just got serious bruises now."

Jeannie waited for him to answer her first question. Finally, Jones started, "Well, Congress is howling as well as everyone from the American Civil Liberties Union to the Montana Militia. It seems that someone has got to take a fall, and it's going to be me." He raised his eyes to hers. "I told you that the Assistant Directorship was a front. With only a hundred people under me, I had fewer agents than a sub office in Los Angeles."

He pursed his lips. "So I lose my Assistant Directorship and the CTU."

Jeannie gasped. "Harley, that's terrible. It's everything you worked for. What's going to happen?"

"Well, the Director and I had a serious heart-to-heart. It appears that the President, the Director of the CIA, and our Director would prefer to be distanced from the 'Boston Incident,' as they call it. The Director and I agreed that I did what had to be done, and apparently the other two know that as well. It would just be political death to admit that they gave me the green light."

"So you get the ax?" Jeannie asked, incredulous.

A faint smile crossed Jones's face. "Well, as you know, all my conversations were recorded. I have those records and these gentlemen know it. Also, they would prefer that I simply take the beating quietly. So, a little give and a little take. I'll be demoted, of course, and placed in charge of another team, a much smaller team. We've agreed that I can speak some of the truth before Congress, let them know what will have to be done in the future if they want to prevent this kind of thing. I'll take some heat, of course, but they've agreed that they'll protect me in my new position. My pay drops, but I'm alive to fight another day."

Curious now, Jeannie leaned forward in her chair. "OK Jones, what's the new position?"

Jones moved his pillow before replying. "I'm head of a unit called the Contingency Planning Unit. We'll have maybe twenty people, the best. Our job is to plan for big problems, like the Boston Incident. There were too many linkages that needed to be made, last-minute fumblings and scrambling. We didn't know about the NSA capability, we couldn't monitor enough phones—it just goes on and on. The Unit will look into that. The CTU will be expanded but will concentrate primarily on intelligence analysis and the development of teams that can be assembled quickly. The U.S. Marshals is one group we could have tapped. Delta Force, Special Forces, and the Navy SEALs were all units that we might have used or used better. There are lots of local tactical units that are really first class. We should have been able to call on them too." Jones looked distant for a moment. "There's a lot to do."

Jeannie sat silent for a moment, then stood up as a smile crept across her face. "Let me get this straight. If a big problem comes along, one that the CTU can't handle, then they call on your unit, right?"

Jones nodded, his smile matching hers. "Yep. If things get really ugly, they call out the old war dogs. Otherwise, we stay in the kennel."

Jeannie laughed. "Did the Director think this up?"

Jones cocked his head slightly. "Some suggestions were made to him by the parties involved. I also suggested that my unit should conduct the investigation of the Boston Incident. It's perfect as a start for our scenario planning."

Jeannie laughed again. "Harley, you can't investigate yourself. That's..." she paused, looking for a phrase, "a conflict of interest."

Jones nodded. "I won't be the Special Agent in Charge of record, but I'll be there."

He turned serious. "It won't be a whitewash, Jeannie; we're going to lay it out like surgeons. We're going to write up every mistake, every branch that we might have taken. I really don't care if I made mistakes then. I want to learn from them now."

He looked up at her, his eyes sad again. "We lost so many, Jeannie. I don't know what we could have done, but I'll find out."

She stood up and moved closer to his bedside. Shyly, she took his hand. "I know you will, Harley Jones. You're one of the last honest men. I know you will."

They watched each other for a moment, then Jeannie brightened up. "I've been transferred back to the D.C. lab. Apparently the Director thought that two people closely involved shouldn't be working together."

Jones searched her eyes. "Is this OK with you? You really wanted to stay with the CTU. Now that I'm out it would be fine."

Jeannie straightened up and paused for a moment. "I thought about how I felt, and I realized that I really enjoyed working with you, but I know that wouldn't work in the long run."

She looked up into his eyes. "It's better this way. We can see each other without ... complications."

A broad smile broke over Jones's face. Jeannie couldn't help but think of the rising sun. He pulled her closer, but she pulled back. "Can you...?"

"Try me," Jones said.

Jeannie Kawai walked to the door, opened it, and said to the uniformed officers outside, "Mr. Jones has just received a call from the President of the United States. He's not to be disturbed by anyone until I tell you. Understood?"

Clearly impressed, they both answered, "Yes ma'am!"

The door closed quietly.

PRINCIPAL CHARACTERS AND TERMS

Government

CIA:

Theodore (Teddy) Browner: Formerly Assistant Director of Operations. Presently second-in-command of the FBI/CIA Counter-Terrorist Unit (CTU).

Department of Homeland Security:

Melody Jane Harmony: Secretary of Homeland Security. Responsible for FEMA, the Secret Service, Coast Guard, Immigration, Border Patrol, and numerous other organizations.

Susan Page: Deputy Secretary of Homeland Security. Formerly with the Justice Department and the United States Marine Corps.

Jerry Price: National Director of the Homeland Fusion Center Program.

FBI:

Harley Jones: Promoted to Assistant Director of the Federal Bureau of Investigation. Agent in Charge of the newly formed FBI/CIA CTU.

Jeannie Kawai: Special Agent of the FBI. A specialist in forensics with a PhD in analytical chemistry.

George Alvarez: Special Agent of the FBI. Electronic surveillance specialist. An early member of the CTU.

Tim Blackwell: Special Agent in Charge of the Boston office of the FBI.

Jessica Williams: Special Agent of the FBI. Data analysis expert. A long-term member of the CTU and its predecessor.

Liz Martin: FBI Technical Services: Linguistics, communications, and surveillance specialist.

Jay Schwartz: FBI psychologist. Based with the Behavioral Sciences Unit and seconded, on occasion, to the Hostage Rescue Team (HRT), Quantico, Va.

Military:

Lieutenant General Thomas Bradley: Deputy to the Chairman of the Joint Chiefs of Staff. Formerly United States Marine Corps commander in Afghanistan.

John Miller: Private. Massachusetts National Guard, Company C, 182nd Infantry Battalion (Mechanized).

J. J. Knight: Captain. U.S. Army Signal Corps. Telecommunications Specialist.

Boston Police Department:

Brian Delaney: Police Commissioner.

Eddy Yeager: Boston Police Deputy Superintendent responsible for the Arrest and Apprehension Team (Special Weapons and Tactics, SWAT).

Paul Andrews: Detective. Boston Police Department

David Maloney: Detective: Boston Police Department

Others

Patrick Henry Johnston: Businessman, big game hunter, gun collector. Resident of Boston.

Pamela Clark: Reporter for WXTV in Boston.

Roz (full name not known): Israeli Intelligence Service. Well known to Harley Jones from his secondment with that service.

The Opposition:

Hassan Bucheri: Homeland: Palestine. Trained as a professional soldier then served as an intelligence officer. Also trained as an intelligence operative in the Soviet Union. Now a professional terrorist. Harvard graduate.

Sharif Al-Hawari: Student. Agent responsible for securing housing and storage sites for Hassan Bucheri.

Dr. Ali Kamal: PhD in synthetic chemistry. Former director of the Al Bahah pesticide plant.

Professor (also General) Montasser: Director of the Bureau of Intelligence (Cover: Assistant Director of Agriculture). Directly responsible for training and financing external operations in support of Revolutionary Council objectives.

Nadia Nikolsky: Former Alpha Group Spetsnaz (Soviet then Russian Republic Special Forces) operative as well as a competitive athlete and high school athletics instructor.

The Leader: Speaker for the ruling Revolutionary Council.

Dieter Schmidt: Leader of the German Team. Former East German *Stasi* (secret police) officer.

Sergeant Besso: Leader of the Somalia Team. A professional soldier.

Terms

APC: Armored Personnel Carrier.

CAP: Combat Air Patrol. Combat aircraft which fly a constant patrol over a fleet. Usually they are configured for air-to-air combat.

CIC: Combat Information Center. The tactical center of a warship where information from all sources is collected and displayed on screens.

Central Intelligence Agency (CIA): The CIA is a civilian intelligence agency of the United States. Its primary mandate is the collection of foreign intelligence. It uses both electronic means, primarily satellite imagery, and human agents in the collection process. Upon occasion it may carry out tactical operations. Other independent agencies collect different types of intelligence (e.g., the National Security Agency [NSA] collects signals [electronic eavesdropping] intelligence). Its annual budget is estimated to be over $40 billion.

CTU: FBI-CIA Counter-Terrorist Unit. A group formed to combine CIA and FBI resources to quickly respond to terrorist threats to the continental United States. The formation was triggered by what is commonly called *The Boston Incident*.

E2: The Grumman E-2 Hawkeye is an all-weather carrier-launch-capable aircraft that is used to provide tactical "early warning" through its sensitive radar systems.

Emergency Operations Center (EOC): An EOC is a command post designed to be activated in the event of an emergency of any kind, including weather-related disasters. EOCs are designed to control operations at a strategic level in a specific geographical region. Tactical local decisions are generally made by local authorities.

F15I Ra'am: A modified version of the U.S. F15 specifically tailored for the Israeli Air Force.

Federal Bureau of Investigation (FBI): The FBI is an agency belonging to the U.S. Department of Justice. It provides both criminal investigation and internal intelligence (counterintelligence) services. The 2011 budget was $7.9 billion dollars. The FBI has approximately 40,000 employees, of whom, roughly 13,000 are special agents.

Fusion center: A fusion center is an information-sharing center created by the U.S. Department of Homeland Security and the U.S. Department of Justice. Such centers are designed to promote locally relevant information sharing between federal agencies. There are 72 fusion centers across the U.S. They are usually linked to an Emergency Operations Center (EOC).

HRT: The FBI Hostage Rescue Team (HRT) is trained to rescue persons held by a hostile force. HRT members compete to join this elite unit, which is believed to be the best civilian force of its type in the United States. Unlike the 56 field office SWAT teams, the HRT members train full-time with techniques ranging from helicopter fast-rope techniques to night techniques. The team can be deployed within four hours to go anywhere in the U.S. or its territories.

M113: A type of armored personnel carrier used extensively through the Vietnam War and beyond. It resembles a box with treads.

Rendition or Extraordinary Rendition: The apprehension and transfer of a person from one nation to another without trial or hearing.

Rockeye bomb: A type of cluster bomb that breaks apart in the air to release many smaller bomblets, thereby covering a large area.

SRU: The FBI Special Research Unit. A group tasked with developing protocols for handling emergencies which require more resources than the FBI can provide.

Stasi: The common name for the Ministry for State Security, the official state security service of East Germany. It was widely regarded as one of the most effective and repressive secret police agencies in the world. Its officers were well trained in both police and military espionage procedures.

www.ingramcontent.com/pod-product-compliance
Lightning Source LLC
Chambersburg PA
CBHW020941260626

47169CB00006B/1763